本书由2024年中国地质大学（武汉）外国语学院外国语言文学学科培育项目（项目编号：162301244815）资助出版

伊迪丝·华顿小说中的世纪之交

新英格兰风景

周诗羽　著

The Turn-of-the-Twentieth-Century

New England Landscape

in Edith Wharton's Fiction

武汉大学出版社

WUHAN UNIVERSITY PRESS

图书在版编目(CIP)数据

伊迪丝·华顿小说中的世纪之交新英格兰风景／周诗羽著．
武汉 ：武汉大学出版社，2024. 12. -- ISBN 978-7-307-24752-9

Ⅰ. I712.074

中国国家版本馆 CIP 数据核字第 2024WA0288 号

责任编辑:李晶晶　　　责任校对:鄢春梅　　　版式设计:韩闻锦

出版发行：**武汉大学出版社**　　（430072　武昌　珞珈山）

（电子邮箱：cbs22@ whu.edu.cn　网址：www.wdp.com.cn）

印刷:湖北云景数字印刷有限公司

开本:720×1000　　1/16　　印张:19.25　　字数:273 千字　　插页:1

版次:2024 年 12 月第 1 版　　2024 年 12 月第 1 次印刷

ISBN 978-7-307-24752-9　　　　定价:79.00 元

版权所有，不得翻印;凡购我社的图书，如有质量问题，请与当地图书销售部门联系调换。

Preface

Landscape is an important element in Edith Wharton's works, and this is closely related to her love of nature, her writing principles, and American literary traditions. The period between the end of the Civil War and the onset of World War II marked a phase of accelerated social transformations in the United States. The United States underwent a series of transformations such as from an agricultural nation to an industrialized nation, from a predominantly rural society to an urban-centric society, from industrial capitalism to the monopoly capitalism of large corporations, and from continental expansion to overseas expansion. Positioning Wharton's fiction within the context of social transformations at the turn of the twentieth century, this book studies the depiction of New England landscape in her six novels *The House of Mirth* (1905), *Ethan Frome* (1911), *The Custom of the Country* (1913), *Summer* (1917), *Hudson River Bracketed* (1929), and *The Gods Arrive* (1932), for the aim of exploring the intricate interplay between the characters and their surroundings during a crucial period in American history.

This book employs landscape theories from cultural geography as the primary research methodology to analyze Wharton's landscape writing about New York City, rural New England, and the Hudson River Valley in the novels. The analytical strategies from landscape studies about urban landscape and the theories of urban studies are applied to the discussion of New York cityscape, while the theories of rural landscape and rural studies are enlightening regarding the analysis of New England countryside. The

Hudson Valley landscape is studied from the lens of landscape phenomenology, ecocriticism, and the Frankfurt School's interpretations of natural beauty.

In *The House of Mirth* and *The Custom of the Country*, the replacement of Old New Yorkers by the new plutocrats, driven by socio-economic restructuring during the turn of the century, paves the way for the transformation of New York cityscape. The representatives of urban landscape—the streets, the opera houses, and the hotels—reflect the rising importance of individuality, the increasing accessibility of leisure, and growing geographical and social mobility in New York's transition from a nineteenth-century Victorian City to a twentieth-century modern one. Landscape plays an active role in forming class and gender identities, legitimizing hierarchical relations, and operating as a signifying system through which social values are reproduced. Shaped by the operation of power dynamics, the urban landscape evokes the characters' various emotions which shed light on the effects of social transformations on their ideologies and aesthetics.

Rural New England experienced a change in the regional identity from a decaying backwater to rural idyll in urbanites' eyes, under the influence of rural social transformations which includes the uneven development between rural and urban regions, European immigration, commercial agriculture, and rural tourism. The different perceptions of rural landscape by city visitors and local inhabitants in *Ethan Frome* and *Summer* illustrate that old New England's transformed image is molded by the notions of class, race, and gender. The characteristic components of rural landscape—the villages, the mountains, and the vernacular architecture—are shaped by the power relations between the urban leisure class and rural poor, US-born Anglo-Saxons and immigrants from Ireland and Italy, and men and women. In the writer's view, resorting to a romanticized old New England which cloaks and perpetuates class, gender, and racial inequalities is an inadequate strategy for dealing with social transformations.

Wharton envisions an idealized landscape in *Hudson River Bracketed* and its sequel *The Gods Arrive* to express her views on how Americans should handle the impacts of social transformations. Her idealized landscape is characterized by the harmony between landscape and technology, integration of natural beauty and artistic beauty, and cross-fertilization of European legacy and American innovation. Wharton elucidates that Americans' domination over nature contributes to their emotional numbness via drawing a stark contrast between the Hudson landscape and the protagonist Vance's bleak Midwestern hometown. The interaction between Vance and the Hudson River Valley landscape which includes the suburb, the forest, and the mansion signifies Wharton's expectation that the aesthetic value of landscape can counterbalance the prevalent negative effects of standardization, mechanization, human alienation from nature, and disregard for history in American society during the 1920s and 1930s.

Through analyzing the six novels in chronological order, this book argues that Wharton's delineation of New England landscape reflects the impacts of social transformations upon Americans' lifestyles and mentalities at the turn of the century. The characters experience dramatic socio-economic, political, and cultural transformations. Power relations among different classes, races, and genders, as well as between men and nature shape individuals' perceptions of landscape and people's emotions emerging from experiencing landscape indicate the effects of social transformations on their ideologies and aesthetic tastes. Wharton's portrayal of the landscape demonstrates that her attitude towards social transformations in the United States changes from skepticism to acknowledging its inevitability and seeking solutions to mitigate its adverse effects. The writer also adopts a more positive attitude towards America in her writing of the 1920s and 1930s. In general, the study of New England landscape in Wharton's novels provides a new perspective on the writer's reflections over the rapid social transformations at the turn of the century, examines the impact of those transformations on Americans, and scrutinizes Americans' responses. This book advances interdisciplinary research that applies theories from cultural geography to Wharton studies as well. Wharton's concerns about the influences of social transformations offer valuable insights for considering relevant issues in contemporary American society, demonstrating her foresight as a great American writer.

Contents

1

List of Abbreviations

Chapter One   Introduction

Edith Wharton (1862-1937), one of the major figures in American literary history, presents intriguing insights into the turn-of-the-twentieth-century American experience. Author of more than 40 volumes which include novels, short stories, poetry, drama, and non-fiction, she is the first woman awarded the Pulitzer Prize for Fiction, an honorary Doctorate of Letters from Yale University, and a full membership in the American Academy of Arts and Letters. Wharton was also nominated for the Nobel Prize in Literature in 1927, 1928, and 1930. With classics such as *The House of Mirth* (1905), *Ethan Frome* (1911), and *The Age of Innocence* (1920), she remains one of the most widely read authors in American literature.

Wharton is primarily known as a novelist who utilized her insider's knowledge of the upper-class New York "aristocracy" to document Gilded Age New York. However, as the leading Wharton scholar Emily J. Orlando summarizes in *The Bloomsbury Handbook to Edith Wharton* (2023), "Wharton studies has evolved to an increasingly global, multidisciplinary enterprise [...] Wharton is now embraced by specialists in not only literary, cultural, and gender studies but also architecture, art history, museum studies, fashion studies, history, sociology, and anthropology" (1).

The writer's influence has reached beyond the realm of academia as well. *The House of Mirth* and *The Age of Innocence* have been adapted into movies. The detective novel *The Edith Wharton Murders: A Nick Hoffman*

Mystery (1997) and children's book *The Brave Escape of Edith Wharton* (2010) introduced Wharton's life and work to a new generation of readers. *The Gilded Age*, an HBO miniseries inspired by Wharton's works, has been renewed for a second season while an Apple TV adaptation of her novel *The Custom of the Country* (1913) is in development. The Mount—her country house in Massachusetts—is a National Historic Landmark in the United States and welcomes approximately fifty thousand visitors every year (Hudson et al., xiv). As we approach the centenary of her demise, Wharton's enduring impact confirms that her corpus will yield far more than we have already known.

1.1   Edith Wharton and Landscape Writing

Wharton had lifelong interests in landscape, which is evident both from her own passion for travel and from the meticulous delineation of landscape in her fictions, travelogues, and guides to gardens and interior decoration. In her autobiography, *A Backward Glance* (1934), she declares that since the age of four, she had an "incurable passion for the road and the scenery" (31). She also repeatedly describes her fascination with the landscape of Lenox, Massachusetts, where The Mount is located: "the joys among fields and woods of my own, and the childish ecstasy of that first spring outing at Mamaroneck swept away all restlessness in the deep joy of communion with the earth" (124).

In addition to her love of nature, Wharton understands landscape as a multiple concept which includes "perception, metaphor, and social myth" (Whaley, 23). In *The Writing of Fiction* (1925), her book on novelistic craftsmanship, she stresses the importance of depicting landscape for writers: "characters and scenic details are in fact one to the novelist who has fully assimilated his material" (84). In her view, landscape makes visible the " inner drama " of the character by demonstrating " the observer's perspective" (*The Writing of Fiction*, 4). Landscape, in her understanding, has "double dimensions of metaphorical space" (Whaley, 24). On the one hand, it provides the localized settings of time and place which reflect particular social conditions; on the other hand, it reveals the psychology of the observing characters (Wharton, *The Writing of Fiction*, 49-52). In this way, landscape in her novels not only works as a depiction of the actual circumstances of characters, but also indicates individuals' relations to social forces and their emotions and ideologies. In short, the depiction of landscape reveals the writer's exploration and evaluation of the interaction between people and their surroundings.

Furthermore, Wharton's landscape writing reflects the effects of social transformations upon turn-of-the-twentieth-century Americans since landscape is embedded within relevant social and historical contexts. In her letters to literary friends, Wharton emphasizes the " cultural and historical implications of landscape" (qtd. in Whaley, 2). Therefore, an analysis of her landscape writing will offer a significant perspective for examining her attitude towards the transformations in American society. In her lifetime, the United States had undergone tremendous transformations. Firstly, America transformed from an agrarian to an industrial nation and emerged as an industrial giant in the second half of the nineteenth century. Meanwhile, with the development of industrialization, the degree of agricultural mechanization was increased and fertilizers were widely used, leading to a significant rise in crop yields. This caused agricultural products to drop in price due to oversupply, coupled with high railway transportation costs and the massive exodus of rural labor, American farmers found themselves in economic distress (Harold Wilson, 99). Secondly, the late nineteenth century saw impressive economic growth and the unprecedented expansion of major cities. In the decades following the Civil War, cities in the United States grew at a dramatic rate and the nation attained urban-majority status between 1910 and 1920 (Scobey, *Empire City*, 16). Thirdly, the rise of transnational tourism shaped the global outlook of the turn-of-the-century Americans when traveling to other countries became an increasingly common feature of their lives. Besides, the rise of the United States as a new world power inspired public debates about how the country should re-examine its relationship with Europe (Endy, 565).

Historians concur that the period between the end of the Civil War and the onset of World War II marked a phase of accelerated social transformations in the United States. Scholars point out that Americans who lived in the early twentieth century strongly felt a rupture from the preceding nineteenth century because they regarded the 1900s as the dividing line between the old and the new. Henry Adams, one of the most outstanding scholars at that time, called the Americans of the twentieth century "new men" who lived in a "modern society" (qtd. in Richard D. Brown, 190). As Jenny Lynn Glennon summarizes, American people at the time saw the new century as "a climactic break with history and aesthetic tradition" (67).

Wharton articulates that landscape adds an "extra dimension of visual meaning" to the "psychological and cultural themes" in her works (qtd. in Whaley, 6). Revealing the impacts of social transformations, the author's landscape writing has been profoundly influenced by American Romanticist predecessors and her contemporary realistic writers. For instance, Washington Irving consistently mourned the changes in the landscape of Hudson River Valley due to intrusions of progress. As early as March 1839, he wrote to the *Knickerbocker* as "Geoffrey Crayon": "I can no longer picture an Arcadia in every green valley; nor a fairy land among the distant mountains; nor a peerless beauty in every villa glistening among the trees"

(104). James Fenimore Cooper portraits the natural landscape of the Puritan settlement to express his perspectives on crucial matters such as the Puritans' relationship with Native Americans and post-Revolutionary patriotism①. Against the backdrop of rapid industrialization sweeping across the United States in the second half of the nineteenth century, Ralph Waldo Emerson attempts to join Americans' enthusiasm for technological progress with their love of landscape, a blending of Machinery and Transcendentalism: " the road with iron bars [...] darts through the country, from town to town, like an eagle or a swallow through the air. By the aggregate of these aids, how is the face of the world changed" (8). Wharton, a fervent reader of Emerson, embraces his belief in the spiritual power of nature to counter the encroaching mechanization within American society. Confronted by the overwhelming influences of urbanization, late-nineteenth-century realistic writers such as William Dean Howells and Theodore Dreiser search for pastoral dream in rural landscape as a temporary relief from urban reality: "Whether it be the tinkle of a lone sheep bell o'er some quiet landscape, or the glimmer of beauty in sylvan places, or the show of soul in some passing eye, the heart knows and makes answer, following" (Dreiser, 898).

Given Wharton's love of nature, her writing principles, and the literary traditions with which she grows as an American writer, the significance of landscape in Wharton's works thus can be justified. This book chooses her six novels *The House of Mirth* (1905), *Ethan Frome* (1911), *The Custom of the Country* (1913), *Summer* (1917), *Hudson River Bracketed* (1929), and *The Gods Arrive* (1932) to explore her delineation of the intricate

---

① For instance, in his masterpiece *The Last of the Mohicans* (1826), Cooper often portrays Native Americans' residence as "the tract of wilderness [...] seemed as if the foot of man had never trodden, so breathing and deep was the silence in which it lay" (373). Native Americans were described as part of the wilderness: "the person of Chingachgook, who sat upright, and motionless as one of the trees, which formed the dark barrier on every side of them" (168).

interplay between the characters and their surroundings during a pivotal period in American history. The reasons for selecting those works are as follows: Firstly, the six novels contain all the New England landscapes portrayed in Wharton's fiction, including New York City, rural New England, and her idealized Hudson River Valley landscape. Given the writer's prolonged residence in the Northeastern United States, these novels present an overall picture of her understanding of New England landscape. Specifically, although Wharton published several novels set in New York, most of them focus on indoor activities, with sparse descriptions of the urban landscape①. For example, in *The Age of Innocence*, the scenes predominantly unfold within the mansions of New York's elite during the 1860s and 1870s. Due to the strict social conventions of that time, characters rarely venture outside to partake in city life. Additionally, the societal transformations experienced by New Yorkers in the post-Civil War period were not as profound as those occurring at the dawn of the twentieth century. By comparison, *The House of Mirth* and *The Custom of the Country* offer more extensive portrayals of the urban landscape. Moreover, with the former set in the late nineteenth century and the latter in the early twentieth, an analysis of these two novels reveals the transitions in New York at the turn of the century. Compared to her New York novels, Wharton's works depicting New England are more limited in number, primarily consisting of short stories published in newspapers and magazines. *Ethan Frome* and

---

① Wharton's New York novels include *The House of Mirth*, *The Custom of the Country*, *The Age of Innocence*, *Old New York* (1924) , *The Mother's Recompense* (1925) , and *Twilight Sleep* (1927). Unlike *The House of Mirth* and *The Custom of the Country* which focus on describing the urban landscape, *The Age of Innocence* and *Old New York* are more concerned with the "the customs, manners, conventions, and subtle distinctions of high society" rather than the city itself (Wang Lin, 29). In *The Mother's Recompense* and *Twilight Sleep*, "the structures and spaces of New York have disappeared almost entirely and the map has faded to irrelevance or unintelligibility" (Benert, 196).

Summer are the only two novels centering on rural life in New England, and they are her most well-known local color novels. In Wharton's works, the Hudson River Valley often appears as a venue for urban elites' entertainment. Only in *Hudson River Bracketed* and *The Gods Arrive*, she devotes much attention to describing the valley's landscape. Secondly, through comparing Wharton's idealized Hudson Valley landscape with the other two types of New England landscape, this book provides insight into her thoughts on how Americans should navigate social transformations and how landscape can serve as an antidote to the negative effects of these transformations. Thirdly, as these works revolve around American life at the turn of the twentieth century, this book's analysis of various landscapes sheds light on the impacts of social transformations on Americans during that period. Besides, because the six novels are roughly arranged in chronological order which starts with Wharton's first bestseller *The House of Mirth* and concludes with her final two completed novels *Hudson River Bracketed* and *The Gods Arrive*, this book's analysis of the landscape illuminates both the transformations in American society over the span of these decades and the shifts in the author's stance on social transformations.

To sum up, Edith Wharton demonstrates a profound understanding of the significance of landscape in both human society and literary creation. In her view, the issues such as the formation and transformation of landscape, the identities of observers, and the ways of seeing are all intricately intertwined with historical and cultural contexts. It is hoped that this book, by scrutinizing various kinds of landscapes in Wharton's fiction, will provide a new perspective to understand her concerns with the dynamic interrelationship between individuals and their surrounding environments when America was rushing into heightened industrialization, urbanization, and globalization at the turn of the century.

1.2   Literature Review

Upon receiving the news of Wharton's demise in 1937, American art historian Bernard Berenson said to their mutual friends: "For me she can never be dead. She will remain while consciousness lasts […] a cultural term of reference" (qtd. in Orlando, *The Bloomsbury Handbook to Edith Wharton*, 1). After nearly a century since Berenson made his observations, Wharton continues to hold her position as a significant literary figure in American history and a discerning cultural critic of her era. The range, quality, and popularity of Wharton's works arouse abundant critical responses from Western and Chinese scholars. Since the establishment of the Edith Wharton Society and the launch of *Edith Wharton Review* in 1984, the body of Wharton scholarship has significantly expanded and the approaches to her works have drawn widely from different critical paradigms.

In the Western academia, more than 10,000 critical articles on Wharton have been published from 1919 to 2023, according to JSTOR database. Based on PQDT full-text, a total of 193 doctoral books, spanning the period from 1904 to 2023, have been devoted to the writer[1]. Generally speaking, Wharton criticism was dominated by feminist, psychoanalytical, and Marxist perspectives throughout much of the twentieth century[2]. Since the 1990s, two significant trends have emerged in academic scholarship. Firstly, instead of concentrating on the theme of patriarchy, the interpretation of the

---

[1]   These data were collected from the library database of Guangdong University of Foreign Studies on March 28, 2023.

[2]   For a comprehensive summary of Wharton scholarship in the twentieth century, see Helen Killoran, *The Critical Reception of Edith Wharton* (Rochester, NY: Camden House, 2001).

characters in Wharton's works has benefited more from gender theories which explore the issues such as masculinity and queer identities. Secondly, cultural studies have provided fresh insights for Wharton criticism. An increasing number of scholars situate the writer in material culture studies, media studies, race studies, disability studies, cosmopolitanism, etc.①

Chinese scholars began their research on Wharton from the 1930s. More essays appeared after the publication of Chinese translations of *The House of Mirth*, *Ethan Frome* and *The Age of Innocence* in the 1980s. Until now, there are seven monographs on Wharton's works which are based on those authors' doctoral books and MA theses. In addition to the monographs, 205 pieces of journal articles, three doctoral book and 172 MA theses on Wharton can be found in CNKI between 1987 and 2023②. Compared with the studies on Wharton in the Western academia, the criticism at home mainly focuses on *The House of Mirth* and *The Age of Innocence*, thus few studies pay attention to the novels published after 1920. Moreover, most studies are centered on the discussion of female characters from a dominant feminist perspective (Xie, 203; Yang & Wang, 48; Xiong & He, 57).

Although there have been significant achievements in Wharton studies, research conducted from the perspective of cultural geography is comparatively limited, predominantly focusing on the spatial politics of New York City. Few researchers have carefully examined and interpreted various landscapes portrayed in the writer's novels. The present review will focus on the following three groups of studies which are related to this book: the

---

① For a detailed analysis of the reviews, see Cheng Xin, "New Directions of Wharton Studies in the 21st Century", *Contemporary Foreign Literature*, 2 (2011): 161-167; also see Jessica Schubert McCarthy, "Modern Critical Receptions" in *Edith Wharton in Context* (New York: Cambridge University Press, 2012): 103-113.

② These data were collected from the library database of Guangdong University of Foreign Studies on March 27, 2023. The doctoral books of the above-mentioned Chinese scholars are not included in the database.

studies on New York City, rural New England, and the Hudson River Valley.

1.2.1   Studies on New York City in Wharton's Works

Wharton is primarily labelled as an Old New York writer. Since she devotes most of her works to the description of New York City life in the late nineteenth and early twentieth centuries, many critics have discussed her presentation of the city, especially in the two most well-known fiction—*The House of Mirth* and *The Age of Innocence*.

Firstly, scholars pay close attention to the rituals of the "Upper Ten Thousand" and thus regard Wharton's fictions as "New York Novels of Manners" (Sarah Wilson, 121-25; Pennell, 93-101). The clashes between the old New York and the *Nouveau Riches* are scrutinized by critics. For instance, Judith Fryer argues that Wharton criticizes the "custom" of the country that threatens "a world of civilized ritual" which is the meaning of "city" (108).

Secondly, studies on New York City mainly center on Wharton's literary representation of interior space because the characters' activities mostly take place inside different houses due to the society's preference for domesticity at that time. Many scholars take notice of the interplay among characters, social history, and domestic aesthetics in Wharton's fictions. Both Whaley and Clubbe argue that interior space in New York City restricts women's opportunities (Whaley, 121; Clubbe, 543) while Chance links interior design to women's pursuit of independence (199). Claiming that Wharton's city is "a city of interiors", Nancy Von Rosk places the writer's description of domestic space in the larger context of urbanization, pointing out that these interiors are "urban phenomenon—domestic theaters made possible by the new urban economy" (329). Xu Hui and Guo Qiqing interpret the connection between interior decoration and characters' personalities and social statuses in *The House of Mirth* (97-101) , whereas Zhu Hejin and Hu Tiesheng focus on the ethical dimensions of buildings through pointing out that their façade and interior decoration reflect the conflicts between individual and collective ethics (155-158).

Thirdly, how urban spaces impact the city dwellers' lives also attracts critics' attention. By illustrating how the apartments and luxury hotels transform the traditional home with history to a consumable commodity, Besty Klimasmith argues that the permeable buildings reflect " modern, mobile, transformable subjectivity " (" Hotel Spirit ", 29). While Klimasmith's study focuses on the urban homes, Irene Billeter Sauter analyzes the streets and theatres to show how public space greatly influences the protagonists' identities and then concludes that Wharton's millionaire heroines are framed by conspicuous consumption in the "gilt cage of their New York City" (254). In a similar spirit, Johnny Finnigan in his book discusses the evolution of New York City between the 1870s and the 1910s by carefully decoding the topographical sites of the houses (5). Examining the author's representation of New York within the larger social and political context of the American Renaissance and City Beautiful Movement, Annette Benert pushes the discussion further by highlighting the presence of one dichotomy in Wharton's use of space that " physical structures that in her architectural and autobiographical works serve to reify the ideals become in her fiction agents of social domination" (58).

Lastly, scholars stress the influences of consumer culture in the Gilded Age in their discussion on urban space. As Olin-Ammentorp suggests, New York City "has long encapsulated the tension between money making and art in a small geographic space" (118). Drawing on the work of economist Thorstein Veblen, Anne-Marie Evans analyzes the utilization of consumerism and the use of different forms of space in *The House of Mirth* and

11

explores "how women are consistently relegated to the status of products for male consumption" (107). Ailsa Boyd draws a similar conclusion by analyzing the showy hotels, shadowy brownstones, and crowded restaurants in *The Custom of the Country* ("Looey Suite", 9). In *Elite Tradition and Culture of Consumption: On Edith Wharton's "Old New York" Novels* (2014), Sun Wei highlights that Wharton's portrayal of New York embodies two pronounced features: "conspicuous consumption as an added value to architectural symbolism" and "home décor as a fundamental expression of social manners", showcasing the influence of materialism on the perspectives and lives of Americans (205).

1.2.2   Studies on Rural New England in Wharton's Works

In addition to New York City, rural New England is also a significant place in Wharton's fiction. She wrote two novels—*Ethan Frome* and *Summer*—and several short stories to describe the scenery of the New England countryside near her summer estate, The Mount. The criticism on Wharton's representation of rural New England undergoes a transition in focus, shifting from an examination of the reliability of her landscape writing to an exploration of the metaphorical meaning of the landscape, and ultimately encompassing an expanding body of interdisciplinary studies in the present era.

Since the publication of *Ethan Frome* and *Summer*, a large number of reviewers debate whether Wharton's New England stories offer a realistic portrayal of local landscape or not. Despite her own denial of writing as an outsider of the region, many critics see the bleak picture of rural place as a distortion due to class prejudice. Acknowledging that the author knows well the New England architecture and distinctive features of local culture, Nancy

R. Leach argues that Wharton sees the rural villages with "slight disdain" and the colorless records of New England scenery are "essentially literary impressions and handled, for the most part, superficially and conventionally" (91). Putting her among a group of the late-nineteenth-century writers who hold a critical, sometimes pessimistic, view of the people and land in the hill country of Western Massachusetts, Perry D. Westbrook concludes that the rural landscape in *Ethan Frome* and *Summer* "exists only in the background, providing the rigid, inhumane forces" that lead her characters into decay (225). Diverging from most scholars' concern on the issue of realistic representation, Ruth Maria Whaley in her doctoral dissertation *Landscape in the Writing of Edith Wharton* (1982) states that Wharton uses landscape as a metaphor for her own life divided between art and society. Whaley's argument sparks subsequent research on the meaning of rural New England landscape in *Ethan Frome* and *Summer*. However, instead of focusing on the landscape, Whaley's study mainly deals with American Transcendentalists' impact upon the writer's opinion about nature.

In their research on the meaning of rural landscape, scholars tend to interpret the landscape as a metaphor. Most reviewers believe that New England landscape symbolizes the characters' pursuit of love. While the mountain covered in white snow symbolizes hopeless love in *Ethan Frome*, the blooming flowers in *Summer* hint at romantic passion in *Summer* (Dean, 130). Critics also relate Wharton's description of landscape to the sexual awakening she feels in her extramarital affair with American journalist William Morton Fullerton (Wolff, "Cold Ethan", 232). In addition to the metaphor of love, scholars propose that the hostile natural environment exemplifies the modern spiritual crisis. Whereas Carol J. Singley emphasizes the influences of Puritanism (*Edith Wharton: Matters of Mind and Spirit*, 107), He Yan concentrates on Wharton's endorsement of naturalism (38).

Recently, interdisciplinary studies that examine New England in Wharton's fiction emerge, with a particular focus on the rural landscape in *Summer*. The latest research employs diverse theories from fields such as tourism and media studies to analyze the representative rural places such as the library and the village in *Summer*, thereby broadening the scope of Wharton studies. Both Liisa Stephenson and Sheila Liming notice the importance of the public library in this novel. Through scrutinizing the relationship of female readers to the library space, Stephenson proposes that "women readers wish to transform the library from a mausoleum of dead authors to a living space of their own" (28). Stephenson further adopts theories of influence and intertextuality to explore Wharton's "modernist impulse to democratize the archive or liberate the library" (27). While Stephenson's thesis focuses on the fictional library, Liming links the novel to Americans' reading habits and the development of public and private libraries in the early twentieth century. According to Liming, the heroine Charity's indifference toward books and reading reveals "Wharton's fears regarding the modern American culture's insistence on newness and its resulting impatience with tradition and with history" (52). The village in *Summer* attracts critics' attention as well. For example, Tara K. Panniter sees the New England village as a fictional representation of the nostalgic summer place at that time. By combining tourism studies with feminist theories, Panniter finds the "intersections between travel and domesticity" in *Summer* (21). Panniter's consideration of the context of rural tourism and analysis on the correlation between Charity's growth and various landscapes in the village are of particular relevance to the third chapter of this book. Nonetheless, Panniter does not pay enough attention to the significance of the New England rural landscape due to her study's emphasis on women's activities in summer vacationing.

1.2.3 Studies on the Hudson River Valley in Wharton's Works

Compared with the studies on Wharton's depiction of New York City and rural New England, the essays about the Hudson River Valley are much fewer. As the valley in *The House of Mirth* and *The Age of Innocence* serves as a stage where the elite characters partake in their recreational activities, some critics pay attention to the relationship between culture and nature in the gardens of the valley's rural estates. Reviewers generally agree that although those gardens are figured as natural landscape, they are actually suffused with artifice. For instance, Sharon L. Dean sees the garden as a decorative element in Wharton's novels (89). By investigating how the garden acts as a stage for the leisure-class's performance, Rosk concludes that nature becomes another commodity in modern society (341). Agreeing with Dean and Rosk on the garden's role as a setting for performance, Benert adds a feminist perspective to the discussion through examining the problematic relationship between women and nature in the nineteenth century (144).

In her last two completed novels—*Hudson River Bracketed* and its sequel *The Gods Arrive*, Wharton devotes considerable space to the portrait of the valley landscape. Since the writer adopts the indigenous architectural style—Hudson River Bracketed—as the title of her novel, critics scrutinize an old house named The Willows in *Hudson River Bracketed* and *The God Arrives* which is built in this style. Although some reviewers such as Benert sees the old house as "a metaphor, a mystic inspiration, rather than a place where people lived", more and more scholars have recognized the importance of the old house (206). Jan Cohn, for example, believes that The Willows is the center of the novel through analyzing its influence upon the protagonist Vance's development of "artisthood and manhood" (548). Agreeing with Cohn on the significance of the house, Stephenson pushes the discussion further by arguing that Wharton inverts the typical nineteenth-century scenario of the gentleman's library in her depiction of The Willows (246).

Seeing the Hudson Valley as an ideal and symbolic landscape which balances open spaciousness and bounded space, Whaley is the first scholar to point out the significance of the natural environment in *Hudson River Bracketed* and *The Gods Arrive* (200). While Whaley stresses the influences of Transcendentalism on the Hudson River Valley, Judith P. Saunders highlights this region's unique cultural-historical roots as the iconic American landscape by concluding that both the natural landscape and cultural history assumes "obvious importance in Vance's story" since Wharton endows "the Mid-Hudson region with creative potency and transformative properties" for her self-educated hero (187). The essay of Saunders inspires the author of this book to research the position of the valley in American literature and art. But Saunders focuses more on the literary allusions in *Hudson River Bracketed* than the landscape of the valley, thus leaving space for further exploration in this book. In his response to Saunders, Gary Totten analyzes how the "lush and creative" landscape of the Hudson River Valley "works as an antidote to" American business culture ("Edith Wharton's Geographical Imagination", 94). In agreement with Saunders and Totten on the uniqueness of the Hudson Valley, Olin-Ammentorp sees Wharton's treatment of the place as "a different vision of America, one in which western energy and eastern refinement can be productively united" (184). However, since none of these studies note the protagonist's emotional and aesthetic experiences of the landscape, they fail to acknowledge how the landscape of the Hudson Valley liberates him from spiritual crisis.

To sum up, Wharton's works are analyzed through an ever-growing array of approaches from the biographical and feminist perspectives in the latter part of the 1900s to the ongoing discussions in the twenty-first century from various perspectives such as space, urban studies, material culture, etc. This literature review demonstrates that critics have already noticed Wharton's representation of New York City, rural New England, and the Hudson River Valley. However, they have not paid enough attention to the significance of landscape in her writing.

Firstly, as most critics hold a dated view on the concept of landscape, they tend to either ignore the important role that landscape plays in Wharton's writing, or merely treat landscape as a metaphor. This lack of analytical depth is clearly demonstrated in the two above-mentioned studies which contain the word "landscape" in their titles: Whaley's doctoral dissertation *Landscape in the Writing of Edith Wharton* and Dean's monograph *Constance Fenimore Woolson and Edith Wharton: Perspectives on Landscape and Art*. While Whaley draws a conclusion that landscape is "a metaphorical expression" for the writer's life divided between art and society (235), Dean emphasizes landscape's relationship to taste and thus regards landscape in her books as "a view of aesthetics" (x). Since landscape in their discussion is taken for granted as an aesthetic framing of certain geographic areas, they fail to recognize its role as an active agent of various power relations in shaping the relationship between human viewers and the material world. The spectators' identities and their specific perspectives of observing the landscape have also been ignored in most previous studies. Moreover, because most reviewers have not recognized the importance of people's emotional experiences while looking at the landscape, so they fail to acknowledge the impacts of the landscape upon the characters' mentalities and ideologies.

Secondly, there are only a few studies focusing on the specific elements of New England landscape in Wharton's novels. Critics tend to view the landscape as an abstract representation of certain values, without paying enough attention to its visual characteristics and cultural-historical connotations. This neglects the uniqueness of the landscape in her novels.

Thirdly, scholars rarely associate Wharton's depiction of landscape with the specific social and historical contexts in turn-of-the-twentieth-century United States. Since they tend to interpret the landscape as something static and changeless, they fail to notice that the formation and transformation of landscape are influenced by complex socio-economic, political, and cultural forces which further mold the characters' perceptions of their surroundings. Moreover, how the writer's delineation of landscape reveals her own stance towards social transformations in a pivotal phase in American history is largely neglected by the previous studies.

Fourthly, the interpretation of Wharton's landscape writing is to some extent affected by the critics' preconceived impression of the writer. In their discussion on *Ethan Frome* and *Summer*, for example, since nearly all the reviewers are greatly influenced by biographical materials, they tend to interpret Wharton's depiction of the rural landscape based on her own emotional life and her characters' experience, thereby overlooking the impacts of social transformations upon New England. Some critics even carelessly label Wharton as an Old New York novelist who does not know New England very well. When analyzing *Hudson River Bracketed* and *The Gods Arrive*, scholars overemphasize Wharton's social status and regard the Hudson River Valley as a nostalgic refuge for the upper-class writer who longs for the bygone days, thus failing to observe Wharton's constant concerns about the social issues in post-WWI America.

Based on the previous studies, this book attempts to explore the significance of landscape in Wharton's writing by investigating how the depiction of New England landscape illustrates her insights into the impacts of social transformations upon turn-of-the-twentieth-century Americans. As the well-known Wharton scholar Olin-Ammentorp says, "Wharton's work has not benefited from quite the same extended attention to place as her contemporary writers", this book's attention to the landscape, therefore, does respond to the growing academic interest in applying cultural geography theories to interpret Wharton's works (12).

1.3　Study Objectives and Research Questions

Adopting landscape theories in cultural geography as chief interpretive strategies, this book studies Edith Wharton's depiction of New England landscape in the selected works, with the aim of elucidating the impacts of social transformations upon turn-of-the-twentieth-century Americans by investigating how power relations among different classes, races, and genders, as well as between men and nature shape individuals' perceptions of their surroundings, and how people's emotions emerging from experiencing landscape indicate the effects of social transformations on their mentalities, ideologies, and aesthetic tastes.

This book intends to answer the following questions:

1. How are New York cityscape, rural New England landscape, and Hudson River Valley landscape represented in the selected works of Wharton in relation to turn-of-the-twentieth-century Americans' experiences?

2. How do various power relations shape the characters' perceptions of New York City, rural New England, and the Hudson River Valley in Wharton's works, and how do the characters' emotional experiences of these landscapes reveal the influences of social transformations on their mentalities, ideologies, and aesthetic tastes?

3. How does the characters' interaction with landscape in the selected

works reflect the changing American society, and how does Wharton's delineation of landscape illustrate her attitude towards turn-of-the-century America and her thoughts on handling social transformations?

1.4   Landscape, Power and Emotion

This book explores the significance of landscape in Wharton's works by analyzing the urban landscape in New York City, rural landscape in New England region, and the writer's idealized landscape in the Hudson River Valley. In order to provide theoretical support for the book, this review will first define the concept of "landscape" and then discuss two major ways of conducting landscape studies in cultural geography, which will be used as chief interpretive strategies in this book.

1.4.1   Defining Landscape

As a pivotal concept in cultural geography, "landscape" is a complex term that cannot be easily defined. The origin of the word "landscape" comes from the Germanic language. The earliest use can be found in the Middle Dutch "landscap" and the Germanic "landschaft" which both refer to a land region or environment. Through the sixteenth and seventeenth centuries, the Dutch word "landschap" migrated into English language, with "landscape" gradually coming to refer to a painting of the countryside. Its etymology shows that the English word "landscape" contains both the material and the representational meaning, which is clearly demonstrated in its definition in *The Dictionary of Human Geography*: "the visual appearance of land, most often countryside, and its pictorial depiction" (Wylie, "Landscape", 409).

Landscapes not only contain the natural land forms such as mountains, lakes, and oceans, but also man-made architectural structures including buildings, streets, cities, etc. According to the *European Landscape Convention*, landscape means "an area, as perceived by people, whose character is the result of the action and interaction of natural and/or human factors" (qtd. in Atha et al., xx). Since they are produced by both the natural processes and human activities, landscapes reflect the distinct characters of people and place in a certain part of the world.

Landscape has long been the essential object of investigation and interpretive vehicle for cultural geographers. Carl Ortwin Sauer introduces the concept of "landscape" into American geography and defines it as a cultural entity produced by the interactions between human cultures and natural environments (316). Based on Sauer's definition, scholars extend the empirical studies on the morphology of landscape to the studies on its symbolic and iconic meanings. J. B. Jackson, for instance, defines "landscape" as at once "an everyday, lived-in world and a repository of symbolic values" (49). His notion that all landscapes are expressions of cultural values inspires theorists to explore how the interpretation of landscape is shaped by our subjectivities. Another influential geographer Kenneth Olwig emphasizes the political meaning of landscape by pointing out the close relationship between landscape and law and relocating an original meaning of the English word "landscape as a nexus of community, justice, nature, and environmental equity" (630-631).

More diversified writings on landscape emerged since the "cultural turn"[1] in the 1980s and theorists began to pay more attention to the

---

[1] According to *The Dictionary of Human Geography*, "cultural turn" refers to a set of intellectual developments that led to issues of culture such as gender, race and sexuality becoming central in human geography since the late 1980s (Barnett, "Cultural Turn", 134).

sociocultural factors in the representation of landscape. Through tracing Western visual traditions of landscape painting and gardening, Denis Cosgrove in his influential book *Social Formation and Symbolic Landscape* (1998) defines "landscape" as "a way of seeing"—produced by the way in which people see the world around them (1). In other words, Cosgrove regards landscape not merely as a geographic area but rather as a visual representation of the relationship between the human viewer and the material world. It is the viewer's imagination that turns a piece of land into landscape.

Sharing with Cosgrove's stress on the visual representations of landscape, James Duncan and Nancy Duncan see landscape as a text to be critically read by drawing upon the theories of structuralist semiotics. In "(Re) reading the Landscape", they argue that landscape operate as a signifying system which is read and interpreted via "an ingrained cultural framework of interpretation" (123).

While the above-mentioned theorists focus on how landscape is interpreted and consumed, Don Mitchell emphasizes that the key to understanding landscape is to investigate the process of its production. As he explains, "any morphology, any patterns, arrangements and looks, any representational act, does not just arise spontaneously in place". Consequently, he understands landscape as "form, meaning and representation" which "actively incorporates the social relations that go into its making" (49). For him, those relations are capitalist and the production of landscapes is a matter of ongoing struggle and conflict among different social and economic groups in terms of labor, value, profit, etc.

Pointing out that landscape is often taken for granted "as an aesthetic framing of the real properties of space and places", W. J. T. Mitchell in *Landscape and Power* (2002) urges cultural geographers to treat "space, place, and landscape as a dialectical triad" in order to activate landscape studies from diversified angles: "If a place is a specific location, a space is a 'practiced place,' a site activated by movements, actions, narratives, and signs, and a landscape is that site encountered as image or 'sight'" ("Preface", x). With a similar focus upon issues of power like Don Mitchell, but in a more discursive and interpretative manner, he defines landscape as a verb, not a noun—that is, as a process by which "social and subjective identities are formed" ("Introduction", 1). That is to say, researchers should not only ask what landscape is or means, but also how it works for the formation of individual and collective identities. It should not be regarded as a fixed object to be viewed, appreciated, or interpreted (the way proposed by Cosgrove). Rather, it is an active agent of power which veils the operation of cultural practices by naturalizing its own social construction and representing an artificial world "as if it were simply given and inevitable" (2).

Whereas the above-mentioned theorists adopt iconographic, discursive, and interpretive approaches to define landscape which emphasize its representational aspects, others focus on exploring human beings' bodily contact with and emotional experience of landscape. In other words, the multi-sensorial, experiential, and emotional dimensions of landscape are paid attention to. In disagreement with the notions of landscape as a way of seeing—an image, representation or gaze, Tim Ingold argues that because those definitions treat it as a scene to view rather than a world for inhabitation, they tend to neglect what landscape means to the people who live in it. What is more, a series of dualities—subject and object, mind and body, and especially culture and nature, have been reinforced in those definitions. He offers an alternative definition by suggesting that landscape can be understood as "an ongoing, reciprocal, bodily process of engagement and involvement, a process in which 'perceiver' and 'world' are enrolled" (153). In a similar manner, Arnold Berleant regards

23

landscape as "a somatic engagement in the aesthetic field" (166).

Richard H. Schein attempts to integrate the humanistic view of thinking landscape as everyday material world in which people live with the discussion on landscape politics. Stressing that it is not only a discursive mediator of cultural values, but also a tangible, visible entity which is experienced by human beings through embodied and multi-sensory encounters, he argues that landscape should be understood as both part of the "material world for human interaction" and a "conceptual framework" through which human beings understand the world ("Normative Dimensions of Landscape", 202). Emphasizing the importance of people's embodied experience and practice, at the same time he acknowledges that the issues of power, identity, inequality, and conflict are central ingredients of everyday landscapes. This eclectic definition of "landscape" is particularly useful for this book.

To summarize, the meaning of "landscape" has expanded from its initial geographical concept to include rich cultural, political, and social connotations. Although its definitions are variegated, the meaning of "landscape" in cultural geography mainly contains the following aspects: firstly, it describes the visible features of land which include both natural and man-made environments; secondly, it is the product of a particular way of seeing which has aesthetic significance; thirdly, it is culturally constructed and represented; fourthly, it can also be thought of as the everyday material world in which people live and interact with each other. The landscapes analyzed in this book include both the visual appearance of land—natural landscapes such as mountains, rivers and forests, and man-made landscapes such as buildings and streets. It is worth noting that both the exteriors and interiors of buildings are regarded as landscapes in this research since they contain the above-mentioned features: the exterior and interior decoration of houses demonstrates the visible features of man-made environment; on the one hand, they represent certain aesthetic and cultural values; on the other hand, they are also part of the everyday material world where people live.

Based on Schein's definition that landscape is both part of the everyday world in which people experience and a "conceptual framing" of the world, this book will investigate not only the geographic features of landscape in Wharton's works, but also explore how social values are reflected and the flow of emotions are produced in people's engagements with landscape ("Normative Dimensions of Landscape", 202). The following review will scrutinize the study of landscape especially with reference to its relations with power and with emotion.

1.4.2 Landscape and Power

Although the traditional aesthetic and historical approaches to landscape tend to overlook or downplay the issue of power, since the 1980s, theories of hegemony and dominant ideology have been applied to analyze landscape's complicated engagement with the social, economic, and political conditions. Landscape studies pay much attention to investigate power disparities in terms of class, gender, and race.

First of all, cultural geographers demonstrate how landscape reflects as well as helps in maintaining class stratification. Cosgrove and Daniels are among the first group of theorists to point out that the long-held "idyllised" vision of rural landscape covers up and conceals the power and control in a hierarchical society by chiming with elite visions of human society and nature ("Introduction", 1-10). Because people's way of seeing is affected by pre-existing concepts and beliefs, Cosgrove draws upon the work of cultural Marxist critics such as John Berger and Raymond Williams to point out the ideological function of landscape images. He proposes that the landscape idea "emerged as a dimension of European elite consciousness and supported a range of political, social and moral assumptions and became a significant aspect of taste" (*Social Formation*, 8). Thus, "landscape" is not a neutral term but an ideological concept because the process of seeing and representing landscape reflects and reproduces the values of a privileged class. The key point here is that the way of seeing creates a distance between the viewer and the viewed landscape which leads to a sense of authority and control for the outside viewer. What is more, those people who work and live within the landscape are reduced to part of the scenery and thus also objectified by the detached observer. To summarize, Cosgrove stresses landscape's role as a way of seeing through which political, economic, and social hierarchies can be veiled.

Sharing with Cosgrove's emphasis on the ideological function of landscape, James Duncan and Nancy Duncan point out that landscapes may "be inculcating their readers with a set of notions about how the society is organized, and the readers may be largely unaware of this" ("(Re)reading the Landscape", 123). In seeing landscape as "text", they dwell upon the manner in which landscape may be understood as expressions of power and authority. As the text of landscape conveys and transmits certain ideological narratives about the organization of society, they propose that cultural geographers should pay attention to the "mechanisms through which dominant ideas and beliefs are reproduced via landscapes" and supply alternative readings from various perspectives (124).

Influenced by the above-mentioned theorists' conclusion that landscape should be treated as a "visual ideology", many cultural geographers pay attention to how class conflicts operate in the rural landscape (*Social Formation*, 47). Rural landscape is most often associated with idyll. As recognized by Paul Cloke, the significance of "the rural idyll lies partly in the ways in which it transports implicit ideologies amongst its iconography, and symbolizes the enrollment of rural landscapes into particular material and political processes in the production of cultural space" ("Rural Landscapes", 229). For example, Harriet Hawkins argues that the peaceful English countryside in John Constable's paintings can be a "class battleground" as his representation of the landscape covers the exploitative labor relations, rural poverty, and political unrest at that time (209). Whereas scholars such as Cosgrove and Daniels attempt to investigate the ideological function of landscape in order to critique the perspective of a particular class, Don Mitchell adopts a more materialist and Marxist vision to claim that the production of landscape is a matter of constant conflicts between different socio-economic groups within capitalist networks (49-56).

In addition to analyzing its role in representing and reproducing class stratification, theorists claim that landscape also functions as a gloss to perpetuate gender hierarchy. Drawing upon psychoanalytic and visual theories to analyze the issues of landscape, gender and visual representation, Gillian Rose argues that the landscape way of seeing is a "masculine gaze" and the "pleasure of looking at landscape" is closely associated with masculine domination (86). For her, the landscape way of seeing involves "a duality between an active masculine eye and a passive, naturalized femininity": firstly, landscapes in geographical discourse are often related to the female body and the beauty of Nature; secondly, the female body-as-landscape forms a metaphorical terrain of desire (87). Based on this duality, she argues that landscape as gaze reveals a tension between rational observation and repressed visual pleasure in the form of voyeurism and narcissism (101). Based on Rose's critiques of the masculinity of the landscape tradition, Catherine Nash further notes that there is a gendered difference in people's relationship to the land: man is often represented as the owner of the land, while woman as "a part of the still and exquisite landscape" (94). Thus, she argues that feminist geographers should attempt to open up possibilities for "subversion, resistance, and reappropriation of visual traditions and visual pleasure" (149).

While Rose and Nash concentrate on the femininization of nature, other theorists analyze the gendering of urban landscape in Western countries. Generally speaking, theorists state that the towns and cities in Western societies have a patriarchal basis and the gendering of space interweaves with the development of built environments. The most well-known example is that the urban landscape demonstrates a gendered division of labor under capitalism and patriarchy by separating masculine public space from feminine private space in the processes of urbanization and industrialization. Apart from the issue of separate spheres, cultural geographers investigate the gendering of urban landscapes such as the streets, buildings, and landmark monuments. David Scobey, for instance, traces how the streets in New York City in the second half of the nineteenth century were portraited as threatening to women from the genteel class and how the anxiety led to broad campaigns aimed at ordering streetscapes (*Empire City*, 177-179). Discussing the cityscapes of New York and Boston in the same period, Mona Domosh uses gender and consumption theories to interpret the manipulation of middle-class women in department stores which function as a site of spectacle (*Invented Cities*, 268-284). Instead of focusing on specific cities, Liz Bondi provides a general analysis on how ideas about gender are historically inscribed on urban landscapes through examining the "interplay between changing gender identities and changing urban landscapes" (157). For example, she proposes that built environments can be viewed as texts which signify "general beliefs about gender relations" (158).

In addition to the dimensions of class and gender, the aspect of race represents another vital component in the scholarly investigation of the relationship between landscape and power. Firstly, theorists pay attention to the close relationship between rural landscape and the important issues such as patriotism, national identities, and racial identities. Cloke, for instance, summarizes that rural landscape is often "associated with white ethnicities [...] representing both a contrast to multicultural cities and potentially a space in which people of other ethnicity experience unease, or out-of-placeness" (Cloke, "Rural Landscapes", 229).

Secondly, the imbrications of race and American landscape are thoroughly investigated by cultural geographers. As Schein argues in *Landscape and Race in the United States* (2006), "all American landscapes are racialized" (4). Scholars examine how racial processes take place and racial categories get made through cultural landscapes. The issues such as the historical importance of racial codes in keeping "order" in urban landscape, the plantation in American antebellum life, and the role of the "New Negro Movement" in stimulating African Americans' racial pride have been scrutinized to reflect over "debates on citizenship, race relations, the nation's immigrant history, and contemporary immigration policy" (Hoskins, 96).

Thirdly, landscape theorists devote significant attention to exploring the intricate relationship between landscape and imperialism. W. J. T. Mitchell extends the focus of landscape studies from national contexts to linkages between the Western perceptions of non-European landscapes and discourses of imperialism. By pointing out that the values and beliefs which emerge from specific landscape practices can travel through space and time, especially from European to non-European countries, he argues that landscape is historically identified with European imperial discourse as the visual mode of European explorers, cartographers, artists, and travelers. In this sense, it can be understood as "a particular historical formation associated with European imperialism" (W. J. T. Mitchell, "Imperial Landscape", 5). As he notes, landscape might be seen as something like the "dreamwork of imperialism" since Europeans' scientific, intellectual, and artistic representation of foreign landscape reflects and reproduces their sense of superiority over other cultures and thus contributes to the belief in their right to govern (10).

Following Mitchell's argument, many cultural geographers have extensively discussed the issues of landscape, transnational travel, and imperialism by drawing widely from postcolonial and post-structural theories. For instance, scholars attempt to investigate the close relationship between landscape as a way of representing and the expansion of European geographical and scientific knowledges such as cartography and navigation①. As Mary Louise Pratt neatly summarizes, the observer is "the European male subject of European landscape discourse—he whose imperial eyes passively look out and possess" (7). While some theorists analyze the relationship between landscape and knowledge, others focus on how European landscape aesthetics such as the pastoral, the picturesque, and the sublime are used by Western colonists and travelers to judge unfamiliar scenes. Those codes and conventions of landscape representation have the effect of "subduing strangeness" and implanting the "Europeanness" into the illegible landscapes with an aim to transform or control them (Wylie, *Landscape*, 131). One important consequence of aestheticizing non-European landscapes is that those regions are often depicted as primitive and untouched and therefore ready for settlement and colonization (Ryan, 157). It is noteworthy that although they emphasize the important role that landscape plays in promoting discourses of imperialism, most cultural geographers point out that local and indigenous practices are incessantly disrupting European imperial visions, which makes imperial landscape a hybrid "contact zone" (Pratt, 6).

---

① See Kearns, 450-472; Barnett, "Impure and Worldly Geography", 239-251; Clayton, 371-401.

To sum up, these studies demonstrate that landscape is closely associated with social, economic, cultural, and political forces. On the one hand, the formation and transformation of landscape is shaped by various power relations in terms of class, gender, and race; on the other hand, landscape works in naturalizing, maintaining, and reproducing the existing power disparities.

1.4.3 Landscape and Emotion

In addition to analyzing the notions of power which serve as the major concerns of the above-mentioned studies, some theorists propose a different way of conducting research by exploring people's emotions which emerge from their engagements with landscape. Generally speaking, cultural geographers propose that emotions are not discrete properties of an individual mind or body; rather, they are generated by the interactions between individuals and their environment. As Steve Pile points out, a core viewpoint of the latest research findings is to see emotions as relational phenomena (10). In other words, researchers are concerned with how emotions shape space, and how space affects people's emotional experiences. Emotions are not only personal feelings but also social construction, closely related to societal structure, culture, power relationships, etc.

The study of landscape and emotion by cultural geographers start early. They pay attention to the different emotions that people feel for space, place, and landscape in specific situations and analyze the multiple ways in which emotions emerge from and reproduce socio-spatial orders. The emotional qualities of place and human life occupy an important position in the work of humanistic geographers. Yi-Fu Tuan, for instance, demonstrates how human beings' fear is projected onto landscapes throughout history and investigates the ways in which authorities devise landscapes in order to instill fear and subservience in their own populations①. While humanistic geographers emphasize the capacity of landscapes to evoke emotions, feminist geographers focus on how differential emotions are repressed in gendered experiences of landscapes. Taking Gill Valentine's much-quoted essay "The Geography of Women's Fear" (1989) as an example, she argues that women's perception and use of public space have long been ignored by male geographers. Through investigating how the association of male violence with certain environmental contexts has a profound effect on women's fear of pubic space, she finds that women are pressured to adopt such "defensive tactics" as avoiding the perceived "dangerous places" at "dangerous times", which leads to their restricted use and occupation of public space (385).

In contemporary cultural geography, particular within the non-representational theories② which have become well-known since the 1990s, the understanding of emotion is influenced by the works of philosopher Martha Nussbaum and neuroscientist Antonio Damasio. Despite their different approaches, the two scholars propose that "emotions are intrinsically cognitive": "emotions undoubtedly transform our attitude(s) towards the world, towards its meaning and worth, and are also transformative of the self, of our judgments and choices" (Locatelli, 78).

---

① See Yi-Fu Tuan, *Landscapes of Fear*, New York: Pantheon Books, 1979.

② Non-representational theories refer to a diverse body of works that emerged during the mid-to-late 1990s as an alternative approach to the conception, practice, and production of geographic knowledge. Initially coined by Nigel Thrift during that time, non-representational theory has sought to reorientate geographic analyses beyond a perceived overemphasis on representations toward an emphasis on practice, embodiment, materiality, and process: a movement away from a focus on the interpretation of the meaning of landscapes toward a consideration of what they "do" in the unfolding of the social world. Some scholars prefer to use the alternative term "more-than representational theory" to suggest that their theories can act as a supplement to the existing approaches to geographic knowledge production (Waterton, 92-95).

Hence cultural geographers interpret human emotions evoked by landscape as indicative of people's cognition, ideologies, evaluative strategies etc.

This understanding about emotion urges cultural geographers to consider individuals' emotional experience of landscape more carefully. Firstly, based on the theories about the politics of emotion, researchers examine how power dynamics influence people's emotion when they interact with various landscapes. For instance, Emma Waterton and Steve Watson analyze visitors' emotional encounters with heritage tourism sites by describing their embodied practices, sensuous awareness and "fleeting moments of belonging and identity" (47). They find that as the visitors' perceptions of landscape are "culturally, economically, politically and historically mediated", "different bodies [...] will have certain emotional responses already mapped onto them, defined by social expectations and structures of feeling that have built up around issues of gender, class, race and so forth" (76). Similarly, Divya P. Tolia-Kelly argues that the tourists' embodied and sensory experiences of the Lake District National Park in England are shaped by "the moral geography of the landscape as embodying a singular English sensibility" which ignores a multi-ethnic British culture (329). Thus, Asian immigrants feel anxious since the Lake District landscape remind them of racial violence and discrimination. In short, politics of identity molds the emotional dimension of landscape.

As the circulation and distribution of emotion can be "engineered" by the powerful, scholars also pay attention to the manipulation of flows of emotions and investigate emotions' engagements with political issues (Pile, 12). Thrift, for example, draws on the theories of biopower and biopolitics to discuss how emotions are manipulated for political ends in the urban planning of Euro-American cities (57). Stressing that emotion is "viscerally political" because it is "infused with power, grounded in place and located bodies", Christine Berberich, Neil Campbell, and Robert Hudson investigate a variety of everyday landscapes such as playgrounds, roadside memorials, and council estates in the UK to analyze how landscapes become bound up with the issues such as neoliberalism, class relations, and the welfare state. Through specifying which emotions can be expressed and whose emotion are valued, landscape is intertwined with "discourses of the state, media, corporatization, and other systems of order and power" (7). They also note that people can disrupt social orders with an alternative way of experiencing landscapes.

Secondly, Tim Ingold and John Wylie emphasize a more phenomenological understanding of landscape and emotion, compared with the above-mentioned theorists. Inspired by the theories of Martin Heidegger and Maurice Merleau-Ponty, Ingold sees landscapes as active forces and participants in the unfolding of life and emphasizes human beings' embodied practices of dwelling and being-in-the-world (154-157). He suggests that landscape can be understood as "an enduring record of—testimony to—the lives and works of past generations who have dwelt within it, and in so doing, have left there something of themselves" (152). In this definition, he stresses bodily performance and perception of landscape by claiming that it is produced by the inhabitants' processual, material, and perceptual engagement of the world.

Based on Ingold's theories, Wylie pushes the discussion further to explore the relations between the sense of self and landscape via the ideas of emotion. For him, emotion should be understood as "describing domains of experience that are more-than subjective and yet at the same time formative of senses of self and landscape" (*Landscape*, 214). He also proposes that landscape might be described in terms of "the entwined materialities and sensibilities with which we act and sense" through phenomenologically and experientially delineating the emergence of distinct senses of self in the process of embodied encounter with landscape ("A Single Day's Walking", 245). For instance, he explores how tactile engagement with the seascape in coastal walking leads to the emergence of distinct senses of self (Ibid., 215).

To summarize, there are two major ways of conducting landscape research in cultural geography: while some theorists regard landscape as an ideological medium to represent the operation of power structures, others focus on how the notions of emotion contribute to landscape studies. Since landscape is both a "conceptual framing" of the world and part of the "material world for human interaction", these two ways together elucidate the symbolic and emotional dimensions of landscape (Schein, "Normative Dimensions of Landscape", 202). The interpretive strategies also shed light on the dynamic interplay between people and their environments: produced and shaped by the operation of power structures, landscape also has the capacity to evoke people's emotions that mold their mentalities and ideologies. This book adopts the landscape theories in cultural geography as chief interpretive strategies to examine New England landscape in Wharton's works. Specifically, this study explores how various power relations function in the formation and transformation of landscape, and further shape the characters' perceptions of their surroundings. It also scrutinizes how the characters' emotional experiences of landscape reveal the effects of social transformations on their aesthetics, psyche, and ideology. Thus, the analysis of Wharton's landscape writing provides insight into her thoughts on the social transformations in America in late nineteenth and early twentieth centuries. In addition to the theories of cultural geography, this book will also adopt the theories from urban studies, rural studies, natural beauty, and ecocriticism to examine the depiction of landscape in Wharton's works.

1.5   Analytical Procedure

This book intends to explore how landscape in Edith Wharton's novels reflect the impacts of social transformations upon turn-of-the-twentieth-century Americans. The New England landscape in the six novels is divided into the following three categories and analyzed respectively in the three chapters: New York cityscape, the landscape of rural New England, and the landscape of the Hudson River Valley.

Chapter Two, "Transitional New York Landscape in *The House of Mirth* and *The Custom of the Country*," places the two novels in the contexts of New York's transition from a nineteenth-century Victorian city to a twentieth-century modern one. Chapter Two first examines how the characters' different ways of experiencing the streetscape display the growing importance of individuality in urbanization. Then it investigates how the opera houses turn from a marker of class and gender privileges into a site of relaxation, which manifests the increasing accessibility of leisure. The role of the opera houses in reinforcing women's self-objectification is also analyzed. The hotels as the embodiment of mobility exemplify how a more public and mobile lifestyle associated with hotel living evokes senses of uncanniness and alienation among its residents. This chapter delves into the class and gender power dynamics driving the changes in urban landscape, as well as the impacts of these changes on characters' tastes, self-perceptions etc., thereby illuminating Wharton's pessimistic perspective regarding the effects of social transformations.

Chapter Three, "Old New England Landscape in *Ethan Frome* and *Summer*," centers on a shift in the regional identity of rural New England. The important issues in rural social transformations such as the uneven development between rural and urban regions, European immigration, commercial agriculture, and rural tourism are discussed in this chapter. Through scrutinizing the different perceptions of rural landscape by city visitors and local inhabitants, specifically their views of the villages, the mountains, and the vernacular architecture, Chapter Three analyzes how the notions of class, race, and gender shape the transformation of old New England landscape and influence the characters' perceptions of the landscape. The individuals' emotions evoked by landscape such as nostalgia shed light on the impacts of social transformations on their ideologies and aesthetics as well. In Wharton's view, resorting to a romanticized old New England is an inadequate strategy for dealing with the challenges of social transformations.

Chapter Four, "Idealized Hudson River Valley Landscape in *Hudson River Bracketed* and *The Gods Arrive*," focuses on Wharton's envision of an idealized Hudson Valley landscape which expresses her views on how Americans should handle the impacts of social transformations. By drawing a stark contrast between the Hudson landscape and the protagonist Vance's dreary Midwestern hometown, Wharton accentuates the notion that Americans' domination over nature contributes to their emotional numbness. Through scrutinizing the interplay between Vance and the Hudson River Valley which includes the suburb, the forest, and the mansion, this chapter examines how the idealized landscape serves as a counterbalance to the adverse effects caused by standardization, mechanization, intellectual parochialism, and disregard for history in American society in the 1920s and 1930s.

It is hoped that this book, by analyzing various categories of New England landscape in Wharton's novels, will provide a new perspective to understand her concerns with the effects of social transformations on Americans at the turn of the twentieth century. Furthermore, this research intends to advance interdisciplinary research that applies theories from cultural geography to Wharton scholarship.

Chapter Two   Transitional New York Cityscape in *The House of Mirth* and *The Custom of the Country*

Edith Wharton is famous for her vivid depiction of New York between the 1870s and the 1920s, covering the years from the postbellum periods to the Gilded Age and beyond into World War Ⅰ. Known as the "chronicler of Old New York①", her fiction about the turn-of-the-century city received the most attention from critics, with *The House of Mirth* and *The Custom of the Country* being the two representative ones (Sauter, 31). The novels are set roughly contemporaneous to their publication time: the former depicts the experiences of the heroine Lily Bart in New York in the 1890s, while the latter focuses on the urban life of Undine Spragg's family in the 1910s. In both novels, the urban landscape is closely tied to the protagonists' life trajectories: whereas the city witnesses the descent of Lily from an Old New York lady living in a Fifth Avenue mansion to an impoverished milliner struggling to survive in a boarding house, it also sees the rise of Undine from a Midwestern arriviste in a West End hotel to the hostess of the high society through multiple marriages.

Although the discussion of New York figures prominently in the criticisms about the two novels, it usually focuses on the manners of the Old

---

① As a major topic in Wharton's works, " Old New York " contains both geographical and temporal connotations. For the writer, " Old New York" mainly refers to a smaller Manhattan between the mid-1870s and the 1890s whose social life was controlled by a group of Old New York families (Sarah Wilson, 123-125).

New York families dominating the city rather than on the urban landscape. As Joseph A. Dimuro points out, "it usually appears as just that—a figure or metonym signifying a small and exclusive 'society' made up of a dozen interchangeable family names" (1). Generally speaking, the literary landscape of New York City in the two novels is the elite segment of Manhattan which covers the area from Washington Square to the Central Park. In his biography of Wharton, R. W. B. Lewis notes that "The physical contours of Edith's New York" stretched from "Thirty-second Street to Forty-fifth between Third and Sixth Avenues" (37). New York in the novels does not merely function as a static background to the plot. Rather, it reflects socioeconomic and cultural transformations at a transitional era when economic and social power shifted from the old money① to the newly minted industrialists, manufacturers, and financiers② who gained stunning

---

① "The old money" refer to a small set of families who constituted New York high society from the first quarter of the nineteenth century to the early decades of the twentieth century. Many prominent families, including the Rhinelanders, the Van Rensselaers, and the Roosevelts, were the descendants of Dutch settlers who accumulated fortunes in trade or real estate investments after immigrating to New York in the seventeenth century. The daughter of George Frederic and Lucretia Rhinelander Jones, Edith Wharton grew up in this exclusive circle (Jaher, 258). The following phrases are used interchangeably in this chapter to refer to this group of people: Old New Yorkers, New York's established elite, Old New York aristocracy, the old guards, the old money, the upper crust of society, the upper echelon, and the upper reaches of society.

② New-moneyed plutocrats poured into New York City during the Second Industrial Revolution, in which incredible wealth was amassed through technological advancement, stocks, and commercialism. Coming from lower-class or immigrant families, the self-made multimillionaires such as James Fisk, Andrew Carnegie, and Jason Gould struggled to push into the high society (Jaher, 259). In this chapter, the following phrases are used alternatively to refer to this group of people: the parvenus, the new money, the new rich, the newcomers, the newer elite, *Nouveau Riches*, robber barons, social climbers, invaders, and upstarts. The clash between the old and new elites in the turn-of-the century New York is widely-discussed by cultural historians. For instance, see Sven Beckert, *The Monied Metropolis: New York City and the Consolidation of the American Bourgeoisie*, 1850—1896 (New York: Cambridge University Press, 2001), pp. 205-322; Clifton Hood, *In Pursuit of Privilege: A History of New York City's Upper Class and The Making of a Metropolis* (New York: Columbia University Press, 2016), pp. 171-250.

wealth in the Second Industrial Revolution. This transformation was the outcome of socio-economic restructuring in the United States at the turn of the century, characterized by a shift from industrial capitalism to the monopoly capitalism of large corporations. More importantly, the writer explores the impacts of social changes upon turn-of-the-century Americans by delving into the interaction between the city dwellers and urban landscape.

According to cultural historians Samuel P. Hays and T. J. Lears, Americans experienced "complex social and cultural changes" at the turn of the century, particular the periods from the 1870s to World War I (Lears, xix). Among the tremendous changes, three aspects are particularly noteworthy: the rising emphasis on individuality, the increasing accessibility of leisure, and the growing levels of geographical and social mobility. First of all, the emphasis on individuality was "regarded as the attribute of [...] the urban milieu" (Chen, 138). In his seminal essay "The Metropolis and Mental Life" (1903), Georg Simmel states that modern cities afford individuals unprecedented personal freedoms and enable them to break free from social constraints: the small circle which was "almost entirely closed against neighboring foreign or otherwise antagonistic groups but which ha[d] however within itself such a narrow cohesion that the individual member ha[d] only a very slight area for the development of his own qualities and for free activity" had gradually lost their influences in the turn-of-the-twentieth-century cities (15). Echoing Simmel's analysis of individuality and urban life, cultural historian Warren Susman observes the growing importance of personality among New Yorkers in the first decades of the twentieth century. According to Susman, "personality was the quality of being Somebody that stressed self-fulfillment, self-expression, self-gratification" and "the transition from Victorian to modern American culture involved the [rise] of the twentieth-century concept of 'personality'"

(280). In *The House of Mirth* and *The Custom of the Country*, the changes in the streetscape demonstrate the rise of individuality in the process of urbanization.

Secondly, analyses that aim to define "what makes twentieth-century American life 'modern' always treat changes in how Americans spend their leisure time" (Fischer, 453). At the dawn of the twentieth century, Americans underwent notable transformations in their understanding of leisure. For quite a long time, American attitudes towards leisure were shaped by Puritan and Protestant beliefs that emphasized hard work and thrift, positioning leisure as a realm primarily accessible to the elite. However, at the end of the nineteenth century, an increasing number of Americans, especially those living in major cities like New York, began to view leisure as an essential break from the pressures of daily life. This shift was made possible by reduced working hours and increased disposable income, both outcomes of unprecedented economic growth and the widespread use of machinery. As Susman notes, one of the principal transformations in early-twentieth-century United States was from "an older culture, often loosely labeled Puritan-republican, producer-capitalist culture" to "a newly emerging culture of abundance and leisure" (xx). In the two novels, opera houses showcase the rising accessibility of leisure and its impacts on class and gender relations.

Thirdly, turn-of-the-century Americans experienced growing geographical and social mobility. Their enthusiasm for geographical movement was demonstrated by extensive networks of railroads and waterways, a diverse array of hotels, and a rising number of automobiles on the roads. As temporary living places, hotels facilitated this geographical mobility by providing essential services such as lodging, food, and drink. Additionally, the rise in social mobility began to chip away at aristocratic standing and challenge the established elite's control. Hotels, particularly the luxurious ones, offered avenues for those aspiring to climb the social ladder. The hotels in the novels reflect the increasing geographical and social mobility in American society and display a more public and mobile lifestyle among New Yorkers.

In the two novels, the process of social transformations is demonstrated by New York's transition from a Victorian city to a modern one. According to Douglas Tallack, modern New York took shape in 1898 when the consolidation of the five boroughs led to an enormous growth in its population, industry, and wealth (12). In 1882, Walt Whitman described the cityscape encountered while pleasure sailing around New York Bay: "V-shaped Manhattan, with its compact mass, its spires [...] the green of the trees, and all the white, brown and gray of architecture well blended" (qtd. in Lindner, 44). By 1904, when Henry James observed the city from the bay, this low-rise New York had turned into a "strange vertiginous" metropolis: "the multitudinous sky-scrapers standing up to the view, from the water, like extravagant pins in a cushion already overplanted" (76). In addition to the morphological changes, the transitional urban landscape, represented by the streets, the opera houses, and the hotels in *The House of Mirth* and *The Custom of the Country*, illustrates immense cultural transformations: the rising emphasis on individuality, the increasing accessibility of leisure, and the growing levels of geographical and social mobility. By analyzing the interplay between the urban landscape and New York citizens in the two novels, this chapter will explore the effects of the above-mentioned social transformations upon turn-of-the-century Americans.

2.1   Streets as the Epitome of Urbanization

New York witnessed its unprecedented development of urbanization at the turn of the century, transforming from a compact and well-ordered Victorian city to an expansive metropolitan one. François Weil regards the years between 1890 and 1920 as the most decisive phase in the city's urbanization when the postbellum economic boom and the consolidation in 1898 led to the formation of modern New York (166). By 1900 its population had swelled to 3.4 million and the urbanized area grew from lower Manhattan to the entire island (Weil, 167). As the "most vital organs" of the city, the streets best reflect this process in a period when the horse-drawn carriages and low-rise brownstones were gradually superseded by the speeding cars, mass transit systems, and steel-framed high-rise buildings (Jacobs, 29).

In the two novels, the transformation of the streets reflects the changing power relations between the old money and the new money. Moreover, the Victorian culture, which stresses boundary, order, and self-control, is giving way to modern urban culture that emphasizes individuality. As N. Kumar argues, "the advent of the individual human being (rather than of the community, tribe, group) as the hub of society" is a fundamental dimension of twentieth-century urban social transformations (qtd. in Galland and Lemel, 169). Through analyzing how Lily in *The House of Mirth* and Moffatt and Undine in *The Custom of the Country* interact with the streetscape, this section aims to explore the impacts of urbanization upon turn-of-the-century New York citizens' lifestyle and mentality.

2.1.1 Class-Divided and Gender-Separated Streets

The House of Mirth was written by Wharton during the first years of 1900s when the industrialization of the late nineteenth century had brought on rapid urbanization across the United States. With the consolidation of the five boroughs in 1898 into an enlarged city, New York became the national capital of finance, industry, trade, publishing, and arts. At that time, New York culture was still governed by Victorian values① which stressed order and boundary. Lily's way of seeing the streetscape reveals that through inscribing social orders into the urban landscape, Old New Yorkers in the novel make the street a class-divided and gender-separated site. This further results in Lily's sense of aimlessness and fear.

The late-nineteenth-century New York in the novel is controlled by Victorian values which place strong emphases on rational order, self-control, and obedience to family and community. According to historian David Scobey, the impact of Victorian values upon the urban landscape is manifested in Old New Yorkers' ideas of city planning and management. They associate the cityscape with civilizational ideal and envision "a cityscape that would separate, discipline, and elevate" the public (*Empire City*, 174). The city builders, reformers, and designers from the genteel class regard the natural and built environment as an instrument for maintaining order and uplifting morality in a chaotic urban life. One of the most representative examples is Central Park which "used techniques of segregation, movement control, and visual occlusion" to ensure class hierarchy and sexual respectability (Scobey, *Empire City*, 236). In a similar manner, the well-ordered streets in the novel with regulated boundaries embody the authority of genteel culture.

New York City in *The House of Mirth* is composed of gridded and

---

① In the history of the United Kingdom, the Victorian Era was the period of Queen Victoria's reign from 1837 to 1901. The American society at this period is usually called as "Victorian America". Victorian values controlled American social life for much of the nineteenth century, especially among the old moneyed families who had dominated economic, social, and political institutions until the final decades of the century. Historian Daniel Walker Howe call the dominant culture as "American Victorianism" which includes a series of values such as "punctuality, rational order, regulated self-improvement" (522).

ordered streets which are demarcated along class and gender lines. The layout of the streets is based on The Commissioners' Plan of 1811 which utilized a rectilinear grid① to divide Manhattan into 2,028 roughly identical blocks. The blocks were further subdivided into standard 25-foot-by-100-foot lots (Scobey, *Empire City*, 122). By erasing the topographical features of privately-owned land and turning irregular land into roughly equal-sized units, the grid turned the city's land into a commodity that could be conveniently bought and sold, thus facilitating the development of capitalism and urbanization in the nineteenth century. As Reuben S. Rose-Redwood notes, the grid not only "served as an ordering scheme for the capitalist commodification of the landscape", more importantly, by inscribing the Cartesian coordinate system into the Manhattan landscape, it disciplined the citizens to rational order which was the core of Victorian values (92). Thus, the characters in the novel are kept in place according to their class and gender.

Wharton's meticulous description of streets vividly demonstrates a geographically hierarchical and economically divided city. In the late nineteenth century, the economic and cultural authority was controlled by a small set of families collectively referred to as Old New Yorkers which are represented by the Penistons, the Gryces, and the Van Osburghs in the novel. Vertically, those wealthy people live in the Upper North as a result of the northward march of New York City throughout the century to escape from the immigrant and working-class neighborhoods of the lower east and west sides (Domosh, "Those 'Gorgeous Incongruities'", 215). In addition to the north-south axis, the other great demarcation in Wharton's New York is the east-west division for which Fifth Avenue serves as the dividing line.

---

① In urban planning, the "grid plan", "grid street plan", or "gridiron plan" is a type of city plan in which streets run at right angles to each other, forming a grid (Lynch, 75).

The East Side is where the fashionable people live while the West Side is where the working class's tenements are located. For instance, while the old money occupy Fifth Avenue, the newly riches live in nearby districts and the most promising among them manage to buy Fifth Avenue mansions. Not rich enough to afford a house on the central spine, the middle-class lawyer Lawrence Selden rents an apartment on 50th Street between Fifth Avenue and Madison Avenue. His poorer cousin Gerty Farish lives in a room farther west. The streets thus form "a kind of class sandwich where riverfront tenement neighborhoods enclosed the fashionable district on either side" (Scobey, *Empire City*, 118).

As the most frequently mentioned street in *The House of Mirth*, Fifth Avenue is depicted as a sphere of order and discipline. The glaring neon lights and large signs are restricted, with more subdued white street lamps designated for use on Fifth Avenue and genteel parts of the East Side. The street is mainly composed of Old New Yorkers' mansions, with few commercial buildings. Houses are primarily constructed of brownstone or marble, often adhering to classical styles. Fifth Avenue is filled with ornately decorated carriages. Peddlers and vagabonds are rarely seen on the sidewalks, with the main passersby being the well-dressed leisure class. During the social season, the avenue becomes "a torrent of carriages surging upward to the fashionable quarters about the Park, where illuminated windows and outspread awnings betokened the usual routine of hospitality" (*HM*, 156). When Selden and another gentleman named Van Alstyne walk down Fifth Avenue, they see the new house of Jewish merchant Simon Rosedale and deride his efforts to push into the high society:

That Greiner house, now—a typical rung in the social ladder! The man who built it came from a milieu where all the dishes are put on the table at once. His façade is a complete architectural meal; if he had omitted a style his friends might have thought the money had given out. Not a bad purchase for Rosedale, though: attracts attention, and awes the Western sightseer. By and by he'll get out of that phase, and want something that the crowd will pass and the few pause before. (*HM* , 207)

The two gentlemen's comment on Rosedale's house reveals the class division on Fifth Avenue. Although Rosedale is one of the few upstarts who manage to own a house on the street, in Old New Yorkers' eyes, his house does not match the streetscape. Old New Yorkers' view of his house implies that it disrupts the elegant ambiance of Fifth Avenue. Far from showcasing his social status, Rosedale's mansion in fact highlights class exclusion.

What most clearly displays the street as a venue of class differences is Lily's southward and westward move due to the decline of her social status: starting from her aunt's Fifth Avenue mansion as an upper-class heiress, she then has to stay in a small hotel on the edge of the fashionable neighborhood after having been disinherited due to her scandal with a married man, then she lives for a short period of time in a tawdry hotel on the West Side as the private secretary for the social-climbing Mrs. Hatch, and finally inhabits a boarding house on the geographical periphery of the city while working as a milliner. The boarding house is located deep into the southwest: when walking back home from Sixth Avenue, she "led the way westward past a long line of areas which, through the distortion of their paintless rails, revealed with increasing candour the disjecta membra of bygone dinners" (*HM* , 333) and " hated every step of the walk thither, through the degradation of a New York street in the last stages of decline from fashion to commerce" (*HM* , 327). For Lily, the streets represent the division of class: the narrow streets with " paintless rails" and " disjecta membra of bygone dinners" are in stark contrast to the fashionable quarters she used to linger. By using the streets to visualize Lily's downward spiral, Wharton

47

displays a city which maintains class hierarchy by spatial demarcation and exclusion.

The above-mentioned differentiation not only displays social hierarchy, but also facilitates the reproduction of class division. In his discussion about the production of social relations in urban landscape, David Harvey argues that residential differentiation " reinforces the tendency for relatively permanent social groupings to emerge within a relatively permanent structure of residential differentiation" and therefore strengthens class stratification (120). By occupying the reputable streets and pushing the less advantaged citizens such as Lily to the margin of the city, the established elite produce class-divided streets and thus naturalize and reproduce the hierarchical power relations. According to Scobey, during the 1860s and 1870s the old guards actively participated in a broad campaign to rid the streets of sidewalk peddlers, unlicensed carters, casualized labor, sexually independent women, and vagrant children (*Empire City*, 177). They even protested horse cars in the respectable neighborhoods such as Fifth Avenue to protect those streets from the pubic traffic and commercial activities (Scobey, *Empire City*, 35). In short, the upper echelon took the socio-spatial separation for granted and thus viewed the street as a medium for projecting their power.

As an epitome of class division, the street is an important site for class identification which embodies the authority of the upper echelon. In the novel, not only the arrivistes are refused by Fifth Avenue mansions, once a person is expelled from the high society, he or she is also excluded from the social activities on Fifth Avenue as well. That Lily is no longer part of the old money becomes evident while she stands on a corner, "look[s] out on the afternoon spectacle of Fifth Avenue" as "familiar faces in the passing carriages" provide a " fleeting glimpse of her past" (*HM*, 336). The "mauve" flowers on both sides of the avenue exude sweet fragrance and lush trees throw a "veil over [...] the side streets and give a touch of poetry

to the delicate haze of green that marks the entrance to the Park" (*HM*,
338). "The afternoon spectacle of Fifth Avenue" refers to the carriage
parades popular in the fashionable society throughout the nineteenth century.
Elite New Yorkers sat in the plush carriages and gravely passed the genteel
boulevards such as Broadway and Fifth Avenue at prescribed time while the
pedestrians looked on with admiring eyes. In her autobiography *A Backward
Glance* (1934), Wharton recalled the grand scene of parades as the
exclusive entertainment for the upper class: "Carriages, horses, harnesses
and grooms were all of the latest and most irreproachable cut [...] The dress
of the young ladies perched on the precarious height of a dog-cart or phaeton
was no less elegant than that of the dowagers" (73). As Scobey
underscored, the parade helped in "the construction of class identity and the
demarcation of class boundaries" ("Anatomy of the Promenade", 204). On
the one hand, it functioned as "a symbolic act of class formation". By
following complex codes of salutation such as nodding to each other in the
stately procession, the genteel passengers recognized each other as a
respectable collectivity. On the other hand, it represented "a symbolic act of
class subordination". The upper crust of society used the promenading to
display their superiority to the crowds who served as invisible audiences on
the margin of the streets. Together the parade inscribed "class and cultural
hierarchy" on the streetscape ("Anatomy of the Promenade", 221).

Scobey's interpretation of the street highlights the function of landscape
as a process by which "social and subjective identities are formed" (W. J.
T. Mitchell, "Introduction", 1). According to Mitchell, landscape as an
instrument of power has a double role with respect to something like
ideology:

it naturalizes a cultural and social construction, representing an
artificial world as if it were simply given and inevitable, and it also

49

makes that representation operational by interpellating its beholder in some more or less determinate relation to its givenness as sight and site. (2)

Understood in this way, the street becomes an active agent of power to legitimize class exclusion in a hierarchical society "as if it were simply given and inevitable". Thus it plays the role as the agent of the dominant class to "address" or "hail" in Louis Althusser's terms, interpellating① Lily in "a material ritual practice" of recognition and exclusion (85). In other words, the street makes her internalize the ideology of class hierarchy and decide her own identity by whether she can partake in the exchange of recognitions the parade offers. This process of "interpellating" makes Lily recognize the insurmountable boundary between her old friends who sit in luxurious carriages and the larger public including her who serve as onlookers.

Before going to the street, Lily still dreams about using her apprenticeship at Mme. Regina's work-room to open a millinery shop and regaining her popularity as an independent lady. However, the street sheds light on her current situation and renders her feel that the plan is unrealistic: "The sense of aimlessness with which Lily at length turned toward home" from Fifth Avenue is in fact caused by her internalization of class hierarchy because she has taken her exclusion from the upper class for granted (*HM*, 337). Regarding herself as "just a crew or a cog in the great machine I called life" (*HM*, 348), she sees her destiny as unescapable: "to look forward to a shabby, anxious middle-age, leading by dreary degrees of

---

① The French philosopher, Louis Althusser, first popularized the word in his essay "Ideology and Ideological State Apparatuses (Notes towards an Investigation)". In his definition, interpellation is the constitutive process where individuals acknowledge and respond to ideologies, thereby recognizing themselves as subjects. The process by which individuals encounter and internalize a culture's or ideology's values constitutes the very nature of people's identities (166-176).

economy and self-denial to gradual absorption in the dingy communal existence of the boarding-house" (*HM*, 358). The street, as the surrogate of the old guards, therefore successfully legitimizes class exclusion and strengthens class division in Victorian New York. Through portraying the protagonist's sense of aimlessness and hopelessness, Wharton expresses her critique of the detrimental effects that the class-divided city imposes on its citizens' quest for individual independence.

In *The House of Mirth*, the streetscape is not only a representation of class division but also reflects gender separation. Following the Victorian Cult of Domesticity①, Old New Yorkers believed that women's place was home, thus saw public space as inappropriate for them. At the late nineteenth century, the presence of women on the streets was still questioned; if unaccompanied by a chaperon or male escort, they were at risk of being thought a prostitute. In Daphne Spain's words, "the idea of separate spheres was encoded within the turn-of-the-century city" (584).

In the opening pages of the novel, when she still belongs to the Old New York society, Lily is portrayed as the embodiment of Victorian propriety. Out of curiosity, she takes a risk in accepting the invitation of Selden—a single gentleman in her circle—to visit his home for a cup of tea. After having left his flat and come back to the streets after five o'clock in the afternoon, Lily notices "her own fears" and decides to find a hansom to

---

① The "Cult of Domesticity" or "True Womanhood" is an idealized set of societal standards placed on middle-and upper-class American women of the nineteenth century. The term was explained by historian Barbara Welter in the 1960s as referring to a belief in which a woman's value is based upon her ability to stay home and perform the duties of a wife and mother as well as her willingness to abide by the four cardinal virtues: piety, purity, submissiveness, and domesticity. Stressing that home is her proper sphere, the ideal of True Womanhood keeps women from participating in urban life. See Barbara Welter, "The Cult of True Womanhood: 1820—1860", *American Quarterly*, 18.2, 1966: 151-174.

leave quickly (*HM*, 48). Her fear of being seen on the streets is due to both the inappropriate time and place of her public appearance. According to Maureen E. Montgomery, the canonical hour for a lady to appear in public in the late-nineteenth-century New York is from 11 a.m. to 3 p.m., which means that Lily's presence on the streets in the late afternoon may cause questions about her respectability (*Displaying Women*, 97).

The street where Lily stands also contributes to her fear. It is where a bachelor flat-house named "The Benedick" is located. According to Johnny Finnigan, The Benedick is based on Wharton's knowledge of a luxury bachelor apartment building of the same name on Washington Square at the turn of the century (118). The building's "Philadelphia red brick and Nova Scotia stone façade " is transformed in the novel into " new brick and limestone house-fronts" which attracts Lily's interested glance. As a type of new urban buildings designed specifically for well-off bachelors in New York since the 1870s, the bachelor apartments were often viewed by the middle-and upper-class Americans as a place "threatening to the institutions of marriage and family " and " the future of domesticity in a rapidly modernizing and urbanizing age " (Snyder, 248-249) , a neighborhood where "the foot of charming woman never falls" (275).

As feminist geographers argue, towns and cities in Western societies have a patriarchal basis and the gendering of urban landscape interweaves with the development of built environments (Valentine, 385). The street where a bachelor apartment building is situated hence represents the borders of the sexual segregated New York City. The symbolic and material gendering of the urban landscape that have a patriarchal, male-dominated basis is the root of Lily's fear since she internalizes the normative ascriptions of gendered spatiality. That explains why she tells a clumsy lie to explain her presence there while encountering the Jewish merchant Rosedale by coincidence. However, after having "glanced up interrogatively at the porch of the Benedick", "the sudden intimacy of his smile" and the "tone which had the familiarity of a touch" all betray that Rosedale associates her with immoral behavior and treats her with a less respectful manner (*HM*, 17). Worrying that he would spread rumors about what he has seen, she is scared to think that "This one, at any rate, was going to cost her rather more than she could afford" (*HM*, 19). The incident makes her the center of male gossip and thus severely harms her reputation. Later in the novel when a married man fails to rape her, he complains that "Gad, you go to men's houses fast enough in broad day light—strikes me you're not always so deuced careful of appearances" (*HM*, 188). The street, as the embodiment of gender hierarchy, therefore helps in punishing those who fail to observe the rules and regulations in Victorian New York.

The class-divided and gender-separated streets are the epitome of the Victorian culture in late-nineteenth-century New York society which is dominated by the old money. As the agent of class and gender hierarchy, the streets naturalize exclusion and strengthen class and gender division to satisfy Old New Yorkers' demands for rational order and self-control, thus resulting in Lily's sense of aimlessness and fear. As Simmel points out, small groups which required "a rigorous setting of boundaries and a centripetal unity" were gradually abandoned by city dwellers at the turn of the twentieth century because the groups could not "give room to freedom and the peculiarities of inner and external development of the individual" ("The Metropolis and Mental Life", 15). Lily's emotions indicate the difficulty in maintaining her independence and individuality against the powers of family and society in Victorian New York. In *The Custom of the Country*, Wharton presents readers with different ways of experiencing streetscape through the perspectives of the new money, thereby shedding light on the growing importance of individuality in New York's urbanization.

2.1.2   The New Money's Transgression Against Class and Gender Exclusion on the Streets

With the specific mentioning of the Elevated and the Subway by which the male characters take to work and the "the steel and concrete tower" on Wall Street where their offices are located, Wharton implies that New York in *The Custom of the Country* is becoming a modern city (70). While the streets in *The House of Mirth* are class-divided and gender-separated which signify the dominant Victorian values, in this novel they are portrayed as undergoing tremendous transformations which result from the upstarts' pursuit of individuality. According to Susman, with the urbanization of the early twentieth century, New York witnessed the rise of a new culture of personality. While Victorian lifestyle " focused on moral concerns and preached the virtues of self-control; the new culture of personality was more concerned with emotional temperament and the techniques of self-expression " (Halttunen, 187). The emergence of " the culture of personality" in American cities affected the social order in the following two ways: it stimulated Americans' need to stand out in a mass society and to distinguish themselves from others in the crowd; the pursuit for leisure and enjoyment replaced that for order and self-discipline (Susman, 275-277). In the novel, the transformation that the new rich bring to the urban landscape is majorly showcased in the office towers on Wall Street and sumptuous mansions on Fifth Avenue. Furthermore, different from Susman's focus on male urbanites, Wharton notes that the cultural turbulence also influences women's manners through depicting Undine's appreciation of Fifth Avenue's night view.

There are majorly two streets mentioned in *The Custom of the Country*: Wall Street and Fifth Avenue. While Fifth Avenue is the center of the New

York society in *The House of Mirth*, Wall Street starts to play a significant role in this novel and even determines the transformation of Fifth Avenue. As the social-climbing protagonist Undine—daughter of a Midwestern arriviste businessman—quickly understands, "Every Wall Street term had its equivalent in the language of Fifth Avenue" (*CC*, 303).

The plutocrats, represented by Undine's third husband Mr. Elmer Moffatt, yearn to "stand out from the crowd" (Susman, 280). Their ambitions are displayed by their skyscrapers in lower Manhattan and opulent palaces on Fifth Avenue. In the first decade of the twentieth century, with the advent of skeleton construction, Wall Street tycoons' need for larger corporate headquarters and ostentatious display of their commercial success were satisfied by soaring office towers. The prominent early twentieth-century high-rises such as the Singer, Metropolitan Life, and Woolworth Buildings were financed by the robber barons to "signal in brash and public ways the growing presence and power of corporations in the modern city" (Lindner, 33). For instance, Mr. Elmer Moffatt—the billionaire Railroad King—establishes his corporation in a "steel and concrete tower" on Wall Street (*CC*, 70). Cultural geographer Mona Domosh proposes that urban landscape can be interpreted in both macro-level (as an expression of corporate capitalism) and micro-level explanations (as an expression of personality) in her iconographic analysis of New York skyscrapers ("A Method", 352). From the macro-level perspective, the buildings in the novel symbolize the rapid economic growth and urbanization at the turn of the century; in terms of the micro-level, they express the *Nouveau Riches'* ambition for economic power and social legitimacy.

Apart from investing in high-rises on Wall Street, the newly riches build sumptuous mansions on Fifth Avenue, gradually breaking down the class segregation of the street. The upper reaches of Fifth Avenue are occupied by their palaces, among which Undine's final home at the pinnacle—5009 Fifth Avenue—after her marriage to Moffatt are the most extravagant. No longer the targets of ridicule, Undine and Moffatt look at their house like "some warrior king and Queen borne in triumph" (*CC*, 59). Whereas the number of the parvenus' houses on Fifth Avenue is quite limited in *The House of Mirth*, in *The Custom of the Country* Undine's first husband Ralph Marvell—a scion of the Old New York aristocracy Dagonets—has already sensed "the social disintegration expressed by widely different architectural physiognomies at the other end of Fifth Avenue" (*CC*, 44). By contrast, the old guards' brownstones are either replaced by commercial architecture or seen as outmoded by the young generation. For example, the family house of the Dagonets in Washington Square implies their social and geographical peripheralization. Washington Square used to be the most honorable place for the Old New York families, but New York's upper class has kept moving northward since the last quarter of the nineteenth-century, thus the fact that the Dagonet family seat is still located at the same area in the twentieth century explicitly tells that "[m] aterial resources were limited on both sides of the house" (*CC*, 42). It is worth noting that the Dagonets of Washington Square also appear in Wharton's *The Age of Innocence* (1920) as the patriarchs of Old New York society in the 1870s. The social devaluation of the region in the 1910s thus illustrates not only the accelerated northward expansion of the city but also reflects that, with power shifting from the old money to the new money, Old New Yorkers are unable to maintain class division. Expressions like "social disintegration" and "widely different architectural physiognomies" reveal Wharton's unease about shifts in the urban landscape, as they highlight the challenges that new wealth poses to Old New Yorkers.

In addition to the changing class relations, the constraints on women's manners on the streets were loosened because the ever-expanding new elites gradually became "fed up with adhering to formal rules of etiquette to prove their worthiness to enter the upper echelon" (Kaplan, 92). In their quest for self-expression and self-gratification, the new rich "abandoned a ' Victorian' model of public culture which elided respectability, sexual regulation and bodily repression in favour of heterosexual companionship, physical expressiveness, and the frank embrace of an emerging culture of sensuous, often strenuous amusement" (Scobey, "Anatomy of the Promenade", 226). Wharton places particular emphasis on the growing importance of individuality and its impact on women. According to Montgomery, from the mid-1890s on, the Victorian rules of women's acceptable behavior in public, particular for the upper-class ones, were most notably challenged by the new rich. In the decades around the 1910s, "a revolt took place against the constraints of Victorian gentility. Part of this revolt was related to the greater physical mobility of women" (*Displaying Women*, 56). More and more middle- and upper-class ladies stepped out of home to shop in malls, eat at restaurants, go to theatres, and visit city parks. Undine is a representative of the *Nouveau Riches* who take tremendous pleasure in "the thronging motors, the brilliant shops, the novelty and daring of the women's dresses" (*CC*, 161). She always spends a whole day in visiting dressmakers and jewelers, having lunches in fashionable restaurants, visiting galleries, and taking afternoon motor-rush to the suburbs. In stark contrast to Lily who seldom walks on the streets and feels scared of being seen alone until her fall from the high society, Undine enjoys " the noise, the crowd, the promiscuity" (*CC*, 224) and "the gaze of admiration which she left in her wake along the pavement" (38).

Undine's boldest transgression on the gender-separated streets is her ride in an open car after eight o'clock in the evening with a married man from the new money set, Peter Van Degan. She understands that her behavior is inappropriate since " it is awfully late" (*CC*, 175) and even Peter asks when they reach the street: "You're not afraid of being seen with me, are you?" (159-160). What is more, the car, as a powerful machine, was

57

perceived as the territory of men at the early twentieth century. It was often associated with female body, which contributed to the driver's sense of control in the masculine domain. For instance, the well-known Model T, the first affordable automobile for Americans, was colloquially known as the "Tin Lizzie" and "Leaping Lena" since it entered the market in 1908. Early terms for automotive parts also derived from women's clothes (Clarke, 23). In general, the gendered connotation of the automobile renders women's access to it detrimental to traditional gender roles. Therefore, Undine's appearance in a man's car late at night on the street challenges the notion of proper female sphere, which showcases her "resistance to conventional gender roles and the strictures of a normative femininity" (Smith, 175).

Furthermore, urbanization, boundary-crossing, and individuality are closely related. Urban sociologist Moritz Föllmer proposes that "the early twentieth century provides further evidence of individual boundary-crossing when city dwellers have claimed the opportunity to explore urban space and broaden their own individuality" (8). Like Lily who recognizes her fear while standing in front of the bachelor apartments, Undine senses her own fear about the power of patriarchy which is symbolized as a sight of her husband Ralph: "his face seemed to rise before her, with the sharp lines of care between the eyes: it was almost like a part of his 'nagging' that he should thrust himself in at such a moment!" (*CC*, 161). Nevertheless, she takes Peter's offer for a ride. While driving through Fifth Avenue, she observes that electricity lights put "yellow splashes" on the "long snow-piled street" and illuminated signs glitter atop the roof of the adjacent shops (*CC*, 159). In the 1910s, Fifth Avenue ceased to be an exclusive residential area reserved for Old New Yorkers. Many shops had already appeared on the street. From the car, Undine sees that the windows of restaurants, jewelry stores, and florist shops gleaming in rapid succession. The white sign of Sherry's restaurant is still flashing. Cars are parked at the entrance, waiting for guests to finish their meals. The illumination of the streetlamps progresses up the street. In the distance, some tall buildings, covered from top to bottom with signs, posters, and advertisements, are illuminated by neon lights, with their outlines intermittently visible.

The streetscape makes Undine "feel the rush of physical joy that drowns scruples and silences memory" (CC, 160). As noted by Richard H. Schein, landscape not only "works to normalize/naturalize social and cultural practice, to reproduce those practices", but also "to provide a means to challenge those practices" ("A Methodological Framework", 383). The "rush of physical joy" derives from Undine's transgression of the confining borderline of gender on the streets. Transgression, as defined by Tim Cresswell, are acts that are judged to "have crossed some line that was not meant to have been crossed" (23). Since the streets function as the surrogates for patriarchal control and power, Undine's transgression of the manners on the streets constitutes a symbolic offence against the forces. As Cresswell notes, acts of transgression gain their power from occurring in front of, and being noticed by, those being resisted. By taking a ride on the street late at night, Undine transgresses the public/private divide which is based on gender hierarchy first in front of Peter and later in front of her husband Ralph when he sees her getting off at their doorstep. The fresh air blows away her scruples about her responsibility as a wife and gives her "the eyes and complexion she needed" (CC, 116), which symbolizes her breaking free of "the social dictum that says that woman's place is in the home—her husband's home" (Clarke, 35). As Mary K. Edmonds points out, Undine's behavior reflects the cultural transformation in the early twentieth century: "she proves to be not only the New Wealth's representative, but also the fictional exemplum of the culture of personality's self-serving victory over [...] Old New York" (4). Unlike male theorists such as Simmel who characterizes urban residents' typical emotion and mentality as "blasé", Wharton focuses on portraying women's joy and excitement as urbanization provides them with more opportunities to express their individuality ("The Metropolis and Mental Life", 14).

In their studies of urban automobility, sociologists point out the connection between car-driving and individuality. For instance, Uwe Schimank argues that urban drivers are joyful because they regard "automobility as a way of extending [...] individuality" (qtd. in Föllmer, 13). A great enthusiast of motor cars, Wharton celebrates this vehicle's liberating power for women. One of the first female car-owners in America, she purchased her car in 1904 with the profits from her novel *The Valley of Decision* (1902). In her lifetime, she travelled in the United States and Europe by car, went to the front as a correspondent in a military car during the First World War and wrote about motoring experiences in her travelogues. In her consideration of *The Custom of the Country*, Deborah Clarke argues that by linking Undine with the new age of automobility, the writer celebrates the car's function in destabilizing the public/private divide and facilitating women's access to the urban life (33). Nevertheless, it is important to note that Wharton dedicates 12 pages to meticulously describe the negative repercussions of Undine's quest for personal joy, which comes at the cost of forgetting her son's birthday party. Her son waits for her since the afternoon and cries all night, her husband leaves work early, her father-in-law gives up his drive and mother-in-law cancels a hospital meeting. By emphasizing that "she had been unconscious of the wound she inflicted", the writer sharply criticizes Undine's extreme apathy and selfishness and highlights the harmful consequences that can ensue when the pursuit of individuality and self-gratification supersedes self-discipline (*CC*, 170).

The delineation of streets in the two novels displays the transformations of urbanization in New York City at the turn of the century. As Tallack proposes, the era from the 1880s to the 1910s can be regarded as a watershed-moment in New York's urbanization history, a moment when "the city was transformed from a poor copy of Victorian London at the tip of Manhattan and from a poor copy of Parisian modernity around Union and

Madison Squares into [...] the modernist city of the twentieth century" (15). The urbanizing process was vigorously discussed by contemporary boosters, politicians, and intellectuals, as can be seen from a series of books published during this period, in which the name "New New York" appeared for the first time in the titles (Tallack, 9).

The streetscape in *The House of Mirth* epitomizes late-nineteenth-century New York when Victorian culture which stressed rigid boundaries still dominated. Influenced by Victorian values which advocates a strong sense of moral order, Old New Yorkers produce class-divided and gender-separated streets and impose strict regulations upon manners on the street. The street, as epitome of class and gender hierarchy, functions in making Lily take her inferiority for granted, which leads to her sense of aimlessness and fear. Lily's emotions illustrate the difficulty of maintaining independence and individuality in Victorian New York. By comparison, the streetscape in *The Custom of the Country* represents the 1910s New York when the rising power of the new money challenged the old money's social and cultural authority. If Moffat's mansion on Fifth Avenue shows an assault on the street's class segregation, then Undine's pursuit of individuality and her transgression on the street constitute symbolic offences against patriarchal power, a defiance that leads to her pleasure in appreciating the street's night view. To conclude, the streetscape reflects New York City's urbanization at the turn of the century from a Victorian city with rigid boundaries, horse-drawn carriages, and low-rise brownstones to a modern city with motors, skyscrapers, neon lights, the Elevated and Subway. The characters' different ways of experiencing the streetscape display the rise of individuality in the process of urbanization. Although Wharton recognizes that an urbanizing New York provides its inhabitants, especially women, with greater freedom, her portrayal of the streetscape reveals her disquiet about the increasing emphasis on individuality and her critique of its detrimental effects.

2.2 Opera Houses as Manifestations of the Increasing Accessibility of Leisure

While the streets reflect the urbanization of New York City, the opera houses witness the growing accessibility of leisure. The early twentieth century saw dramatic expansion of leisure in American history when both time and resources grew significantly for recreational activities. According to cultural historian Gary Cross, the period between 1900 and 1930 was "an era of 'Common Enjoyment' and soon leisure rather than work would be the core of personal experience" (163). The "accessibility of leisure" or "democratization of leisure" refers to the "greater use of discretionary time for cultural pursuits, formerly only the province of the elite" (Robinson, 207). According to Cross, leisure as "a topic of study" is closely related to issues of class and gender identities ("Crowds and Leisure", 631). One of the major venues for upper-class entertainment in New York, the opera house was "a contested site" since the 1870s (Montgomery, *Displaying Women*, 31). On the one hand, the struggle between New York's established elites and wealthy newcomers over the ownership of opera boxes led to the Metropolitan Opera House's replacement of the Old Academy of Music, which manifested shifts in the notions of leisure. On the other hand, the opera house was "an area of contestation between men and women" (Montgomery, *Displaying Women*, 11). The opera houses encouraged women's self-objectification through facilitating male gaze. As cultural geographer James Duncan notes, "landscape as an objectifier" plays an important role in reproducing the social order, the opera houses as urban landscape function in maintaining patriarchal power in *The House of Mirth* and *The Custom of the Country* (*The City as Text*, 19).

62

A member of Old New York society, Wharton is quite familiar with opera houses. Her diaries and letters include accounts of various performances she watched in America and Europe. Carmen Trammell Skaggs argues that in opera "Wharton discovered a social institution that illustrated both the customs of the old guard and the consumption of the new wealth" (98). Moreover, in the two novels, by delineating the role of the opera houses in shaping female audiences' self-perception, the author highlights that the expansion of leisure opportunities does not significantly mitigate gender inequalities in leisure activities. It is worth noting that although she does not specify the names of the opera houses, Wharton scholars, based on the social life of the upper class at the turn of the twentieth century, generally agree that the characters watch operas at the Metropolitan Opera House (1883—1967) on Broadway (Lee, 594).

2.2.1 Opera House as a Marker of Class and Gender Privileges

The opera house acts as a turning point in the social life of Lily, the heroine in *The House of Mirth*, when she uses the venue to attract potential suitors. Her presence there leads to a misunderstanding that she is Gus Trenor's mistress, which tarnishes her reputation in the upper-class circle. Wharton's depiction of the opera house's interior illustrates that this venue of leisure serves as a marker of class and gender privileges.

The emergence of New York's opera houses in the nineteenth century was driven by Old New Yorkers' need for demonstrating their exclusiveness by displaying leisure. When most Americans were preoccupied with their weekly work routines, interrupted only by religious activities, "leisure time was considered a marker of class" (Hays, 41). In his classic work *The Theory of the Leisure Class* (1899), American economist and sociologist

Thorstein Veblen proposes that the gentlemen and ladies consumed their time in non-productive activities such as accumulating knowledge of dead languages, music, manners, proprieties of dress, games and sports "as an evidence of pecuniary ability to afford a life of idleness" (33). Enjoying leisure thus became a way in which they could display status and hold the esteem of others. Before the first opera house in New York was opened in 1833, opera used to be performed in theatres that offered a hodgepodge mix of plays, farces, and other entertainments. The ritualization of operagoing by the upper echelon in the first half of the nineteenth century made watching opera an important way for them to display leisure. Bruce A. McConachie summarizes that the elite in New York developed three strategies which gradually separated opera from the everyday world of popular entertainment between 1825 and 1850. Firstly, they separated opera from promiscuous theaters by establishing buildings specifically for its performance with more expensive tickets. Secondly, they formulated codes of behavior which deemed proper while attending the opera. In keeping with Victorian frugality and Protestant self-denial, the old money preferred elegant but unobtrusive clothing. Finally, they insisted that only foreign language opera especially Italian ones could meet their standards of excellence (182). By building the venue and controlling the social practices within it, the upper class made the opera house a symbol for their cultural capital. In her autobiography, Wharton describes the leisure that Old New Yorkers enjoyed on the "Opera night": "the Opera, then only sporadic, became an established entertainment, to which one went (as in eighteenth century Italy) chiefly if not solely for the pleasure of conversing with one's friends" (*A Backward Glance*, 56).

One feature of the opera house, the opera box, served to stratify the audience by creating a visible distinction between insiders and outsiders. Ownership of a box was a clear indicator of an individual's social position. Separated entrances, access routes, and public spaces shielded the owner of the boxes from other audiences. Between 1854 and 1886, the Academy of Music was the exclusive site for Old New Yorkers. Although the four thousand seats arranged on five levels (orchestra, parquette, balcony and first, second and third tiers) were sold to the public, the thirty boxes were owned by the most prominent Knickerbocker families and passed down from fathers to sons. The newly minted multimillionaires of the industrial boom, including the Vanderbilts, Goulds and Morgans, had to sit in the orchestra stalls below the boxes and endure the humiliation of being excluded from the high society (Dizikes, 214-216). Therefore, the opera house served not only as the stage for the musical and dramatic performance by the opera stars, but also functioned in enabling the complex performance of class relations.

Since landscape is "form, meaning and representation" which "actively incorporates the social relations that go into its making", the production of opera houses is thus a matter of ongoing struggle and conflict among the old guards and newly riches (Don Mitchell, 49). While the opera house could be used as a mechanism of distinction and exclusion by the Old New Yorkers, it conversely could be a tool employed by the social climbers in their pursuit of higher status. Eventually, Old New Yorkers could no longer prevent the powerful new group of corporate financiers and industrial entrepreneurs from founding the Metropolitan Opera and Realty Company and launching the construction of the Metropolitan Opera House in 1880. Calling the Metropolitan Opera House as "the opera house of Wall Street", John Dizikes notes that its construction epitomized the supremacy of finance capitalism over commerce when the United States were moving towards "centralized national business control in the era of the trusts, sugar and petroleum, meat packing and tobacco and banking" (284). Unable to afford the fierce competition, the Academy of Music was forced to close two years after the opening of the Metropolitan Opera House. The old elites thus had moved to the new opera house, which "symbolically acknowledging the new power relations" (Beckert, 247).

The triumph of the new money illustrates the declining exclusivity of opera attendance as a form of leisure. Firstly, the location, exterior, and interior decorations of the Metropolitan Opera House— "the semiotics of theatre architecture" in Marvin Carlson's words—all represent this change (10). In contrast to the Academy's small scale and inconvenient location, the new opera house occupied the entire western side of the block between 39th and 40th Streets on Broadway. According to Surdam, in the early years of the twentieth century, Broadway played a pivotal role in the rapid growth of "modern American leisure industry" (201). Broadway was a key hub for entertainment, where "a riot of electric lighting signif[ied] new and exciting leisure-time activities" (202). Thus, since its inception, the new opera house had been at the heart of leisure activities in New York. Different from the grand opera houses of Europe or the previous ones in New York, the Metropolitan Opera House had an industrial looking exterior rather than the more-commonly-seen neo-Baroque style:

> there was no Greek pediment or portico to hallow the entry place, no Greek or Latin inscription, no Corinthian columns. Rather, a pair of sevenstorey apartment buildings (or were they offices?) faced with yellow brick [...] the "new yellow brewery on Broadway". Overall, however, this building spoke not of art but of money. (Snowman, 278)

In addition to the façade which celebrated the victory of money over art, the building was famous for its lavish interior because the stockholders demanded that the inside be more extravagant than the Academy of Music. Opulently bedecked with gold trimming, glittering chandeliers, and plush red velvet, it was intended to challenge the more subdued Academy and the exclusivity of the old elite for which it stood. Most importantly, with 122 boxes which were able to contain 750 people, the Metropolitan Opera House offered the prestige of box seating to those who would afford to purchase one (Snowman, 280).

Secondly, the upstarts not only dominated the construction of the Metropolitan Opera House but also changed the code of conduct for opera-going. In order to assert their entitlement to the elevated position, they more conspicuously displayed leisure than Old New Yorkers. For instance, the affluent audiences dressed up to watch opera, which cost both time and money. The close relationship between leisure and social class imposed an obligation on female opera-goers to reinforce their husbands' social standing through public displays of leisure and wealth since "at the stage of economic development at which the women were still in the full sense the property of the men, the performance of conspicuous leisure came to be part of the services required of them" (Veblen, 119). As major places of nightly entertainment that were accepted by the genteel society, the Metropolitan Opera House on the one hand provided women opportunities to participate in leisure activities. On the other hand, society women signified with their bodily presence and appearance not only class privilege but also their male provider's wealth. The attention to appearance and behavior which made women into an object of desire for the aim of appealing to male opera-goers reveals a commercial aesthetic of display, or in Saisselin's words, the women "exhibiting herself to advantage in the same way that commodities were shown to advantage in the boutiques" (55).

In *The House of Mirth*, self-made financier Rosedale successfully purchases a box at the opera house. However, his confidence is not solidified until he invites members of Old New York families such as Lily, Gus Trenor, and Mrs. Fisher to join him in his box for the opera's opening night. As Lily observes, "it was a relief to find [...] supported" (*HM*,

67

149). This insecurity exhibited by Mr. Rosedale suggests that even though the opera house has become less exclusive, attending the opera as a form of leisure remains tied to social class.

When Lily is invited to watch an opera, the first thing she thinks of is not the performance, but how to attract the attention of her admirers. Her reaction reflects the importance of the opera house as an arena for social competition, where female beauty is the object on display. Moreover, opera-goers' clothes reveal the gender differences in the relationship between seeing and being seen. As Tamar Garb notes, while women, knowing that they were there to be looked at, would wear dresses such as décolletage that showed the appropriate amount of skin and sit at the front of their boxes, men would wear black to disappear within the box so that they could look without being seen (224). Additionally, the raised location of the box and glittering background not only facilitated the occupants' view but also "functioned as a glorious jewel box to set off its prize" (Solie, 208). Opera etiquette required that ladies would not stare around through a glass, appear to be conscious of being looked at, or return the gaze of an admirer, "as to do so would signal the type of sexual availability associated with prostitution" (Montgomery, *Displaying Women*, 128). Therefore, both the spatial organization and social code of the opera house made women the target of a non-reciprocated male gaze.

In her analysis of the female opera-goers in the novel, Montgomery pinpoints women's self-objectification: they are "subject to the scrutiny of unobserved spectators who have the power to label them as dangerously sexual" (*Displaying Women*, 134). Their self-objectification reveals gender inequalities in the realm of leisure activities. In the late nineteenth century, patriarchal society dictated the types of recreational pursuits in which women could engage and the manners in which they should comport themselves during leisure time. "Cultivated pursuits [...] such as reading, singing, small-scale hospitality, and visiting artists' studios, or with traveling to see the sights of ancient European civilizations" constituted the primary leisure activities for ladies. Although women were allowed to have fun in the opera house, their behavior was subject to stringent restrictions. There were numerous etiquette manuals providing women with guidelines on appropriate conduct while engaging in leisure activities. In *The House of Mirth*, the patriarchal power is enabled and amplified by the self-objectification the opera house imposes upon women, which is demonstrated by Lily's pleasure due to her internalization of the social demands for feminine propriety and ideals of attractiveness.

When she appears in Mr. Rosedale's box on the opening night of the opera season, Lily eclipses the other ladies with her impressive beauty and exquisite attire. Like a diva on stage, she attracts all the gentlemen's attention. In "The Deep Surface of Lily Bart: Visual Economies and Commodity Culture in Wharton and Dreiser", Bärbel Tischleder adopts Laura Mulvey's theory of "male gaze" to discuss "the quasi-cinematic staging of feminine beauty" in the opening of the novel when Lily is surveyed by Selden and other male travelers at the Grand Central Station (70). There are also parallels between this opera scene and Mulvey's analysis of the sexualized esthetics of Hollywood films. Mulvey describes how the films often "open with the woman as object of the combined gaze of spectator and all the male protagonists in the film. She is isolated, glamorous, on display, sexualized" (811). This comment applies to the opera scene which opens with Lily standing alone as object of "the general stream of admiring looks" from several hundred audiences (*HM*, 149). The fact that she is sexualized by the men in the house is clearly demonstrated by Trenor whose observation connotes sexual desire: having been aroused by her display, with "the dark flush on his face and the glistening dampness of his forehead", he asks for sexual favors as repayment for his previous financial assistance when the two are alone in the box (*HM* , 150). Through offering a critical reflection of the gendered spectatorship, Wharton predates feminist film theorists' discussion on the ubiquitous patriarchal power.

More importantly, Wharton also reveals the impacts of the opera house upon Lily's self-perception. Looking around, she is pleased with the opera house as its interior decoration highlights her beauty: while the crystal chandeliers and "shifting of lights" add "a general brightness of the effect" to her hair, the crimson silk walls set off her skin as white as ivory (*HM* , 149). "Always inspirited by the prospect of showing her beauty in public", Lily feels satisfied with being the center of attention at the opera house: "Ah, it was good to be young, to be radiant, to glow with the sense of slenderness, strength and elasticity, of well-poised lines and happy tints, to feel one's self lifted to a height apart by that incommunicable grace which is the bodily counterpart of genius!" (*HM* , 149). Sitting in the most conspicuous box, she feels like a "superfine human merchandise" in a luxurious jewelry case (*HM* , 294). According to Duncan, landscape has "the impact of objectification", which refers to "the effectiveness of the landscape as a concrete, visual vehicle of subtle and gradual inculcation" by persuading observers of the legitimacy of the social order (*The City as Text* , 19). In other words, Lily's pleasure reveals that the opera house makes her take for granted her role as an object of male desire.

Psychologists Barbara Fredrickson and Tomi-Ann Robert name the effect of women's tendency to "internalize an observer's perspective on self ", especially men's, as "self-objectification". As they explain, this perspective on self can lead to "a form of self-consciousness characterized by habitual monitoring of the body's outward appearance " (180). Understood in this way, Lily is controlled by this perception of self because she is always seen examining her face in front of mirrors, worrying that "petty cares should leave a trace on the beauty which was her only defence against them" (*HM*, 63). Based on the theory of Fredrickson and Robert, Dawn Szymanski, Lauren Moffitt, and Erika Carr further argue that certain environments contribute to women's self-objectification. They summarize the specific attributes of those environments that encourage and deepen women's self-objectification: the environments are the ones where traditional gender roles exist, where a high degree of attention is given to the display of women's bodies, and where male gaze is approved and acknowledged (20-21). Therefore, the opera house can be understood as a "sexually objectifying environment" (20) that leads women to perceive themselves as objects of male desire. A 29-year-old single girl who needs a husband to support her precarious economic situation, Lily knows well that her visibility in the opera box proves her value in marriage market. Her pleasure thus articulates that she takes her self-objectification for granted, depending her value on presenting herself as a highly prized object. Unfortunately, what Lily fails to notice is that her display is interpreted by the opera-goers in a different way from her expectation:

> If Lily's poetic enjoyment of the moment was undisturbed by the base thought that her gown and opera cloak had been indirectly paid for by Gus Trenor, the latter had not sufficient poetry in his composition to lose sight of these prosaic facts. He knew only that he had never seen Lily look smarter in her life, that there wasn't a woman in the house who showed off good clothes as she did, and that hitherto he, to whom she owed the opportunity of making this display, had reaped no return beyond that of gazing at her in company with several hundred other pairs of eyes. (*HM*, 149-150)

According to Montgomery, women's public display "was intended to provoke in other men the envy of the women's 'possessor'—the man who paid for her clothes and jewelry" (*Displaying Women*, 128). Consequently, in the other audience's eyes, Lily's behavior suggests that she is the mistress of Trenor who pays her opera cloak. Through the mouth of the narrator, Wharton exposes the perilous situation of women's objectification in the opera house and articulates her critique of gender disparities in leisure activities.

To conclude, the transformation of the opera houses in New York is made possible by the increasing economic and social authority of the *Nouveau Riches*. In *The House of Mirth*, the opera house as a locale for leisure serves as a marker of social status, evidenced by Mr. Rosedale's attempts to secure an opera box. Additionally, the opera house functions in reinforcing women's self-objectification through facilitating a non-reciprocated male gaze. By probing deeply into Lily's pleasure in the opera house, Wharton discloses women's perilous position as the object of male desire and condemns gender inequalities in leisure activities such as attending the opera. Overall, Wharton's portrayal of the opera house demonstrates that in late nineteenth century, leisure was an indicator of class and gender privileges.

2.2.2   Opera House as a Site of Relaxation

While the opera house in *The House of Mirth* functions as a marker of class and gender privileges, in *The Custom of the Country*, the venue serves as a site of relaxation. In tandem with the transformation in the notions of leisure in the early twentieth century, the social status of opera audience expanded to include the middle classes and the ownership of opera boxes was on longer exclusive to the established elite (Snowman, 286). For the new audiences from the middle and upper middle classes, going to the opera was less a matter of social obligation than a way to spend their money for entertainment. Used to be the exclusive domain of the elite, leisure gradually became "accepted in the United States as a natural right of people [...] by the opening of the twentieth century" (Dulles, 288). In her essay about *The Custom of the Country*, Cheng Xin states that middle-class women who wear ready-made clothes in the opera house exemplify the "democratization of fashion" ("Fashionable Things", 199). Through securitizing the location, façade, and interior of the opera house in the novel, this book proposes that shifts in the landscape of the opera house display the growing accessibility of leisure.

Unlike such European capitals as Paris and Vienna, in New York, opera's status as "the plaything and projection of the elite" was already destabilized in early twentieth century (Aspden, 8). In addition to providing a chance for the new elites to display their leisure and wealth, the opera house as a large venue of leisure must attract more audiences to watch performances. While the opera house's managers paid more attention to the marketplace, its audiences expanded to contain less socially distinguished citizens.

The location, exterior, and interior of the opera house in *The Custom of the Country* all reveal the growing availability of leisure activities to a wider audience. Firstly, the Metropolitan Opera House's location on Broadway places it at the epicenter of New Yorkers' leisure life. Around the 1910s, Broadway had become an elegant avenue filled with theaters, clubs, restaurants, and stores. The theatrical district of New York gradually extended up Broadway from the 20th and 30th to 42nd Street near Times Square. During afternoons and evenings, a large crowd of New Yorkers "descended on the theater district, crowding the highways, thoroughfares, streetcars, subways, and elevated trains as they rushed to meet their friends outside one of Broadway's" many places of leisure (Schweitzer, 35). In the novel, when Undine and her middle-class friends go to see an opera, they see a queue of music enthusiasts waiting to purchase tickets at the box office. The street is aglow with neon signs. Adjacent to the opera house is a theater whose advertising billboards display the "pictures from *Oolaloo* and *The Soda-Water Fountain*", the shows that "Undine has seen fourteen times". A short distance away stands a towering building covered from top to bottom with a sign of "Broadway" (*CC*, 30). Secondly, the façade of the opera house is characterized by advertisements, posters, and electric light to capture the interest of passers-by on Broadway. The dazzling lights, colorful posters announcing tonight's performance, bustling carriages and cars, and well-dressed audience makes the opera house a prominent sight of the cityscape. Thirdly, the opera house reorganizes its interior to cater to a wider range of audiences. In the 1910s, "the pit, and gallery arrangement [...] gave way to an arrangement of stalls with [...] balconies above" (Carlson, 157). Less visible boxes and better, cheaper seats for the middle class were introduced. New staircase provided "access to all parts of the house", including the previously separated opera boxes (158).

Early in the novel, Undine goes to the opera house with her middle-class friends, Mabel Lipscomb and Henry Lipscomb, on a Friday evening after Henry has finished his work for the week. While Henry wants to relax after a week of labor, the two ladies are eager to see celebrities in the audience, about whom they have read in newspapers. Before going to New York, Undine's knowledge about the Metropolitan Opera House is from newspapers and magazines. She enjoys reading reports on the decorations of the opera house and the attire of its audiences. After moving to New York City, she immediately asks her father to buy a box when she sees advertisements of the opera house. Unlike Mr. Rosedale in *The House of Mirth* who regards opera-going as a way to solidify his newly-acquired position in the elite society, the trio from *The Custom of the Country* view this leisure activity primarily as a form of relaxation. Far from feeling insecure in their opera box, they talk, wag, and wave conspicuously. They "shout above the blare of the wind instruments" and "make conspicuous outbreak of signaling", which constantly draws attention from other audiences. When the opera reaches its middle part, Henry even "lean[s] back on the sofa, his head against the opera cloaks, continue[s] to breathe stertorously through his open mouth and stretche[s] his legs a little farther across the threshold" (*CC*, 52). It is worth noting that Undine tries to exercise her own gaze as soon as she enters her box. In *The Ladies' Book of Etiquette and Manual of Politeness* (1860), Florence Hartley explains the rules and regulations for women's visual behavior in the opera house: women should "not look round the opera house with your glass", "never turn your head to look at those seated behind you, or near you", and "avoid carefully every motion or gesture that will attract attention" (173-174). However, Undine and Mabel violate all the above-mentioned instructions. When the curtain falls after the first act, Undine, "for the moment unconscious of herself, swept the house with her opera-glass, searching for familiar faces" (*CC*, 61). Mabel, also searching the crowd, makes "large signs across the house with fan and play-bill" (*CC*, 63). They curiously observe the operagoers who they have read in newspapers, magazines, and society columns. An active female spectator, Undine challenges the opera etiquette's demand that women should play a passive role as the object of male gaze. Her spectatorship thus can be interpreted as an attempt to resist self-objectification which the opera house imposes on women.

The behavior of the three characters reflects the growing accessibility of leisure. In the early twentieth century, notions of leisure underwent significant transformation in the United States. As Susman points out, one of the most significant transformations in early-twentieth-century America was the transition to a burgeoning culture of "plenty, play, leisure, recreation" (xxiv). The Victorian ideals of diligence and thrift, once dominant in the nineteenth century, gave way to the notion that "having fun" was beneficial to one's health and overall well-being. Rather than being exclusive privileges for the elite few, leisure "increasingly was considered a necessary release from the pressures of city life and the workplace" (Husband & O'Loughlin, 180-181). Throughout much of the nineteenth century, the general attitude towards leisure in America was that leisure was "tolerated rather than encouraged" (Surdam, 20). Americans' unease about pleasure-seeking was rooted in the Puritan legacy. The Puritans feared that entertainment "could become so attractive, so compelling, so seductive—so enchanting as an alternative ritual—that to allow any aspect of it to separate from the rest of society would inevitably break all the boundaries and break all the rules" (Surdam, 19). As Max Weber contends, the Protestant work ethic was also characterized by "the dominance of work and the neglect of leisure" (qtd. in Surdam, 20). The shift in Americans' attitudes toward leisure at the turn of the century was prompted by an expansion of leisure time, a rise in discretionary income, and the introduction and widespread adoption of new leisure technologies in the United States, such as bicycles, streetcars, automobiles, telephones, movies, and radios (Fischer, 453). The prosperity of the early twentieth century extended to a broader segment of the population. What used to be considered a luxury expenditure on leisure was increasingly becoming a norm, even for less affluent Americans. With the emergence of a more affluent middle class, leisure activities that were once exclusive to the wealthy became more accessible:

> At the dawn of the twentieth century, the American economy was almost unrecognizable from that of 1800, and even the economy of 1860 seemed primitive. At the beginning of the industrial era, only the wealthy were likely to devote substantial time and money to the few public

amusements that were available. But by the turn of the century the landscape of most American cities had been transformed into a world of phonograph and kinetoscope parlors; of vaudeville halls and ten-twenty-thirty melodrama theaters; of world's fair midways; of amusement parks, ballparks, dance halls, and picture palaces. (Husband & O'Loughlin, 187)

American women participated more actively in leisure activities as well. They read fiction, joined various clubs, and frequented downtown stores for shopping. Specialty stores and department stores elevated the shopping experience by offering amenities like tearooms, upscale restaurants, and delivery services. Increasingly, younger women also participated in sports, encouraged by physicians and female physical educators who advocated physical exercises to enhance both health and beauty. Sports traditionally considered " feminine", such as golf, tennis, horseback riding, cycling, and ice skating, saw a marked increase in participation. Working-class women, even those with limited means, also sought excitement in dance halls, cheap theaters, and amusement parks (Piott, 108).

From Wharton's satirical delineation of Undine and her two friends, whom she labels as " intruders" in the opera house, we can see that the writer holds a critical attitude towards the increasing accessibility of leisure (CC, 49). When the opera house as a place of leisure welcomes a larger range of audiences and its codes of conduct continues to be violated by newcomers, Wharton, as a member of the elite, regards the expansion of leisure as a threat to upper-class exclusivity and a debasement of taste. Moreover, she exposes that the growing accessibility of leisure does not significantly mitigate existing gender inequalities by showcasing how Undine transforms from a spectator into an object of male desire in the opera house. Although Undine manages to temporarily exercise her own female gaze, she remains entrapped within and defined by patriarchal values.

While looking at neighboring opera boxes, Undine notices that some private boxes are adorned with portraits of women. They were bought from the society painter Popple who has also requested to draw her portrait in his studio. The portraits make her feel that women become part of the ornament of the opera house and an essential element of its interior. When Undine looks around with her opera-glass, the female opera-goers' clothes heighten her sense of women as part of the interior decoration: "In all the boxes cross-currents of movement had set in [...] black coats emerging among white shoulders, late comers dropping their furs and laces in the red penumbra of the background" (*CC*, 48). "White shoulders" conveys that the female audience wear the décolleté gowns which emphasize their sexuality. The contrast between men's and women's clothes thus reveals the observer/observed dichotomy which is similar to that in the opera house in *The House of Mirth*.

The portraits in fact demonstrate the objectification of women in the society. The pictures on the wall reminds Undine of Popple who often calls her "auburn beauty". Seeing her as a portrait which will hang in his gallery, he uses her body parts such as the hair and skin to represent her entire being, calling her "Brunette" and even "a mere bit of flesh and blood" (*CC*, 55). In the painter's eyes, she is "a good thing for the spring show" to attract wealthy male clients (*CC*, 56). According to Sandra Lee Bartky, sexual objectification occurs whenever a woman's body or body parts "are separated out from her person", or "regarded as if they were capable of representing her" (35). In other words, when objectified, women are treated as bodies, in particular as bodies that exist for the pleasure of others. Although Undine regards herself as a powerful participant in leisure activity, the decoration of the opera house clearly signals that women continue to be viewed as objects of male desire.

Looking at the portraits, Undine responds with "cheeks burned with resentment", "the leaden sense of failure" and an overwhelming feeling of being "helpless and tired", which all indicate her shame that results from feeling others' negative perspective on her (*CC*, 53). Benjamin Kilborne defines "shame as involving discrepancies between the way one wants to be seen and the way one feels or imagines one is being looked at" (35). Therefore, Undine's sense of shame arises from the discrepancy between her self-perception as an active participant in leisure activities and her realization that she is viewed by men as an object of their desire. Instead of looking around, she quickly lowers her eyes and turns to "the haughty study of her programme" (*CC*, 49). Her behavior shows that although she manages to play the role as an active female spectator, the opera house, a "sexually objectifying environment" (Szymanski et al., 20), prevents her from escaping self-objectification. Jean-Paul Sartre explains how the internalization of another's judgement is central to the experience of shame: "[shame] is the recognition of the fact that I am indeed that object which the Other is looking at and judging. I can be ashamed only as my freedom escapes me in order to become a given object" (261). Pointing out that the source of shame is unequal power relation in terms of race, class, and gender, Joseph Adamson and Hilary Clark emphasize that "whenever a person is disempowered on the basis of gender, sexual orientation, race, physical disability, whenever a person is devalued and internalizes the negative judgment of an other, shame flourishes" (3). Therefore, the opera house imposes the unequal gender relation upon Undine, forcing her to debase herself and lose her subjectivity. Shame thus functions in dismantling female autonomy and solidifying gender inequalities in the opera house.

To summarize, the transformation of opera houses is shaped by the shift of power from Old New Yorkers to the newly wealthy. The changes in the landscape of opera houses in the two novels manifest the rising accessibility of leisure in America at the turn of the twentieth century. As cultural geographers emphasize, "the nature of gender and class relations in a particular place are likely to influence, and even dictate, the social behaviour of individuals in that place including what is considered to be the appropriate and acceptable leisure behaviour" (Mowl & Towner, 106). The opera house in *The House of Mirth* functions as a marker of class and gender privileges. On the one hand, the opera house serves as an indicator of social standing. On the other hand, it encourages women to internalize the gendered ways of seeing, thereby reinforcing their self-objectification. Lily's pleasure in the opera house reveals that she takes her self-objectification for granted. The opera house in *The Custom of the Country* becomes a site of relaxation for its middle-class audiences. Undine initially enjoys an active spectatorship. However, her experience of collapsing into an object of male desire indicates that the increasing accessibility of leisure fails to effectively mitigate gender inequalities in such activities. Her shame reveals that she remains bound and defined by patriarchal values.

Wharton's delineation of the opera houses in the novels illustrates her critical attitude towards the growing accessibility of leisure. In terms of class relations, Wharton views the democratization of leisure as undermining the exclusivity of the upper class and debasing cultural tastes. In terms of gender, while Wharton acknowledges that leisure venues like opera houses provide women greater access to urban life, she contends that this change does not rectify gender inequalities in leisure activities.

2.3 Hotels as the Embodiment of Mobility

The hotel is another iconic urban landscape in the two novels. Widely regarded as a unique symbol of American culture since the early decades of the nineteenth century, distinctively American architecture which was "nourished and brought to flower solely in American soil and borrowed practically nothing from abroad" (Williamson, 5), the hotel not only changed the urban landscape of American cities, but also influenced Americans' lifestyles when an increasing number of people lived in hotels as long-term residents between 1880 and 1930, the period when hotel life was most vigorous (Groth, x). Named as "the greatest hotel city in the world" at the turn of the century, New York witnessed the prevalence of grand hotels which were invested and inhabited by the *Nouveau Riches* (Fick, *New York Hotel Experience*, 14). As cultural geographers point out, urban landscape can be read as revelatory texts (Duncan, "Landscape Taste as a Symbol of Group Identity", 355). In *The House of Mirth* and *The Custom of the Country*, while the hotels' façades symbolize the power of corporate capitalism, their interiors display a public and mobile lifestyle among New Yorkers. The popularity of hotel living reflects the growing geographical and social mobility in American society.

The rise of American hotels was closely tied to the expansion of rail travel and innovations like the automobile, all of which were byproducts of the intense industrialization at the turn of the twentieth century. The advances in transportation facilitated an unparalleled level of mobility among Americans. As historian Sandoval-Strausz notes, the popularity of hotels during this period demonstrated that Americans' "relationship to geographic locations was becoming more tentative and temporary than ever before" (2). Hotels supported this geographical mobility by offering travelers essential services like lodging, food, and drink—amenities usually found within one's own home. Hotels also made crucial contributions to the places in which they were located; they helped "integrate newcomers into expanding networks of commodities, capital, and information that were vital to community prosperity in the formative decades of national and international capitalism" (3). Moreover, hotels acted as catalysts for social mobility. They were the key witnesses and products of major power-shifts in the United States, especially in large Northeastern cities such as New York, where the balance of power shifted from the old money to the *Nouveau Riches*. With the ascendancy of the newly wealthy and the advent of train travel, luxury hotels, once the domain of the old money, were invaded by the new rich. The hotels built and inhabited by the upstarts, which were once avoided by the upper crust, eventually gained acceptance among the established elite as well. Thus, hotels provided opportunities for the social aspirants who sought upward mobility in social status. In short, hotels embodied an American culture of personal mobility. Though the era saw the construction of a variety of hotels (resort and beach hotels, artistic hotels, etc.), this section focuses on a specific category: the ones commonly known as grand hotels, palace hotels, or luxury hotels. Often serving as landmarks in the cities, luxury hotels contained "a series of interior public locations—the lobby, the bar, the dining room, the ballroom, the terrace— that were known to virtually everyone in the city and that were generally accessible only to the truly elite" (Groth, 37). These architectural marvels, grand in both scale and scope, were essential elements of the urban landscape, showcasing the rising influence of the new money.

From a young age, Wharton has had a keen understanding of the impacts of houses upon human emotion. Her "sensibility to the interaction" between people and their surroundings dates to her earliest memories and lasts a lifetime (*A Backward Glance*, 28). The sensitive perception of her environment results in a professional interest in houses and their interior decoration. She built homes for herself both in America and France, published books about architecture and interior decorating, and created a variety of houses in her fictions. As Els Van Der Werf notes, her fictional houses are "emotional architecture, a fusion of material and mental dwelling places" (187). Wharton's attention to the dynamic interplay between people and their surroundings is clearly demonstrated in the two novels, exemplified by the emotional impact of the hotels on the occupants.

In a letter to her friend Sara Norton in 1904, the writer complained about the New England hotel where she stayed: "Such dreariness, such whining sallow women, such utter absence of the amenities, such crass food, crass manners, crass landscape! And, mind you, it is a new and fashionable hotel" (*The Letters of Edith Wharton*, 93). In her analysis of the hotels in Wharton's novels, Susan Koprince concludes that "Wharton consistently portrays the hotel as the antithesis of what she considered to be the ideal home" because she cannot bear the vulgar taste in architecture and the questionable repute of guests (13). What Koprince overlooks is that, from the author's perspective, the characteristics of permeability and transience make the hotel the antithesis of an ideal home, undermining Americans' respect for morality, tradition, and history. Through analyzing both the material and emotional dimensions of the hotels which serve as temporary residences for the characters in the two novels, this section intends to explore the influences of increasing mobility on the psychological and cognitive experiences of New York citizens.

2.3.1 Senses of Uncanniness in the Permeable Emporium Hotel

Having been disinherited by her aunt and expelled from Old New York society, Lily—the heroine of *The House of Mirth*—moves to the Emporium Hotel where she makes a living by working as the private secretary of the oft-divorced Mrs. Hatch from the West. The hotel serves as the home for the wealthy newcomers who revel in material indulgence and aspire to climb the social ladder. As a permeable private/public venue in the eyes of Lily and

Mrs. Hatch, the Emporium elicits their senses of uncanniness.

The development of American hotels reflected the increasing influence of corporate capitalism and the power of the *Nouveau Riches* since the second half of the nineteenth century. Although the word "hotel" originated from the French term "hôtel" which referred to the residence of a nobleman, the modern hotel run by standard systems and professional staffs was an American creation as the result of the transportation revolution, the urbanization, the rise of tourism, and geographical and economic expansion in the nineteenth century (Sandoval-Strausz, 48). Different from European inns and taverns which were usually converted from landlords' private houses, American hotels were financed by businessmen as a way of investment not different to that of railroads and industrial plants ever since the construction of the first establishment to be called "hotel" in America—the City Hotel of New York (1794)—was built by a stock company when New York was a thriving town with a population of about 30,000 (Williamson, 10). For the aim of capitalizing on the booming real estate industry and showcasing their incredible wealth, the upstarts served as both the investors and guests for the urban hotels. Catering to their pursuit of geographical and social mobility, the hotels epitomized the parvenus' lifestyle during this period.

Since the last decades of the nineteenth century, many people, particularly wealthy newcomers to major cities like New York, have resided in luxury hotels. The popularity of grand hotels in New York was mainly related to the upstarts' mobile lifestyle. In terms of geographical mobility, the advancement of transportation made domestic and international travel more accessible for Americans. The new rich always traveled, rather than settling in one place for an extended period. In *The House of Mirth*, the residents of the Emporium Hotel are perpetually on the move. Men journey from New York to other cities for business, while their wives and daughters spend weekends in suburbs, summers in Europe, and winters in Newport. According to urban historian Groth, the soaring rents and shortage of servants resulted from New York City's expansion and population boom in the second half of the nineteenth century made hotel life a strong attraction, especially for the new arrivals who were too busy to consider household management (116-117). The hotels liberated them from domestic obligations and enhanced their geographical mobility. More importantly, the hotels facilitated the parvenus' pursuit of upward movement in social status. In addition to providing meeting places for politicians and businessmen, the turn-of-the-century palace hotels were primarily used for social life such as holding banquets and balls. Living in hotels eliminated the need for the time-consuming construction and decoration of a costly house in the respectable neighborhood, the incremental cultivation of good reputation, or the strenuous effort to gain acceptance into the appropriate social clubs and dinner circles. As soon as they moved into palace hotels, newcomers had the opportunity to both see and be seen by the local elite. Upper-class dances, feasts, and weddings provided more opportunities for upward movement. "Through palace hotel life, nouveaux riches could buy reliable entry to high society" (Groth, 27). Therefore, the guests most often encountered in New York hotels were newly successful entrepreneurs in retail, investment, industrial, or mining enterprises, especially the affluent families from the West.

An " exemplary of the modern ", the hotel was at the forefront of technological, social, economic, and cultural transformations between the 1860s and 1930s (Moore, 17). American hotels installed technological conveniences such as telephones, communal heating and vacuum cleaning systems before they became commonplace. Industrial building materials, modern plumbing, elevators, and electricity were widely used to construct skyscraper hotels. The hotels were also pioneers in adopting chain and franchise structures as well as branded and standardized spaces. Their organizational structure was revolutionary in terms of labor organization and information control (18). As cultural geographers articulate, urban landscape can be "read as a text" which represents the social relations producing the landscape (Bunnel, 280). Understood in this way, hotels embodied the power of corporate capitalism in American society.

In *The House of Mirth*, Wharton uses the Emporium Hotel as a representative of the luxury hotels in New York. Located within the fashionable district, the hotel is firmly rooted in the urban life. Since 1890, the high-rise hotels and skyscrapers in Manhattan had formed the skyline of New York City, serving as remarkable visual representations of urban social transformations (Lindner, 26). In 1910, Ezra Pound described the spectacle of New York hotels at night: "It is then that the great buildings lose reality and take on their magical powers [...] Squares after squares of flame, set and cut into the aether. Here is our poetry, for we have pulled down the stars to our will" (qtd. in McQuire, 132).

According to Koprince, Wharton's depiction of the Emporium is based on the Fifth Avenue Hotel (16). This hotel was located near the writer's childhood home and its residents' promiscuous lifestyles often drew criticism from Wharton's family. Built by real estate investor Amos Richards Eno in 1859 and run by hotelier Paran Stevens, the Fifth Avenue Hotel was one of the first hotels on Fifth Avenue when hotel living had not yet been widely accepted by Old New Yorkers. Covering 16 building lots and the Fifth Avenue block from 23rd to 24th Street, the seven-story white marble building stood in stark contrast to the neighboring residential areas. In comparison to the surrounding brownstone dwellings, the hotel appeared immense. It spurred development of additional hotels to the north and west, transforming the neighborhood into a hub for entertainment activities, including restaurants, studios, and clubs. The overall design of the exterior adopted the Italian style, with the entrance characterized by large white pillars, and the hotel's name marked with Corinthian capitals. Entering through the main entrance, beneath the portico at the front, visitors were welcomed into the grand entrance hall. The floor of the entrance hall was adorned with a diamond pattern of white and dark red marble, while the counter was crafted from solid white marble. The first floor housed various shops and offices for travelers' convenience, including a reading room, telegraph office, barber shop, washroom, and restaurant. The second floor contained the main dining room, an additional dining room for early meals and breakfasts, and the ladies' tea room, all framed by corridors lined with double rows of Corinthian columns. The tea room was elegantly carpeted, painted, and illuminated with sidelights, mirroring the hall below, serving as a gathering place for the ladies in the evening. Starting from the third floor, there were accommodations for guests. The suites were thoughtfully arranged to meet the needs and sizes of families or individual guests. Each of these rooms was furnished with wardrobes, bureaus, and lounges (Steen, 279-284). In addition to its massive exterior and luxurious interior, the hotel was also famous for its technological conveniences. It was reported to be the first hotel in the United States to introduce a passenger elevator, a feature that New Yorkers described as "a little parlour going up by machinery" (284).

In *The House of Mirth*, the Emporium, equipped with electric light, modern plumbing, and heating systems, is described as "a world over-heated, over-upholstered, and over-fitted with mechanical appliances for the gratification of fantastic requirements, while the comforts of a civilized life were as unattainable as in a desert" (358). The interiors are decorated with "the excesses of the upholstery or the restless convolutions of the furniture" under "the blaze of electric light" which "impartially projected from various ornamental excrescences on a vast concavity of pink damask and gilding"

(*HM*, 357-358). The long-term residents, especially ladies, indulge "in a haze of indeterminate enthusiasms, of aspirations culled from the stage, the newspapers, the fashion journals, and a gaudy world of sport" (361). At the entrance of the hotel, lines of "high-stepping horses and elaborately equipped motors" wait to transport the hotel guests into "vague metropolitan distances" (358).

For Old New Yorkers, the mobile lifestyles of the Emporium's residents imply corruption, indulgence, and sexual promiscuity. The Emporium as a permeable public/private venue is of greatest concern to the Old New Yorkers. Serving as a gathering place, the Emporium is characterized by its gregariousness and mixed-gender sociability. Its inherently public nature—teeming with transient residents unfamiliar to each other—and its uniform interior design underscore a diminished sense of privacy for those who consider the Emporium as their temporary home. Old New Yorkers are doubtful about the social events in the hotel, such as banquets organized by Mrs. Hatch to attract the heirs of the Old New York families. When Selden, one of the gentlemen from Old New York families, comes to the hotel for visiting Lily, he is shocked by the residents' constant and chaotic motion. In his eyes, the Emporium cannot be separated from the streets. The ground floor of the hotel appears like a vast cage, flinging gaslight into the street and absorbing the passers-by promiscuously. The noises and movements outside diminish the grandeur of the building, leaving it vulnerable to the vulgar assault of the street life. The crowded space of movement and overstimulation suggests the gregarious state of hotel life and the occupants' sexual misconduct. As soon as Selden enters Mrs. Hatch's drawing room, he notices "the sofa in question and the apartment peopled by its monstrous mates" (*HM*, 364). He cautions Lily that Mrs. Hatch's gregarious life mirrors her disregard for responsibility and her indifference to social conventions. From the perspectives of Old New Yorkers, the geographical and social mobility exhibited by hotel dwellers signifies the erosion of boundaries, leading to a loss of social norms and identity.

The characters who are mostly influenced by the new money's mobile lifestyle are Lily and Mrs. Hatch. Gazing at the Emporium from the street, Lily experiences both fascination and uneasiness: she is fascinated by the vertical grandeur, but feels uneasy about the unfamiliar urban spectacle. The occupants "who drifted on a languid tide of curiosity from restaurant to concert-hall, from palm-garden to music-room, from ' art exhibit' to dress-maker's opening" display a mobile life that Lily is unfamiliar with. In his 1919 essay on the uncanny, Sigmund Freud proposes that it is a mixture of feeling both familiar and unfamiliar to the surroundings. He points out the contradictory connotation of the uncanny through tracing its etymological root in the German word *unheimlich*: the meaning of *unheimlich*'s antonym *heimlich* overlaps that of *unheimlich*, which can be defined as either feeling "belonging to the house, not strange, familiar, tame, dear and intimate, homely" or feeling strange, unfamiliar, and unhomely (122). He further articulates how architecture produces the uncanny, which emphasizes the interplay of environment and human emotion. Building on Freud's argument, Anthony Vidler suggests that the uncanny is a phenomenon associated with modern cities: "the uncanny, as Walter Benjamin noted, was also born out of the rise of the great cities, their disturbingly heterogeneous crowds and newly scaled spaces" (4). Vidler names this "condition of modern anxiety" as the "architectural uncanny", referring to a sense of "estrangement" that is intrinsic to the process of urban social transformations and closely tied to the spatial formations and social experiences of large cities (6). Thus, Lily's emotion stirred by the hotel can be understood as a sense of uncanniness that she feels in urban social transformations.

When Lily first moves into the Emporium, she feels the advantages of mobile and free life. Since the residents keep coming and going, nobody cares about her scandal and rejection by the Old New Yorkers. The anonymity and freedom provided by the hotel comfort her: "The sense of being once more lapped and folded in ease, as in some dense mild medium impenetrable to discomfort, effectually stilled the faintest note of criticism" (*HM*, 357). However, the guests' mobility soon makes her feel uneasy. Lily repeatedly refers to the Emporium as a haunted house. The inhabitants "float together outside the bounds of time and space" and even the most "substantial" Mrs. Hatch "still floating in the void, showed faint symptoms of developing an outline" (*HM*, 359). The female guests are "wan beings as richly upholstered as the furniture" who "drifted on a languid tide of curiosity" from the hotel to other parts of the city and "whence they returned, still more wan from the weight of their sables, to be sucked back into the stifling inertia of the hotel routine" (*HM*, 358). In Lily's eyes, the hotel is like Dante's *Inferno* where the residents "had no more real existence than the poet's shades in limbo" (*HM*, 358-359). The permeable hotel catalyzes her sense of estrangement and terror. Such feelings are explained by Freud as features of the uncanny: "the quality of feeling" that arouses "dread and creeping horror" which is often associated with the images of death and ghosts (121).

Lily's sense of uncanniness reaches its peak when she attends Mrs. Hatch's ball. Seeing decorations in the drawing room that are akin to those of New York's established elite, she has "an odd sense of being behind the social tapestry, on the side where the threads were knotted and the loose ends hung" (*HM*, 361). After knowing that the purpose of the gathering is to entice Freddy Van Osburgh, the heir of an old family, into marrying Mrs. Hatch, Lily realizes that Mrs. Hatch's continual movement between hotels is a strategic effort to ascend the social ladder through sexual misconduct. Underlying the lady's mobility, Lily discerns, are irresponsibility and immorality. Hotel patrons like Mrs. Hatch are preoccupied with material indulgences and individual desires, disregarding moral obligations and social norms.

It is noteworthy that Mrs. Hatch also sees the Emporium as a haunted house. Despite being a beautiful and wealthy divorcee from the West who appears even younger than Lily, Mrs. Hatch feels that the hotel life makes her suffer from " the fixity of something impaled and shown under glass" (*HM*, 358). Her feelings suggest that the extreme mobility of her lifestyle strips her of the meaning of life and leads to spiritual emptiness. Both Judith Fryer and Ailsa Boyd point out that the hotel experience throws light on the frightening similarity between Lily and Mrs. Hatch. " Mrs. Hatch is merely a more vulgar representation of Lily, an ornamental woman, spending her time in a ' jumble of futile activities', angling to marry a distinguished member of the high society" (Fryer, 86; Boyd, *Home of Their Own*, 311). In this sense, Mrs. Hatch can be understood as Lily's double who symbolizes her fear of emptiness and rootlessness. Many scholars believe that Lily's rootlessness is the main reason for her tragedy, but they tend to analyze the fictional buildings metaphorically rather than pay attention to their material and emotional dimensions (Clubbe, 554; Jacobsen, 518; Singley, *Edith Wharton: Matters of Mind and Spirit*, 81). At a time when a growing number of Americans were embracing mobile lifestyles, Wharton, by examining the hotel's influence on the psyches of Lily and Mrs. Hatch, highlights that the anonymity and freedom of hotel life may lead residents to indulge in material pleasures and individual desires, thus resulting in a disarray of values and a decline in moral integrity.

Being permeable between familiarity and unfamiliarity, neither wholly public nor wholly private, the Emporium hotel is thus closely associated with the uncanny. As noted by Gail McDonald, in the 1900s many Americans regarded " buildings' permeability as representative of their modernity" since architectural permeability signified the rise of a fluid and malleable self which was suitable for urban life (233). According to the well-known psychologist William James, for example, architectural permeability demonstrated that the "model of consciousness as a wavelike succession of fields with their indeterminate margins" had replaced the nineteenth-century model of consciousness as "a perduring substantial entity" (qtd. in Gail McDonald, 244). However, the senses of uncanniness evoked in Lily and Mrs. Hatch by the Emporium reveals that a mobile lifestyle does not necessarily lead to liberation. The hotel guests' mobility disrupts the boundaries between the public and the private, making the Emporium a permeable site. The excessive freedom afforded by the hotel leads to irresponsibility and immorality, and even engenders spiritual emptiness.

2.3.2　Senses of Alienation in the Transient Hotel Stentorian

In *The Custom of the Country*, heroine Undine Spragg and her parents spend most of their time residing in New York's grand hotels. Mr. and Mrs. Spragg circulate among half the hotels of the city. Undine is perpetually in motion, driven by her unending pursuit of wealth and social status: starting from the Hotel Stentorian on Manhattan's Upper West Side, progressing to a small house on West End Avenue, and then moving on to hotels and estates in France before ultimately splitting her time between New York and Paris. The restless mobility enabled by hotel living undermines the Spraggs' regard for tradition and history, which results in their senses of alienation.

The turn of the twentieth century saw the explosion of luxury hotels which transformed New York's cityscape. Sumptuous high-rise hotels began to appear in the skyline since the massive Waldorf-Astoria (built in two parts by millionaire cousins William Waldorf Astor and John Jacob Astor IV), the world's largest hotel at that time, opened on Fifth Avenue in 1893 and 1897. Upon returning to New York in 1904, after nearly two decades residing in Europe, Henry James discovered that the low-rise brownstones of his childhood had been replaced by vertical office buildings and palace hotels. Looking from New York Bay on the ship, he described the tall buildings as "standing up to the view, from the water, like extravagant pins in a cushion already overplanted [...] like the flare, up and down their long, narrow faces" (76).

The emergence of luxury hotels in New York paralleled the triumph of the robber barons who gradually obtained dominance in the high society in the early decades of the twentieth century. The hotels satisfied their demands for geographical and social mobility. Whereas the members of the upper class in *The House of Mirth* such as Selden and Lily see the stylish hotel as a horrible place, the old moneyed families in *The Custom of the Country* have already used the grand hotels as their favored venues for sociability. The hotels facilitated geographical and class mobility by providing new kinds of spaces for interaction. Their public rooms, especially the impressive ballrooms, grand restaurants, and exotic roof gardens, encouraged the elites to move out of their private parlors and into the hotels, which led to the mixing between the old and the new money. The middle class was also able to participate in the new social rituals as long as they could afford the expenses. The hotels not only changed the social life of the upper class, more importantly, they "encouraged processes that opened up the exclusive Four Hundred, democratized them to a certain degree, and encouraged Americans to live their lives more in the public" (Fick, "The Waldorf-Astoria and New York Society", 137). In other words, the hotels provided the newly wealthy with more opportunities to enter and even influence the once exclusive high society. The luxury hotels thus reflect the transformation of power from the dominance of the old families to that of the parvenus, or in Joseph A. Ward's words, they are "the evidence of [...] conquest by the new barbarians" (158).

In *The Custom of the Country*, the Spraggs live in the Hotel Stentorian at the upper west side shortly after having arrived the city from the Midwestern town of Apex, Kansas. It is Undine who persuades her father to give up the house they have bought and move into the hotel because "all the fashionable people she knew either boarded or lived in hotels" (*CC*, 12). Her preference for the hotel as their home captures a unique feature of urban life in the United States since the middle of the nineteenth century: both wealthy and middle-class Americans increasingly chose to live in hotels rather than rent or buy houses, especially in big cities such as New York. The New Yorkers' interests in making hotels their homes reached the apex between 1880 and 1930, which made New York City "the capital of palace hotel living" (Groth, 44). Be able to get rid of the routine responsibilities of managing a large house and obtain instant social position the hotels conferred on their residents, the newly wealthy, most often successful entrepreneurs from the West often lived for a long time in urban hotels. As Montgomery summarizes, large hotels were "strategic sites" for the new money class to "network, build up its group identity, and enhance its socio-economic power" ("The Testimony of the Hotel", 160). According to *King's Handbook of New York City* 1892: *An Outline History and Description of the American Metropolis*, there were over 100 good hotels where New York families made their homes in them all year around to avoid the annoyances attendant upon housekeeping.

It is this assurance of permanent patronage that has done much to promote the excellence of New York hotels during the present generation, and particularly during the last decade. Several of the best American-plan hotels are sustained chiefly in this way, and the tendency among many well-to-do people is more and more toward that style of living. (King, 216)

Located on West Seventy-second Street overlooking the Central Park, the Stentorian where the Spraggs live is a massive building with "aglow façade", "monumental threshold", "marble vestibule", and "mirror-lined lift" (*CC*, 91). Taking the description of its location and architecture into consideration, several scholars postulate that Wharton modelled the Stentorian on the Waldorf-Astoria and a similarly named hotel—the Majestic which stood at the address in the novel (Boyd, "'Looey Suite'", 20; Finnigan, 168). Opened in 1894, the Majestic was one of the representative family hotels targeting at permanent residents. Catering to the needs of wealthy families, the 600-room building made up of six massive joined towers was famous for its suites of luxurious decoration. A British hotel guest wrote about the difference between the Majestic and British hotels: "The inn is with us, proverbially, the travelers' home, but here it is the home of a great many besides travelers" (Sandoval-Strausz, 267).

In the novel, the Stentorian, an important landmark in New York, attracts many tourists to see its magnificent façade, visit its gigantic lobby, and enjoy the view of Central Park from its roof garden. The manager of the Stentorian even employs a group of young men to guide people through the splendor of the hotel, placing the Stentorian on par with popular tourist attractions. Invested by the self-made millinery magnate Victor Henry Rothschild, the hotel is located at Central Park West, between 71st Street and 72nd Street on the Upper West Side of Manhattan. Not far from the elevated railway, the Stentorian is one of many grand hotels along Central Park. The hotel's location is convenient, standing near the entrance to the park and offering easy accessibility to railroad stations, steamboat piers, and shopping districts. As a result, it is highly popular among newcomers to New York. West 72nd Street in front of the Stentorian connects the carriage drives of Central Park with Riverside Drive. The street bustles during the day with traffic heading to the park and pedestrians taking walks. At night, after Central Park descends into darkness, the main sources of light on this street come from the windows of the hotels and advertising boards on their exterior walls. Nearby commercial buildings include the Dakota apartment immediately to the north and other hotels. Central Park West is a low-rise thoroughfare where the most notable buildings are grand hotels. The only other structures in view are white stone-fronted Gothic-style row houses. The hotels thus define the character of the neighborhood. In the early twentieth century, the West End where the fictional Stentorian is located was the hub of New York grand hotels which hosted almost half of the city's hotel population. Half of the leading hotels of the metropolis were in that territory which was less than two miles long by a half mile wide (King, 216). Imposing apartment houses and towering palace hotels made the landscape of this quarter quite different from that of the older residential areas at East Side. Lloyd Morris summarizes the uniqueness of this hotel district: "It was like a city in itself; it had its own distinctive social tone. Nowhere else in the city was there a neighborhood that so eloquently expressed the spirit of the times [...] the fine, carefree sense of 'easy come, easy go' (201)".

The sense of "easy come, easy go" vividly conveys the transience of the hotels. Henry James expresses a similar impression of New York hotels in *The American Scene* (1907): "Thus, as you are perpetually provisional, the hotels and the Pullmans—the Pullmans that are like rushing hotels and the hotels that are like stationary Pullmans" (300). While James juxtaposes the hotels and trains, Wharton in *The Custom of the Country* highlights the similarity between the hotels and ships: "the lofty hotels moored like a sonorously named fleet of battleships along the upper reaches of the West

Side" (*CC*, 18). Her depiction not only emphasizes the number and size of the hotels, but also points out their transience by linking them to the movement and speed of fleets. Besides, the luxury hotels usually did not last long due to the fierce competition in the industry. The investors kept demolishing outdated hotels and rebuilding new ones with more massive exteriors and advanced facilities. In spite of their initial popularity, the Waldorf-Astoria and the Majestic were torn down in 1929 and replaced by new buildings. As provisional urban landscape, the hotel epitomizes the city's "will to move—to move, move, move, as an end in itself" (James, 65).

The scale of the Stentorian is enormous: three twelve-story sections are divided by courtyards which allow abundant light and air into the interior rooms. The façade is primarily made of white marble, decorated with sandstone trim and terracotta detailing. The main entrance features a double-height archway on the street. The hotel contains about 600 rooms, several bowling alleys, and the only roof garden in New York. The first floor includes a marble-lined lobby, a main dining room, a reception, parlors, drawing rooms, billiard rooms, and private dining rooms and ballrooms. Most of the rooms for guests are rented in suites which comprise drawing rooms, bedrooms, and bathrooms. A significant portion of its residents are long-term occupants, primarily consisting of wealthy families from the West.

Since urban landscape can be viewed "as readable and revelatory texts" (Gail McDonald, 228), the hotel in the novel operates as a signifying system which conveys the inhabitants' identities. Naming interior decoration as a " living-room scale microlandscape ", James Duncan points out that landscapes of houses is of great importance in the formation and performance of individual, familial, and community values (" Landscape Taste as a Symbol of Group Identity" , 355). Both the spatial location and architectural elements of the Stentorian are therefore "tropes that allegorically represent" the shift in social and cultural powers from Old New Yorkers to the new money (Duncan, *The City as Text*, 6). Undine's notion of home, her choice for interior decoration, and her judgement of other characters in the novel are all shaped by what she sees in the hotel. Her " white and gold bedroom with its blazing wall-brackets" are arranged based on the suites in luxury hotels (*CC*, 13). The first time she realizes that Old New York is no longer the center of the high society is when she regards their houses as being "rather shabby" because "there was no gilding, no lavish diffusion of light" (*CC*, 21). Apparently, her reading of the interiors is shaped by the decorating styles she learns from the Hotel Stentorian. As Duncan argues, landscapes are read and interpreted via " an ingrained cultural framework of interpretation [...] if they are often read ' inattentively' at a practical or nondiscursive level, then they may be inculcating their readers with a set of notions about how the society is organized " (" (Re) reading the Landscape", 123). By inculcating the inhabitants such as Undine with the new money's ideas about how home should be, the hotel amplifies the influence of the upstarts on New York culture.

As geographers point out, the cultural meaning of urban landscape can be ichnographically interpreted in terms of macro-level as well as micro-level explanations (Domosh, " A Method ", 352). The Stentorian hotel's monumental and vertical façade which eclipses the old elites' mansions symbolizes the power of corporate capitalism and the *Nouveau Riches'* ambition for social legitimacy. The hotel combines room-to-room telephones, electric elevators, and lighting with Renaissance ornaments such as turrets, gables, and finials, thereby embodying the integration of old and new, traditional and modern. While the Emporium Hotel in *The House of Mirth* features in its permeability, the most striking characteristic of the Stentorian is its transience.

Anthropologist Marc Augé sees the hotels as typical architectures which are not "relational" or "historical" (77). He regards hotel chains as the examples of "transit points and temporary abodes [...] proliferating under luxurious or inhuman conditions". Although the hotel chains had not appeared in the United States when the novel was published, his theory is applicable for analyzing the impacts that the "fleeing, the temporary and ephemeral" hotel imposes upon the psyche and cognition of Undine and her parents (78).

In Augé's opinion, the hotel makes residents feel free and liberated because it engenders new beginnings and relieves the guest of "his usual determinants", mainly his past (103). Providing an escape from the weight of the past and freedom from social conventions, the hotel thus becomes an emancipatory space; as Augé explains, "the relative anonymity that goes with this temporary identity can even be felt as liberation" (101). The Spraggs relocate to New York to escape their stifling hometown and the scandals they are embroiled in. Undine's failed first marriage to Elmer Moffatt generates rumors that tarnish her reputation. After Mr. Sprag's business misconduct comes to light, the Spraggs leave their hometown to try their luck on Wall Street. The residents of the Stentorian are indifferent to the family's past; they view the Spraggs simply as affluent Westerners attempting to break into the upper echelon of New York society. In the hotel, Undine experiences a disconnection from her past and feels that a new sense of self begins there. Indeed, the hotels enable her to launch a new life every time when she seeks change: she encounters her first husband Ralph Marvell at a dance held in the Stentorian; later, she meets her next husband, Raymond de Chelles, in the busy dining room of the Hotel Nouveau Luxe in Paris, which is a transplanted first-class New York hotel; and ultimately, she accepts her third husband Moffatt's proposal in his suite at a French hotel. Akin to Augé's argument that in hotels "what reigns there is actuality, the urgency of the present moment" (104), Wharton calls the

Spraggs' life in the Stentorian is an "abundant present" (*CC*, 162).

In addition to the erasure of individual past, the hotel represents the early-twentieth-century Americans' lack of concern for family history and more generally, their lack of concern for tradition. The décor and furnishings in the hotel rooms demonstrate the erasure of historical contexts. While old families such as the Dagonets and de Chelles put family portraits and artifacts in their homesteads for the remembrance of their ancestors and family history, the ancient portraits of Marie Antoinette and the Princess de Lamballe and valuable objets d'art in the Spraggs' Looey suite have nothing to do with the inhabitants' personal or familial past. Instead, those objects' value depends on their status as commodities which signify the hotel patrons' wealth.

The evisceration of history from home that the hotel encourages is most strikingly displayed when Undine tries to remove history from the ancestral houses of her two old money husbands by redesigning her rooms in the style of the Looey suit and selling family heirlooms for profiteering. After being married to the railroad king Elmer Moffatt, her ultimate home is as provisional as the Stentorian. The billionaire couple divides their time between a Paris hôtel and a Fifth Avenue mansion which are both decorated with valuable objects collected and removed from old families. As Betsy Klimasmith notes, their home becomes "mobile, ahistorical, temporary" which is in fact a hotel in the most American sense (*At Home in the City*, 132). Undine's marriages therefore reflect hotels' detrimental effects on American society: the geographical and social mobility facilitated by hotel life erodes Americans' respect for tradition and history. Through the words of Undine's French husband Chelles, Wharton expresses her attack on the lack of concern for history in American culture: "you come from hotels as big as towns, and from towns as flimsy as paper, where the streets haven't had time to be named, and the buildings are demolished before they're dry, and the people are as proud of changing as we are of holding to what we have" (*CC*, 307). Chelles clearly links Americans' hotels to their passion for transience which results in the devastating consequence of the eradication of tradition in modern society.

As Augé points out, the temporary abodes create "neither singular identity nor relations; only solitude, and similitude" (103). Although it provides the Spraggs with freedom and mobility, the hotel as home causes alienation among the Spraggs due to the removal of history. Firstly, the Spraggs feel an alienating sense of nothingness in the Stentorian. Since Mr. Spragg divides his day between his office and the hotel lobby, and Undine is busy attending various social events, Mrs. Spragg either spends her time alone or converses with her only friend in the hotel—her masseuse. Her sole form of entertainment is to sit motionless by the window of her suite and "watch the nightly lighting of New York": "the lights spring out down the long street and spread their glittering net across the Park" (*CC*, 41). By pointing out the unsettling continuity between Mrs. Spragg and materials in the hotel rooms, Wharton implies that the furniture and interior decoration smother the inhabitants' activity. Mrs. Spragg is described as a mannequin not different to other decorations in her drawing room: "Mrs. Spragg herself wore as complete an air of detachment as if she had been a wax figure in a show-window. Her attire was fashionable enough to justify such a post [...] suggested a partially melted wax figure" (*CC*, 5). Like the heavily gilt furniture, ornate tapestry and portraits surrounding her, she is reduced to a lifeless model who passively displays the wealth of her husband, indistinguishable from the ornament-filled room.

The fluctuation between comfort and oppression is emphasized in Mr. Spragg's description of the row of hotels on the street: "the expressionless faces of the buildings against an opaque, bright blue sky" (*CC*, 20). His description implies that the sense of nothingness overpowers the built structures and their occupants. Mr. Spragg feels a sense of alienation in the

101

hotel lobby as well. Although the hotel provides openness, mobility, and freedom, he thinks that it reduces the occupants into indistinguishable "American types", a "group of puppets" (*CC*, 25). The guests either quickly walk in and out of the lobby, or sit in the chairs with their faces hiding behind newspapers. Looking around, Mr. Spragg sees " the emblazoned ceiling and the spongy carpet", "pallid families, richly dressed, and silently reading", and "a knot of equally pallid waiters, engaged in languid conversation, turned their backs by common consent on the persons they were supposed to serve" (*CC*, 26). Mr. Spragg's view of the lobby reveals the conflicts between freedom and homogenization, as well as between mobility and stasis in the hotel. In his eyes, the lobby is homogenizing and the individuals become unidentifiable in the faceless crowd. Mr. Spragg's sense of alienation peaks when he attempts to engage a gentleman in conversation, only to find the latter avoiding eye contact. He feels "a sense of being caged into this crowded emptiness" —an oxymoron that highlights the alienating sense of nothingness.

In his study of the hotel lobby, sociologist Siegfried Kracauer explains the alienation which is provoked by hotels. He argues that the twentieth-century urbanites have become lifeless in relation to their surroundings and that the hotel represents an extreme example of how environment can overpower an individual. Regarding the lobby as "impersonal nothing", "vacuum" and "void", he focuses on the lack of emotional connection between the hotel guests and their surroundings (290-291). Since the hotel is a temporary living place, the residents do not bother to develop intimate relationship with each other. In Kracauer's opinion, acting as a powerful emblem of transience, the hotel makes the guests "vanish into an undetermined void" and become alienated from each other (293).

Secondly, the Spragg family experiences a sense of alienation amongst themselves. There are vast deserts of silence in their suites. Undine only takes the initiative to converse with her parents when she needs to request financial support. Bettina Matthias points out that "as a modern economic phenomenon", the hotel represents "the workings of the money-based economy" (3). The operation of the hotel is based on the power of capital, with money securing a guest's stay. Not only goods and services, but interpersonal relations become quantifiable in monetary terms, creating a distance between the individual and the surrounding world. As Simmel elucidates, this distance is simultaneously liberating and alienating: while money enables geographical and social mobility, it also erodes the unmediated connections between people, commercializing human interactions and rendering genuine experiences increasingly elusive (*The Philosophy of Money*, 80). For Undine, under the influence of the transient hotel, even the closest family members are uncapable of maintaining emotional bonding with each other. Undine's father labors to meet her material desires, while her mother plays the role of a mediator, convincing her father to pay the daughter's bills. Even when she sees that her parents seem "much older, tired and defeated", Undine ruthlessly compels her father to betray his business partner just to finance her trip to Italy.

The sense of alienation engendered by hotel living produces extreme lifelessness—the incapacity to act in any meaningful way. It is through the life of the Spragg family that Wharton makes evident the ultimate sterility of modern life. Undine "perpetually dash[es] over to New York and back, or rushes down to Rome or up to the Engadine" (*CC*, 457). Whenever she resides in a place, she is always uneasy, sensing that there is still something more to achieve. Her parents drift from hotel to hotel and depend on the change of abodes as the only variety: whereas Mrs. Spragg "shrinks from the thought of 'going back to house-keeping'", Mr. Spragg is completely "disconnected from any fixed habits and domestic sentiments" (*CC*, 177). The empty lives of the Spraggs highlight the psychological toll that abandonment of the past can have on Americans.

Elaine Showalter points out that Undine embodies the hotel culture: her "natural milieu is a hotel" (qtd. in Klimasmith, *At Home in the City*, 170). The initials of her name "U. S." shows that for Wharton the transient hotel is a synecdoche of the American society. Thus the title of the novel—*The Custom of the Country*—can be interpreted as referring to Americans' mobile lifestyle. While Henry James suggests in *The American Scene* that the "hotel-spirit" may be the American spirit—passion for supreme gregarious social life, Wharton emphasizes a temporary home without history, whose popularity destroys the past (Despotopoulou, 504). In *The Custom of the Country*, the transient hotel reinforces the early-twentieth-century Americans' lack of concern for tradition and history. By tracing history's dwindling force in a culture dominated by transience and exploring the psychological effects of the hotel's provisionality on its occupants, Wharton expresses her anxieties about the fate of the past in a modern urban nation.

In conclusion, as one important urban landscape in Wharton's novels, the hotel develops under the influence of the new money. The exteriors of the hotels represent the dominance of corporate capitalism, whereas their interiors reflect a more public and mobile lifestyle among New Yorkers. The Emporium Hotel in *The House of Mirth*, which is a permeable public/ private site, evokes the residents' sense of uncanniness as the anonymity and freedom of hotel life leads to a disarray of values and a decline in moral integrity. The Hotel Stentorian in *The Custom of the Country*, a transient site which erases history, makes the Spraggs feel alienated, a sense of emptiness caused by being disconnected from the past. Altogether, the hotels embody the growing geographical and social mobility experienced by New Yorkers. Seeing New York hotel as a mirror of American society at large, the writer cautions that although Americans' mobile lifestyle offers expanded freedoms and prospects, it undermines their reverence for morality, tradition, and history.

2.4 Summary

The urban landscape in *The House of Mirth* and *The Custom of the Country reflects New York's transition from a nineteenth-century Victorian city to a twentieth-century modern one. The changes in the urban landscape*, represented by the streets, the opera houses, and the hotels, lead to the following social and cultural transformations at the turn of the twentieth century: a rising emphasis on individuality, an increasing accessibility of leisure, and growing geographical and social mobility.

In this chapter, the changes in the cityscape, and the interactions between the urban landscape and New York citizens in the novels are analyzed to explore the impacts of social transformations upon urban dwellers at the turn of the century. Firstly, the streetscape reflects the urbanizing process of the city. Following the Victorian emphasis on order and boundary, Old New Yorkers produce the class-divided and gender-separated streets. The streetscape helps Old New Yorkers to legitimize class and gender exclusion, represents hindrance to Lily's pursuit of independence and individuality and consequently contributes to her aimlessness and fear. By comparison, Mr. Moffat's Fifth Avenue mansion represents a challenge to the street's class segregation, while Undine's transgression leads to her pleasure in enjoying the street's night view. The three characters' different ways of experiencing the streetscape showcase the increasing importance of individuality in urbanization. Secondly, the opera houses demonstrate the rising accessibility of leisure. The production of the buildings is a matter of ongoing struggle between the old guards and newly riches. The opera house in *The House of Mirth* serves as a marker of class and gender privileges. Lily's pleasure in the opera house reveals that she takes her self-objectification for granted. The opera house in *The Custom of the Country* turns into a site of relaxation for its middle-class audiences. However, Undine's shame suggests that the expansion of leisure does not effectively mitigate gender inequalities in such activities. Thirdly, the hotels display the growing levels of geographical and social mobility. The popularity of hotels as temporary residences is fueled by the parvenus' need for sociability and mobility. While the hotels' façades represent the dominance of corporate capitalism, their interiors exemplify a more public and mobile lifestyle among New Yorkers. The permeable Emporium hotel in *The House of Mirth* evokes senses of uncanniness among its residents, as the anonymity and freedom associated with hotel living contribute to a breakdown of values and a decline in moral integrity. The transient Hotel Stentorian in *The Custom of the Country* erases history and results in the Spraggs' senses of alienation.

The urban landscape in the two novels functions as an ideological medium to represent the operation of power structures, and it also constitutes a part of the material world for human beings' sensorial experiences. The changes in the urban landscape represented by the streets, the opera houses, and the hotels are enabled by the replacement of Old New Yorkers by the newly riches when Victorian New York is transforming into a modern city. Landscape plays an active role in forming class and gender identities, legitimizing hierarchical relations, and operating as a signifying system through which social values are reproduced. Shaped by the operation of power, the urban landscape evokes the characters' various emotions which reveal the effects of social transformations on human psyche and ideologies. The relation between people and the urban landscape is thus a two-way street: people act as much as they are acted upon. All in all, Wharton's delineation of the urban landscape illuminates the dynamic interplay between turn-of-the-century Americans and their surrounding environments, reflecting the impacts of social transformations.

106

The transitional urban landscape in the two novels exemplified the dominant role of commercial culture in New York City at the dawn of the twentieth century. Unlike Paris, which was modernized under the command of a local government led by Baron Haussmann and whose boulevards embodied the imperial power, the cityscape of New York was largely shaped by the needs of its "mercantile and financial elite class" (Domosh, *Invented Cities*, 2). Different from Boston whose commercial districts were carefully limited for the aim of underscoring its image as "a center of intellectual society", the development of New York's streets and commercial buildings, both horizontally and vertically, exhibited "the ultimate material expression of a capitalist city" (Domosh, *Invented Cities*, 1).

To summarize, the urban landscape in the two novels should not be oversimplified as a metaphor for elite values. Instead, it demonstrates the changes of the citizens' lifestyles and mentalities resulting from New York's morphological and cultural transformations. Wharton's delineation of the urban landscape in the two novels reveals her pessimistic perspective regarding the effects of social transformations upon the tastes and psyche of Americans at the turn of the twentieth century. The description of the characters' interactions with streetscape demonstrates that an increasing emphasis on individuality may lead to selfishness and irresponsibility. Her delineation of opera houses showcases that the rising accessibility of leisure debases cultural taste and does little to alleviate gender disparities effectively. The portrayal of hotels displays that growing mobility undermines Americans' regard for morality, tradition, and history. She watches anxiously as the changing cityscape pushes New York culture toward individualism, indulgence, and disregard for tradition, which further influences modern American culture. Although she acknowledges that societal shifts provide Americans, especially women, with greater freedom, she is more worried about the negative influences.

Chapter Three Old New England Landscape in *Ethan Frome* and *Summer*

Wharton produced a sizeable body of fiction set in rural New England which often deal with the lives of the poor and middle class, including a dozen short stories and two novels, *Ethan Frome* and *Summer*. Her New England, like New York in Chapter Two, was a society in transformation, when "economic, cultural, and structural changes transformed the nation from an agrarian state to one that was urban, industrial, and economically interdependent" between 1840 and 1920 (Hays, 120). The writer, who lived in Western Massachusetts every summer after building a country house called The Mount in the town of Lenox in 1902, stated that she knew the New England countryside very well: "'Ethan Frome' was written after I had spent ten years in the hill-region where the scene is laid, during which years I had come to know well the aspect, dialect, and mental and moral attitude of the hill-people" (*A Backward Glance*, 210).

The literary landscape of rural New England in the two novels is based on Wharton's understanding about the hill villages in Western Massachusetts. In her autobiography *A Backward Glance*, the writer articulates that the two stories were inspired by the actual landscape of old New England near The Mount: "For years I had wanted to draw life as it really was in the derelict mountain villages of New England [...] In those days the snow-bound villages of Western Massachusetts were still grim places, morally and physically" (208). Fryer highlights the importance of landscape by categorizing the two books as Wharton's "novels of situation" (178)—the kind of novels relying heavily on environment which "instead of being imposed from the outside, is the kernel of the tale and its only reason for being" (Wharton, *The Writing of Fiction*, 133).

Ethan Frome and *Summer* are often discussed together by critics because Wharton famously calls the latter as "the Hot Ethan" (*The Letters of Edith Wharton*, 385). Since her extramarital affair with William Morton Fullerton between 1906 and 1909 was discovered in the 1980s, scholars have tended to analyze biographically by connecting the two stories to her emotional life①. Thus, most reviewers read rural landscape in the books in terms of its association with the protagonists' pursuit of love: while *Ethan Frome* tells the story of the eponymous hero's renunciation of passion in a lifeless winter landscape, *Summer* traces the heroine Charity Royall's sexual awakening in a vibrant summer landscape (Whaley, 64; Dean, 135). However, critics fail to notice that the landscape exemplifies the transformed identity of old New England: whereas *Ethan Frome* focuses on the bleak picture of the remote rural region in the postbellum era, the landscape in *Summer* reflects the rising popularity of old New England in the twentieth century when urban Americans increasingly saw the region as a refuge from the annoyances of social transformations. Old New England was believed to be preindustrial and ethnically homogeneous, becoming "new geography of the imagination that dominated representations of regional identity into the twentieth century" (Conforti, 204). Serving as the antithesis of "all that

---

① Cynthia Griffin Wolff provides a representative interpretation by concluding that the two novels express Wharton's "emotional quandaries" when her relationship with the two important men in her life—her husband Teddy Wharton and lover Morton Fullerton— "was thrown into chaos" ("Cold Ethan", 232). In Wolff's opinion, while *Ethan Frome* conveys the anguish of the writer who is trapped by her duty to manic-depressive Teddy, *Summer* is imbued with both her passion awakened by Fullerton and her bitterness of being deserted by him (236-244).

was most unsettling in late nineteenth-century urban life", it changed into the reification of a tranquil past which featured the white village, homogeneous Anglo-Saxon population, and virtuous household (Donna Brown, 9). As historian Harold Wilson notes, while "in the last three decades of the nineteen century" rural New England "went through a severe winter season" due to the desertion of farms and decline of rural population, the years between 1900 and 1930 can be regarded as its "spring" period of adjustment and development when the "very backwardness" of the countryside became its most valued attributes (95, 211). With this socio-historical context in mind, we can see that the landscape which shifts from winter to summer in the two novels actually echoes the changes in rural New England at the turn of the century.

Economists and sociologists in the twentieth century generally regarded social transformations as "both the cause and the potential solution to rural poverty" (O'Connor, 215). On the one hand, the process of social transformations caused a significant reduction in the agricultural workforce and brought an end to traditional rural lifestyles. On the other hand, the theorists argued that social transformations presented a solution to the challenges faced by the impoverished rural population through enhanced agricultural productivity, economic expansion and diversification, migration to the cities, etc. Walt Whitman Rostow and Richard David Brown, for example, attributed the decline of rural places like the hill country in *Ethan Frome* to their "inefficient and unproductive economies that failed to grow in a modernizing world because of traditional values and practices that prevented successful adoption of new technologies and new institutions" (Tickamyer, 415). New England farmers were left behind in the prosperity that came from industrialization and urbanization because the local economy failed to unfold or to "take off" in the development of social transformations (Rostow, 55). Rural sociologists also pointed out that when social transformations intensified public anxiety by 1900, Americans turned to "nostalgia for a calmer, less perplexed, preindustrial life" as their "ways of adjustment" in a swiftly modernizing age (Hays, 5). In *Ethan Frome* and *Summer*, old New England's transformed identity is the result of this adjustment.

Moreover, rural landscape often represents class, racial, and gender ideologies. For instance, it is closely associated with nativism, white ethnicities, and traditional gender and class relations. As cultural geographer Paul Cloke contends, the importance of rural landscape "lies partly in the ways in which it transports implicit ideologies amongst its iconography" ("Rural Landscapes", 229).

In the two novels, the impact of social transformations is displayed by rural New England's transformation from a decaying backwater to a romanticized site of retreat from the city. This chapter aims to analyze three representatives of old New England landscape—the villages, mountains, and vernacular architecture—for the purpose of examining the power relations between the urban leisure class and rural poor, US-born Anglo-Saxons and immigrants from Ireland and Italy, and men and women. Through exploring the interactions between the characters and landscape, this chapter will delve into the effects of social transformations upon turn-of-the-century rural New Englanders.

3.1 Villages from a Stagnant Backwater to Rural Idyll

In his influential monograph on the development of New England literature from the American Revolutionary era to the end of the nineteenth century, Lawrence Buell underscores the "double vision" of the New

England village as "backwater" and "utopia" for regionalist writers due to the changes in the economic and cultural milieu of nineteenth-century New England (318). As he explains, during the postbellum years, the rapid growth of cities was in striking contrast to the relative stagnation of the countryside, leading to widely-spread concerns about rural inferiority and backwardness. The villages were thus often described as being unattractive and obsolete, and the farmers as social problems in need of remedy and reform. However, the negative opinion of the New England village gradually shifted to a nostalgic one when urban Americans suffered from the side effects of social transformations (304-318). Thomas D. Rowley notices the change in the image of rural areas across the United States at the turn of the century: "as the Nation became increasingly urban, rural America's cultural stock continued to climb" (3). As cultural geographers emphasize, rural landscape can be used to maintain class stratification since it often chimes with the values of a privileged class (Cosgrove, *Social Formation and Symbolic Landscape*, 15). This section will explore the transformed image of old New England in urbanites' eyes through analyzing the depiction of the two villages in *Ethan Frome* and *Summer*, with the purpose of investigating power relations between the urban leisure class and rural poor.

3.1.1   Desolate and Backward Starkfield

The narrative of *Ethan Frome* spans twenty-four years from the 1880s to the early twentieth century. Except the introduction and the final chapter, the main body of the novel is the anonymous narrator's description of a decaying New England village called Starkfield in the last decades of the nineteenth century. The narrator is an engineer who comes to the village from a nearby city for a railway project. Historian Harold Wilson calls the years between 1870 and 1900 the "severe winter season" of rural New

England, as this period witnessed the worst farmland desertion and rural depopulation in the region's history (96). Competition from the Midwestern farm products and the lure of the West and neighboring cities contributed to the exodus of farmers, with 33.5 percent of New England farmland abandoned between 1880 and 1930 (Bell, 463). The crisis for New England countryside became so disturbing that "scarcely a major periodical appeared in the last decade of the nineteenth century without at least one reference to the abandoned farms of New England, and the haunted houses" (Harold Wilson, 112). The desolate village in *Ethan Frome* epitomizes the decline of old New England when America was transforming from an agricultural to an industrial nation. The narrator's view of the village landscape reflects the impact of contemporary poverty discourse upon power relations between the urban middle class and the rural poor.

Rural sociologists attribute the problems that New England faced in late nineteenth century such as the plight of agriculture, farm abandonment, and out-migration of rural population to the impacts of social transformations, particularly the effects caused by unprecedented urbanization and industrialization (Tickamyer, 415). The most rapidly urbanizing region in the United States, New England as a whole attained urban-majority status by 1890, with 51 percent of its inhabitants living in towns and cities which contained a population of more than 2,500 (Harold Wilson, 107). Urbanization attracted farm youths to factory towns and nearby cities, making New England villages in the stony countryside forsaken places where only women, children, and the elderly remained. In the northern New England state of Vermont, for example, by 1880, 163,325 mountain natives had migrated to urban areas, while by 1900, the number was 223, 496, an increase of 36.8 percent in twenty years (Harold Wilson, 140-141). The lament that New Englanders were abandoning the countryside was heard insistently in the last quarter of the nineteenth century.

In addition to the appeal of urban life, New England farmers were faced with the transformation of agriculture when industrialization rendered technology and new mode of transportation significant for agricultural success. On the one hand, the peasants in small family farms who failed to adopt new machines and management skills found it difficult to compete with the owners of industrial farms which emerged after the Civil War. On the other hand, the expanding national railway network following the completion of the first transcontinental railway in 1869 brought vast quantities of cheap agricultural produce from the Midwest to the Northeast, forcing New England farmers to compete in a national market. The growing reliance of agriculture on modern transport thus disadvantaged the rural areas which were without access to railroads. Unable to keep pace with industrialization, large numbers of New Englanders had to abandon their land and move to cities or the West to make a living. The out-migration of rural population exacerbated the degradation of New England villages (Joseph Wood, "New England's Legacy Landscape", 262).

According to rural sociologists, the decline of old New England in the latter half of the nineteenth century exemplified the adverse effects of social transformations. Rural poverty was "the result of inequalities created and promoted by uneven development between the countryside and city" which led to urban exploitation of impoverished regions (Tickamyer, 416). However, the poverty discourse during that time generally blamed farmers for failing to adopt new technologies and urban lifestyles, rather than acknowledging the exploitation of rural areas by cities. In her study of discourse on rural inferiority in New England, Farland found that there was "vast scientific literature on rural degeneracy" ranging from family case studies to regional studies and official surveys ("Modernist Versions of Pastoral", 906). The peasants were regarded as social problems that needed scientific intervention. In other words, poverty was believed to stem from their inability to adjust to a rapidly industrializing and urbanizing society. In *Ethan Frome*, the narrator's description of the village landscape reflects the influence of the aforementioned discourse on rural poverty.

Starkfield, where the protagonist Ethan Frome lives, is a decaying New England village which faces the challenges of urbanization and industrialization. Starkfield is "a shadowed country, under the growth of industry and the cities" (Raymond Williams, 196). Its main street, rows of white farmhouses, and "slim white steeple of the Congregational church" constitute a picture of the quintessential New England village. Mr. Varnum's mansion with "classic portico and small-paned windows" implies the village's prosperous past (*EF*, 9). Ethan mentions the busy sight of Starkfield years ago when merchants and travelers must pass there to travel to nearby towns. By the 1880s, nevertheless, Starkfield has been left behind. As the narrator observes, there are no trolley, bicycle or rural delivery in the village and the youth of the hills have nowhere for recreation. In the urbanite's eyes, the village is, as its name conveys, a stark field. It lies under "a sky of iron", with points of the Dipper hanging "like icicles" and Orion flashing "cold fires" (*EF*, 23). The countryside is "gray and lonely", with farmhouse being "mute and cold as a grave-stone" (*EF*, 43-44).

The village's decline is caused by the following reasons. Firstly, its location in the hill region prevents the use of agricultural machinery. The rocky land makes farming in Starkfield difficult, rendering being a farmer unattractive for the young generation. Secondly, the long winter hinders the village's communication with the outside world. Starkfield is cut off from the outside by heavy snow for six months. In warm days, villagers drive their own horses to go outside or depend on the only stage between Starkfield and Bettsbridge—the neighboring town—to take the trains. During the winter months, however, the stage stops and trains are slow and infrequent.

Therefore, the location up on the hill, the long winter, and the lack of transportation all contribute to Starkfield's predicament. The migration of countrymen to the nearby cities and the West further results in the loneliness of the village. As one villager named Harmon explains to the narrator, "Most of the smart ones get away" (*EF*, 6). Ethan is among the ones who dream of getting away. Before being called back to Starkfield by his ailing parents, he took courses at a technical college in Worcester, a major industrial city of central Massachusetts, and worked in engineering in Florida. Later in the story when he plans to elope with his wife's cousin Mattie, the first place that comes to his mind is the West. By delineating the landscape of Starkfield, Wharton vividly portrays the plight of old New England when America was rushing into an age of urbanization and industrialization during the postbellum years.

The water-powered sawmill and newly-built railroad in the novel—the former serving as the marker of premodern world and the latter as the icon of industrialization and urbanization—represent the tension between rural and urban America. For the narrator, Ethan's water-powered sawmill reflects his lack of access to contemporary technological innovations. The sawmill has been a feature of the vernacular landscape in rural New England since the earliest years of European settlement: the first water-powered sawmills were built by the colonists in the 1630s near Berwick, Maine. In order to utilize the region's abundant water resources for cutting and transporting lumber, sawmills were built on nearly every river and stream—by 1840 there were about 5, 500 in New England (Penn & Parks, 6). Sawmills changed significantly during the Industrial Revolution of the nineteenth century. One of the most important advancements in technology was the introduction of steam engines, which led to the replacement of water-powered sawmills by steam-powered ones in mid-nineteenth century (Gschwend, 10). "[E] xanimate enough, with its idle wheel looming above the black stream dashed with yellow-white spume, and its cluster of sheds sagging under their white load", Ethan's water-powered sawmill in the village suggests his failure to keep up with the update of industrialization (*EF*, 17).

In contrast to the obsolete sawmill, the newly-built railway in the nearby town which brings the narrator—an engineer who works in the big power-house at Corbury Junction—to Starkfield is the emblem of social transformations. The "magician's rod" in Ralph Waldo Emerson's words (qtd. in Bush, 279), the railroad was viewed by the postbellum Americans as symbol of industrial might which nationalized the economy, made possible the rise of a network of giant cities, and opened new markets for farmers and manufacturers (Gordon, vii). James Walter Goldthwait comments on the importance of the railroad in rural New England: "In the three decades 1840-1870 the railway was perhaps the strongest single factor affecting life" (538). In *Ethan Frome*, the coming of the train to the hill country, nevertheless, exacerbates the isolation of Starkfield rather than facilitating communication between the villagers and a larger world, as travelers no longer need pass through Starkfield to the surrounding towns. The loss of contacts with passersby cuts off inhabitants' connection to the outside world. Moreover, as the train gives local merchants better access to urban markets, no one stops in Starkfield for business anymore. Consequently, for the residents of Starkfield, the train signals their stagnation and accelerates their slide into deeper economic and psychological crises. As Ethan complains about the village's status quo,

> We're kinder side-tracked here now [...] but there was considerable passing before the railroad was carried through to the Flats [...] I've always set down the worst of mother's trouble to that [...] after the trains begun running nobody ever come by here to speak of, and mother never could get it through her head what had happened, and it

preyed on her right along till she died. (*EF*, 19)

The Fromes' experience displays the negative effects brought by the railroad; while Ethan's mother suffers from loneliness due to the loss of interaction with passersby, then develops psychological problems and eventually dies, Ethan fails to find a buyer for his farm and ends up in being trapped in the village because the nearby merchants stop coming there. The Fromes' tragedy is a microcosm of the challenges faced by rural New Englanders in the late nineteenth century when railroads created uneven development between the countryside and city. According to Harold Wilson, "A number of localities bordering on a lake or on a large river which had formerly served as a means of outlet for their products also found themselves isolated, as the railroad, passing them by, went through a neighboring township" (51). The negative effects that the railway causes in Starkfield thus manifests the impacts of industrialization and urbanization upon the countryside's marginalization. However, by emphasizing the backwardness of rural culture, the narrator's delineation of the sawmill and the railroad reveals his belief that the rural poor are incapable of adapting to the requirements of the modern world, thereby attributing poverty to the individuals rather than considering it as a result of uneven development. In short, the narrator sees the landscape of Starkfield as an indication of the villagers' failure to adapt to social transformations.

In the narrator's eyes, the village in *Ethan Frome* reflects the impacts of social transformations upon rural New England in the last three decades of the nineteenth century. Farmers who were unable to adapt to the transformations brought about by industrialization and urbanization found themselves in a tragic state of backwardness and marginalization. The way in which the urban engineer sees the landscape suggests that he attributes poverty to the deficiencies of the rural poor themselves and their

118

environment. Influenced by social Darwinism and environmental determinism, the middle and upper classes of the postbellum era tended to regard the countryside as a different world where people's hardships were determined by the rural environment. Sociologists claimed that "the rural poor lacked the values and aspirations essential for success in the modern, urbanized middle-class society and thus were unable to benefit from social transformations" (O'Connor, 216). As Cloke pointed out, the middle class and the rich deliberately employed "discursive tactics which sought to undermine the concept of poverty by blaming the [...] victims" ("Rural Poverty and the Welfare State", 1006). The narrator's response to Starkfield's landscape thus demonstrates the influence of contemporary poverty discourse which marginalizes and stigmatizes the poor and ultimately reinforces power disparities between the urban middle class and the rural poor.

Moreover, the narrator regards the villagers' reticence as evidence of their inability to adapt to social transformations. He repeatedly mentions the overwhelming silence in Starkfield and ascribes the villagers' taciturnity to their feeblemindedness caused by the environment. For example, he thinks that the winter landscape functions in "retarding still more the sluggish pulse of Starkfield" and Ethan "seem [s] a part of the mute melancholy landscape, an incarnation of its frozen woe" (*EF*, 8, 13). The narrator's depiction of the farmers' insular life and psychological problems mirrors contemporary conceptions of rural inferiority and backwardness. As Farland argues, by the last decades of the nineteenth century, the countryside had become "modern America's Other, cut off from urban industry and innovation, tethered to rituals, traditions, and habits seen as increasing outmoded and outside the culture's mainstream" ("Modernist Versions of Pastoral", 911). Nevertheless, the farmers' reticence in fact implies a sense of shame in their belief that they are inferior to urban residents. Lev Raphael pinpoints that "shame over a lifetime of disappointments" silences Ethan, but she does not identify the origin of shame (284). The prevalent reticence among the villagers stems from social exclusion and stigma brought about by the discourse on poverty. As explained before, urbanites such as the narrator attributes rural poverty to the farmers and exacerbates class inequality. The villagers thus perceive themselves as inferior and experience shame regarding their inadequacies. They lament the gap between themselves and urban dwellers, and feel reluctant to talk about their sufferings as if poverty were their blemish. As Gershen Kaufman points out, "the affective source of silence is shame, which is the affect that causes the self to hide. Shame itself is an impediment to speech" (qtd. in Raphael, 284). The villagers' reticence thus indicates the impact of poverty discourse upon their self-perception.

To summarize, Starkfield's desolate landscape in *Ethan Frome* exemplifies the economic and psychological challenges brought by industrialization and urbanization to old New England's farming villages in the second half of the nineteenth century, a result of inequalities created by uneven development between the countryside and city. The novel is dominated by the tension between the backward countryside and progressive city, which is represented by the antithesis between the obsolete water-powered sawmill and newly-built railroad. Influenced by the discourse on rural poverty, the narrator—an engineer from the city, a man of progress who is associated with the power of electricity and railway—sees the landscape of Starkfield as an indication of the villagers' failure to adapt to social transformations and attributes poverty to the deficiencies of the farmers and their environment, thereby reinforcing power disparities between the urban middle class and the rural poor. The poverty discourse also stigmatizes the villagers and impacts their self-perception, which results in their reticence due to a sense of shame. Therefore, Wharton expresses her attention to rural impoverishment and her denunciation of class inequity through describing Starkfield's landscape.

3.1.2 North Dormer as the Exemplar of Pastoralism

While Starkfield in *Ethan Frome* epitomizes rural New England that was hit by industrialization and urbanization in the postbellum era, North Dormer in *Summer* serves as a representative of the quaint villages which were nostalgic retreats from social transformations for urban visitors in the twentieth century. By portraying the different ways in which urbanites and locals view the village, Wharton criticizes that romanticized old New England landscape veils rural impoverishment and reinforces the class inequality between the urban leisure class and the rural residents.

New England witnessed a significant shift of its regional identity at the turn of the twentieth century when the United States became more industrialized, urbanized, and characterized by increasingly Roman Catholic immigration. Kent C. Ryden summarizes that as American cities grew larger, "rural New England was reimagined as the antithesis of modernity" (45). Likewise, Donna Brown finds that urban tourists did not pay much attention to New England countryside until the last quarter of the 1800s (10). As the least modernized region which was bypassed by the nineteenth-century growth and development detailed in the previous section, the hill country of New England became popular tourist destinations for the vacationers from the Northeastern cities. The widespread Country Life Movement① of the Progressive Era even monumentalized the New England

---

① In response to the increasingly desolate look of the countryside, especially in rural New England, since the late nineteenth century progressive reformers made efforts to tackle rural problems by organizing the Country Life Movement. It received official sanction and considerable aid in 1908 when President Theodore Roosevelt appointed the Country Life Commission to investigate the deficiencies of American country life. He reiterated "the importance to the nation of the material and moral welfare and character of the 'great farmer class'" and demanded that the Commission help New England farmers make their hometowns attractive places (Peters and Morgan, 293).

village as an archetype for all rural America to emulate. The quaint villages were seen by urbanites as the emblem of old New England—a simple, pure, and stable world insulated from the chaotic urban life.

The centennial celebrations of American independence in 1876 not only inspired a nationwide interest in American history and culture, but also deeply attracted urban residents to the charm of old New England, especially the middle and upper classes. As Joseph Conforti points out, "Old New England or the 'old times' signified more than the colonial past; such terms conjured up images of nineteenth-century America before railroads, mill complexes, immigrant hordes, urban squalor, and conspicuous displays of wealth" (228). Urbanites sought after an imagined past that was thought to remain intact in remote rural areas, especially in the mountain villages of northern and western New England where railroads, new technology and consumer culture had not yet penetrated. Empty streets, dilapidated buildings, and outmoded lifestyles were read as something antique and timeless other than poverty and backwardness. Historian George Street recorded the transformation of rural New England at the turn of the century: "It was certainly at a fortunate time [...] that the summer business began [...] the hills had been stripped of the last trees suitable for sawing, the thin soil of the farms was practically exhausted. With the coming of the new population [...] the whole aspect of affairs changed" (326). Street's observation shrewdly captures the phenomenon that the villages' failure to adapt to social transformations has converted into their advantages in attracting urban visitors.

Wharton was familiar with the shift of old New England's regional identity at the turn of the century, as Lenox in the Berkshire Hills of Western Massachusetts, where The Mount was located, is a prime example. Berkshire endured a turbulent time for much of the nineteenth century due to the unprofitable farming and failure of glass manufacturing in the competition with iron companies in Pennsylvania and the Midwest. Encountered by the challenges of social transformations, Berkshire welcomed the arrival of urban travelers which peaked between the 1880s and 1920s when the area's solitude and isolation had been deemed as representing the serenity of the old days. Once considered desolate wilderness, Lenox's beautiful hills drew writers, artists, and journalists throughout the second half of the nineteenth century. Its tranquil villages which were summer homes to such influential writers as Nathaniel Hawthorne and Herman Melville were called America's "Lake District①" (Birdsall, 328). By 1900 Lenox had been the summer place of choice for wealthy residents of Boston and New York.

The author's delineation of the New England village North Dormer in *Summer* is based on the actual landscape surrounding Lenox, where she spent her summers from 1902 to 1911. The novel's depiction of landscape and community in North Dormer at first glance presents a quaint New England village, but its real purpose is to reveal the power asymmetry between urban visitors and local residents in shaping the landscape.

The novel challenges the ideal of the New England village from two aspects. Firstly, the representation of the landscape seems to echo the stereotypes of an idyllic New England, but it in fact subverts the imagery through juxtaposing the different views of the landscape by the heroine Charity Royall and urban visitor Lucius Harney. Wharton opens the book with a typical landscape in the remote mountainous region. Charity, a village

---

① The Lake District, also known as the Lakes or Lakeland, is situated in the northwestern uplands of England. A popular resort, it is famous for its natural scenery, old villages, and associations with the Lake Poets and other intellectuals such as John Ruskin (Darby, 147). Lenox had become what the renowned clergyman Henry Ward Beecher called America's "Lake District" since the 1850s when writers such as Catharine Maria Sedgwick, Henry Wadsworth Longfellow, Oliver Wendell Holmes, Hawthorne, and Melville lived in its villages and towns (Birdsall, 328-355).

girl in North Dormer, sees the rural landscape when she goes out of home:

> It was the beginning of a June afternoon. The springlike transparent
> sky shed a rain of silver sunshine on the roofs of the village, and on the
> pastures and larchwoods surrounding it. A little wind moved among the
> round white clouds on the shoulders of the hills, driving their shadows
> across the fields and down the grassy road that takes the name of street
> when it passes through North Dormer [...] at the other end of the
> village, the road rises above the church and skirts the black hemlock
> wall enclosing the cemetery. (*S*, 1)

With its hills, trees, pastures, winding country road, white church and
farmhouses, North Dormer seems like a representative of the bucolic New
England village as geographer Joseph Sutherland Wood summarizes: "the
village of tree-shaded green surrounded by a tall-steepled church and white-
clapboarded shops and dwellings" (*The New England Village*, 136). The
New England village has been widely thought as the best embodiment of
American pastoralism① since the nineteenth century, as B. D. Wortham-
Galvin notes (24). However, instead of celebrating the pastoral ideal, the
writer pinpoints the class inequality cloaked by the landscape. Her
description of North Dormer demonstrates that the rural idyll is essentially a
fabrication of the elite class.

---

① Pastoralism is a major theme in American literature. In Marx's definition,
American pastoralism is "a desire, in the face of the growing power and complexity of
organized society, to disengage from the dominant culture and to seek out the basis for a
simpler, more satisfying mode of life in a realm 'closer,' as we say, to nature" (Leo
Marx, "Pastoralism" ,54). Though the pastoral ideal had been deployed to define America
since the age of discovery, it was not until the end of the eighteenth century that "a fully
articulated pastoral idea" emerged in the nation (Leo Marx, *The Machine in the Garden*,
73).

Wharton immediately interrupts the idyllic landscape by introducing New York architect Harney to the scene when Charity is on her way to work. His "city clothes" and "careless laugh" makes her feel "the shrinking that sometimes came over her when she saw people with holiday faces" and then quickly go back into the Royall house (S, 1). The reason why the girl returns home is that she must check her clothes in the mirror. In a study of New England's turn-of-the-century tourism, Donna Brown points out that "the industry's growth enforced profound class divisions" since it widened the gulf between the urban vacationers who could enjoy this leisure and the local farmers who must work to serve them (7). The conflicts over class, money, and power between city visitors and rural residents were widely recorded by contemporary writers and correspondents①. Taking the above-mentioned tension into account, we can understand that Charity reacts so oddly because Harney's ease reminds her of the unequal social and economic status between the urban leisure class and the poor farmers. She "felt the distance between them [...] divided them by a width that no effort of hers could bridge" (S,66). The "shrinking" comes over her, therefore, in fact derives from the sense of inferiority caused by her lowly class standing.

When Charity goes outside and sees the same landscape once again, her response alters dramatically: "How I hate everything!" (S, 32). Her bitter exclamation tells that at this moment she re-examines her surroundings through the eyes of the outsiders like Harney instead of her own eyes as an

---

①   A widely circulated report on *The Inquirer* cites a protest by a farm girl as a typical example of local dissatisfaction with the urban people's condescending attitude: "We don't like to be regarded as curiosities, or have strangers come just to play for fun at a sort of life we live in sober earnest the year round. People don't like to have what is practical to them patronized as amusement by others" (qtd. in Donna Brown, 126). For more examples about the conflict written by contemporary writers, see William Dean Howells's "Confessions of a Summer Colonist" (1898) and "The Problem of the Summer" (1902), and Henry James's *The American Scene* (1907).

insider (Panniter, 130). The presence of an urbanite in her familiar environment makes Charity critically examine North Dormer to imagine how it looks like to people from cities. To her surprise, Harney regards North Dormer as a lovely village which is worthy of tourists' interest. He is charmed by the remote village which does not have any signs of modernity: "no shops, no theatres, no lectures, no ' business block' " (*S*, 31). Different from the narrator in *Ethan Frome* who sees Starkfield's landscape as evidence of rural inferiority, Harney tries to convince the residents of North Dormer's value. While Charity regards the empty village as a sign of abandonment caused by economic failure, Harney takes it as a perfect representative of the peaceful rural life.

Nevertheless, Charity's perception of the landscape denies the authenticity of this pastoral imagery in Harney's eyes. For her, the place is in fact "a weather-beaten sunburnt village of the hills, abandoned of men, left apart by railway, trolley, telegraph, and all the forces that link life to life in modern communities"—a decaying village which is not very different from Starkfield in *Ethan Frome* (*S*, 31). On the hot afternoon, the "few able-bodied men" work in the fields and the women are "engaged in languid household drudgery" (*S*, 32). The different attitudes of Charity and Harney towards the same landscape thus demonstrate the chasm between the outside observer and the inside inhabitant, which reveals that the romanticized vision of the New England village in fact veils the power and control in a hierarchical society by chiming with elite notions of human society and nature (Cosgrove, *Social Formation and Symbolic Landscape*, 262). Such visions of the privileged urbanites like Harney in the novel are "distant from the actuality of working and living in landscape, and should be understood as imposing an aesthetic and moral order from afar" (Wylie, *Landscape*, 62). In this sense, North Dormer's landscape can be regarded as a "visual ideology" because its formation not only reflects the socio-economic inequality between urbanites and villagers, but also reproduces the values of the privileged class—the pastoral ideal of city dwellers at the turn of the century (Cosgrove, *Social Formation and Symbolic Landscape*, 266). By depicting the New England village, Wharton does not praise the idyllic landscape, but criticizes the vision of pastoral New England for beautifying the difficult life of the farmers and naturalizing the power of the urbanites.

In addition to questioning the ideal of pastoralism embodied by the New England village, Wharton challenges contemporary Americans' belief in the New England village as an ideal community. D. W. Meinig points out that since the nineteenth century the New England village has become one of the most influential symbolic landscapes in the United States which was "widely assumed to symbolize for many people the best we have known of an intimate, family-centered, Godfearing, morally conscious, industrious, thrifty, democratic community" (165). This conception of the village community is akin to Ferdinand Tönnies's definition of Gemeinschaft (community)— "a living organism in its own right" which is comprised of close ties and in-person interactions defined by blood and clan relationship (19). In other words, the New England village was seen by turn-of-the-century Americans as an organic and nucleated type of social organization which contrasted with the atomized cities where individualism and materialism dominated.

In *Summer*, what city visitors such as Harney think of North Dormer fits perfectly with the aforementioned beliefs about old New England community. They eulogize the close links among the villagers who know each other: kindly old people, industrious young men, and pious girls create an atmosphere of "homely sweetness" (*S*,128). Nevertheless, the villagers are in fact conservative and hypocritical. When Charity seeks help from old Miss Hatchard, the guardian of morality in North Dormer, after her foster father Mr. Royall tries to break into her bedroom at night, the venerable lady refuses to talk with her about the scandal, let alone offer help. Besides, the villagers always monitor the behavior of female members in the community. Though Charity fails to notice, Mr. Royall warns that her contact with her lover Harney is constantly watched by the neighbors: "The whole place is saying it by now [...] You know there's always eyes watching you" (*S*,84). Charity points out to Harney the pervasive hostility in North Dormer: "anyway we all live in the same place, and when it's a place like North Dormer it's enough to make people hate each other just to have to walk down the same street every day. But you don't live here, and you don't know anything about any of us" (*S*, 50). The villagers are tied together not because they have emotional connection to each other, but because they live in the same place and have nowhere to go. Through Charity's rebuttal, Wharton satirizes the urbanites' imagination of a harmonious rural community which serves as an antidote to their unsatisfying city life.

Harney's praise of North Dormer as the embodiment of pastoral simplicity and intimate community reflects the cult of the New England village① that prevailed in the United States at the turn of the twentieth century. The romanticized images of the white villages were widely circulated and most typically displayed in the field of historic preservation

---

① In Conforti's explanation, "cult of the New England village" refers to the transformation of village landscape into "a visual and literary icon that selectively portrays the region as a pastoral, homogeneous, and stable world. This cultural invention not only excludes industrialization and its attendant alterations of the region; it also obscures the energetic commercialism of the white village itself" (149). Considering the importance of the New England village in American literature and culture, Buell argues that literary depictions of the villages should be approached "semiologically, as a codification of a repertoire of motifs built up over time, and mimetically, as referring to a historical reality, however transmuted that reality may have been in the process of literary embodiment". In this sense, to "study the cult of the New England village is to study the most distinctively New Englandish contribution to the American social ideal" (305).

and local color literature. According to Wortham-Galvin, the New England village, "a mixture of fact and fiction", has become a "myth", "one of America's enduring mythological cultural landscapes" by the 1900s (22). Harney's task in North Dormer—to prepare a book about the charming village for a New York publisher—is such a myth creation: his sketches of the old houses and introductions to the village's history will fuel urban readers' nostalgia for New England and thus help in creating a whitewashed vision of the rural landscape. As rural geographers propose, representation of pastoral landscape can be understood as "discursive strategies which obscure rural problems and even filter them out altogether in the various constructions of idyll-ized rural life as the spatial expression of self-supporting [...] existence in a market place economy" (Cloke et al.,351). The cult of the New England village not only concealed problems, but also exacerbated poverty by perpetuating rural deprivation as it was the state of deprivation—lack of transportation and employment opportunities, etc.—that rendered rural areas enticing to urban residents.

Furthermore, urban dwellers' nostalgia for the New England village in fact reflected their efforts to maintain class hierarchy in an era of social upheavals. On the one hand, the concentration of political, economic, and cultural power in cities in the early twentieth century intensified the wealth disparity and class conflicts between rural and urban regions. On the other hand, the influx of a large population from rural areas to urban centers in search of employment opportunities resulted in housing shortages, environmental degradation, and ongoing labor disputes. For example, New York City witnessed 1,652 strikes during the ten-year period between 1907 and 1916 (Hays, 78). Donna Brown neatly summarizes that nostalgic tourism in rural New England offered urban people an opportunity to "recapture the class stability and harmony of a world without industrial conflict, the graciousness and dignity of aristocrats whose claims to authority

129

had never been challenged" (187). In *Summer*, the cult of old New England conceals the class division and wealth disparity brought about by the rapid development of capitalism. It also fosters the perception among farmers that their hardships are compensated by the benefits of residing in the idyll, thereby perpetuating their confinement within poverty and ensuring a distance between them and urban elites.

As an emotion which refers to a yearning for the past and a sense of loss in the face of change, nostalgia is "not only connected to time, history, and memory, but also to space, home, and affections felt for an environment" (Colin & Olivares, 296). According to Fred Davis, despite its focus on the past, nostalgia is more revealing about present circumstances than any past reality since the emotion is always caused by the loss of control over the present events (9). Latest nostalgia theories further propose that nostalgia is not just a longing for the good old days or the warm homeland, but a cognitive strategy: "an adaptive response" derived from human emotion and cognition to the changes of the environment (Batcho, 170). Hence the widespread nostalgia for New England among the genteel class served as "a defense mechanism" which indicated their attempts to reconstruct a stabler society in symbolic time and space to compensate for their own senses of lack and insecurity (Boym, xiv). City dwellers' nostalgia can be called "restorative nostalgia" in Svetlana Boym's term①,

---

① Boym divides nostalgia into two categories: restorative and reflective. While restorative nostalgia shows the past in an idealized manner and seeks to reconstruct and preserve it, reflective nostalgia treats the past more critically. In her view, restorative nostalgia led to a series of "national and nationalist revivals all over the world which engaged in the antimodern myth-making of history by means of a return to national symbols and myths" when the pace of social transformations accelerated in the late nineteenth century (41). The cult of the New England village apparently belongs to those "invented traditions" and national myths (Hobsbawm, 263-307).

helping them to cope with the effects of social transformations and create a sense of continuity and security in the face of discontinuity. Thus, North Dormer, as Harney's nostalgic object, is essentially a space and time away from rural reality fabricated for meeting his own class-based needs.

The depiction of North Dormer in *Summer* reveals the distance between the reality of rural New England and the perceptions of city dwellers like Harney. Through the creation of this village, Wharton illustrates the class inequality between the urban leisure class and the rural poor, resonating with the claim that Raymond Williams makes about nineteenth-century British writers' attitudes towards the countryside. Williams points out that the writers such as George Eliot and Jane Austen cast the country as "other" by creating it as "a site devoid of industry, livelihood, or action, [...] as a strategic respite" (33). Similar to him, Wharton suggests that considering the countryside as a nostalgic retreat fixed in the past not only ignores the real needs of rural communities but also advocates in favor of their continued backwardness, thereby reinforcing class inequality. According to her biographer Hermione Lee, Wharton noticed the bleak side of the rural New England landscape: "The grimness of the remote, inaccessible New England farms", "desolate little hill villages", "hard times of the industrial workers in the region", and "vast contrasts" between the opulent vacationers and "the deprivation of the rural poor" (195). A prominent supporter of Lenox's Village Improvement Society and the Lenox Library, the writer used to take part in projects such as donating books, burying electricity lines, and planting shade trees while living in The Mount. Her experience shows her belief that helping the rural poor to improve their situation is more important than extoling their quaintness.

To sum up, the depiction of Starkfield in *Ethan Frome* and North Dormer in *Summer* reflects the New England village's transformation from a decaying backwater into the embodiment of pastoralism for urbanites at the turn of the twentieth century when the uneven development between the countryside and city caused class division and wealth disparity. Impacted by the discourse on rural poverty, the narrator of *Ethan Frome* sees the landscape of Starkfield as evidence of the farmers' inability to adapt to social transformations. In *Summer*, the urbanites' nostalgic view of the village conceals rural deprivation and maintains power disparities between urban tourists and rural dwellers. The portrait of the village landscape in the two novels thus illustrates Wharton's concern about rural poverty and her criticism of class inequality.

3.2   Mountains from the Symbol of Racial Decline to That of Anglo-Saxon Superiority

While old New England's villages signify pastoralism, its mountains are closely associated with the belief in the superiority of Anglo-Saxons because of Massachusetts Bay governor John Winthrop's seminal sermon of 1630 about "city upon a hill". This founding image of New England intertwines the mountains in this region with the "Puritan origins of national identity" and the conception of "American moral superiority" (Conforti, 27). Through analyzing its place within the United States' national narrative and its influence on New England's regional identity, Abram Van Engen argues that Winthrop's statement "led to the whole idea of a ' Puritan stock'—the belief that special traits descended from the precious blood of the Puritans to their various descendants and heirs spread all across the United States" (179). New Englanders, especially those living in small villages of the hill country, were regarded as the offspring of the old Puritan stock. The domain of New England mountains was seen as "homogeneous settlement composed entirely of Anglo-Saxons, and its virtue depended on maintaining that racial and cultural purity" (Van Engen, 177). Anglo-Saxon Americans' perception of New England mountains reveals, to a certain extent, their views on the issue of race, as rural landscape is closely tied to nativism, "national identity construction", and "notions of belonging" (Askins, 365).

However, turn-of-the-twentieth-century industrialization and urbanization throughout the United States attracted successive waves of immigrants[1]. The first federal census in 1790 showed that 26 percent of New England's population was born in the United States. That number fell to eight percent in 1880, with non-English-speaking immigrants a rapidly growing presence (qtd. in Conforti, 9). By then, old New England which was believed to consist of homogeneous Anglo-Saxons had emerged as "an object of nostalgia and veneration" (Conforti, 205). As Zhou Ming notes, "New Englanders believed that their regional and ethnic identity served as the cornerstone for resisting the cultural impact of foreign immigrants and for upholding Anglo-Saxon civilization" (55). Focusing on the depiction of the two mountains in *Ethan Frome* and *Summer*, this part intends to scrutinize

---

[1]   The immigrants who arrived in the United States at the turn of the twentieth century mainly came from Southern and Eastern European countries. Before the mid-nineteenth century, the American population was predominantly composed of white Anglo-Saxon Protestants. The influx of Catholic Irish immigrants between the 1840s and 1870s shocked the American society. In the 1880s and early 1890s, as the flow of Irish immigration began to wane, Italians, Poles, Slovaks, and other immigrants from Southern and Eastern Europe started arriving in the United States in greater numbers, which made Anglo-Saxon Americans feel that their hegemony was under threat. See Matthew Frye Jacobson, *Whiteness of a Different Color: European Immigrants and the Alchemy of Race* (Cambridge, MA: Harvard University Press, 1998), pp. 39-90.

US-born Anglo-Saxons'① perception of whiteness② and figure out Wharton's views on the issue of race③.

3.2.1   The Barren and Lifeless White Mountain

US-born Anglo-Saxons in the postbellum period saw a rising number of foreigners in New England—the most rapidly industrializing and urbanizing region in the United States whose expanding mills and factories were supported by a supply of immigrant labor from Europe. Western Massachusetts, for instance, by 1900 had the highest proportion of foreign born and of foreign parentage in the country. It had become a region of immigrants, particularly of immigrants from Ireland and French Canada (Golden, 12). The rapid pace of industrialization, urbanization, and most

---

① Between the 1840s and 1920s, US-born Anglo-Saxons are described as "American white Anglo-Saxon Protestants of long lineage" (Meagher 12). They supported a pseudoscientific intellectual trend that gained popularity during the height of immigration from Eastern and Southern Europe to the United States. They claimed that the American way of life was threatened by the presence not just of nonwhite people but of non-Anglo-Saxon white people. Their beliefs shaped the racist immigration-restriction laws of the early twentieth century. In *Ethan Frome* and *Summer*, US-born Anglo-Saxons refer to the descendants of English immigrants who settled in New England before the mid-nineteenth century.

② According to Eric Arnesen, while the notion of "whiteness" may initially evoke connotations related to skin color, it actually pertains to a particular racialized social identity that occupies a superior position within a hierarchical system of race (6-9).

③ It should be noted that at the turn of the twentieth century, the word "race" was often used to conceptualize both the "physical characteristics" of different groups of humans and their "cultural, psychological and social characteristics" (Gindro, 94). For Wharton, both native-stock white Americans and immigrants such as the Irish or Italians were spoken of as races. As Kassanoff summarizes, the writer applied the term "race" to "a diverse array of possible identifications [...] from national origin, religious affiliation and aesthetic predilection, to geographic location, class membership and ancestral descent" (3-4).

134

importantly, ethnic transformation undermined Americans' confidence in the future of New England and the United States. New Hampshire poet Thomas Bailey Aldrich composed a well-received poem entitled "Unguarded Gates" (1895) which perfectly encapsulated Americans' resentment towards the influx of foreigners. "Wide open and unguarded stand our gates", the poem began, "And through them presses a wild motley throng" (qtd. in Donna Brown, 189). In *Ethan Frome*, even the desolate Starkfield is under the influence of immigration. As cultural geographers summarize, rural landscape is often associated with "white ethnicities", "nationalist politics", and nativism (Cloke, "Rural Landscapes", 229). Wharton echoes the widespread anxiety about racial decline among US-born Anglo-Saxons by depicting how the narrator observes the barren and lifeless white mountain where the Fromes live.

In the narrator's eyes, what is striking about the mountain inhabited by Ethan is its barrenness. The villagers' farms are arid: Ethan's land is "always 'bout as bare's a milkpan when the cat's been round" (*EF*, 12). The apple trees in the orchard are "writhing over a hillside among outcroppings of slate that nuzzled up through the snow like animals pushing out their noses to breathe" (*EF*, 17). The barren farms and orchards exemplify the villagers' failure in farming, especially Ethan's. The agricultural predicament is mainly caused by natural factors such as the topography, soil, and climate of the region. Firstly, since Western Massachusetts features the Berkshire Mountains, a broad belt of steeply rolling hills and ridges, the fields developed on the hill locations are therefore usually small and irregular, unsuitable for using agricultural machinery. Secondly, New England's "combined glacial and geologic history produced a landscape decidedly lacking in flat, well-drained, fertile soils" (Irland, 55). The stoniness and infertility of soils make agriculture difficult for peasants, particularly those in the hardscrabble hill farms such as

Ethan. Thirdly, long and harsh winters result in shorter growing seasons for crops compared to other states, and the variable summer weather imposes additional hardships on the farmers' cultivation.

Apart from the failure of agriculture, the narrator feels that the barren mountain also suggests the infertility of the villagers. Through analyzing the symbolic meaning of the dead vegetables and plants on the mountain, Candace Waid states that *Ethan Frome* is "a story of female barrenness and relentless infertility" (60-61). It is noteworthy that no children are mentioned in the novel. Take the only young couple in Starkfield—Ned Hale and Ruth Varmun as an example, Ned dies not long after their marriage, leaving Ruth a middle-aged widow who lives with her mother. Given that there are only the two women in the house, it is fair to speculate that the Hales do not have any offspring. The most striking case comes from Ethan's family. The only son of the Fromes, Ethan has no children after his seven years' marriage to Zeena. Moreover, since Zeena falls ill within a year of their marriage and Ethan is severely injured after a failed suicide attempt with Mattie, obviously the Fromes will never have a next generation. The couple's broken wedding gift—a red pickle dish—reveals their broken sexual relationship. As many Wharton scholars point out, the color red① implies sexuality in the writer's works. In the novel, Ethan repeatedly associates the

---

①   Rhonda Skillern traces Wharton's repeated association of the color red with female sexuality in her novels to the author's unforgettable encounter with " New York's first fashionable hetaera" on Fifth Avenue at the age of seventeen (122). Though her mother ordered sternly that she immediately turned her head away, Wharton caught a glimpse of a lady who was "dark-haired, quietly dressed, and enchantingly pale, with a hat-brim lined with cherry color which shed a lovely glow on her cheeks". She wrote about the woman again and again, memorializing her as "my first doorway to romance" and "the mirage of palm trees in the desert" in contrast to the "impoverished emotional atmosphere of Old New York" (*The Uncollected Critical Writings*, 276). Apart from Zeena's pickle dish and Mattie's scarf and ribbon which have been explained in the book, in *Summer* Wharton also uses Charity's cherry-colored hat to connote her budding sexuality.

cheery color with Mattie's sexual attraction. The cherry scarf sheds a lovely glow in her lips and cheeks and the crimson ribbon makes her "taller, fuller, more womanly in shape and motion" (*EF*, 71). Elizabeth Ammons notes correctly that the smashed red dish not only suggests the barrenness of Zeena, but also "predicts the broken bodies and lost fertility of Ethan and Mattie" ("Myth", 27).

In addition to the barren landscape, the narrator is impressed by the mountain's lifeless whiteness. Since snow is everywhere in the story, the landscape is dominated by "glaring whiteness" (Ammons, "Myth", 9). The ubiquitous whiteness is closely connected with the deadness of the mountain. As the narrator depicts, on their way back from the church at night, Ethan and Mattie walks up the hills to Ethan's house:

Sometimes their way led them under the shade of an overhanging bank or through the thin obscurity of a clump of leafless trees. Here and there a farmhouse stood far back among the fields, mute and cold as a grave-stone. The night was so still that they heard the frozen snow crackle under their feet. The crash of a loaded branch falling far off in the woods reverberated like a musket-shot. (*EF*, 44)

The "leafless trees", "grave-stone", "frozen snow", and "crash of a loaded branch" all convey the overwhelming silence and deadness of the landscape. The way the narrator portrays the lifeless white mountain alludes to the widespread anxiety among US-born Anglo-Saxons about the decline of the white population, when the nation's social transformations at the turn of the twentieth century attracted more and more immigrants. The fiction is about "white people trapped in a white landscape"—a "nativist myth of imperiled whiteness", as Ammons argues ("Myth",6).

Towards the end of the nineteenth century, the influx of European immigrants and their high fertility rate alerted US-born Anglo-Saxons who felt the threat of being outnumbered by the newcomers. At that time, the total population of the United States and the ratio of the number of various ethnic groups in the country were seen by politicians and eugenicists① as the important indicators which were closely related to the survival of the nation and the Anglo-Saxon race. As President Theodore Roosevelt stressed, "All the other problems before us in this country, important though they may be, are as nothing compared with the problem of the diminishing birth rate and all that it implies" (qtd. in Dyer, 150). However, the fertility rate of the US-born white women was far lower than that of immigrants. The United States census of 1900 showed that there were approximately "666 children under five years of age per 1,000 white women aged twenty to forty-four", a decline of about a quarter since 1850 (Whelpton, 278). The American society worried that the situation would lead to race suicide of US-born Anglo-Saxons. The highly racist concept of "race suicide" was introduced by sociologist Edward Alsworth Ross in 1901. In the sociological terminology of the time, a race committed suicide when its birthrate dropped below its death rate, with the ultimate consequence that the race would become extinct. Distorting the framework of social Darwinism, Ross claimed

---

① Eugenics, a set of beliefs and practices aimed at improving the genetic quality of the human population, played a significant role in the United States between the 1890s and the 1940s. The term "eugenics" was first coined in 1883 by English sociologist Francis Galton who proposed a selective breeding program designed for encouraging reproduction in humans with desirable traits and discouraging reproduction in those with negative traits. The eugenics movement took root in America in the early 1900s and quickly adopted the racist and xenophobic discourses of the time. American eugenicists believed in the genetic superiority of Nordics, Germans, and Anglo-Saxons, supported immigration restriction and anti-miscegenation laws, and advocated forced sterilization of the poor, disabled and so-called "inferior races" (Allen, 105-128). For a discussion on Wharton's attitude to eugenics, see Dale M. Bauer, *Edith Wharton's Brave New Politics* (Madison: University of Wisconsin Press, 1995), pp. 28-51; 83-112.

that lower birth rate of the white couples and the competition among different races meant that "less-civilized" races would eventually replace "more-civilized" Anglo-Saxon Americans (qtd. in Lovett, 86).

The anxiety about "race suicide" was prevalent among the Northeastern politicians and intellectuals, including Wharton's friends Henry James①, Henry Adams, Senator Henry Cabot Lodge and so on, among which Roosevelt② was the most fervent propagandist of the theory of race suicide. The racial crisis first became apparent to him in 1892 when he read the newly released census of 1890 and saw a dramatic increase in the birth rates of Irish and French-Canadian immigrants who were moving into New England in large numbers. In a letter to historian Francis Parkman, Roosevelt clearly expressed his worries that the immigrants might "in many

---

① In *The American Scene* James explicitly expressed his fear of the European immigrants who threatened the existence of traditional American culture and the position of US-born Anglo-Saxons: "The children swarmed above all—here was multiplication with a vengeance [...] As overflow, in the whole quarter, is the main fact of life" (94). For a discussion on James' attitude towards the immigrants in the Northeastern America, see Sara Blair, *Henry James and the Writing of Race and Nation* (New York: Cambridge University Press, 1996), pp. 158-210.

② Born into the same upper-class New York milieu and be related distantly by marriage, Wharton and Roosevelt had known each other since their youth. They exchanged visits (including at the White House) and letters on literary and political subjects until Roosevelt's death in 1919. Wharton composed an elegy for him and wrote to his sister, stating that "No one will ever know what his example and his influence were to me" (qtd. in Kirsch, 200). Roosevelt appears in the final chapter of *The Age of Innocence* and serves as the protagonist Newland Archer's model of good citizenship. Roosevelt was a firm believer in the theory of race suicide and used his various political offices to bring the issue before the American people. For Wharton's friendship with Roosevelt, see Geoffrey R. Kirsch, "Innocence and the Arena: Wharton, Roosevelt, and Good Citizenship", *American Literary Realism* 51.3 (2019): 200-219. For Roosevelt's opinions about race suicide, see Thomas G. Dyer, *Theodore Roosevelt and the Idea of Race* (Baton Rouge: Louisiana State University Press, 1992), pp. 143-167.

places supplant us" (qtd. in Dyer, 144). In his influential *The Passing of the Great Race* (1916), Madison Grant also associated New Englanders' decline in population with the coming of immigrants throughout the nineteenth century: "During the last century the New England manufacturer imported the Irish and French Canadians and the resultant fall in the New England birthrate at once became ominous" (11).

According to Daylanne English, the theory of race suicide was "a central national ideology" in America during the late nineteenth century, "so widely accepted that it might be considered the paradigmatic modern discourse" (Watson, 174). The influx of Irish, Southern, and Eastern European immigrants "opened up a rift in US whiteness" and changed Americans' perception of whiteness (175). As Matthew Frye Jacobson pointed out, the mass immigration in late nineteenth century "announced a new era in the meaning of whiteness in the United States"—what he calls the "fracturing of monolithic whiteness" or "variegated whiteness" (38). Between the 1840s and the 1920s, a time of extensive foreign immigration and prevalent prejudice against immigrant groups, there arose a pattern of "variegated whiteness" in which specific groups were deemed to be whiter and better than others. To put it simply, skin color no longer guaranteed white identity as Americans began to believe that in addition to the binary line of white and black, there was a racial hierarchy among white people as well. Contemporary scientific racism provided the language and the models for understanding the differences within the "white race". Grant, for instance, divided "European populations into three distinct subspecies of man"—the Nordic/Baltic, Mediterranean/Iberian, and the Alpine subspecies, and stressed the superiority of the Nordic (19).

In *Ethan Frome*, Wharton draws readers' attention to the issue of whiteness by demonstrating a contrast between the diminishing Fromes, representatives of native New Englanders, and the prospering Irish immigrant family of the Eadys. From the first page of the story, the narrator points out Ethan's physical characteristics as Anglo-Saxons: "It was not so much his great height that marked him, for the 'natives' were easily singled out by their lank longitude from the stockier foreign breed" (*EF*, 3). According to Ammons, the turn-of-the-century anti-immigration advocates often regarded height as a marker of Anglo-Saxonness ("Myth", 10). Ross, for example, claimed that the average Americans were "an inch or an inch and a half taller than the foreign-born", while the "dull, fat-witted immigrants" from "the lesser breeds" were "undersized in spirit, no doubt, as they are in body" ("The Value Rank", 1062-1063). The "undersized" or "stockier" immigrants in the novel are not only referred to as foreigners, but also described by an animalistic word "breed" which suggests their fecundity① and unstable white identity.

The only foreign-born villagers mentioned in the story are the Irish family of Michael Eady, an ambitious grocer "whose suppleness and effrontery had given Starkfield its first notion of 'smart' business methods, and whose new brick store testified to the success of the attempt" (*EF*, 27). In marked contrast to Ethan who is impoverished by failing to keep pace with industrialization and urbanization, the Irish merchant thrives by serving as the representative of modern business. Furthermore, unlike the dwindling Fromes, the Irish family expands. Michael's son Denis Eady not only follows in his steps to conquer the local market, but also applies "the same

---

① The propagandists of race suicide always used "breed" in a derogatory manner to imply the fertility of the turn-of-the-twentieth-century immigrants, emphasizing that unlike US-born white Americans, the newcomers could reproduce at an alarming rate like animals. For instance, in "The Value Rank of the American People", Ross wrote that the immigrants in New England "throng to us, the beaten members of breeds" (1063).

arts to the conquest of the Starkfield maidenhood" (*EF*, 27). The Catholic
Denis leads in a Virginia reel① in Starkfield's Protestant church with Mattie
on his arm, having "taken on a look of almost impudent ownership" (*EF*,
27). His audacious usurpation of Anglo-Saxon space and women sparks the
wrath of an emotionally retarded Ethan: "Hitherto Ethan Frome had been
content to think him a mean fellow; but now he positively invited a horse-
whipping" (*EF*, 28). Considering Ethan's emphasis that Denis has "Irish
blood in his veins", we can see that Ethan feels furious not only because he
adores Mattie; more importantly, he senses the threat of being taken over by
the "stockier foreign breed" (*EF*, 27). Ethan's wrath implies his identification with the notion of "variegated whiteness". He perceives the Irish as
an inferior race in comparison to Anglo-Saxon Americans, which reflects the
trend of an "increasing fragmentation and hierarchical ordering of distinct
white races" in late-nineteenth-century United States (Matthew Frye
Jacobson, 41).

Ethan's attitude exemplifies US-born Anglo-Saxons' perception of
whiteness and their hostility to the turn-of-the-twentieth-century immigrants,
especially the Irish. The Irish dominated the immigrant stream from the
1840s to 1870s, particular in New England, before the massive waves of
immigrants from Southern and Eastern Europe arrived after 1880. Due to
their poverty and Catholic faith, the Irish's identity as the white was not

---

. ①　Phil Jamison finds that in the late nineteenth century the Virginia reel was
promoted as "the most representative American folk-dance" by such hereditary patriotic
organizations as the Daughters of the American Revolution for the aim of reaffirming
"America's Anglo-Saxon colonial heritage and identity" (99). The dance was usually
performed by Anglo-Saxon boys and girls in colonial costumes at nationalist events. Through
portraying the Irishman Denis's role as the lead in a Virginia reel, Wharton highlights his
challenge to US-born Anglo-Saxons' authority.

widely accepted until the postbellum period①. Despite their white skin color and European ancestry, the Irish were considered as racially inferior. In order to integrate into mainstream American society, they actively participated in labor unions and political activities. The Irish controlled many important government positions in cities across the nation and managed to move up the social ladder into the middle class in the 1880s and 1890s. They captured the mayor's office in Boston in 1884 and boasted that "New England is more Irish today than any part of the world outside Ireland" (Kinloch, 205-206). The Irish's success in politics and growing number of Catholic churches made white Anglo-Saxon Protestants feel their position threatened, which led to a series of nativist movements mainly targeting the Irish. Following the Know Nothing Party popular in the mid-1850s, the American Protective Association, the largest anti-Catholic organization in the United States in the latter half of the nineteenth century, aimed to curb the growing Irish control over public schools and political institutions. Ethan's hostility towards Denis thus demonstrates US-born Anglo-Saxons' conception of whiteness and their anxiety about the decline of hegemony.

Wharton became acquainted with the anti-immigrant sentiment when she visited a Berkshire mill town named North Adams to collect materials

---

① By the 1860s the Irish were categorized as "a sort of racial *other*, neither white nor black" (Roediger, 162, original emphasis). They were thought to have some repulsive traits similar to African Americans that limited their possibilities for integration into American society. Only in the latter decades of the nineteenth century did a combination of acute political skills and a strong sense of community enable the Irish to "be admitted into the ranks of American white people, with the psychological and practical privileges that came with being white" (162). For an account of the process by which Irish immigrants were accepted as full-fledged white Americans, see Matthew Frye Jacobson, *Whiteness of A Different Color: European Immigrants and the Alchemy of Race* (Cambridge, MA: Harvard University Press, 1998), pp. 39-135.

about factory workers for her novel *The Fruit of the Tree* (1907). At the time of her visit, the factories employed many immigrants, mostly French Canadians and Irish, who made up more than a third of the town's population. The immigrants lived in segregated areas in the town due to frequent clashes with the local residents (Ammons, " Myth ", 14-16). Wharton endorsed discrimination against the Irish and complained about their negative influence on American culture: "the interchangeable use of ' shall' and ' will' has passed from Irish-English speech to our own, and is finding its way into newspapers and books" (*The Uncollected Critical Writings*, 61).

As Kassanoff proposes, before the First World War, Wharton held " a deeply conservative, and indeed essentialist model of American citizenship": "If her native land generously welcomed the world's huddled masses, then the novel, under Wharton's neo-nativist laws of ' pure English' [...] formed an architectural, aesthetic and political bulwark against the menacing possibilities of democratic pluralism" (5). In *Ethan Frome*, the writer reveals her concern about the diminishing power of US-born Anglo-Saxons through portraying the manner in which the narrator observes the barren and lifeless white mountain. In the latter half of the nineteenth century, old New Englanders were threatened not only by the social transformations brought about by industrialization and urbanization, but also the immigrants drawn to the United States by those transformations. The danger of race suicide prompted Anglo-Saxon Americans to embrace the notion of whiteness that was characterized by a hierarchical ordering of white races. Thus, Wharton laments the passing of Anglo-Saxon New England and implicitly supports nativist sentiments of the time by delineating the mountain landscape.

3.2.2 Harney's Picturesque Way to Tame the Wildness of the Mountain

Most critics regard the Mountain in *Summer* as an ominous backdrop to the story, in contrast to the more civilized North Dormer. Ruth Maria Whaley, for example, argues that the Mountain symbolizes "a sullen and threatening nature" which foreshadows the disillusion of Charity's love with Harney (78). However, reviewers fail to notice that the Mountain implies Italian immigrants' threat to the ethnically homogeneous New England. Through describing how the villagers and the urbanite Harney look at the Mountain, as well as displaying their conception of whiteness, Wharton satirizes the xenophobic and nativist sentiment among US-born Anglo-Saxons in the early twentieth century.

When New England cities were increasingly populated by Southern and Eastern European immigrants, old New England, particularly the remote hill country, was believed to preserve its racial purity because immigrants were not interested in places that offered few jobs. New England farmers were often portrayed as the Pilgrim Forefathers' descendants, "sturdy members of the ' Anglo-Saxon race'" and "the vigorous guardians of democratic traditions" (Donna Brown, 146). For those Americans who were beset by foreign faces and languages, New England mountains, where Anglo-Saxon purity still prevailed, could provide a refuge from the heterogeneous cities.

In *Summer*, urban visitors like Harney's view of North Dormer fit the above beliefs about old New England's homogeneous mountain community. They extol the families who have settled in New England since the colonial era: "All the old names ... all the old names [...] Targatt ... Sollas ... Fry" (*S*, 114). The village, however, is in the shadow of the Mountain inhabited by a group of racially ambiguous outcasts.

Mr. Royall tells Harney that although the Mountain falls under the jurisdiction of North Dormer, it is a chaotic and uncivilized world, with a group of alcoholics, thieves and outlaws living separately from the villagers. For people in North Dormer, the Mountain, with its oppressive height, bare rock, and year-round fog, is a "blot" on the tranquil rural landscape.

> from the scarred cliff that lifted its sullen wall above the lesser slopes of Eagle Range, [the Mountain] making a perpetual background of gloom to the lonely valley. The Mountain was a good fifteen miles away, but it rose so abruptly from the lower hills that it seemed almost to cast its shadow over North Dormer. (*S*, 32)

Words like "the scarred cliff", "sullen wall", "perpetual background of gloom" and "shadow" illustrate that in the villagers' eyes, the Mountain arouses sublime or even gothic terror. Both Dale Bauer and Gary Totten point out that the villagers' distaste for the Mountain stems from its residents' racial otherness (Bauer, 39; Totten, "Inhospitable Splendour", 61-62). The ambiguous racial identity of the Mountain people, including Charity who was brought down to North Dormer from the Mountain by Mr. Royall as a child, is first implied by their "swarthy" complexion (*S*, 30). On the opening page of the novel, Wharton hints at Charity's racial otherness by juxtaposing her swarthy skin, dark hair and eyes with the blonde hair and blue eyes of the city girl Annabel Balch. When Charity sees Harney for the first time near her home, she immediately goes into the house to look critically at "her small swarthy face" in the mirror, "wish[ing] for the thousandth time that she had blue eyes like Annabel Balch" (*S*, 5). Although Charity's ethnicity is not specified in the novel, the emphasis on the differences in the two girls' physical features creates a racial dichotomy between dark Charity and fair Annabel, which suggests the former's

146

ambiguous racial identity. Furthermore, at the turn of the century, the word "swarthy" was widely used in describing immigrants from Southern and Eastern Europe who had darker skin than Anglo-Saxons. For instance, Grant claimed that the Mediterranean and Alpine people had "very dark or black eyes and hair" and "more or less swarthy skin" (20). The same usage is frequently seen in the fiction of the period, such as in William Dean Howells's novel *A Hazard of New Fortunes* (1890). The protagonist Basil March is depicted as being interested in the "picturesque raggedness" (67) of Southern European immigrants and he particularly "liked the swarthy, strange visages" of the Italians (65).

Wharton draws from "stereotypes associated with the Italian immigrants who settled in Western Massachusetts at the turn of the twentieth century" ("Inhospitable Splendour", 70) in portraying the "swarthy Mountain" (*S*, 120) and its swarthy inhabitants, according to Totten's research. The description that the Mountain community is composed of "a gang of thieves and outlaws" (*S*, 63) coincides with the contemporary stereotypes about Italian immigrants who were often believed to be nonwhite, morally and intellectually inferior as subhuman, prone to alcoholism and "the ferocious crimes that go with a primitive stage of civilization" (Ross, "Italians in America", 440-444). Mr. Royall's disdainful comment on Charity's biological parents is consonant with these popularly held beliefs about the Italians: her father "ran amuck, the way they sometimes do [...] ended up with manslaughter" and her mother "ain't half human up there" (*S*, 64). After Harney leaves the village, Charity finds that she is pregnant with his child and then goes to the Mountain in the hope of seeking help from her mother. The depiction about what she sees there clearly stresses the residents' alcoholism, feeble-mindedness, and animality. There is "no sign [...] of anything human": her mother "lay there like a dead dog in a ditch", the anguished heads of the drink-dazed people are "like the heads of nocturnal animals", and their children roll up like "sleeping puppies" (*S*, 154).

Moreover, the Mountain people's previous experience as railroad workers is reminiscent of the large number of Italian immigrants in Western Massachusetts who had constructed and maintained railroad lines since the 1880s. Harney mentions that "the first colonists are supposed to have been men who worked on the railway that was built forty or fifty years ago between Springfield and Nettleton" (*S*, 60). By the early twentieth century, Italian immigrants had replaced the Irish as the major ethnic group working on the rails (Ross, "Italians in America", 441).

Through underscoring the Mountain people's alcoholism, animality, swarthy complexion, innate criminality, and their connection to railroad jobs, Wharton invokes a racial narrative familiar to early-twentieth-century readers who felt anxious about their hegemony while facing an unprecedented mass immigration from Southern and Eastern Europe. From the 1880s, Southern and Eastern European immigrants began to flow into the United States in greater numbers when Irish immigration gradually slowed. According to Hilda H. Golden, by 1900 more than sixty percent of the population in Western Massachusetts was either foreign-born or of foreign parentage (1), with an increasing number coming from Eastern or Southern Europe, particularly Italy (12). The Southern and Eastern European immigrants were known as the "new immigrants" to be distinguished from the so-called "old immigrants" who came primarily from Northern and Western Europe. Differing more radically in religion, language, and culture from Anglo-Saxons than the earlier arrivals such as the Irish, the new immigrants were thought by US-born Anglo-Saxons as challenges to "New England's Anglo-Puritan colonial heritage" (Conforti, 209). When we consider the racial characteristics of the Mountain people, then Harney's delineation of them— "a handful of people who don't give a damn for

148

anybody" and "they seem to be quite outside the jurisdiction of the valleys. No school, no church, and no sheriff ever goes up to see what they're about"—can be understood as suggesting those immigrants' refusal or failure to be assimilated by the law of Anglo-Saxon Protestants represented by North Dormer (S, 60). Thus, the swarthy Mountain that looms menacingly over the village suggests the Italian immigrants' threat to the social order of New England. In this sense, the villagers' distaste for the Mountain manifests US-born Anglo-Saxons' perception of racial variegation within whiteness. Like Ethan in *Ethan Frome*, they believe in the hierarchy of whiteness which places Anglo Saxons at the apex. Nevertheless, instead of endorsing US-born Anglo-Saxons' anxiety as what she has done in *Ethan Frome*, Wharton attacks Anglo-Saxon supremacy in *Summer* through satirizing Harney's efforts to tame the wild Mountain by using the protocols of picturesque landscape appreciation.

In strike contrast to the locals, Harney keeps describing the Mountain in romantic phrases such as "a curious place", "a queer colony up there", and "a little independent kingdom" and repeatedly expresses his interest in going up to see the mountain people who "must have a good deal of character" (S,60). In his view, those people lead an independent life which is free from the worries of modern society. According to Donna Brown, the equation of mountain and freedom is characteristic of the nineteenth-century tourists' picturesque way of seeing the hill regions in old New England (Donna Brown, 146). If New England villages like North Dormer are the embodiment of the pastoral landscape in the eyes of urban visitors such as Harney, then the wild mountains belong to the category of the picturesque.

Originating in the seventeenth-century Italian and Dutch painting, picturesque as an aesthetic category was introduced into England by such theorists as William Gilpin, Uvedale Price, and Richard Payne Knight in the last quarter of the eighteenth century and soon established itself as a principal mode for landscape appreciation. It then migrated to America and became a dominant way of viewing and representing landscape in the nineteenth century①. First introduced by Gilpin in *An Essay on Prints* (1768), the picturesque was defined as "a term expressive of that kind of beauty which is agreeable in a picture". Gilpin sees rugged mountains as typical picturesque landscape: "the wild and rough parts of nature produce the strongest effects on the imagination; and we may add, they are the only objects in landscape which please the picturesque eye" (qtd. in Siddall, 29). An intermediate term between Edmund Burke's the beautiful and the sublime, which emphasizes "variety, intricacy, wildness and decay", the picturesque way of seeing landscape enables the viewer to take the craggy irregularity of the daunting mountains into something wild but charming (Brook, 42). In his essay on the development of mountain landscape in New England from 1830 to 1930, Kimberly A. Jarvis enunciates that the rocky hills which used to be dismissed as inaccessible wasteland had been reinterpreted by explorers, artists, writers, and tourists in the terms of the picturesque since the late eighteenth century (71-76). Closely associated with the Romantic aesthetic convention, the mountains in New England then "long evoked fantasies of freedom and vigor" and the granite "was imagined as representing the independence" of its inhabitants (Donna Brown, 146). Harney's romanticized imagination of the Mountain thus conforms to the aesthetic conventions of appreciating New England landscape. As Malcolm Andrews points out, the picturesque enables the viewers to be "engaged in an experiment in controlled aesthetic response to a

---

①　For a review of the definition and development of picturesque as an aesthetic ideal in Britain, see Xiao Sha, "Picturesque: A Keyword in Critical Theory", *Foreign Literature*, 2019 (5): 71-84. For a comprehensive investigation of the picturesque in nineteenth-century American literature, art, and landscape architecture, see John Conron, *American Picturesque* (University Park: The Pennsylvania State University Press, 2000).

range of new and often intimidating visual experiences" (67). Following the picturesque mode of landscape appreciation, Harney transforms the menacing Mountain into the charming mountain scenery, with the impoverished inhabitants into romantic anarchists.

Harney's positive comment on the Mountain does not indicate his respect for racial otherness; on the contrary, his picturesque way of seeing the landscape reveals the same view on the hierarchy of whiteness as the villagers. The picturesque is more than an aesthetic formula, for it has powerful ideological significance. From its emergence, the American picturesque has been intertwined with the issue of race. Unlike the garden-like landscape and happy farmers on which the European tradition relied, the American picturesque was confronted with daunting wilderness and dangerous Indians. The continuing popularity of the picturesque in nineteenth-century America, as Brigitte Bailey argues, "is due to its usefulness in encountering images of 'others'" such as natural power and alien races[1]. The picturesque as an "aesthetically hegemonic approach" enables the observer to "harmonize conceptually a diverse and heterogeneous landscape (geographical or social), that is, to manage the impact of a range

---

[1] Tracing the origin of the American picturesque to the turn of the nineteenth century, Larry Kutchen argues that the post-Revolutionary writers such as Charles Brockden Brown adapted Gilpin's aesthetic formulas to assert control over untamed nature and suppress the radical energies of Native Americans (396). The picturesque then enabled well-known Romantic authors like Washington Irving, James Fenimore Cooper, and Henry David Thoreau to erase the "residual presences of Native Americans and the colonial past" from American landscape (Evelev, 17). Similarly, the aesthetic masked the "ongoing deprivations and brutalities" suffered by African-Americans who were often represented as comically or exotically picturesque in articles and cartoons published in postbellum Northern newspapers (Conron, 227). When American cities were crowded with Southern and Eastern European immigrants at the turn of the twentieth century, writers and journalists again adopted the picturesque mode to impose order upon the urban space that "was becoming highly differentiated according to race, ethnicity and class" (Bramen,447).

151

of potentially disorienting images" (183). The selection and organization of landscape components thus enable the spectator to take control of untamed landscape and its inhabitants.

In the novel, the reason why Harney sees the Mountain as "a curious place" is that its residents' swarthiness adds variety to the picturesque landscape (*S*, 60). Unlike the villagers who fear the Mountain, he aestheticizes the Mountain people by seeing their swarthiness as picturesque charm. He even regards Charity as part of the landscape when she confides her origin from the Mountain. Ignoring that this secret brings the girl a great sense of shame, he looks at her with newly inspired interest: "You're from the Mountain? How curious! I suppose that's why you're so different ..." (*S*, 61). Applying the same words such as "curious" and "different" which are used in his depiction of the Mountain to describe Charity, he instantly sees her as part of the landscape instead of listening to her story with patience. The Mountain people such as her are thus objectified by the detached spectator. In his eyes, the immigrants serve as the counterpart of peasants, gypsies, and beggars in eighteenth-century landscape painting who add variety to the quaint rural landscape. Zhang Hui notes that the picturesque taste for "outlaws and exiles" exists because the viewer "only regards people as objects of aesthetic pleasure, perceiving them as things rather than humans" (27). In a similar way, the suffering of the Mountain poor is naturalized and beautified. When social and racial inequities "become the irregularities, variety, and ruggedness of nature", Harney as the viewer can "gain the proper distance" to indulge in the illusion that he brings "order to the scene of near-chaos" with his own mind (Kutchen, 399).

Harney's view of the Mountain and Mountain people reflects US-born Anglo-Saxons' perception of whiteness at the turn of the century. Due to the unprecedented immigration between 1880 and the First World War, the conception of American whiteness changed from " the unquestioned hegemony of a unified race of white persons" that encompassed diverse nationalities to "a contest over political fitness among a fragmented and hierarchically arranged series of distinct white races" (Matthew Frye Jacobson, 42-43). Scholars of American studies find that American middle class in the early twentieth century often employed the discourse of the picturesque to delineate Eastern and Southern European immigrant enclaves in cities. The middle class frequently used the word "picturesque" to describe immigrants and their impoverished living conditions, even giving rise to a trend of slumming as a form of voyeuristic pastime. Dirty alleys, overcrowded rooms, shattered windows, and disheveled immigrants were all transformed into the observers' aesthetic objects. However, the romanticization of Eastern and Southern European immigrants by the middle class was not a sign of racial equality; rather, it reinforced existing racial hierarchies. In his research on the American city sketches at that time, John Evelev summarized that the picturesque provided the writers and readers with a privileged position to view the immigrants (71). Brandon Rogers and Carrie Tirado Bramen push the discussion further by focusing on the picturesque delineation of immigrants in turn-of-the-twentieth-century novels and periodical sketches about New York City. While Rogers claims that "the concept of the picturesque functioned as a political tool" for Anglo-Saxon writers such as William Dean Howells and Henry James (77), Bramen argues that by presenting Southern and Eastern European immigrants' swarthiness as picturesque, the authors instructed their readers to "turn the urban realities of class disparity and ethnic heterogeneity into potentially pleasant aspects of the modern experience" and transform their concerns about immigration into an aesthetic pleasure of roughness (444). In *Summer*, the New York architect Harney similarly turns the Italian immigrants on the Mountain from racial threats to delightful varieties of New England landscape. As John Wylie argues, the visual structure of conventional landscape aesthetics such as the picturesque "has the effect of subduing strangeness", which can be understood as "a sort of taming, preserving a sense of difference, but only within a known idiom" (*Landscape*, 131). Harney employs the picturesque as a strategy to tame the wildness of the Mountain and Mountain people by inscribing their alienness within the familiar aesthetic parameters, thereby imposing order on their unsettling otherness. The way in which he views the Mountain reveals his endorsement of the divisions and rankings within white people, as well as his belief in Anglo-Saxon supremacy.

Harney's romanticized imagination ends, however, when he and Charity visit a man who comes down from the Mountain. In order to satisfy his curiosity, she takes him to meet Bash Hyatt who marries a farmer's daughter and lives on the periphery of North Dormer. When Harney walks into their house and sees the poor families, he responds with "a slight shiver of repugnance" and tells her that "We won't stay long" (*S*, 68). After going out, he no longer mentions his former plan of going up the Mountain; instead, he asks her why those people "came down to that fever-hole". Seeing the dramatic change in his attitude, she ironically responds: "To better themselves! It's worse up on the Mountain" (*S*, 71). Through Charity's retort, Wharton reveals Harney's superficiality and expresses her criticism of his attitude towards the immigrants. As John Ruskin points out, it is the distance from the landscape that guarantees the picturesque viewer's sense of control and aesthetic pleasure (7). Harney's behavior falls exactly into what Ruskin calls "the lower picturesque" in *Modern Painters* (1856): the spectator takes delights in poverty and dilapidation instead of sympathizing with the needy (6). Just like the heartless observer denounced by Ruskin, Harney does not possess "any regard for the real nature of the thing [...] any comprehension of the pathos of character hidden beneath" (7). A passionate Ruskin reader who learned "the language with which to analyze and critique visual culture" from *Modern Painters*, Wharton, by depicting Harney's way of viewing the Mountain, satirizes his lack of compassion since he can merely see the outward picturesque qualities on the surface rather than forming a sympathetic resonance with the human sufferings beneath (Orlando, "One Long Vision of Beauty", 29).

In conclusion, the influx of Irish, Southern and Eastern European immigrants into the United States prompted a redefinition of whiteness at the turn of the twentieth century. The ways in which the characters in *Ethan Frome* and *Summer* view the New England mountains shed light on a new perception of whiteness: questioning the notion of a unified white race, Americans thought that there was a contest over fitness for American citizenship among hierarchically ordered white races. The New England mountains in the two novels imply the threat of Irish and Italian immigrants to US-born Anglo-Saxons, but Wharton transforms the terror of racial decline from a tragedy into a satire. The ominous tone of *Ethan Frome* turns into an ironic one in *Summer*. While in the 1880s the issue of race suicide appeared to be a crisis for Anglo-Saxon intellectuals, including Wharton, by the late 1910s it had become, in her eyes, a manifestation of the excessive nativism and xenophobia prevalent in the United States. In a letter to Lapsley, Wharton attached three documents about "The Library League" and its "Creed of CHRISTIAN Citizenship", an anti-immigrant organization dedicated to preserving racial purity. She underlined the sentence "an inheritance received from our Anglo-Saxon ancestry whose traditions were based not partly but wholly on the fundamental faith of the Christian religion" and wrote with a sarcastic tone: "Walter [Berry] and I thought that the enclosed wd interest you. It is an amazing commentary on the chaos là-bas, & makes me long for Holy Church & the long arm of the Inquisition" (qtd. in Bauer, 87-88). Wharton explicitly articulates her attack against Americans' nativist sentiment in the early twentieth century through ironically equating the League's endeavor to root out the immigrants with the Catholic Church's brutal execution of heretics.

The change in Wharton's attitude towards the issue of racial decline is due to the impact of the First World War. According to Bauer, the writer started to question America's "fears of racial degeneracy—expressed in old cultural catch-phrases like 'good stock' and 'racial purity' [...] as a result of the staggering jolt of the war and of her sympathy for what R. W. B. Lewis tellingly described as 'the wretched of the earth— ... for the victimized, the uprooted, the sick and the shattered'" (31). She composed *Summer* in 1916 while raising money for relief work in France and establishing shelters for European refugees. Before the United States finally entered the war in 1917, she wrote many articles to criticize Americans' obliviousness to the sufferings of Europeans which for her demonstrated "the damaging limitations of an inward-looking, defensive, and parochial" culture (Lee, 789). Before writing *Summer*, Wharton told Theodore Roosevelt that "she will allegorize it [America's neutrality] in a story—my only weapon" (Mindrup, 16). By delineating the ways in which the villagers and Harney see the Mountain, she uses the novel as a weapon to shatter the illusion of racially homogeneous New England and attack American nativism.

3.3   Vernacular Architecture from the Symbol of Emasculated Masculinity to Virtuous Household

Since the colonial era, New England households had been regarded as shrines of Puritan and republican virtues which were vital to social and moral order. The Puritans believed that male control over the household was a prerequisite for creating a disciplined and orderly society: "It was the man at the head of the family who embodied God's authority in the daily life of each person" (Rotundo, 11). A typical colonial New England family consisted of a male household head who had supreme power at home and a wife who served as the custodian of virtue. Early New Englanders' patriarchal conception of family life had a profound impact on their descendants' view of gender relations. Singley points out that "the restriction of women" was "part of the New England inheritance": "Although Calvinist doctrine considered women the spiritual equals of men, it upheld a strict social hierarchy in which man ruled over woman, as God ruled over man" (*Edith Wharton: Matters of Mind and Spirit*, 111).

At the turn of the twentieth century, nevertheless, patriarchal authority was challenged by cultural and economic transformations that gave women more control in domestic and social arenas. American men experienced frustration and bewilderment as they tried to cope with the rapidly changing world. Since the 1890s, old New England, seen by urbanites as characterized by traditional households which comprised powerful husbands and submissive wives, had emerged as a model of domesticity (Donna Brown, 147). New Englanders, especially those living in remote villages, were thought to preserve "the old New England idea of home, with its cheerful simplicity, quiet atmosphere, strong ties of affection and ruggedness of virtue" (qtd. in Donna Brown, 153). This section analyzes two types of vernacular architecture—the L-shaped farmhouse in *Ethan Frome* and the colonial houses in *Summer*, with the aim of investigating social transformations' influence upon gender relations in rural New England and exploring Wharton's attitude towards the issue of gender.

3.3.1   Diminished Farmhouse and Emasculated Masculinity

During the latter half of the nineteenth century, industrialization and

157

urbanization in America led to an exodus of the young and able population (mostly male) from rural New England. Men's traditional role as head of the household was challenged as women assumed more responsibility for family management. Additionally, with the influence of a growing market economy, the society placed more value on men's wealth in defining masculine identity. One result of these shifts was concern over male authority. Francis B. Cogan summarizes the pattern of "weak male characters and strong heroines" frequently seen in late-nineteenth-century American regionalist novels which depict incompetent husbands unable to provide for their families (6). In *Ethan Frome*, Wharton investigates the effects of agricultural commercialization on male authority amid rural social transformations by portraying the narrator's view that links Ethan's emasculated masculinity to his diminished farmhouse.

Ethan's farmstead consists of two fields, an orchard of apple trees, and a farmhouse. Situated on a slope "against the white immensities of land and sky", Ethan's farmhouse is "one of those lonely New England farmhouses that make the landscape lonelier" (*EF*, 17). "The black wraith of a deciduous creeper flapped from the porch, and the thin wooden walls, under their worn coat of paint, seemed to shiver in the wind that had risen with the ceasing of the snow" (*EF*, 18). Seeing from the orchard, the narrator finds that the house is "unusually forlorn and stunted" because it lacks an essential part of farmhouses which is known in rural New England as the "L": "that long deep-roofed adjunct usually built at right angles to the main house, and connecting it, by way of store-rooms and tool-house, with the wood-shed and cow-barn" (*EF*, 18). According to architectural historian Thomas C. Hubka, by the middle nineteenth century New England farmers have widely adopted this L-shaped plan for their houses by adding the ell which "linked a series of rooms in an increasingly standardized arrangement that usually included a kitchen, a kitchen workroom, a wagon house, a wood house, and a workshop" ("The New England Farmhouse Ell", 161). The organizational scheme became the dominant arrangement for vernacular architecture in northern New England during the latter half of the nineteenth century and continued to impact farm construction in the early twentieth century before it was gradually replaced by detached agricultural buildings.

This type of vernacular architecture was a product of adaptation to the natural environment of rural New England. Landscape theorist J. B. Jackson defines "vernacular architecture" as "the traditional rural or small-town dwelling [...] that is built with local techniques, local materials, and with the local environment in mind: its climate, its traditions, its economy— predominantly agricultural" (85). The forests in rural New England provided abundant wood for construction, whereas the horizontal layout of the farmhouses suited the hilly landform. Moreover, the L-shaped building was designed to deal with the bleak New England winter. In the heavy snows of long winters, "the connected farmstead allowed for reduced heating costs through shared walls and permitted farmers to move through their farmsteads without being exposed to harsh winter conditions" (Ford, 61). As the narrator notes, the removed ell should have been "the chief sources of warmth and nourishment" which enabled "the dwellers in that harsh climate to get to their morning's work without facing the weather" (*EF*, 18).

Furthermore, the L-shaped farmhouse exemplified rural social transformations in turn-of-the-century New England. Firstly, the connected farmstead brought a new sense of efficiency to agricultural life, "similar to the increased systematization of urban life manifested in the imposition of grid street plans and more formal business arrangements" (Ford, 61). The structure was supported by the progressive movement because it provided a well-organized and streamlined arrangement of workspaces which effectively accommodated most farm activities. In short, it helped in streamlining the entire farm and thus provided efficiency for farmers. As noted by rural sociologists, this type of farmhouse was "considered modern and scientific

159

in the late decades of the nineteenth century" as it displayed " the formulation of a mindset governed more by systems and a systematic way of using spaces" in rural New England (Ford, 70).

More importantly, the connected farmstead reflected the shift to commercial agriculture in rural New England. The reorganization of the farmhouse structure was a result of the peasants' need to accommodate the transformation in agriculture throughout the nineteenth century when farm production shifted "from a self-sufficient economy to one increasingly structured by multiple commercial enterprises" such as the production of butter and handicrafts for both home consumption and commercial sale (Hubka, "The New England Farmhouse Ell", 161). Confronted with agricultural competition from the West, New England farmers had little choice but to abandon traditional self-sufficient practices in favor of a commercialized, mixed-farming and home-industry system. They embraced the ell because it was well-suited to this diversification by providing a compact and efficiently arranged set of workspaces where the vast majority of farm activities could take place (Ford, 61). The connected farm building plan was particularly well suited to a more market-oriented farm and home-industry production. In a nutshell, the flexible, multipurpose ell in New England farmhouses was an innovation that responded to the agricultural commercialization in the nineteenth century (Hubka, *Big House*, 13). Therefore, in the narrator's view, Ethan's diminished house whose ell has been dismantled signifies his failure to keep pace with the development of rural capitalism.

The rise of commercial agriculture in rural social transformations brought about not only economic but also social and cultural transformations. On the one hand, it alleviated gender inequalities in New England farms. The connected farmstead enabled peasants to diversify their income streams beyond their primary agricultural products. For example, home industry and

160

garden production could provide extra earnings. "The work, including textiles and clothing, cheese, eggs, butter, leather goods, basket making, and a variety of handicraft products, was frequently associated with the women of the farm" (Hubka, *Big House*, 152). In other words, the new type of farmhouse gave rural women more opportunities to participate in business activities, allowing them to attain higher positions within their households and engage more actively with the outside world. In the novel, Ethan's mother and wife used to take part in home industry and sell their products to nearby merchants. His mother could talk with peddlers, while his wife Zeena was energetic enough to tell him to "go right along out and leave her to see to things" (*EF*, 61). Nevertheless, after the workrooms were removed, the women are compelled to stay indoors as they are not physically fit to labor in the sawmill or field. As Ammons argues, Zeena's bad temper is in fact caused by her "solitary, monotonous domestic lives" from which the "only escape is madness or death" (*Edith Wharton's Argument*, 72). By highlighting the farmhouse's impact upon the women's fate, Wharton expresses her view that isolation from rural social transformations is detrimental to people in the countryside.

On the other hand, agricultural commercialization redefined rural masculinity, placing more emphasis on farmers' "business acumen" (J. L. Anderson, 5-6). The demand of commercial agriculture for farmers' ability to produce for business and market resulted in a heightened appreciation of male wealth among rural inhabitants. "Conventional masculine identities based on values of physical strength, hard work and land ownership were re-worked in a context where commercial success became the dominant measure of success as a farmer" (Laoire, 298). In the novel, the emphasis on financial gain has a profound impact on Ethan's self-perception and how others judge him. His ability to provide for his family financially becomes the fundamental criterion for assessing his worth. However, because the diminished farmhouse symbolizes his inability to keep pace with the development of commercial agriculture and his isolation from the market economy, so it displays to all villagers his economic failure. Whenever Ethan's neighbors discuss his financial problems, they invariably refer to his farmhouse.

Ethan explains to the narrator that after Ethan's father's death, he must take down the "L" due to poverty. As the narrator observes, the "L" symbolizes "a life linked with the soil" (*EF*, 18). Now that the "L" has been removed, Ethan can barely support his family through farming. Understanding that the ell serves as the center of production in the farm, the narrator points out its economic significance: "it is certain that the "L" rather than the house itself seems to be the centre, the actual hearth-stone of the New England farm" (*EF*, 19). Moreover, the narrator links the building's loss of the "L" to its owner's disability: "see in the diminished dwelling the image of his [Ethan's] own shrunken body" (*EF*, 19). In Farland's view, through metonymically connecting Ethan's body to his diminished house, the novel represents "his lack of physical and sexual potency as a direct effect of his economic powerlessness" ("the 'Springs' of Masculinity", 713). Boyd further notes that "more than his visible disability is evoked here: Ethan's unhappy marriage, disastrous and unconsummated love affair and subsequent entrapment in a house of paralysed and ill women [...] point to his emasculation, and the dismantling of the 'L' as symbolic of castration" (*Home of Their Own*, 312). This book contends that Ethan's emasculation is not only physical, but it is psychological. As the narrator describes, Ethan is "the most striking figure in Starkfield [...] the ruin of a man", which implies that his masculinity is emasculated (*EF*, 3). Emasculated masculinity refers to his powerlessness in gender relations due to his failure to meet the standards of ideal masculinity owing to financial inadequacy and spatial restriction.

Agricultural commercialization gives rise to the belief that one's masculinity depend on his ability to demonstrate his financial prowess. In terms of the farmers like Ethan, the ability to provide for his family is critical to his self-perception as a man. However, Ethan constantly struggles with a lack of money. Although all the villagers in Starkfield are not well-off, he is the only one who is in a bad want of money because his farm and sawmill yield scarcely enough for his household. The living condition of the Ethan family is the worst in Starkfield: their farmhouse is the remotest and smallest, with "the furniture [...] of the roughest kind" (*EF*, 151). Ethan's relationship with his wife Zeena is strained by their financial difficulties. For instance, every time she goes to the doctor, he feels anxious about the expensive medical bills. He even must endure her complaints about his incompetence of supporting the family like the other men in the village. When her request to hire a girl for housework is rejected by Ethan,

> She broke in: "You're neglecting the farm enough already," and this being true, he found no answer, and left her time to add ironically: "Better send me over to the almshouse and done with it ... I guess there's been Fromes there afore now."
>
> The taunt burned into him, but he let it pass. "I haven't got the money. That settles it." (*EF* 99)

Ethan's power within the traditional patriarchal structure is clearly challenged, as not having the money is an indication that he cannot fulfill his expected role as his wife's provider. While Zeena's criticism of his work in the land calls into question his competency as a farmer, her satiric suggestion that she should be sent to the almshouse to relieve his responsibilities belittles his worth as a breadwinner. Her complaints are

163

humiliating because late-nineteenth-century American society deemed men as failures if they could not support their families financially and "American men discovered what happened to men [...] who failed as breadwinners" (Kimmel, *Manhood in America*, 156). In Ethan's case, he feels emasculated— "The taunt burned into him"—which means that his self-esteem is hurt by his economic circumstances and his wife's perception of him. Ethan's reaction indicates that his self-perception as a man is largely dependent on his economic status. Unable to assert his male authority by making more money, he becomes passive and taciturn: "he had first formed the habit of not answering her, and finally of thinking of other things while she talked" (*EF*, 64). As Li Jin proposes, Ethan's feeling of inadequacy leads to his suicide which results in the final tragedy—disabled and disfigured, he becomes as broken as his farmhouse (42).

To sum up, as a manifestation of agricultural commercialization, the L-shaped farmhouse demonstrates the impact of rural social transformations upon New England. Ethan's diminished farmhouse whose L-shaped workrooms are removed on the one hand deprives women of opportunities to engage in commercial activities and interact with the outside world; on the other hand, the farmhouse displays Ethan's economic failure. As commercial agriculture increasingly emphasizes the material wealth of rural men, the diminished farmhouse that limits Ethan's economic prospects influences his self-perception as a man and other people such as the narrator's evaluation of him as a capable husband. Ethan's inability to reach the standards emasculates his masculinity, hurts his self-esteem, and damages his marriage. Through delineating the narrator's perspective on Ethan's farmhouse, Wharton examines the impact of agricultural commercialization on gender relations in rural New England and exposes the negative consequences of isolation from rural societal transformations.

3.3.2 Restoration of Domesticity by Revitalizing the Colonial Houses

If the farmhouse in *Ethan Frome* epitomizes social transformations' challenge to male authority when New England faced the growing influence of rural capitalism during the postbellum years, then the colonial houses in *Summer* serve as representatives of the virtuous households in old New England which were regarded by urbanites as the model of domesticity in the early twentieth century. Although *Summer* is "a novel rich in architectural detail and the imagery of houses, enclosures, and walls", critics have not paid enough attention to the buildings in the book (Christine Rose, 16). Most recently, through using archival material to prove that the architect Harney may be inspired by Wharton's coauthor of *The Decoration of Houses*—Ogden Codman Jr., Emily J. Orlando argues that *Summer* expresses the writer's critique of "an authoritative and arguably arrogant male homosocial aesthetic culture that relegates characters like Charity Royall and women like Edith Wharton to second class citizens" ("The 'Queer Shadow'", 224). While such explanation accurately captures Wharton's lifelong engagement with architecture, shifting the analytical focus toward the old houses that attract Harney to North Dormer unlocks new interpretative options for the novel. As noted by cultural geographers, rural idylls are often "recognized as shoring up traditional gender [...] formations [...] through implicit assertion of patriarchal norms in gendered identity, domesticity, and familism" (Cloke, "Rural Landscapes", 229). This section proposes that by exposing the different ways of seeing North Dormer's old houses between male and female characters, particularly through the eyes of Harney and Charity, Wharton criticizes gender inequality in the village and lays bare the fabricated nature of old New England.

Harney's mission "to make a study of the eighteenth-century houses in the less familiar districts of New England" (*S*, 52) for a New York publisher, his interest in the history of the village and "architect's passion for improvement" (34) of the Hatchard Memorial Library all imply his close tie to the Colonial Revival which peaked in popularity in America between 1880 and 1940. Tracing its birth to the centennial of 1876, the Colonial Revival expressed national fervor for early American culture, primarily the built environments of the eastcoast colonies. Motivated by a range of societal and cultural factors, particularly new immigration and accelerating industrialization, it enabled Americans to express nostalgia for the colonial and Revolutionary eras through architecture, landscape design, material culture, etc. (Richard Guy Wilson, 1-8). Just like the renowned Colonial Revival architects such as Wharton's partner Codman who studied old houses in New England at the turn of the twentieth century, Harney comes to North Dormer for sketching colonial buildings and preparing a book about this region.

Proponents of the Colonial Revival were "principally concerned with preserving early American architecture", with the aim of promoting "white Anglo-Saxon Protestant values [...] through environmental reform and aesthetic moralism" (Junod, 17). Among all those values, domesticity in colonial families was one of the most important things that they tried to restore. Facing the changes to the family life of Anglo-Saxon Americans— falling birthrates and an expanding female workforce, for instance—colonial revivalists "deployed old New England to shore up domesticity" (Conforti, 215). In order to instill proper family values in turn-of-the-century Americans, colonial revivalists celebrated the old New England household as a model of gender relations. Based on the ideological conventions of

Republican Motherhood① and the Cult of Domesticity, old New England households were thought as places where classical republican virtues such as self-denial, restraint, and order were preserved. Consequently, looking to the colonial houses in old New England was a means of legitimizing white Anglo-Saxon men's power and soothing male anxieties in the face of immigration and social movements②.

Whereas rural social transformations are manifested as commercial agriculture in *Ethan Frome*, in *Summer* the most significant impact of social transformations on North Dormer is the emergence of rural tourism. In the early twentieth century, with the construction of railways and highways providing convenience for urban tourists, travel agencies vigorously promoted rural vacationing. Rural areas such as old New England thus became increasingly integrated into the market economy. Since it yielded faster and greater returns compared to farming, tourism was highly favored by villagers. According to Donna Brown, the summer tourist industry had

---

① The term "Republican Motherhood" was first used in 1976 by historian Linda K. Kerber to describe the ideal womanhood in Revolutionary America. Women were considered as guardians of civic virtue who were responsible for "raising sons and disciplining husbands to be virtuous citizens of the republic" (Kerber, 203). Although it increased educational opportunities for American women, the concept of "Republican Motherhood" reinforced the idea of women's sphere separate from the public world. It was modified and used by Progressive women reformers in the early twentieth century to argue that the "obligations of women to ensure honesty in politics, efficient urban sanitation, pure food and drug laws were extensions of their responsibilities as mothers" (204).

② The turn-of-the-twentieth century witnessed many important structural changes that altered gender relations and led to a "crisis of masculinity" among white middle-class men in the United States. Factors such as industrialization, urbanization, immigration, frontier closure, and women's increasingly visible public presence made many men feel threatened by the "erosion of male dominance". In all efforts to reinvigorate masculinity, a return to the patriarchal family of the past and a celebration of women's domestic responsibilities were regarded by antimodernists as methods to restore the "natural order of things" (Kimmel, "The Contemporary 'Crisis'", 138-143).

become a major business in rural New England since the 1890s (155). She further pointed out that traditional gender relations in rural areas attracted urban visitors. For example, because many tourists enjoyed seeing rural women perform household duties, so farmers arranged their wives and daughters to cook, lay tables, and make beds through the open doors and windows, so as to satisfy urbanites' imagination of virtuous households. Pictures of frugal mothers and innocent daughters cooking in the kitchen and making handmade objects by the hearth were the most common illustrations in brochures advertising rural vacations during that period. In *Summer*, the local residents often boast about the village's value to attract boarders from cities: " it was so important, in a wealthy materialistic age, to set the example of reverting to the old ideals, the family and the homestead" (*S*, 115). As Sarah Elizabeth Junod argues, the popularity of old New England in tourist industry " reified a national narrative centered on [...] white patriarchy" (49).

Charity's home, the Royall house, is the most popular old house in the village for city visitors and a noteworthy feature of the rural landscape. Located at the foot of the Mountain, the building has a " red front divided from the road by a yard with a path bordered by gooseberry bushes, a stone well overgrown with traveller's joy, and a [...] Crimson Rambler tied to a fan-shaped support" (*S*, 13). Behind the house, " a bit of uneven ground with clothes-lines str [inging] across it stretches up to a dry wall, and beyond the wall a patch of corn and a few rows of potatoes stray vaguely into the adjoining wilderness of rock and fern" (*S*, 13). As Kassanoff observes, the red dwelling is reminiscent of " Lenox's most famous landmark—the old red farmhouse of Nathaniel Hawthorne " (130). In colonial revivalist writer George Hibbard's words, Hawthorne's house was still " one of the show places of Lenox" at the early twentieth century: " [I] n this place where materialism may be said to offer one of its finest and most luxurious displays, the remains of the 'small red house' are, and long will be, distinguishable and distinguished" (qtd. in Kassanoff, 130). This historical association further enhances the traditional and rustic atmosphere of the Royall house. In urban vacationers' eyes, the red house with its scrubbed floor, a dresser full of china, and the peculiar smell of yeast, coffee and soft-soap seems to be "a vision of peace and plenty" and "the very symbol of household order" (S, 70). Nevertheless, the novel reveals that for Charity the old house in fact symbolizes patriarchy.

Due to his profession as the only lawyer in North Dormer and his role as Charity's guardian, Mr. Royall represents the power of law and patriarchy in *Summer*. His study, which is the most meticulously decorated room in the house, garners significant attention from tourists. For example, the architect Harney visits the room with great interest: he particularly admires "the high-backed horse-hair chair, the faded rag carpet, the row of books on a shelf, the engraving of 'The Surrender of Burgoyne' over the stove, and the mat with a brown and white spaniel on a moss-green border" (S, 70). "The Surrender of Burgoyne", John Trumball's oil painting about the American Revolutionary War, invokes the masculine image of Ebenezer Stevens— Wharton's great-grandfather who figured prominently in the picture and in honor of whose Long Island country home she named The Mount. Moreover, there are many works of Daniel Websters—a famous nineteenth-century lawyer, statesman and orator. Webster, an advocator of old New England, was known for his speeches which eulogized "republican origins" of the region, "communalism of the white villages" as well as the virtue of Puritan families (Conforti, 185). Mr. Royall's choice of interior decoration for the study thus conforms to urban tourists' imagination of colonial houses, which reflects the importance of male authority.

While male characters such as Harney view the Royall house as an exemplar of virtue and tradition, in Charity's eyes, it reminds her of patriarchal power. The Crimson Rambler in the yard, which urbanites find romantic, only serves to evoke memories of Mr. Royall's incestuous desire in her mind. Like the red pickle dish in *Ethan Frome*, the color crimson signifies sexuality, which implies that while Charity regards the lawyer as her adoptive father, he regards her as his own property. Both a lawyer and a father, Mr. Royall is the embodiment of the Law of the Father in the novel. He uses Charity's name to assert his right of possessing her. After being brought down from the Mountain, she is "christened Charity to commemorate Mr. Royall's disinterestedness" and "to keep alive in her a becoming sense of her dependence" (*S*, 39). According to Jacques Lacan, language is a phallocentric system which embodies the Father's Law, capable of "inscribing the bodies of males and females with specific values and meanings" (Grosz, *Sexual Subversions*, 25). In other words, lawyer Royall uses Charity's name as a disciplinary tool to train the girl's obedience: she is constantly reminded of her inferior origin and the need to be thankful for him.

However, the symbolic order of North Dormer is resisted by Charity. Although everyone calls her Charity Royall, the name is not successfully inscribed on her for the following two reasons. In the first place, she understands that because he never legally adopts her, so the name is not actually recognized by law. Her resentment of the name given by lawyer Royall and her curiosity throughout the novel about the names of her biological mother and her own demonstrate her resistance to the symbolic order. Additionally, the most remarkable features that distinguish Charity from other villagers are her inarticulateness and her inability to understand various modes of cultural representation, as several critics have noted (Skillern, 121; Wolff, "Cold Ethan", 243). In other words, Charity cannot be incorporated into the phallocentric system of representation; instead, she embodies the "noncodified feminine" which rebels against the

170

Law of the Father—lawyer Royall (Skillern, 121).

Charity resists the lawyer's hegemony by seeking pleasure in natural landscape as well. She experiences the landscape "in a polysensory way" with all her senses (Westphal, 133). In addition to the visual perception, she revels in the smell and taste of "the thyme into which she crushed her face", touch of the "the dry mountain grass under her palms", and sound of the wind and the creak of the larches.

> She often climbed up the hill and lay there alone for the mere pleasure of feeling the wind and of rubbing her cheeks in the grass. Generally at such times she did not think of anything, but lay immersed in *an inarticulate well-being*. (*S*, 37, emphasis added)

Charity's emotion indicates that her "access to the world occurs through the active powers of *embodiment*" instead of signification or representation (Ben Anderson, 456, original emphasis). The vibrant and sensuous landscape echoes Julia Kristeva's semiotic *chora*—a space of "the rhythmic, energetic, dispersed bodily series of forces which strive to proliferate pleasures, sounds, colours, or movements experienced in the [...] body" (Grosz, *Jacques Lacan*, 152). Nursed by *chora*, Charity feels " an inarticulate well-being "—an unspeakable and unrepresentable feminine power which enables her to defy Mr. Royall.

It is worth noting that the threshold of the Royall house which appears prominently at the beginning of the novel indicates that Charity is going through a liminal stage from a girl to a socially inscribed woman: "A girl came out of lawyer Royall's house, at the end of the one street of North Dormer, and stood on the doorstep" (*S*, 30). Her resistance to Mr. Royall's power thus demonstrates her refusal of the patriarchal system of representation. During this " betwixt and between " stage, she encounters architect Harney who is quite familiar with various representations because of his gender and profession (Victor Turner, 95). In their short-lived love affair, he contributes to her initiation into the symbolic order through making her feel shameful about her embodied way of experiencing landscape and teaching her the picturesque mode of seeing the old houses in North Dormer.

When Harney meets Charity for the first time in the library, he laughs at her lack of knowledge about the social codes of appreciating colonial houses and tells her that the reason why North Dormer has not yet attracted tourists' attention is because there are not any books on the old houses: "They all go on doing Plymouth and Salem. So stupid. My cousin's house, now, is remarkable. This place must have had a past—it must have been more of a place once." (*S*, 35) Plymouth and Salem were representative quaint places "where old houses were sought out and catalogued as the sites of romantic tales or the homes of eighteenth-century heroes" when old New England had become the center of a "cult of the past" since the late nineteenth century (Donna Brown, 133). Harney's words insinuate that he not only records the houses, but also attempts to incorporate the village and its inhabitants into the world of established catalogues and codes. Playing the role as a shaper of cultural meaning for North Dormer, he also shapes the way Charity examines her surroundings: she starts to learn symbolic representation rather than depending on her intuitive understanding.

Harney teaches Charity the verbal and visual vocabulary of the picturesque when she guides him to see the old houses in North Dormer. She gradually knows the "typical" features of the colonial houses that attract the architect's attention, such as "the fan-shaped tracery of the broken light above the door, the flutings of the paintless pilasters at the corners, and the round window set in the gable" (*S*, 68). Though she cannot fully understand why the dilapidated buildings are regarded as picturesque,

Charity convinces herself that "for reasons that still escaped her, these were things to be admired and recorded" (*S*, 68). Under his influence, she relinquishes her previous embodied way of experiencing rural landscape; instead, when his words confuse her, as if she were confronting the books in the library, she feels ashamed about her slowness in studying the cultural codes: "a sense of inadequacy that came to her most painfully when her companion, absorbed in his job, forgot her ignorance and her inability to follow his least allusion, and plunged into a monologue on art and life" (*S*, 58). Since the "proper knowledge" of landscape "gleaned through correct visualization" is constructed and therefore can be "power-laden", Harney's representation of landscape which has the air of accuracy and reliability gives him authority over her (Wylie, *Landscape*, 116). As landscape theorist Gillian Rose contends, the embodied way of experiencing landscape offers "a 'feminine' resistance to hegemonic ways of seeing which dissolves the illusion of an unmarked, unitary, distanced, masculine spectator" (112). Harney thwarts Charity's resistance to hegemonic ways of seeing which is adopted by male spectators and therefore contributes to her initiation into the symbolic order.

Charity's initiation into the symbolic order climaxes in the Old Home Week① ceremony in the Town Hall. In the narrator's words, she begins "her tragic initiation" when she discovers during the celebration that Harney has been engaged to Annabel Balch, a girl of more privileged class, and she also finds out that she is pregnant with his child (*S*, 159). As the organizer of the holiday, Harney not only endows the Town Hall with an air of

---

① Old Home Week is a festival that was created in 1899 by New Hampshire governor Frank Rollins to stimulate tourism in rural New England by inviting former residents of the villages and towns to visit their ancestral household. Appealing to urbanites' nostalgia for old New England families, Old Home Week organizers announced that "the pageant [...] upholds the sweetness, charm, and sanctity of the home, on which America was founded and has been preserved" (qtd. in Kassanoff, 185).

revitalization by redecorating the old house, but also assists Miss Hatchard in restoring domesticity in North Dormer. In order to underscore his function of revitalizing the village, Wharton not only mentions how he plans Old Home Week festivities as tourist attraction to stimulate the village's sagging economy, but also meticulously describes his influence upon the villagers with such expressions as "illuminated by this sudden curiosity" (*S*, 57) and "roused us all to a sense of our privileges" (115). Like the colonial revivalists who attempted to "awaken civic spirit and inject new energy and civility into the communal lifeblood" of New England villages, Harney awakens Charity's sexuality, injects energy to lawyer Royall and other villagers, and eventually contributes a new life to the Royall house by impregnating Charity (Conforti, 241). In short, Harney rejuvenates old New England.

It is lawyer Royall's speech about "coming home for good" that finally draws Charity into the symbolic order (*S*, 125). Harney's teaching about cultural signs prepares her for the effects of the speech: no longer the girl who feels confused about lectures, she for the first time "found her attention arrested by her guardian's discourse" and "noticed that his gravely set face wore the look of majesty that used to awe and fascinate her childhood" (*S*, 125). Lawyer Royall's conclusion that the young people who are planning to leave the quiet hills will be sent back to the old homestead someday by the things they cannot foresee foreshadows Charity's return to the Royall house after Harney leaves North Dormer. The heat of the Town Hall, the discomfort of her pregnancy, and the heartbrokenness of discovering her lover's engagement make Charity faint and fall face downward at Mr. Royall's feet, which symbolizes her submission to the Law of the Father. As Sandra M. Gilbert succinctly puts it, "Harney has really performed as culture's messenger [...] whose glamour seduces the daughter into the social architecture from which she would otherwise have tried to flee" (368).

The novel's ending has sparked heated debate among critics since its publication. After Harney leaves North Dormer when the Old Home Week comes to an end, Charity seeks her biological mother on the Mountain, but only sees her dead body. Lawyer Royall takes advantage of Charity's vulnerability and marries her in a nearby city. The novel closes with Charity returning to the red house as the newly-wed Mrs. Royall, standing on the doorstep where she steps out when the story begins and looking around at the scenery in the autumn moonlight. While Wolff offers an optimistic interpretation by arguing that Charity's return " is no surrender and no regression, but the act of a mature adult " (A Feast of Words, 294), Ammons sees the cycle as an ill omen for Charity's everlasting confinement in North Dormer (Edith Wharton's Argument, 140). But because neither considers the liminality of the threshold, both readings fail to notice the doubleness of the ending since Charity still possesses the potential for resisting the symbolic order. It should be noted that Wharton highlights the heroine's liminality by ending the novel with Charity standing on the threshold rather than crossing it. As Victor Turner points out, " liminality is frequently likened to death, to being in the womb, to invisibility, to darkness" (95). Charity's liminal state is implied by her pregnancy and the imageries of death in the last scene such as the dark sky and her memory of her mother's funeral. Turner further argues that " the attributes of liminality or of liminal personae (' threshold people') are necessarily ambiguous, since this condition and these persons elude or slip through the network of classifications that normally locate states and positions in cultural space " (95). The threshold hence suggests that although she has married to Mr. Royall, Charity will still look for the possibility of " slip [ping] through the network of classifications". The liminality of the threshold in fact signals the double meaning of the denouement: while Charity succumbs to the Law of the Father, she retains the potential for subversion. Therefore, it is not quite convincing to state that by making the ending "an uplifting account of [...] timely legitimization and [...] restoration", Wharton expresses her conservative opinion of gender in *Summer* (Kassanoff, 113). This section demonstrates that Wharton does express her critique of gender inequality by depicting the different ways of seeing the colonial houses between Harney and Charity, even though the writer knows well that opportunities for female rebellion are limited.

To sum up, the vernacular architecture in the two novels reflects social transformations' impacts upon gender relations in old New England. Ethan's farmhouse displays his failure to keep pace with agricultural commercialization. Under the influence of rural tourism, the colonial houses in *Summer* are seen by urbanites such as Harney as an exemplar of domesticity. In *Ethan Frome*, Ethan's diminished farmhouse influences how he sees himself as a man and how others judge him based on his economic status. In *Summer*, Wharton criticizes gender inequality in old New England through contrasting the perspectives of Harney and Charity towards the colonial houses and tracing Charity's resistance to the symbolic order. In both books, Wharton expresses her concern about the detrimental effects of patriarchy, as she does in her New York novels.

3.4   Summary

The rural landscape in *Ethan Frome* and *Summer* reflects the transformation of the regional identity of old New England when the rural region faced the uneven development between the countryside and city, waves of immigration, agricultural commercialization, and a boom in rural tourism between the postbellum era and the early twentieth century. Old New England shifts from a decaying backwater to a romanticized retreat from the tumult of social transformations. While old New England landscape in *Ethan Frome* epitomizes the left-behind rural places in the late nineteenth century, in *Summer* the landscape turns into a reification of Arcadia in urbanites' eyes when this region's backwardness became its most valued attributes in the twentieth century. By comparing the different perceptions of rural landscape by city visitors and local villagers, Wharton exposes the class, racial and gender inequalities underlying old New England landscape.

In this chapter, old New England landscape in the two novels, represented by the villages, the mountains, and the vernacular architecture, is examined and compared to explore the impacts of social transformations upon rural New Englanders at the turn of the twentieth century. In the first place, the villages manifest power disparities between the urban middle class and the rural poor when the villages change from stagnant backwater to the embodiment of pastoralism in urbanites' eyes. The antithesis between the obsolete water-powered sawmill and newly-built railroad in *Ethan Frome* symbolizes the tension between backward countryside and progressive city. Ignoring the uneven development between rural and urban regions, the narrator views the landscape of Starkfield as indicative of the farmers' incapacity to adjust to social transformations. By comparison, North Dormer in *Summer* serves as the embodiment of pastoral simplicity and intimate community for the urban leisure class. The urbanites' nostalgia for the village landscape conceals rural poverty and exacerbates power inequity between them and the farmers. Furthermore, the mountains indicate US-born Anglo-Saxons' perception of whiteness when the mountains change from the symbol of racial decline to that of Anglo-Saxon superiority. The barren and lifeless white mountain in *Ethan Frome* alludes to the race suicide of native New Englanders, which is exemplified by the contrast between dwindling Fromes and expanding Irish households. The Mountain in *Summer* signifies Italian immigrants' threat to the racially homogeneous natives. The villagers' hostility and Harney's attempt to tame the Mountain's otherness by adopting the picturesque mode display their notion of whiteness that is characterized by hierarchically ordered white races, thereby epitomizing the nativist sentiment among US-born Anglo-Saxons. Last but not least, the vernacular architecture reflects the impacts of commercial agriculture and rural tourism upon gender relations in old New England when the houses shift from the symbol of emasculated masculinity to virtuous households in the eyes of urbanites. The diminished farmhouse influences Ethan's self-perception as a man and other people's evaluation of him as a capable husband. In *Summer*, while Charity sees the Royall house as a manifestation of patriarchy, male urban vacationers such as Harney believe that the colonial houses represent old New England's virtue. Through making the rebellious Charity relinquish her embodied way of experiencing landscape and teaching her the picturesque mode of seeing the old houses, Harney dissolves her resistance to hegemonic ways of seeing which are adopted by male spectators and contributes to her initiation into the symbolic order. In conclusion, old New England's transformed identity, with its idyllic villages, homogenous Anglo-Saxon population, and virtuous households, is an invention of city dwellers as an antidote to the ills of social transformations.

Old New England landscape in the two novels is not merely a backdrop for the storylines; instead, it represents the way in which people understand themselves, their surroundings, and other human groups. Constructed by a series of power relations, the rural landscape molds human emotions, thereby shedding light on the impacts of social transformations on the characters' aesthetics and ideologies. To be more specific, old New England landscape is shaped by the power relations between the urban leisure class and rural poor, US-born Anglo-Saxons and Irish, Italian immigrants, and men and women. Thus, this chapter's study of rural landscape demonstrates how old New England is perceived, experienced, interpreted, and represented are socially grounded in historically specific notions of class, race, and gender in turn-of-the-century America.

Wharton's depiction of old New England landscape in the two novels expresses her concern about the issues of class, race, and gender. Firstly, for the power asymmetries between the urban dwellers and rural residents, she attacks class inequality and takes the view that urbanites' praise of quaint countryside veils rural deprivation. Secondly, in terms of immigrants, she shows a shift in attitude influenced by the First World War, from endorsing US-born Anglo-Saxons' anxiety about racial decline to satirizing American nativism. Thirdly, with regard to gender relations, she criticizes the harmful effects of patriarchy on both men and women. To sum up, the writer believes that turning to a romanticized old New England which cloaks and perpetuates class, gender, and racial inequalities is not an effective way to cope with social transformations. This is because the very possibility of the rural idyll is itself dependent upon modern travelers' eyes and their metropolitan idealism. Wharton presents her solution by creating Hudson River Valley landscape in the last two novels published before her death— *Hudson River Bracketed* and *The Gods Arrive*.

Chapter Four   Idealized Hudson River Valley Landscape in *Hudson River Bracketed* and *The Gods Arrive*

In addition to New York City and rural New England, Wharton meticulously sketches the landscape of the Hudson River Valley in her works. In most novels, such as *The House of Mirth* and *The Age of Innocence*, the valley is used as a setting for the vacations and social events of the elite characters. However, the writer devotes considerable space to the portrait of the valley landscape in her last two completed novels—*Hudson River Bracketed* and its sequel *The Gods Arrive*. As Saunders points out, both novels emphasize the importance of landscape, which serves not merely as "backdrop for action", but, in fact, as the novels' "subject" (188). The stories take place in Paul's Landing, a fictional suburb in the valley, an hour and a half by train from Manhattan. "A long crooked sort of town on a high ridge" which overlooks "turfy banks sloping down" toward lustrous water, it resembles various small communities along the Hudson that Wharton is familiar with (*HRB*, 39).

The Hudson River Valley held a significant place in Wharton's mind. In *A Backward Glance*, she recalled that her earliest memory of architecture was about the house of her aunt Elizabeth Jones at Rhinebeck on the Hudson. Since she first visited the valley at the age of three, the building, named Rhinecliff by her aunt, had been "a vivid picture in the gallery" of her little girlhood (36). While writing her autobiography in 1934, Wharton

180

still remembered "everything at Rhinecliff". The "specimen of Hudson River Gothic" inspired *Hudson River Bracketed* and *The Gods Arrive* and turned into an old mansion named the Willows which figured prominently in the landscape of Paul's Landing (37). The author's familiarity with the area was reinforced by numerous excursions she took during her youth and married life. Even after having moved to France, every October, she missed the "wonderful colors of foliage" in the valley (R. W. B. Lewis, *Edith Wharton: A Biography*, 172).

Apart from her longtime acquaintance with the beautiful scenery of the Hudson Valley, Wharton was impressed by its rich historical and cultural legacy. In *A Backward Glance*, she mentioned that the Hudson River landscape inspired some of America's greatest writers such as Washington Irving and Walter Whitman. As Donald Anderson and Judith Saunders suggest, Wharton's depiction of Paul's Landing in *Hudson River Bracketed* and *The Gods Arrive* was based on her reading of the works of literary predecessors about the valley (2). "Sustained by cultural-historical roots that North America otherwise conspicuously lacked", the region, according to Wharton, was a place that inspired and nourished artistic vision (Saunders, 210). In the two novels, she correspondingly empowered the history, architecture, and natural environment of Paul's Landing with mystery and creativity.

Hudson River Bracketed and *The Gods Arrive*, Wharton's bildungs-romane, traces the development of the protagonist Vance Weston, a young American writer in the 1920s and 1930s. Vance's growth as a writer corresponds with his journey from Midwestern America to New York State and Europe and his final return to the Hudson River Valley. Arriving in the Northeastern United States as a complacent college graduate from the Midwest, Vance experiences his artistic awakening and begins writing in Paul's Landing. His access to European literature in the Willows opens his horizons and prompts him to travel in Europe for three years. In the last scene of *The Gods Arrive*, he comes back to the Willows with a more mature image, which implies his potential of being an outstanding American novelist.

The two books, published just five years before Wharton's demise, are largely regarded by scholars as the author's summary of her long career and her insight into the methods of writing, with Vance serving as her spokesman to criticize a younger generation of modernist writers (Singley, *Edith Wharton: Matters of Mind and Spirit*, 195). The landscape of the Hudson Valley is often seen as a metaphor for Wharton's longing to return to the premodern age, a testament to her outdatedness as a nostalgic writer who approaches the end of her life. Critics state that she employs the idealized landscape to create romantic refuges from social problems of post-World War I America. For example, Whaley concludes that Wharton "endowed the Hudson River Valley with an atmosphere of romantic nostalgia": her inability to address the questions of her era and her retreat to the past suggest that she "moved from a liberal to a conservative position" in the final stage of her writing career (215). In a similar manner, Annette Benert claims that Wharton's scathing critiques in prewar books have faded into "flabby fantasies" as Paul's Landing serves as "a metaphor, a mystic inspiration, rather than a place where people lived, loved, hated, suffered, enjoyed" (206). Nevertheless, reviewers have not noticed that far from showcasing her detachment from the reality of American society in the 1920s and 1930s, the idealized landscape of Paul's Landing in fact conveys Wharton's reflections on how Americans should respond to the negative effects of social transformations and her search for a balanced development between nature and human society, demonstrating her profound concern for modern America.

When Wharton wrote these two novels, it was in the midst of the famous Roaring Twenties in American history. Though the period from World War I to the Great Depression of 1929 was a time of unprecedented economic prosperity, some Americans were keenly aware of the spiritual emptiness lurking beneath the surface of the materialistic world, and Wharton was one of their representatives.

First and foremost, this era was characterized by the increasing standardization of industrial society. The impact of new technologies such as mass production, electricity, advertising, telephone and telegraph, automobile, radio, and film transformed every aspect of American life. Although Americans enjoyed tremendous technological progress in the first decades of the twentieth century, many doubted whether technological advances had made life aesthetically or emotionally better. According to Richard H. Pells, "concern with the impact of science and technology on human behavior" reached its peak in American society when the Great War demonstrated the destructive uses of technology and machinery (27). In the 1920s, it was widely believed that American life was becoming more and more standardized and mechanical. Historians Charles and Mary Beard commented on the American society in their influential book *The Rise of American Civilization* (1927): "The technology of interchangeable parts was reflected in the clothing, sports, amusements, literature, architecture, manners, and speech of the multitude. The curious stamp of uniformity [...] sank deeper and deeper into every phase of national life—material and spiritual" (728). In *Hudson River Bracketed* and *The Gods Arrive*, Vance's repressed emotion showcases the adverse effects of standardization and mechanization.

Secondly, with the rapid growth of the capitalist economy came human alienation from nature. According to the famous American scholar Samuel Phillips Huntington, many Americans in the early twentieth century believed that the principal difference between traditional society of the nineteenth century and their modern society of the new century lay in "the greater control which modern man had over his natural [...] environment" (28). Americans' instrumental way of viewing nature led them to treat it as a provider of unlimited resources, which legitimized their wanton transformation of nature and destruction of environment. American novelist Willa Cather, a contemporary of Edith Wharton, once denounced Americans' domination over nature by describing the scarred Midwestern landscape in 1927: "gentle hills and valleys are turned into 'blackened waste[s]' by industry; 'virgin soil' is torn by the 'chilled products' of the mills' 'red forges'; timber is 'ruthlessly torn away' from mountains, leaving 'wounds in the earth'" (qtd. in O'Brien, 389). The excessive development of instrumental rationality not only damaged the natural environment on which Americans depended for survival, but also eroded their spiritual world. In the two novels, Vance's emotional distress manifests modern Americans' alienation from nature which was caused by their instrumental perspective of it.

Thirdly, this period witnessed an increasing interconnectedness between the United States and the rest of the world. Globalization played an important role in the process of social transformations. On the one hand, the growing trend of globalization changed Americans' perception of national identity. On the other hand, the spread of U. S. economic, political, and cultural influences fueled Americans' blind confidence in their own culture. As American culture's global impact continued to grow, some Americans advocated for a rejection of history and aesthetic tradition, particularly those from the Old World. In the two novels, for example, Vance's families only read American writers' books and always feel glad that there are no old families in their "go-ahead" neighborhood (*HRB*, 53). Their disregard for European heritage results in intellectual parochialism and neglect of history.

In the final stage of her writing career, by creating the idealized landscape of the Hudson River Valley, Wharton expresses her concern about the effects of social transformations in the United States and presents her own solution to handle its detrimental influences upon human spirit. This chapter examines three significant elements of the Hudson landscape in *Hudson River Bracketed* and *The Gods Arrive*—the suburb, forest, and old mansion—to explore the power relation between man and nature, and the role of landscape in redeeming Americans from emotional and aesthetic starvation. By delving into the interaction between the protagonist Vance and the landscape of the Hudson River Valley, this chapter discusses Wharton's views on how Americans should respond to social transformations and the limitations of her perspective.

4.1 Blending of Nature and Technology in Hudson Valley Suburb

The American intelligentsia in the 1920s and 1930s paid significant attention to assess the impact of social transformations on individuals, particularly in terms of standardization and mechanization. American society embraced a fast-paced machine civilization and new forms of industrial organization (Fordism) and efficiency (Taylorism). Terminology that adopted mechanical metaphors for human behavior, emotion, and cognition first came into use during this period: like a train, for instance, people could get "steamed up" or "in gear" (Dinerstein, 220). As noted by Pells, an expert in twentieth-century American cultural history, many scholars in the 1920s felt that the United States was heading towards " an inhuman civilization" that " glorified machine processes and calculated success in terms of material acquisitions ", " a conveyor-belt society preaching individualism while reducing everyone to a cog in the wheel of

185

industrialism" (29). Perhaps no book published in the 1920s offered a more extensive analysis of the American society than Harold Stearns's *Civilization in the United States* (1922) which included essays written by thirty influential scholars such as Lewis Mumford and Van Wyck Brooks. In the preface, the editor announced that Americans were afflicted with a mechanistic view of life: "the most moving and pathetic fact in the social life of America to-day is emotional and aesthetic starvation, of which the mania for petty regulation, the regimentating standardization [...] the firm grasp on the unessentials of material organization of our pleasures and gaieties are all eloquent stigmata" (Stearns, vii). In short, the contributors pointed out that Americans' worship of science and technology resulted in the mechanization of humanity and depletion of emotion.

Sharing similar concerns, Wharton commented in 1925 on the state of modern life in America: "America has indeed deliberately dedicated herself to [...] a dead level of prosperity and security" (*The Uncollected Critical Writings*, 154). Through comparing the uniform Midwestern suburb with the idealized Paul's Landing, this section investigates Wharton's attitude towards the standardization and mechanization which pervade American life. Furthermore, this part will explore her vision of reconciling nature and technology in *Hudson River Bracketed* and *The Gods Arrive* by analyzing Vance's experience of the suburban landscape in the Hudson River Valley.

4.1.1   Hudson Valley as New York City's Backyard

Since the nineteenth century, the Hudson River Valley has become a suburb of New York City due to its proximity, famously referred to as "New York City's Backyard" by nineteenth-century American novelist Nathaniel Parker Willis (D'Amore, 363). Originally inhabited by wealthy businessmen and then by middle-class commuters after public transportation connected the valley to Manhattan, the area was widely seen as a model that combined natural beauty with urban conveniences. Drawing on the history of the valley as a suburb of New York and the suburban ideal in American literature, in the two novels, Wharton portrays Paul's Landing as an idealized suburb which embodies the advantages of both city and country. More importantly, the Hudson Valley suburb reflects the writer's dream of blending technology and nature.

As one of the earliest suburban regions in the United States, the Hudson River Valley had been the retreat of choice for New York's upper class since the nineteenth century. Located alongside rivers, lakes or in picturesque locations, the elites' mansions served as venues for hunting events and other extravagant forms of entertainment, as well as providing the quiet pleasures of gardening. According to Kenneth Jackson, Andrew Jackson Downing, a popular architect and landscape gardener in the nineteenth century, was "the most influential single individual in translating the rural ideal into the suburban ideal" by promoting the cottages in the Hudson River Valley as the exemplars of suburban living for Americans (85). By the 1850s, "the combination of efficient steamship travel [...] and frequent railroad access had transformed communities along the Hudson River into bustling New York suburbs, highly desirable to men of means who worked in the city a few days a week but preferred to live close to nature" (D'Amore, 370). The well-known editor Nathaniel Willis introduced the suburban life of this region's commuters: "a steamer will take the villager to the city between noon and night, and bring him back between midnight and morning [...] There is a suburban look and character about all the villages on the Hudson [...] They are suburbs; in fact, steam has destroyed the distance between them and the city" (qtd. in Stilgoe, 5). The decreased costs of public transportation in the 1870s resulting from the revolutionary technological advances rendered travelling between the Hudson

River Valley and New York City affordable for the middle class. In "the suburban boom of the 1920s", the Hudson region experienced dramatic changes, particularly in areas adjacent to New York City: they became less agricultural, while rapidly gaining population as a result of suburban development fostered by the wide usage of trains, trolleys, and automobiles (Kenneth Jackson, 218).

Dutchess County, where the two novels are set, is situated in the Mid-Hudson Valley region, north of New York City. Before the wave of mass-scale transformation of farmlands into residences following the Second World War, Dutchess County had started to become suburbanized since late 1890s because of its proximity to New York City. In 1898, Grand Central Station received approximately 118,000 commuters daily from three main passenger railroad lines that ran along the Hudson River, Harlem River Valley, and Long Island Sound, in addition to several minor routes. The reason for the increase in commuters was that Dutchess County's population nearly doubled from 1890 to 1910 (Kenneth Jackson, 122). During the twentieth century, agriculture gradually lost its significance in the economy of the county. "The amount of 'improved' land or cropland dropped rapidly between 1910 and 1940, from two-thirds to about one-third of the county's land area. More of the southwestern part of the county became a part of suburbia, with much of the commercial agriculture remaining in the north and east" (Jackson, 38).

Calling American suburbs as "borderlands", John R. Stilgoe states that they combine the advantages of both urban and rural lives (9). Less than an hour and a half by train from New York City, Paul's Landing, where the protagonist Vance's relatives live, are facing the arrival of suburbanization. As Vance observes, "The suburb, evidently uncertain of its future, awaited in slatternly unconcern the coming of the land-speculator or of the municipal park-designer" (*GA*, 416). Located on a high ridge and surrounded by big trees, Paul's Landing is a developing suburb where agriculture is giving way to residential development. Trees and fences between the houses give each family a feeling of isolation in nature, while open space in front accommodates views of distant hills and the Hudson River. Like the nearby cities, Paul's Landing has a main street, several shops, garages, and business buildings (*HRB*, 39). Moreover, the inhabitants frequently go to cities by car, trolley, and train. For instance, Vance's cousin Laura Lou learns French in New Jersey while her elder brother Upton works as a gardener in Westchester County—a famous commuter suburb in the State of New York. Later in *Hudson River Bracketed* when Vance works for a high-brow review called *The Hour*, he commutes between Manhattan and Paul's Landing by train. Even for the locals who still make a living from farming, their life is built on "the interconnectedness of city and suburb along the Hudson": they sell butter, cheese, and cattle to New Yorkers and buy groceries from urban stores, including goods imported from Europe (D'Amore, 369). In short, soldered together with New York City, Paul's Landing is a successful integration of country and city.

Formerly referring in a general way to the outskirts of urban areas, the word "suburb" has come to denote a positive union of urban and rural characteristics in American literature since the middle nineteenth century (Archer, 139). The suburban ideal was first made influential by American Romantics who "set the ideological stage for an elite migration to the suburbs, a new kind of settlement that merged the advantages of urban life with the pleasures of the countryside" (Nicolaides and Andrew, 14). Ralph Waldo Emerson commented in 1844 that his home in Concord, a suburban town twenty miles from Boston, provided "rural strength & religion for my children" as well as "city facility & polish" (87). He stated that the advantage of a suburban residence over one isolated in the country was the suburb's proximity to cities and the facilities it afforded of participating in those sources of instruction and enjoyment which could only be obtained in cities (17). Summarizing Emerson's life in Concord as " a product of the convergence rather than the polarity of city and country", Jacob Risinger argues that he "was one of the first eloquent spokesmen of a new suburban sensibility" that formed "at the intersection of the urban and the rural" (4).

In a similar manner, Henry David Thoreau's lakeshore experiment at Walden expressed his suburban ideal. Far from a rural backwater, the lake was "a recently logged clearing in an intensively used landscape just fifteen miles from downtown Boston" (Maynard, 303). When Thoreau moved to Walden Pond in 1845, the area was experiencing the transformation from village to suburb which enabled middle-class Americans to enjoy the exciting advantages of the city without having to live there. By participating in the suburban way of living, Thoreau creatively translated wilderness values to a suburban location as part of his desire "to live a primitive and frontier life, though in the midst of an outward civilization" (11).

In the mid-nineteenth century, Nathaniel Hawthorne expressed his ideal of blending the urban and rural lifestyles by creating a utopian farming commune in *The Blithedale Romance* (1852). As Edward Christopher Hudson argues, the novel " lays the formal foundations for suburban discourse" because it discusses issues such as " Puritanism, the agrarian ideal, ideal communities, pastoralism, transcendentalism, and the cult of domesticity—all of which are encompassed by the suburban ideal" when the United States experienced its first real surge in suburban growth with the establishment of the Victorian suburb during the final thirty years of the nineteenth century (57-58).

Later in William Dean Howells's *Suburban Sketches* (1871) which published as a serial in *The Atlantic Monthly* during the heyday of the streetcar suburbs, the narrator describes his neighborhood in Charlesbridge— a fictional suburb based on Cambridge, Massachusetts—as " a frontier between city and country" (12). He extols the suburb as "appear[ing] to us a kind of Paradise" : "In the city, even, it is oppressive; in the country it is desolate; in the suburbs it is a miracle" (89). For the narrator and Howells, the suburb was the last outpost of civilization.

In addition to the above-mentioned writers, landscape architect Downing, who was a Hudson River Valley native, utilized the daily lives of the region's typical commuters as an example to advocate a suburban aesthetic for a broad American audience :

> An industrious man, who earns his bread by daily exertions, and lives in a snug and economical little home in the suburbs of a town, has very different wants from the farmer, whose accommodation must be plain but more spacious, or the man of easy income, who builds a villa as much to gratify his taste, as to serve the useful purposes of a dwelling".
> (*The Architecture of Country Houses*, 40)

Downing's promotion made the landscape of the valley a nationally well-known model that blended natural beauty with urban conveniences. As perhaps the most celebrated proponent of early suburbanization in the nineteenth century, he helped popularize the notion that the suburb had the benefit of being both nostalgic and forward-looking : on the one hand, it allowed individuals to feel connected to a simpler, less hurried or less complicated past; on the other hand, it took full advantage of the newest developments in transportation and the most popular trends in home design.

In the two novels, the suburbanization of Paul's Landing mainly benefits from the revolution in transportation technology. By the middle nineteenth century, the inhabitants were either poor farmers who seldom went out of the region or wealthy elites who could afford private carriages for travelling between Paul's Landing and Manhattan. It was not until the

1880s, with the introduction of affordable steamships and trains, that the promoters' market really took shape, expanding the suburban focus from the wealthy families' estates to local houses. When Vance comes there in the 1920s, the suburban landscape comprises the farmers' cottages, the villas of the elites who travel by car, and the cozy bungalows of the middle-class residents who commute by trolley and train. The access to public transportation not only draws city dwellers to live in Paul's Landing, but also results in better roads and more business buildings. The locals take advantage of the mobility the public transportation offers to explore other counties that has previously been as foreign to them as another nation. During the weekends and holidays, the families usually have an outing to New York City for visiting theaters, parks, and public libraries.

The suburbanization of Paul's Landing is related to the problem of population concentration in New York City. In the 1920s and 1930s, despite a process of population deconcentration that had been underway for half a century in some neighborhoods, congestion in many sections of the city remained high. One solution was to spread out the population toward open land and the advance in transportation technology made that movement possible. As a leading reformer claimed in 1912, "better streetcar lines to the suburbs would reduce disease and death rates and combat all social ills by decentralizing the inner city population" (qtd. in Kenneth Jackson, 149). Though he only lives in New York for a short period of time, Vance expresses his comfort in Paul's Landing which relieves him from the "huge towering wilderness of masonry where Vance Weston of Euphoria was of no more account to any one among the thousands inhabiting it [New York City] than a single raindrop to the ocean" (*HRB*, 37).

What makes the suburban landscape of Paul's Landing unique is the harmony between technology and nature. Since the suburbanization of Paul's Landing is closely associated with the advance in transportation, the railway station is the most obvious symbol of technology and progress. While Nathaniel Hawthorne calls the whistle of the locomotive in the woods as "the long shriek, harsh, above all other harshness" which cannot be mollified into harmony by natural landscape (qtd. in Marx, *The Machine in the Garden*, 13), and Sinclair Lewis in *Main Street* depicts the station in a Midwestern town as "a monster of steel limbs, oak ribs, flesh of gravel, and a stupendous hunger for freight" (192), Wharton highlights the blending of Paul's Landing's railway station with the landscape. Surrounded by "some crooked-boughed locust-trees", the station which connects the suburb with New York City is "under the pale green shade" (*HRB*, 38). When Vance walks out of the station, he catches a glimpse of "lustrous gray waters spreading lake-like to distant hills" (*HRB*, 39). Wharton's depiction of the harmony between the railway station and the suburban landscape echoes Emerson's appeal that writers and artists have a special responsibility to incorporate into their work "such new and necessary facts" as mill and railroad. For Emerson, machinery and landscape can "agree well" because there is nothing inherently ugly about factories and railroads (216). Instead, it is the dehumanizing impact of mechanization that is truly ugly. When machinery is seen from the empirical mode of consciousness that always measures and calculates for material gains, then it represents the mechanization of human soul. In other words, whether technology and machinery can blend with nature or not depends on the way human beings handle those powerful instruments. As long as humans treat technology and machines as tools for the betterment of life, rather than modes of thought and feeling, "mechanical power is to be matched by a new access of vitality to the imaginative, Utopian, transcendent, value-creating faculty" which comes from nature (Marx, *The Machine in the Garden*, 236).

The landscape of the Hudson River Valley played a prominent role in Wharton's own life, "all the indulgence of affection [...] the setting of my own youth," as she told her friend Elisina Tyler in 1930 (*The Letters of*

Edith Wharton, 525). When Wharton was a toddler, her father had taken her to Dutchess County by steamboats and ferries for visiting his sister Elizabeth Schermerhorn Jones. After the development of railroads made travel easier since the second half of the nineteenth century, many of the writer's relatives, friends, and acquaintances bought suburban properties in the region. By train and later by automobile, Wharton participated in house parties and enjoyed pleasure-excursions throughout the Hudson River Valley. Feeling satisfied with the area's landscape and its closeness to Manhattan, she claimed that the Hudson Valley suburb was an "attractive, refined, soundly wholesome" form of domestic life (Fishman, 127). This section's analysis of the suburban landscape in Paul's Landing displays that Wharton does not advocate a return to the premodern age. It is noteworthy that she never suggested a retreat to an isolated farming life in the countryside, like the old New England villages in *Ethan Frome* and *Summer*. On the contrary, she consistently argued for an incorporation of "the older morality, the genteel ethical code, and the recapture of traditional values through renewed contact with the land" into the conveniences of modern life (Bratton, 10). Her own home in the 1920s and 1930s was a suburban villa named Pavillon Colombe near Paris which had the advantages of both city and country. It was a "welcome...retreat from the bustle of business and the din and the dust of the streets" and "surrounded by noble scenery, yet within a short distance" of the urban amenities (Archer, 145).

To summarize, by depicting the landscape of Paul's Landing, the suburb of New York City, Wharton suggests that as an integration of city and country, the suburb can be an ideal landscape where technology is in harmony with nature. In order to emphasize her vision of reconciling technology and nature, she further compares Paul's Landing with the Midwestern suburb in Vance's hometown and highlights the role that the suburban landscape of the Hudson Valley plays in liberating humans from the standardizing and mechanical influences of social transformations.

4.1.2 Paul's Landing as a Counterforce to Standardization and Mechanization

In the two novels, Wharton compares Vance's home in Euphoria, Illinois—a Midwestern suburb—with Paul's Landing. While the suburban landscape of the former reflects the standardizing process of social transformations as a result of Midwesterners' worship of technology and efficiency, the suburban landscape of the latter expresses Wharton's expectation that technology and machinery can coexist with natural beauty. Furthermore, Vance's interaction with the landscape of Paul's Landing reveals the author's hope that nature's aesthetic value can act as a counterforce to standardization and mechanization, thus helping Americans alleviate the side effects of social transformations.

The protagonist Vance's childhood home which boasts "lawn, garage, sleeping porch and sun-parlour" is photographed for the architectural papers as a model of middle-class suburban house (*HRB*, 4). The sleeping porch, a popular amenity which provides privacy and fresh air for the house, associates Vance's home and lifestyle with the typical American middle class of the 1920s. Historians often view the 1920s as a watershed in the development and promotion of American suburb: the " road-building revolution " opened up remote areas to cars and new residential development; between 1922 and 1929 new homes were built at a rate of 883,000 units per year, more than doubled that of any previous periods. During the 1920s, population growth rates in the outer reaches of U.S. cities exceeded those in the center, 33. 2 percent versus 24. 2 (Jurca, 44). Meanwhile, during this decade the " suburban ideal " was subjected to " commodification and mass production ", as builders working from "standardized plans gained control of the single-family housing market from architects" (Jurca, 45). The popularity of American suburb was made possible by technological advances: mass production, especially the emergence of the ready-made house components between 1905 and the late 1920s, promised greater efficiency and lower costs by replacing handwork with standardized mechanization in house construction (Banta, 241). However, mass production resulted in the uniform look of suburban landscape. In a review essay entitled "The Great American Novel" published in 1925, four years before the publication of *Hudson River Bracketed*, Wharton pointed out that the most obvious feature of American suburb was its "standardization": the monotonous "Main Streets" and "little suburban houses at number one million and ten Volstead Avenue" (*The Uncollected Critical Writings*, 152, 157).

The suburban landscape—the " chief source of pride " and " only criterion of beauty " in Midwestern Euphoria—is the creation of the protagonist's father Mr. Weston, the brightest realtor in the county (*HRB*, 10). Like the real estate developers and boosters for planned suburban communities in the 1920s, Mr. Weston "buy[s] up nearly the whole of the Pig Lane side of the town, turn[s] it into the Mapledale suburb" and builds a row of detached houses with the help of prefabricated construction and rationalized labor (*HRB*, 5). His pursuit of architectural harmony makes Mapledale a typical homogeneous suburb which emerged in the early twentieth century as Robert Fishman summarized: " The pattern of tree shaded streets, broad open lawns, substantial houses set back from the sidewalks was a pattern of prosperity [...] that represents the culmination of the suburban style" (145-146). The houses and lawns in the Mapledale suburb are so uniform that newcomers would have trouble finding their unit in the neighborhood were it not for the different paint colors. Even the cars in the garages are either Fords or Buicks.

As D. W. Meinig points out, suburbia is not merely a physical environment. The landscape of suburbia can be read, in his words, as reflecting "cultural values" and "social behavior," as presenting "at once a panorama, a composition, a palimpsest, a microcosm" of the dominant culture (qtd. in Beuka, 4). In short, suburban landscape implies the set of

values, state of mind, and spiritual condition of its inhabitants (Beuka, 1).
The suburban ideal in the early twentieth century reflects a combination of
"the traditional values of midcentury [mid-nineteenth-century] domesticity
and Republicanism and the modern values of professionalization [...]
management and [..] marketplace" (Sies, 85). The values of rationality,
efficiency, and professional management were the new features of planned
suburbs. Extending Bourdieu's notion of the habitus to the realm of
landscape studies, cultural geographer Martyn Lee speculates that what he
calls a "habitus of location" generates place-specific actions and cultural
predispositions, and contributes to the "cultural character" of specific
regions (qtd. in Beuka, 18). Taking the connection between landscape and
the inhabitants' cultural predispositions into consideration, we can see that
the identical appearance of the Midwestern suburban homes in the novels in
fact reflects the uniformity and conformity of the residents. In the eyes of the
inhabitants in Euphoria, the suburb which consists of neatly lined houses
with identical sun parlors signifies the promise of progress. Despite its
material prosperity, Vance's hometown is depicted as "a standardized
world" in which "the social classifications [...] were based on telephones
and bath-tubs" (*HRB*, 221, 269). In "The Great American Novel",
Wharton criticized that the standardized suburban landscape "Taylorized①"
the residents' mindset: "Inheriting an old social organization which provided

---

① Synonymous with modern industrialism, American engineer Frederick Winslow
Taylor (1856-1915) was widely known during the first two decades of the twentieth century
for his method of scientific management which standardized industry to maximize
productivity and improve efficiency. His method of scientific management is referred to as
Taylorism. In his introduction to *The Principles of Scientific Management* (1911), Taylor
declared that "The same principles [of industrial management] can be applied with equal
force to all social activities" such as home management, charity work, and education. He
succeeded in popularizing an ethos of standardization "that would come to inhere in sectors
of society well beyond the confines of the factory and would ultimately constitute the
dominant system of norms operative in American culture as a whole" (Ball, 3).

for nicely shaded degrees of culture and conduct, modern America has simplified and Taylorized it out of existence, forgetting that in such matters the process is necessarily one of impoverishment" (*The Uncollected Critical Writings*, 154). As Diane Lichtenstein argues, Taylorized mindset refers to "machine-based utilitarian values [...] that upheld science and technology as the solutions for all sorts of physical, psychological, and social problems" in the early twentieth century (66). By associating the suburban landscape with Taylorized mindset, Wharton warns that technological advances such as mass production have made modern American life increasingly homogenizing, mechanical, and dehumanizing.

Firstly, the suburbanites have uniform ambitions to succeed in business: they regard upward mobility and material prosperity as the purpose of their lives and see their houses and cars as markers of social status. They fear being associated with "such phrases as 'back number', 'down and out', 'out of the running'" and believe that "A fellow ought to be up on Society and Etiquette, and how to behave at a banquet, and what kind of collar to wear, and what secret societies to belong to" (*HRB*, 5, 15). The small group of people who are not in accord with the community's whole-hearted devotion to business are derided as "the byword of Euphoria" who "could serve the rising community of Euphoria only as the helots served the youth of Sparta" (*HRB*, 14). What is more, the destruction of nature for commercial development is taken for granted by the Midwesterners. For example, they cleared the land to create the uniform suburban landscape. As Mindy Leigh Buchanan-King notes, people in Euphoria "moved through nature and life as bulldozers, razing all in the name of expedient progress" (13). In other words, they believe in man's ownership over nature.

Secondly, the suburbanites worship new technology and machines. Their idea of good life is based on cars, telephones, gramophones, and bath-tubs. Wharton points out that although they provide Americans with material comfort, technology and machinery lead to the mechanical lifestyle and withering of inner life:

> She [Modern America] has reduced relations between human beings to a dead level of vapid benevolence, and the whole of life to a small house with modern plumbing and heating, a garage, a motor, a telephone, and a lawn undivided from one's neighbor's. Great as may be the material advantage of these diffused conveniences, the safe and uniform life resulting from them offers to the artist's imagination a surface as flat and monotonous as our own prairies. (*The Uncollected Critical Writings*, 154)

Vance's home is such a house "with modern plumbing and heating, a garage, a motor, a telephone, and a lawn undivided from one's neighbor's". The standardizing ethos of the suburban landscape infiltrates the domestic realm. His mother Mrs. Weston Taylorizes the family life by applying strategies of scientific management to the home in order to promote domestic productivity and efficiency. The American mechanical engineer Frederick Winslow Taylor declared in his influential book *The Principles of Scientific Management* (1911) that the principles of industrial management such as "breaking tasks into ever smaller movements, managing work through scientific methods, and standardizing the ways in which any task was completed" could be applied with equal force to all social activities including home management, which led to the popularity of home economics in the early decades of the twentieth century (qtd. in Lichtenstein, 68). Regarding the running of the household as her profession, Mrs. Weston is an expert in all the latest household appliances such as refrigerators, electric cookers, electric cleaners, and electric cold-storage. She admires efficiency and the "orderly establishment" of her house

199

is the envy of the neighborhood (*HRB*, 11). Ironically, the carefully managed organization of daily life and assistance of machines do not produce an orderly family life; instead, Mrs. Weston's worship of machines makes Vance feel that she has been mechanized to the point where she cannot experience pain or pleasure. Since her belief in scientific management controls the family's action and renders the house resemble a Ford production line, Vance always feels repressed in the Mapledale suburb: although he "respected efficiency, and even admired it; but of late he had come to feel that as a diet for the soul it was deficient in nourishment" (*HRB*, 17). What he tries to escape from is the standardized and mechanical life resulted from his parents' worship of technology and the machine.

By delineating the standardized Midwestern suburban landscape, Wharton presents a Taylorized society in which all facets of life are reducible to a mechanical scale: human bodies function as machines, interpersonal relationships as business arrangements, and homes as factories. Wharton's view of suburbanization in Vance's hometown echoes that of Sinclair Lewis and Lewis Mumford: while Lewis makes the suburb a synonym for "mass production, standardization, and [...] the specter of conformity" (Jurca, 13), Mumford criticizes the spiritual bleakness of the suburb where "bathtubs and heating systems and similar apparatus play such a large part" in the suburbanites' "conception of the good life" and where machinery is given more respect than the people it is meant to serve ("The Wilderness of Suburbia", 45). They are all concerned about the spiritual emptiness among modern Americans when machines "suppress many of the most essential characteristics of organisms, personalities and human communities" (Mumford, *Pentagon of Power*, 37). To put it another way, what Wharton attacks is neither the suburb nor Midwest, but the mechanization of humanity demonstrated by Vance's repressed emotion when the mania of technology and machinery reduces human life to standardized components. Her description of Vance's emotional repression in standardized Midwestern society prefigures Herbert Marcuse's argument about the repression of Eros in a "one-dimensional" world after the Second World War. According to Marcuse, while it brings great convenience to humans, the development of science and technology "is tied to progressive manipulation and control of human beings", leading to conformist consciousness and constraint of the life instincts ("Ecology and the Critique of Modern Society", 33). Thus, Vance's subdued emotion manifests technology's destructive influence upon human beings' life instincts.

When he arrives in Paul's Landing—the Hudson River Valley suburb, Vance notices that the greatest difference between the local inhabitants and his Midwestern neighbors is that the locals do not regard technology and machinery as the priority of a good life. Expecting "taller houses, wider streets, fresher paint, more motors, telephones, plumbing, than Euphoria possessed, or could ever imagine achieving" in a suburb close to New York, he feels disappointed at the landscape of the Hudson Valley suburb (*HRB*, 42). The protagonist's initial disappointment reflects his Taylorized mindset that regard science and technology as the solutions for all the problems: he is struck by the lack of uniform buildings and roads in the valley and the locals' tolerance of ramshackle houses along the Hudson River, the coexistence of automobiles and horse-drawn carts on "rutty lanes", and his relatives' simple life which does not depend on electric lighting or telephone. He interprets the locals' harmonious relationship with nature as a manifestation of "an absence of initiative" since they do not "hustle around" to acquire the "luxuries" a Euphorian would take for granted (*HRB*, 42). His attitude towards the Hudson Valley suburb demonstrates the effect on human perception as social transformations moves toward standardization and mechanization: technology and the machine have become the ends of human life rather than the means to improve it.

However, Vance soon learns that technology and machinery can coexist with natural beauty. Different from the uniform buildings and lawns in Vance's Midwestern hometown, the suburban landscape of Paul's Landing is diversified, reflecting the dwellers' personality and pursuit of beauty. Some suburbanites have gardens full of big trees while some plant pretty flowers (*HRB*, 39). The locals use machines to beautify the landscape: for example, instead of using land mowers to make their yards identical to the neighbors', the inhabitants of Paul's Landing apply the latest tools bought from New York to improve their gardens based on their own criteria of beauty and appreciate each other's creativity. In addition, they do not regard the brand and size of cars as signs of social status, but use the cars mainly for exploring wild landscape in the valley. In this sense, the role of technology and machines is to pursue the beauty of nature and realize the diversity of human potential, rather than as the purpose of human life. Their attitudes towards technology and machinery echo Mumford's philosophy of biotechnics which emphasizes the combination of technology, nature, and art, and technology's potential benefits for human beings' pursuit of spiritual fulfillment. Mumford claims that when the machine becomes not only an instrument of practical activity but a valued way of life for beauty, then it is possible for humans to move away from "monotechnics" centered on quantified production and the pursuit of efficiency to "biotechnics" which is in harmony with aspirations of human life and ecological balance (*Pentagon of Power*, 155). For him, if technology is not harnessed for a money culture, then it can be used for improving the quality of American life. In a similar manner, Marcuse proposes "the aestheticization of technology": a new technological rationality "oriented toward the long-term preservation and enhancement of human life and nonhuman nature" which gives rise to appreciation of beauty in the world (*Counter-Revolution and Revolt*, 65). In her travelogue about French landscape, Wharton expresses her expectation that machines such as automobiles can provide better access to natural spectacles and help travelers appreciate natural beauty (Totten, "Dialectic", 141). In the novels, through delineating the coexistence of machines and the Hudson Valley suburban landscape, the writer suggests that when technology and machinery are used for pursuing natural beauty, they can contribute to the aesthetic aspect of human existence instead of rendering human life mechanical and standardized.

Pointing out that nature is part of human body and life experience, Marcuse divides nature into inner and external nature: while inner nature refers to man's emotions and senses "as foundation of his rationality and experience", external nature means "man's existential environment" (*Counter-Revolution and Revolt*, 59). He argues that whereas the destruction of nature results in "psychological destructiveness within individuals", the human experience of natural beauty has the function of resisting technology's detrimental impacts upon the standardization and mechanization of humanity ("Ecology and the Critique of Modern Society", 29). As part of the aesthetic dimension which resists business practices' "aggression on the domain of the life instincts", nature is "not committed to the functioning of a repressive society and its aesthetic values are "strong protectors of Eros in civilization" (Marcuse, *Negations*, 201). Thus, understanding the relation between man and nature is necessary for understanding human sensuousness: recognizing nature's aesthetic values enables man to regain "the life-enhancing forces in nature, the sensuous aesthetic qualities which are foreign to a life wasted in unending competitive performances", thereby reactivating the imagination, creativity and subjectivity repressed by the standardizing and mechanical ethos of social transformations (Marcuse, *Counter-Revolution and Revolt*, 60). In Vance's eyes, different from the monotonous Midwestern suburb, the suburban landscape in Paul's Landing has an ineffable enigmatic quality, unique in that it has not been standardized by mass mechanical production. Though initially he is disappointed by the locals' indifference to technology and machine, he is drawn to their love of the landscape. Under the influence of the Tracy family, he notices blooming lilacs and syringas which he seldom pays attention to in his Midwestern hometown, feeling "a burning inward excitement" unfamiliar to himself (*HRB*, 42). His mind is "so packed with the frail and complicated life of birds, insects, ferns, grasses, bursting buds, falling seeds, all the incessantly unfolding procession of the year [...] only to watch himself, to listen to himself, to try and set down the million glimmers and murmurs of the inner scene" (*HRB*, 511). His shift of attention from automobiles and telephones to the landscape symbolizes his recognition of nature's aesthetic values, thereby reawakening his creativity which is suppressed by standardized Midwestern suburb.

In conclusion, through contrasting Paul's Landing's landscape with Vance's Midwestern suburban hometown, Wharton provides her stinging satire of the Taylorized modern American life. From the Midwestern suburban landscape, she detects the standardization and mechanization of modern life. Her chief objection to suburbia in Vance's hometown is its standardized quality, the disheartening sameness and monotony of everything from its landscape to the manners and mores of its inhabitants. The destruction of nature further causes the withering of Midwesterners' life instincts. Wharton's description of the Midwestern landscape and lifestyle captures the standardizing ethos of social transformations in the 1920s. "Arriving around 1900 and gaining momentum after 1910", according to Robert H. Wiebe, "the orientation did not reach its peak of success until the 1920s" (149). This impulse—referred to at various times throughout the twentieth century as Fordism, Taylorism, scientific rationalism, and bureaucratic management—aimed to construct a streamlined, efficient, and rational nation which Wharton criticizes.

In the two novels, Midwesterners' admiration for technology and machinery results in the mass-produced suburb. The uniform suburban landscape reflects the standardization and mechanization of humanity which are epitomized by the conformity of Vance's families and neighbors. They all prioritize financial success and regard owning the most advanced machines as the purpose of life. Although accustomed to the uniform lifestyle, Vance always suffers from emotional repression and longs to escape from the standardized suburban landscape of the Midwest. By contrast, based on the history of the Hudson River Valley as a suburb of New York and the suburban ideal in American literature, Wharton portrays Paul's Landing as an idealized suburb which is characterized by not only the integration of city and country but also the harmony of technology and natural landscape. Vance's initial disappointment with the landscape of Paul's Landing reflects his Taylorized mindset that worships science and technology. By understanding the harmonious relationship between the local inhabitants and the suburban landscape, he realizes that technology and machinery can coexist with natural beauty. Appreciation of the diversified Hudson landscape liberates him from the standardizing influences of social transformations and revitalizes his sensibility, which is essential to his growth as a creative writer. Therefore, the depiction of the landscape in Paul's Landing expresses Wharton's suburban ideal which blends technology and nature. The above analysis indicates that Wharton does not advocate a return to premodern agricultural society, but hopes to achieve harmony between technology and nature through inspiring people's aesthetic perception. Consequently, the claim made by critics like Whaley that the romantic Hudson River Valley is indicative of Wharton's inability to address the questions of her era and her retreat to the past is unconvincing (215). Wharton's countermeasure against the standardized society reflects her attention to the spiritual life of Americans in the Roaring Twenties, an era of unprecedented material abundance.

4.2   Union of Natural Beauty and Artistic Beauty in Hudson Valley Scenery

With the economic development of the nineteenth and twentieth centuries, Americans' exploitation and utilization of nature had also increased significantly. According to Roderick Frazier Nash, throughout the nineteenth century most Americans held an instrumental perspective of nature which regarded it as " simply a storehouse of materials to be used and tamed" (qtd. in Bryan McDonald, 193). Amidst the rapid acceleration of industrialization and urbanization, natural resources were heavily exploited, especially in the West. Environmental historian Donald Worster pointed out that the westward expansion fueled an instrumental perspective of people-environment relations[1] in the United States: " Americans commonly assumed that the land is a form of capital and must be used to turn a profit" (101).

At the turn of the twentieth century, the instrumental view of nature led to serious resource depletion and environmental problems. From 1850 to 1910, Americans cleared 800,000 square miles of forests. By 1920, the Northeast and Midwest had lost 96% of their old-growth forests (Whitney, 191). Accompanying the disappearance of timber was the loss of rich biodiversity, with species such as beavers, white-tailed deer, and bison pushed to the brink of extinction. Unrestrained exploitation of natural resources caused one of the greatest ecological disasters in the history of the American West—the Dust Bowl of the 1930s, which resulted in reduced or

---

[1]   In environment philosophy, the instrumental perspective regards " physical settings as ' tools' for supporting individual productivity and organizational effectiveness—as the physical means for achieving key behavioral and economic goals" (Stokols, 641).

complete crop failure on vast farmlands and forced a large number of Westerners to migrate elsewhere. In 1939, editors of the *Dallas Farm News* lamented that the land of hope had turned into a land of despair: "the prairies of the West, once the home of deer, bison, and antelope, is now the home of dust storms" (qtd. in Worster, 35).

According to Max Weber, the rise of instrumental rationality①, one important feature of modernity, led to the notion that "the subjugation of nature" was a marker of "the progress of civilization" (qtd. in Dyreson, 463). It was until the latter part of the nineteenth century that the first environmental conservation movement in the United States emerged. Then in the early twentieth century, as a response to the problems brought about by industrialization and urbanization, an intense discussion concerning the relationship of nature, human energy, and mental health became popular. An influential group of American thinkers, including the legendary psychologist and philosopher William James, argued that human organism stored up physical and mental resources that they called human energy. Believing that human energy came from nature, they feared that modern people's estrangement from nature would dry up the wellspring of human vitality (Dyreson, 447). Thus, following their Romantic predecessors, Americans once again saw contact with nature "as a way to improve the spirit, to achieve a civilizing effect on human behavior, and to instill a sense of dignity" (Dunwell, 447). The quest to balance nature and human life, prevent loss of human energy, and conserve vitality in an industrialized, mechanized, and standardized society became "one of the central dilemmas

---

① In Weber's definition, instrumentally rational action or action based on instrumental rationality mainly involves deciding how to use the resources one has as instruments to fulfill his or her goals. Instrumental rationality is "determined by expectations as to the behavior of objects in the environment and of other human beings" and "these expectations are used as 'conditions' or 'means' for the attainment of the actor's own rationally pursued and calculated ends" (24).

facing consciously modern Americans" (Dunwell, 448) .

This section discusses Wharton's views on the negative impact of unbridled instrumental rationality upon nature and human emotion by comparing the disenchanted Midwestern prairies with the mysterious scenery of Paul's Landing. In addition, by analyzing Vance's engagement with the forest in the Hudson River Valley, this part delves into Wharton's idea that the power of nature and art can liberate humans from the constraints of instrumental reason and emotional distress.

4.2.1   Hudson Valley as the Iconography of American Nationhood

Since the mid-nineteenth century, the landscape of the Hudson River Valley has been viewed as a symbol of American nationhood due to its close association with the Hudson River School, the first national school of art in the United States. Based on the valley's cultural importance in America, Wharton imbues the fictional landscape in the two novels with aesthetic significance and a sense of the divine. By contrasting the sterile Midwestern prairies to the enchanted scenery of Paul's Landing, the writer underscores the cultural superiority of the East when the influence of the American West grew across the country in the early twentieth century. Moreover, she criticizes Midwesterners' instrumental view of nature which results in their spiritual crisis.

At the turn of the twentieth century, the Midwest① were increasingly

---

① Today, the Midwest consists of twelve states between the Northeastern and the Western United States: Illinois, Indiana, Iowa, Kansas, Michigan, Minnesota, Missouri, Nebraska, North Dakota, Ohio, South Dakota, and Wisconsin. However, since her life in the United States revolved around New York, Wharton often called the areas west of New York State collectively as the West. In *Hudson River Bracketed* and *The Gods Arrive*, she used both the Midwest and the West to refer to Vance's hometown in Illinois.

equated with the "real" America. In order to weaken the cultural dominance of the Eastern United States, historian Frederick Jackson Turner and his disciples meticulously documented the development of the West and the Midwest and brought to life an impressive corpus of regional history. According to Joanne Jacobson, in American literature and art from the end of the nineteenth century through the decade following World War II, the Midwest served as " a sustaining symbol of national strength ": "Traditionally associated with the frontier values of movement and promise and with the rural values of fertility, order and stability, the Midwest has been invested in unique ways with the symbolic freight of national consensus, of the quintessentially 'American'" (236, 243).

In addition to serving as a symbol of frontier spirit, the Midwest witnessed a great evolution of capitalist expansion. During the late nineteenth and early twentieth centuries, Chicago and other Midwestern cities dominated the United States' economy through industrial production and agricultural commodities. "One of the greatest monuments to capitalism the world has ever seen", the Midwest produced a wealth of tycoons such as Henry Ford whose beliefs of wealth accumulation, practicality and efficiency became increasingly important to the rest of the country. Ford, for instance, called the Midwest "the world of business" and praised the Midwesterners' "relentless entrepreneurial drive" (qtd. in Barillas, *The Midwestern Pastoral*, 158).

Proponents of the West claimed that what Westerners contributed to the American economy compensated for their lack of intellectual nuances and artistic sensibilities compared to the people in the Eastern states. The rise of the West led to questions about American identity: whether "civilization and sophistication encapsulated in the eastern seaboard" or " the innovative frontier" was more American? "Which, indeed, was the 'real' America" (Olin-Ammentorp, 153)? The question concerned Wharton, as well. In her autobiography *A Backward Glance*, the writer highlighted the West's growing influence upon the East at the turn of the century: "big money-makers from the West, soon to be followed by the lords of Pittsburgh [...] greatly affect old manners and customs" (23). Many Americans thought that energetic West would replace the overcivilized and effete East as the embodiment of American progress: "Westerners had promoted equality... and reacted as a check to the aristocratic influences of the East" (qtd. in Barillas, *The Midwestern Pastoral*, 158). The experience of Vance, who is from the Midwest and called as "the cousin from the West" by his relatives in the Hudson River Valley, symbolizes the encounter of the West and the East in the two novels (*HRB*, 67).

While delineating Vance's hometown in Illinois, Wharton highlights its natural landscape, especially the prairies, saying that the protagonist comes from "the prairies of the Middle West" (*GA*, 12). In "Middle Western Pioneer Democracy" (1920), Turner regarded the Midwest and Midwestern prairies as symbols of American nationhood, due to their association with the frontier, pioneers, and westward settlement. He proposed that the massive expanses of flat or rolling grasslands cultivated the distinctive American characteristics:

> That coarseness and strength combined with acuteness and inquisitiveness; that practical, inventive turn of mind, quick to find expedients; that masterful grasp of material things, lacking in the artistic but powerful to effect great ends; that dominant individualism, working for good and for evil, and withal that buoyancy and exuberance which comes with freedom. (398)

Historian Lewis Atherton summarizes the most representative value in the Midwest during the early decades of the twentieth century as a "cult of the immediately useful and the practical [...] that originated with the exigencies of frontier survival and matured in the market oriented society of small towns " (qtd. in Barillas, " Aldo Leopold and Midwestern Pastoralism", 62-63). Implicit in Midwestern " cult of the immediately useful and the practical" was a proprietary view of nature which justified the exploitation of nature for material gain. Wharton's depiction of the Midwestern landscape in Vance's hometown reveals her criticism of Americans' instrumental control over nature.

In the novels, the most striking feature of the Midwestern landscape is its sterility. The landscape has nothing grand to show: the prairies are sparse, the river in marshy fields is polluted by real estate projects, and the flowers such as the lilacs and roses are " straggling " and " neglected " (*HRB*, 11). The barren landscape is the product of Midwesterners' lack of appreciation for natural beauty: people in Euphoria see the land merely as capital. The most representative example is Vance's father who regards the land as lucrative resource for real estate. His dream is to turn every acre of vacant land into a profitable suburb, even at the cost of destroying prairies and polluting rivers. In short, landscape is stripped of aesthetic and moral value in the eyes of Midwesterners, only possessing pecuniary significance. The landscape epitomizes a disenchanted world where people no longer find nature mysterious, sacred, or worthy of reverence. As Max Weber points out, instrumental rationality is the major cause of the disenchantment of nature as it " encourages disrespectful and narrowly instrumental attitudes to nature" (qtd. in Stone, 231). Since the frontier provided the American economy and society with seemingly inexhaustible resources, the instrumental view of nature which believed that " nature should be used to raise individual and collective standards of living" guided the Westerners' and even Americans' attitudes toward the environment in the nineteenth and early decades of the twentieth century (Culhane, 2-3). Americans saw the world as a collection of entities that could be manipulated. Nature was thus reduced to the object of consumption—standing in wait for humans to utilize and dominate; in other words, a tool and means for human beings to achieve their own goals.

Karl Marx points out that the idea of mastery over nature essentially stems from "the expansionist logic of a capitalist system that makes the accumulation of wealth in the form of capital the supreme end of society" (Foster, 9). The capitalist system leads humans to regard natural resources as unpaid productive forces of capital, causing them to overlook the fact that humans are only part of nature and to neglect the interdependent relationship between humans and nature. In other words, human beings are alienated from nature. According to Marx, human alienation from nature means that "We are natural beings, dependent on natural forces for our existence, yet we treat nature as if it were something distinct from us and as something we could (and should) master" (Vogel, 187). Understood in this way, the sterile landscape in Vance's hometown reflects Midwesterners' alienation from their natural environment.

More importantly, Wharton draws readers' attention to the association between the landscape and American national identity by depicting the Fourth of July celebrations in the prairies where Midwesterners commemorate "the priceless qualities the pioneers had brought with them into the wilderness". By pointing out that "To Vance it sometimes seemed that they had left the rarest of all behind", the author clearly questions the national characteristics represented by the Midwestern landscape and the pioneers (*HRB*, 338). She takes the view that the individualism and diligence of the pioneers have turned into unrestrained instrumental rationality which alienates Midwesterners from nature. As Jayne E. Waterman points out, Wharton comments on more than the Midwest: "Wharton explored what she saw as the standardization, vulgarity [...] that had consumed America and used the Midwest as her template to portray these concerns" (79). In other words, the Midwest allows the author to express her concerns about twentieth-century America. For Wharton, human alienation from nature not only floods the Midwest but spreads across the whole nation, while the hope of redemption lies in the East, embodied by the enchanted landscape of the Hudson River Valley in the novels.

Wharton's depiction of the Hudson Valley landscape in the novels is characterized by the association of the scenery with nineteenth-century American Romantic poets and the Hudson River School painters. For instance, when Vance stands on the hill and appreciates the sunset in the valley on a June evening, "twilight floats aloft in an air too pure to be penetrated by the density of darkness" and "the precipitate plunge of many-tinted forest, the great sweep of the Hudson, and the cliffs on its other shore" lay before him (*HRB*, 77). The local inhabitants tell him that not only the famous poet William Cullen Bryant but also the Hudson River School artists have visited Paul's Landing to see the scenery. As the first native school of painting in the United States, the Hudson River School was used to identify a group of New York City-based landscape painters who came to fame in the mid-nineteenth century by drawing the landscape of the Hudson River Valley. The school's style was strongly nationalistic in its proud celebration of the natural beauty of the United States. American landscape artists that followed Thomas Cole—the founding father of the school—attempted to express American identity " as a culture rooted in nature, drawing its virtue from the soil of the continent itself" (Miller, 22). As Stephen Daniels notes, landscape "gave shape to the ' imagined community'" of the United States (5). The Hudson River Valley landscape served as one of the most important iconographic hallmarks of American identity which cultivated a sense of national belonging and strengthened national cohesion. Since the 1820s, admiring the river and its scenery had been almost a national duty for Americans. Tourists left New York on the steamboats which were emblazoned with patriotic motifs and sailed 150 miles along wide tidal waters to Albany. The impenetrable forests, steep mountains, and pastoral riverscapes impressed numerous nineteenth-century artists such as Cole:

> The Hudson for natural magnificence is unsurpassed. What can be more beautiful than the lake-like expanses of Tapaan and Haverstraw, as seen from the rich orchards of the surrounding hills? What can be more imposing than the precipitous Highlands; whose dark foundations have been rent to make a passage for the deep-flowing river? And, ascending still, where can be found scenes more enchanting?" (5)

As the patrons and promoters of the landscape paintings, the Northeastern elites attempted to make the Hudson River Valley landscape a national icon and secure the Northeast's cultural dominance during the years between 1820 and 1870. Scholars have long associated the Hudson River School's paintings with American identity, but what is worth noting is that this national identity was defined by the Northeasterners. As Tricia Cusack comments on the rise of the school, "conscious efforts were made by a group of Northeastern artists and their influential patrons to consolidate and to represent an American national identity through shaping an image of the homeland" (20). The significance attributed to the valley and its artistic representations, and its role in the construction of national identity, depended heavily on the hegemonic economic and cultural status of the Northeastern elites. The status of the Hudson River School as a national school was mainly owing to the powerful New York patrons among "rich Federalist families, landowners, merchants, and lawyer-politicians [...], a kind of American squirearchy" (Cusack, 24) through "institutions of cultural production—publishing and book distribution, exhibition, criticism, and other forms of promotion" (Miller, 209). Facing the internal antagonisms between North and South during the antebellum years, Northeasterners "actively shaped the definition of nationalism" by offering "the promise of a complete and unitary landscape" and "policing national life through aesthetic norms and conventions of propriety" (Miller, 210). In short, Northeasterners enjoyed the power of defining a national landscape and artistic form of national culture.

The reason why Wharton describes the Hudson River Valley landscape in the novels set in the 1920s and 1930s with references to Romantic poets and the Hudson River School painters who were popular in the middle nineteenth century is worthy of our attention. For Northeastern writers such as Wharton and Henry James, the landscape of the valley signifies the cultural superiority of the East: "returning in the spring-time from a few weeks in the Far West, I re-entered New York State with the absurdest sense of meeting again a ripe old civilization. [The valley and river] took their place in the geography of the ideal, in the long perspective of the poetry of association" (James, *The American Scene*, 146-147). James further states that "the wonder of Rip Van Winkle" and "the Hudson River School of landscape art" enhanced the glamour of the valley (154). Like him, Wharton, through describing the landscape and emphasizing its connection to the first national school of painting, reveals her intention to highlight the importance of the Northeast as the center of art and culture in the United States at a time when the region's influence was challenged by the West.

Another characteristic of the Hudson River School is that the artists depicted the landscape of the valley as imbued with a sense of the divine which was morally uplifting for Americans. Inspired by American Transcendentalism of Emerson, Cole and the other Hudson River artists believed that " God or a divine presence deeply resided in nature" and landscape was "the work of God in the visible creation" (Guardiano, 100, 101). In their eyes, the valley was "a spiritual entity of rich beauty" filled with silent divinity. Their works endowed the Hudson Valley landscape with national celebrity for "its inherent beauty" and "aesthetic uniqueness", thereby "effectively shining a sublime light upon" the landscape (Guardiano, 27). The mountains were equated with things from another world, leaves and branches were pages written by Creation, and light in the woods God's radiance. Echoing the artists' transcendental reverence for nature, in the novels Vance feels an inner sense of divinity in the landscape of Paul's Landing: "What I want is to find out how to release that god, fly him up like a kite into the Infinite, way beyond creeds and formulas, and try to relate him to all the other ... the other currents ... that seem to be circling round you [...] and carried beyond Time and Space" (*HRB*, 18). By associating Paul's Landing with the sacred landscape in the Hudson River School paintings, Wharton emphasizes the landscape's religious and aesthetic significance, which is in sharp contrast to the disenchanted Midwestern prairies.

In addition, the painters used the landscape of the Hudson River Valley to critique the instrumental treatment of nature in American society. The landscape artists often associated the forests with personal potency and trees with artistic fecundity in their writings about the valley. For instance, while denouncing the deforestation of the Catskill Mountains West of the Hudson River for settlement, Cole wrote that the destruction of nature resulted in spiritual sterility among Americans: "the wasted places resulted from the quest for gain would produce the barrenness of mind, sterile desolation of the soul, in which sensibility to the beauty of nature cannot take root" (qtd. in Miller, 61). In a similar manner, Wharton links the disenchanted landscape in Vance's hometown to Midwesterners' spiritual crisis which is demonstrated by the protagonist's neurasthenia. More significantly, she finds

216

in the Hudson River Valley landscape a redemptive potential of counteracting the negative impacts brought about by the alienated relation between humanity and nature.

4.2.2 Hudson Forest as a Remedy for Human-Nature Alienation

By linking Vance's neurasthenia to the disenchanted Midwestern landscape, Wharton notes that Midwesterners' perception of nature as a means for capitalistic gain is indicative of a social phenomenon in which excessive development of instrumental rationality prevails, leading to Americans' spiritual crisis. In stark contrast to the Midwest, the enchanted forest of the Hudson River Valley, a combination of natural beauty and artistic beauty, awakens Vance's long-repressed passion and serves as a remedy for human-nature alienation.

After recovering from a serious illness, Vance comes to Paul's Landing for recuperation. He falls ill with a high fever from drinking polluted river water in Euphoria, Illinois, combined with the emotional shock of seeing his girlfriend's affair with his own grandfather. His sickness is also the result of long-term neurasthenia. After graduating from college, the young man often feels listless and bored for no reason in his Midwestern hometown, has no interest in doing anything, and "ha[s] an unutterable weariness" (*HRB*, 27). He experiences emotional distress and profound exhaustion, which leads to a failed suicide attempt.

> The oppression was intolerable. He was like a captive walled into a dark airless cell, and the walls of that cell were Reality. The impulse to end it all here and now possessed him. He had tried out the whole business and found it wanting; been the round of it, and come back

217

gorged with disgust. The negativeness of death would be better, a million times better. (*HRB*, 30)

While he is the most extreme example, Vance is not the only Midwesterner who is suffering from a spiritual crisis. His aunt and grandmother, for instance, turn to religion for psychic harmony. Their depression was representative of the mental state of Americans in the early twentieth century. Neurasthenia was not only a psychological disease, but also a social phenomenon. American society at that time, according to Lears, displayed a waning of human energy and "a lowering of the mental nerve" when Americans felt that "the old springs of simple sentiment are dying fast within us. It is heartless to laugh, it is foolish to cry, it is indiscreet to love, it is morbid to hate, and it is intolerant to espouse any cause with enthusiasm" (47, 48). The New York neurologist George Miller Beard popularized the term "neurasthenia" in *American Nervousness* (1881), which referred to a disease of the nervous system due to lack of nerve force. The disease manifested as symptoms including headaches, fatigue, deficient mental control, a feeling of hopelessness, and pathological fear, etc. Beard claimed that neurasthenia was, above all, a consequence of social transformations, characterized by "steam-power, the periodical press, the telegraph, the sciences" (Campbell, 162). Corresponding to the view of thinkers such as William James that modern man's alienation from nature impaired his vitality, physicians believed that modern life drained an individual's reserves of emotional energy: in turn-of-the-century medical theory, neurasthenia was "construed as both an individual and a broader cultural reaction to various features of modernity, including urbanization, industrialization, and bureaucratization; the faster, technologically enhanced pace of modern life [...] and the psychological repercussions of capitalist competition" (Schaffner, 9). The emergence of neurasthenia hence gave rise to Americans' new interests in "nature's therapeutic properties as a source of energy for depleted nerves [...] and the revitalization of humans" (Jean Mitchell, 113).

Mental crisis was not a phenomenon unique to Americans. In *Modern Painters* (1856), John Ruskin pointed out the prevalent fatigue and depression among the Englishmen when England was undergoing rapid industrialization and urbanization: "On the whole, these are much *sadder* ages than the early ones; not sadder in a noble and deep way, but in a dim, wearied way, —the way of ennui, and jaded intellect, and uncomfortableness of soul and body" (252, original emphasis). Ruskin attributes the root of Englishmen's emotional distress to their alienation from nature when they increasingly saw nature as mere material for practical manipulation. In a similar manner, by describing the disenchanted Midwestern landscape, Wharton points out that Midwesterners' instrumental treatment of nature manifests the disenchantment of the world, which drains the wellspring of human vitality, depletes their emotional energy, and leads to neurasthenia. In her view, the aesthetic experience of natural beauty can help modern people get rid of depression and regain the intimacy between self and the world in a more and more alien society.

On his first day in Paul's Landing, Vance notices that the forest is different from the Midwest: "trees everywhere, trees taller, fuller and more heavy-branched, he thought, than those of his native prairies. Up the hillside they domed themselves in great bluish masses, one against the other, like the roofs of some mysterious city built of leaves" (*HRB*, 46). The trees inspire him to write a poem about a mysterious city built of leaves which is "arcane, aloof, and secret as the soul". While looking at the trees and smelling the scent of lilacs, Vance is awakened from emotional distress and feels that his own soul is "a stranger speaking a language he had never learned, or had forgotten":

In a clump of trees near the road a bird began over and over its low tentative song, and in the ditches a glossy-leaved weed, nameless to Vance, spangled the mud with golden chalices. He felt a passionate desire to embrace the budding earth and everything that stirred and swelled in it. (*HRB*, 47)

Vance's "passionate desire to embrace the budding earth" indicates that the trees activate his passion, make him gain a sensitive perception of the world, and thus help him get rid of depression. Stilgoe notes that the value of trees was heightened immeasurably at the turn of the century when Americans were confronted by varieties of nervousness associated with industrialism and technological advance: they believed that trees "had a message half divine" and "injected spirituality into everyday life and so strengthened the soul" (189-190). Wharton's depiction of the trees in the Hudson Valley not only echoes the contemporary belief in therapeutic landscape, but also associates the therapeutic power with the Northeast.

The relationship between nature and human soul demonstrates the influence of Romanticism upon Wharton. Though she was regarded as one of the most important American realist writers in the nineteenth century, Wharton was deeply immersed in Romantic literature and influenced by Romantic writers on both sides of the Atlantic. For instance, both Johann Wolfgang von Goethe and Ralph Waldo Emerson exerted great influences upon her writing career. In her unpublished memoir "Life and I", Wharton wrote that "I plunged with rapture into the great ocean of Goethe. At fifteen I had read every word of his plays and poems" (quoted in Waid, 226). Her interest in Goethe was lifelong and she used a quotation from his *Wilhelm Meister* as an epigram at the very beginning of her autobiography *A Backward Glance*. Moreover, in *Hudson River Bracketed* and *The Gods Arrive* Vance frequently quoted from Goethe. One of the most important and influential figures of European Romanticism, Goethe criticized the mechanistic and atomistic models of the universe proposed by Newtonian physics and Cartesian rationalism. Instead, he celebrated a pantheistic nature which was "the expression of God's divine immanence" (Nicholls, 37). In his view, as a recipient and translator of God's message, man knew and reinvented himself in the process of understanding nature. In terms of Emerson, Wharton began reading his works at a young age as well. She even took the title of *The Gods Arrive* from the last line of Emerson's poem "Give All to Love". According to Emerson, "Nature is the symbol of spirit" and man, nature, and the soul were all in one (14). He believed that by enjoying landscape human beings could commune with God, understand themselves, and realize the importance of wisdom, love, and beauty, thereby cultivating spiritual strength to resist the materialism of the American society. Akin to her Romantic predecessors, Wharton connects the human spirit to the sacredness of landscape and reenchants nature in her delineation of the mysterious trees in the Hudson River Valley.

Apart from advocating humans' spiritual connection with God in nature, Wharton emphasizes nature's aesthetic value as a revitalizing antidote. The forest inspires Vance's artistic creation, and his widely circulated poem in New York's literary circles endows these trees with artistic value, thus making the landscape of the Hudson Valley a combination of natural beauty and artistic beauty. In his discussion about natural beauty and aesthetic redemption, Theodor W. Adorno argues that in the modern society where instrumental rationality is rampant, natural beauty is often suppressed and thus cannot be truly appreciated. It is in this sense that Adorno believes that the beauty of nature should be experienced via art, so that natural beauty can play an effective role in liberating humans from the rule of instrumental reason (Stone, 244). In Vance's hometown, shaped by the expansionist logic of a capitalist system, Midwesterners' instrumental view of nature reduces nature to the object for material exploitation and prevents people from appreciating natural beauty. For example, Vance only cares about the uses of plants and tries to name the animals he sees. He even feels irritated when he does not know the names of some birds and flowers: "I should like to give everything its right name, and to know why that name was the right one" (*HRB*, 12). In other words, he used to see nature as something secondary and subordinate to human beings, something to be dominated by human will.

According to Adorno, the aesthetic impulse inspired by natural beauty can neutralize the influence of instrumental rationality. Vance's perception of the trees in Paul's Landing echoes Adorno's explanation of the interaction between nature and human beings: nature attracts humans through its aura, that is, the temperament emanating from the uniqueness of nature—what Adorno calls the "non-identical" (73). The aura of nature enables human beings to temporarily abandon conceptual thinking and get rid of the domination of instrumental rationality in modern society, thereby restoring human freedom and dignity, and redeeming human beings from spiritual numbness. On the one hand, the arcane, aloof, and secret trees echo the "essential indeterminateness" of natural beauty which cannot be fully understood by humans (Adorno, 70). On the other hand, Vance's poem captures "the being-in-itself of nature" (Adorno, 77). The combination of natural and artistic beauty in the Hudson River Valley thus liberates the hero's passion and creativity suppressed by instrumental rationality. Vance's "exaltation" and "his imagination [...] drenched with the wonder of the adventure" display that the power of nature and art in aesthetic redemption allows him to break free from the grip of instrumental reason and restore his emotional energy (*HRB*, 105). "A reconciliation of culture and nature would, in this view, redeem human beings from the grip of rational domination" (Siddall, 12).

222

Adorno's explanation about the aura of nature is clearly influenced by Walter Benjamin's concept of aura. Benjamin's key example of aura is drawn from natural landscape:

> The concept of aura which was proposed [...] with reference to historical objects may usefully be illustrated with reference to the aura of natural ones. We define the aura [...] as the unique phenomenon of a distance, however close it may be. If, while resting on a summer afternoon, you follow with your eyes a mountain range on the horizon or a branch which casts its shadow over you, you experience the aura of those mountains, of that branch. (qtd. in Siddall, 13)

Benjamin later extended the definition of aura to the field of poetic creation in "On Some Motifs of Baudelaire" (1939), pointing out that a poet can activate the gaze of man, animals, or natural objects and give them the ability to return the viewer's gaze from a distance. According to David Roberts, aura of natural landscape is produced by human beings' "aesthetic response to [...] natural beauty" which rests on "a reciprocity between man and nature" (131). In this sense, both the Hudson Valley landscape and Vance's poem about the forest have their own aura. Jillian M. Rickly-Boyd further argues that aura emerges in an intersubjective relationship between the viewer and landscape when landscape "disrupts established routines, habits and conventions and bring about renewed emotional experiences" (280). Instead of concentrating on the utility of nature, Vance is stimulated and aroused by the aura of the landscape into "a state of heightened receptivity" and feels that there is "something deeper, something which must have belonged to flowers and clouds before ever man was born to dissect them" (*HRB*, 13). The landscape of Paul's Landing hence disrupts Vance's instrumental way of seeing the world learnt in his Midwestern

223

hometown and evokes his long-forgotten passion, thereby helping him regain his emotional energy which has been drained by modern life.

Wharton further emphasizes the fusion of natural beauty and artistic beauty in the Hudson River Valley landscape by connecting it to Xanadu in Samuel Taylor Coleridge's poem *Kubla Khan*. Several weeks after his arrival to Paul's Landing, Halo Spear, who is the heiress of an old Dutch family in the county and who becomes Vance's lover at the end of *Hudson River Bracketed*, takes Vance to a mountain ridge called Thundertop for viewing the sunrise over the Hudson River. The enchanted river, forests, hills, and caves remind Halo and Vance of the magical world of Xanadu in the poem they read together:

> Again they turned westward, looking toward the Hudson, and now the tawny suffusion was drawing down the slopes of the farther shore, till gradually, very gradually, the river hollows also were washed of their mists, and the great expanse of the river shone bright as steel in the clear shadow. Vance drew a deep breath. His lips were parted, but no word came. He met Miss Spear's smiling eyes with a vague stare. "Kubla Khan?" she said. He nodded. (*HRB*, 99)

In her close reading of correspondences between the poem and *Hudson River Bracketed*, Saunders discovers plentiful details about the parallels between the vibrant landscape of the Hudson River Valley and the scenery of Xanadu which include rivers, hills, trees, houses etc. (198-199). While the landscape of the valley transfers Vance to the magical world of poetic creation and activates his artistic energy, the changefulness and transience of nature is made permanent through art, as happens in both Coleridge's "Kubla Khan" about Xanadu and Vance's poem about the valley. Through "borrow[ing] magically transformative properties [...] from Coleridge in particular—and from the world of poetry in the largest sense", Wharton represents the Hudson River Valley as a site that combines natural beauty and artistic beauty (Saunders, 187). A key figure in English Romanticism and a mentor of Emersonian transcendentalism, Coleridge believed in the power of nature and art in aesthetic redemption. In his view, man, nature, and God were integrated in art, and art pointed towards a reconciliation between man and nature. In his essay "On Poesy or Art" (1818), Coleridge emphasized "a bond between nature in the higher sense and the soul of man" (332). In the preface to "Kubla Khan", he complained about the conflict between creativity and business, and described Xanadu's redemptive function for his artistic visions. Later when Vance moves from Paul's Landing to live in New York City, he gains courage and power to resist materialistic culture in American society every time when he thinks about the enchanted Hudson River Valley landscape. As Qiao Xiufeng argues, "the memories formed by experiencing landscape can bring human mind to a state of tranquility yet full of vitality" (194). Vance's interaction with the forest displays Wharton's hope that with the combined power of nature and art, Americans can be liberated from the grip of instrumental rationality.

To sum up, when the West is increasingly regarded as the representative of American national character, Wharton points out that the pioneers' individualism and diligence have turned into unrestrained instrumental rationality through depicting the sterile Midwestern landscape in Vance's hometown. In contrast, the writer associates the Hudson River Valley landscape with the first national school of art in the United States and highlights the importance of the East in defining American identity. The description of landscape in the two novels indicates that for Wharton, the regional differences between the East and the West represent the more intangible conflicts between art and business, between culture and money. The author believes in the significant position of the East as the center of art and culture in America.

By contrasting the disenchanted Midwestern landscape with the vibrant Hudson River Valley scenery, Wharton criticizes Midwesterners' instrumental view of nature, a view of nature stemming from capitalism's expansionist logic. Midwesterners' alienation from nature drains their nerve energy, hence results in emotional distress, with Vance's neurasthenia being a representative example. As a combination of natural beauty and artistic beauty, the lush and mysterious forest of the Hudson River Valley cultivates an intersubjective relationship between Vance and nature, inspires his artistic creativity, and works as an antidote to human alienation from nature, thereby redeeming him from emotional distress. As evidenced by the delineation of landscape in Paul's Landing, Wharton suggests that the combined forces of nature and art possess the potential for aesthetic redemption, which can serve as a means of resistance against the pervasive influence of unbridled instrumental rationality.

It is worth noting that Wharton expects a productive balance between the East and West rather than ignoring the West altogether. Vance's rebirth in the Hudson River Valley landscape, his potential as a great American writer, and romantic relationship with Halo, the heiress of the most respectable Hudson Valley family, all suggest that Wharton's idealized vision of America is the one which unites Western energy with Eastern refinement. As Olin-Ammentorp shrewdly observes, Advance Weston, Vance' full name, is in fact symbolic: "any advance must come from the West" (184). Yet in order to offer a complete solution to the problem of balancing culture and energy, Wharton looks further to the cross-fertilization of American and European cultures.

4.3 Cross-Fertilization of American and European Cultures in Hudson Valley Mansion

At the turn of the twentieth century, Americans became increasingly aware of the growing interconnectedness of the world. Remarkable events such as the global expansion of American businesses, revolutions in technologies of transportation and communication, rise of transnational tourism industry, implementation of world time, arrival of global competitions including the modern Olympic Games and the Nobel Prizes, and First World War shaped all domains of Americans' lives as well as their understanding of their relationships with other countries. As many theorists have pointed out, "globalization is not exclusively a phenomenon of the post-World War II period" since many similar developments have taken place from the late nineteenth century to the Great Depression (Marsh, 333). For instance, Jeffrey G. Williamson states that before the Depression forced the nations of the world to retreat into isolationism and autarky, "between 1870 and 1930 […] there was rapid globalization—cross-national flows of capital, commodities, and migrants—which led to impressive convergence among the Atlantic nations of Europe and the United States" (qtd. in Marsh, 335). In 1927, Wharton has already noticed that while Americans' contacts with foreign countries in earlier years were "brief and superficial" at best, by the early twentieth century, "innumerable links of business, pleasure, study, and sport join together the various races of the world" (*The Uncollected Critical Writings*, 157).

On the one hand, growing ties around the world prompted Americans to reconsider their concept of national identity. Thinking "beyond the territorially bounded nation-state", many American politicians, writers, and public intellectuals proposed that their own national identity should be viewed in relation to other nations (Croucher, 171). For example, on April 20, 1915, before the United States entered the war, President Woodrow Wilson said in a speech:

> We are compounded of the nations of the world; we mediate their blood, we mediate their traditions, we mediate their sentiments, their tastes, their passions; we are ourselves compounded of those things [...]. We are, therefore, able to understand all nations; It is in that sense that I mean that America is a mediating Nation. (qtd. in Cadle, 25)

Clearly, Wilson called on his audience to rethink American identity in the face of a nascent "globalized America" (qtd. in Cadle, 26). According to Meredith L. Goldsmith and Emily J. Orlando, shaped by her experiences as an internationally renowned writer who crossed the Atlantic sixty-six times in her life, Wharton's attitude towards American identity was characterized by "[a] heightened self-awareness gained through contact with other cultures" which is "not inherently in conflict with a strong sense of national identity" (4).

On the other hand, as the United States rose to global prominence through overseas imperial and economic expansion, as well as increased engagement in international diplomacy, a significant number of Americans began to equate globalization with Americanization and tended to disparage the cultural traditions of other nations, particularly those of Europe. In the 1920s, a prevailing viewpoint emerged in America that the twentieth century represented a rejection of the nineteenth century and the Old World (Glennon, 56). Wharton perceived intellectual parochialism and repudiation of history as serious problems in American society during the 1920s and

1930s.

Through analyzing the temporality of the Hudson Valley landscape, this section explores Wharton's perspective on the dialectic relationship between the past and the present. In addition, this part delves into Wharton's expectation about the cross-fertilization of European heritage and American innovation by examining Vance's view of the mansion in the Hudson River Valley which fuses European heritage with the vitality of America.

4.3.1 Hudson Valley as a Birthplace of American Literature and Art

Because of its multiethnic and multicultural history, the Hudson River Valley was characterized by linguistic diversity and heterogeneous architectural styles. Long regarded as a birthplace of American literature and art which nurtured the United States' first writers, painters, and architects, the valley not only inspired these celebrities' artistic creation, but also provided them with a stage for integrating European cultures into American landscape. Their works about the valley and their houses in the region exemplified the cross-fertilization of European heritage and American innovation.

Since the first Europeans led by British explorer Henry Hudson sailed into the region in 1609, the Hudson River Valley had become America's first "melting pot". Unlike the other areas of North America settled in the seventeenth century, the valley was occupied by many different national groups. While New England and Virginia witnessed the transplanting of English villagers, often from the very same villages and towns in England, to the New World, the Hudson River Valley was settled by several distinct ethnic and cultural groups (Wermuth & Johnson, 1). The valley's early inhabitants consisted of the Dutch, Germans, French Huguenots, Danes,

Swedes, Belgians, Norwegians, and a significant number of African slaves. As the region passed under English control, Scottish, English, and Irish settlers also moved to the valley.

The cultural and ethnic diversity resulted in the use of multiple languages and heterogeneous architectural styles in the Hudson Valley. In 1926, a French missionary travelling in the valley reported that he had heard more than ten languages spoken by the locals. According to William P. McDermott, there was an impressive phenomenon in Duchess County that four languages—English, Dutch, French, and German—were actively used during the early twentieth century (5). In *Hudson River Bracketed* and *The Gods Arrive*, Vance's cousin Laura Lou speaks English and French. Vance's well-educated lover Halo speaks fluent French and German while talking about European literature and art with New York intellectuals.

In addition to linguistic diversity, the landscape of the Hudson River Valley typified heterogeneous architectural styles. The valley featured distinctive Dutch houses which were "the only examples of Dutch architecture in North America" (McDermott, 7). The pitched roofs with gable ends and prominent roof beams displayed the marks the Dutch culture left on the region. While the Dutch built "low, one or one-and-a-half story symmetrical buildings of stone", the English settlers preferred wooden architecture which typified "such Georgian features as symmetry, well-proportioned arched windows and a prominent centralized bell tower" (Ghee, 14, 31). Besides, the French Huguenots who emigrated to the banks of the Hudson favored stone houses that "combined Northern European and medieval building traditions with those of their Dutch neighbors": the architecture was "of local stone, with steeply pitched shingled roofs and Dutch jambless fireplaces" (Ghee, 27). In Wharton's two novels about the valley, the houses in Paul's Landing preserve Dutch features such as "gambrel roofs, overhanging eaves, and compact layout designs" (Ghee, 26). For example, the Lorburns, the most distinguished family in the area, live in a "low-studded old house of gray stone" built by their Dutch ancestors in 1680 (*HRB*, 72).

As Tom Lewis summarizes, the Hudson River Valley gave birth to "the first American literature that gained the attention of readers in Europe (Washington Irving), the first indigenous school of art (the Hudson River School), and one of the first outlines of architectural precepts that sought to shape American taste (Andrew Jackson Downing)" (195). Scholars always name the valley as a birthplace of American literature, art, and architecture, but it is worth noting that Irving, Thomas Cole, and Downing all benefited from European legacy and succeeded in integrating European cultures into American landscape.

The impact of the Hudson River Valley on Washington Irving's aesthetic sensibilities started in the year of 1800 when he took his first trip up the river. He described the spell of the landscape as having "the most witching effect upon his boyish imagination":

> Never shall I forget the effect upon me of the first view of them predominating over a wide extent of the country, part wild, woody, and rugged; part softened away into all the graces of cultivation. As we slowly floated along, I lay on the deck and watched them through a long summer's day; undergoing a thousand mutations under the magical effects of atmosphere". (qtd. in Tom Lewis, *The Hudson*, 196)

Irving's first major literary success, Knickerbocker's *History of New York* (1809), and his two most famous stories, "The Legend of Sleepy Hollow" and "Rip Van Winkle", were all inspired by the quaint Dutch houses, old churches and burial ground, and local Dutch history in the Hudson Valley. Based on the characteristics of the valley, he adapted Dutch and German folklore, such as legends of water, earth, fire spirits, demons, and ghosts, and endowed the landscape with mystery and romance. An enthusiast of Dutch culture, he portrayed Dutch customs in architecture, attire, culinary practices, courtship, smoking, and drinking—exploring topics such as demonism, witchcraft, songs, ghost lore, and tall tales. The first writer to give the valley a new kind of meaning, he combined the magnificent landscape with imaginative Dutch legends about goblins and ghosts and humorous tales about local Dutch life, thereby inventing a literary version of the Hudson River Valley which left a deep impression on American memory. As Frances F. Dunwell states, Irving's writing of the landscape "helped imprint a new image of the valley as a place haunted by the spirits of the Dutch past, but also alive with the promise of a new country" (91).

Irving found artistic inspiration not only in Dutch culture but also in British culture. Judith Richardson argues that Irving's sojourn in Europe between 1815 and 1832 had a formative influence on his writing career: "It was in England that Irving discovered how to synthesize his Hudson Valley experiences and his literary and philosophical sensibilities in such a way that they not only achieved for him international acclaim but would define the Hudson Valley for centuries to come" (48). During his seventeen years in Europe, Irving's immersion in European Romanticism, his contacts with distinguished British writers such as Walter Scott and Coleridge, exposure to usable models in European writings, and "nostalgia-conducive distance from his domestic scene" were all beneficial to his writing about the Hudson River Valley (Richardson, 49).

After having returned to the United Stated from Europe, Irving purchased a country house on the eastern shore of the Hudson near Tarrytown and named it Sunnyside. The renovation of the house reflected Irving's interest in European cultures and his efforts to adapt European architectural styles to American landscape. In order to highlight Dutch heritage in Hudson Valley history and culture, he gathered several Dutch-style weather vanes from demolished houses in New York and Albany and incorporated them into the roof of Sunnyside. He even invented a tradition for his weather vanes, claiming in *The Knickerbocker* that one had "battled with the wind on the top of the Stad-House of New Amsterdam, in the time of Peter Stuyvesant". Irving thus "positioned his house as a repository for the colonial Dutch history and as a monument to the entirety of the Hudson River Valley's cultural heritage" (Faherty, 103).

Unsatisfied with the original building, Irving remodeled the farmhouse and reshaped the grounds and foliage. He added stepped gables at each end to imitate the Dutch dwellings in New York City, and chimneys to give the house an English-rustic-style exterior. The idea for "a stepped gable portico at Sunnyside's entrance, the steeply pitched roofs, and the distinctive chimney pots" were borrowed from Abbotsford, Walter Scott's estate on the River Tweed in Scotland. The ivy clippings in the garden were imported from Melrose Abbey, the first Cistercian monastery to be founded in Scotland, with the aim of organically linking the medieval past of Scotland to the Hudson Valley. As Historian Adam Sweeting notes, the ivy served as "a remarkable associational web involving Scottish history, Dutch legend" and "Irving created a useable literary and historical past that existed outside the commercial present" (qtd. in Carso, 35). Irving also learned from Spanish and Italian architecture, building "a small tower patterned on a monastery to the east side of his house and a delicately columned piazza on the west and north" (Tom Lewis, *The Hudson*, 201). By remodeling Sunnyside, Irving created a unique American version of European architectural ideas. Sunnyside stood out for its harmonious blend of European architectural styles and genteel traditions within the American landscape.

The progenitor of the Hudson River School, Thomas Cole found artistic inspiration in the Hudson River Valley as well. His professional career officially started with the unexpected success of the paintings he drew on a sketching trip up the valley in 1825. Since then, the landscape captured his imagination: "from the moment when his eye first caught the rural beauties clustering around the cliffs of Weehawken, and glanced up the distance of the Palisades, Cole's heart had been wandering in the highlands, and nestling in the bosom of the Catskills" (Dunwell, 79). According to art historian Elizabeth Jacks, Cole's major achievement was "to embrace and reimagine European, and specifically British, modes of landscape painting for the United States" (qtd. in Barringer et al., 1). Schooled in the European traditions of the picturesque and sublime, Cole deeply admired the landscape of the Hudson River Valley and encouraged Americans to view the landscape with a new aesthetic appreciation. His American landscape paintings were influenced by European artists such as Claude Lorrain, Salvator Rosa, J. M. W. Turner; theorists like William Gilpin, Richard Payne Knight, and Edmund Burke; and English Romantic poets Wordsworth and Coleridge (Barringer et al., 2).

More significantly, in addition to inheriting the European landscape aesthetics, Cole adjusted it according to the characteristics of American landscape and emphasized the wild charm of the Hudson Valley. Different from the softness and serenity of European classical landscape paintings, Cole's works departed from the pastoral mode usually adopted by European painters, no longer focusing on farms, fields, squires, and peasants, but paying more attention to the wilderness. His paintings about the Hudson Valley portrayed the mountains, lakes, and forests that had not been developed or transformed by human activities, or integrated limited man-made objects into the wild nature, thus emphasizing the wildness of American landscape and the power of nature, and reflecting the vitality of the young nation.

Akin to Irving's Sunnyside, Cole's home in the Hudson Valley demonstrated his efforts to apply European cultures to American landscape. Cedar Grove, as the artist called his homestead, was a Federal-style yellow brick house whose features were borrowed from Georgian architecture popular in the reigns of England's King George I, II, and III. He also designed the house to be "a sort of Italian looking thing", drawing on the visual language of Italianate villas that he learned from his extensive travels in Italy (Coleman, 27). Based on the work of English architect Sir Christopher Wren, Cole modified the Georgian-style exterior in order to make Cedar Grove match the undulating peaks, rushing waters, and dense forests of the Hudson Valley.

The third celebrity who brought national fame to the valley is landscape gardener and architect Andrew Jackson Downing. As a Hudson River Valley native, he made the aesthetic value of the Hudson River Valley an indelible part of American landscape by writing about this region's buildings and gardens. Downing's first book, *A Treatise on the Theory and Practice of Landscape Gardening*, *Adapted to North America* (1841), was the best-selling and most influential book about landscape and architectural design published in nineteenth-century America and continued to sell many copies in the twentieth century. The *Treatise* drew heavily on eighteenth-and early nineteenth-century English writings about landscape design, notably the works of designers Humphry Repton and John Claudius Loudon, but as its subtitle "Adapted to North America" suggested, Downing consciously attempted to "make Old World ideas about the proper design of gardens and homes appropriate to the climate and republican social structure of the New" (*Treatise*, 298). In architecture design, this usually meant smaller space than that of English dwellings due to the emergence of a large middle class and the transience of fortunes in America, and specific features of houses that catered to local geography such as porches, roof pitch, and types of materials used. Downing conducted extensive research on the estates and cottages of the Hudson Valley, contributing greatly to the development of landscape and architectural design in the United States. According to the topographic characteristics, hydrogeological conditions, and cultural customs of the Hudson Valley region, he proposed the beautiful and picturesque styles for designing American homes and gardens. Whereas the beautiful style emphasized "easy, flowing curves, soft surfaces [...] classical design", the picturesque highlights "bold projections, deep shadows, and irregular outlines" (Downing, *Treatise*, 74-75). The Willows in *Hudson River Bracketed* and *The Gods Arrive*—an old mansion in Paul's Landing—falls into the picturesque style in Downing's definition with its hilly site and irregular surface. Abandoning the formal, geometric, and highly stylized landscape design that was popular in America at the time, he advocated a fluid "natural" approach that emphasized the harmony of buildings with the surrounding landscape rather than distinguishing them from nature.

Furthermore, Downing learned from Englishmen's belief in the association between landscape aesthetics and the dwellers' morality. In the preface to The *Treatise*, he pointed out Americans' spirit of unrest: "tendency towards constant change, and the restless spirit of emigration, which form part of our national character" (viii). In his view, the example of the Hudson Valley cottages could serve as a counterbalance to Americans' propensity for change: the harmony of buildings and scenery displayed the importance of growing roots, which "leads man to assemble the comforts and elegancies of life around his habitation [...] to increase local attachments, and render domestic life more delightful; thus not only augmenting his own enjoyment, but strengthening his patriotism, and making him a better citizen" (*Treatise*, ix). The architect's guidelines about the natural and built environment were embraced by all segments of

American society. He brought an appreciation of landscape—once the privileges of artists and writers—into the domain of the average homeowner. By applying English landscape and architectural design to American landscape, he made the Hudson River Valley the site of an idealized way of life, popularized "the idea that the Hudson Valley landscape was the example the rest of the nation should follow", and fostered the recognition that the Hudson Valley was "the incubator of a national taste in landscape and architectural design" (Schuyler, 91).

In sum, because of its multicultural background, the Hudson River Valley provided artistic inspiration for Irving, Cole, and Downing. As representatives of America's first writers, artists, and architects, they successfully incorporated European cultures into American landscape and gave the landscape new meanings. Benefiting from the Dutch culture in the region, Irving endowed the valley with an air of mystery and romance. Cole applied the motifs and techniques of European Romantic landscape painting to the scenery of the valley, making the wild landscape a symbol of America's vigor. Downing transformed English landscape and architectural ideas into designs suitable for the valley and promoted the area's houses as models of idealized human dwelling. Their examples illustrate the importance of European heritage to the development of American culture, which is further demonstrated in Wharton's depiction of the Hudson River Valley mansion where European heritage fuses with the vitality of America.

4.3.2　The Willows as a Counterbalance to Americans' Intellectual Parochialism

As the ancestral home of the oldest family in Paul's Landing, the Willows is characterized by a blend of European legacy and American landscape in its architectural design, harmony with the natural environment, and association with European literary classics. Through these elements, the mansion embodies the historic significance of the Hudson Valley and its connection to European cultures. While the temporality of landscape teaches Vance the importance of the past, his attachment to the Willows and identification with European cultures counterbalance his intellectual parochialism. Vance's view of the Willows thus illustrates Wharton's belief that the cross-fertilization of European heritage and American innovation can serve as a counterbalance to intellectual parochialism and repudiation of history in American society.

On August 29, 1927, Loren Palmer, the editor of *The Delineator*, wrote to Wharton's editor at D. Appleton and Company and asked the latter to "suggest to Mrs. Wharton that the title [of her novel in progress, *Hudson River Bracketed*] was perhaps unfortunate. I believe any title to be unfortunate that requires explanation" (qtd. in Buchanan-King, 10). Wharton, nevertheless, made clear in her reply that the title was of great importance: "As to the title you will remember how much ' Twilight Sleep' frightened [editor Arthur] Vance, and you will also note that it has been much praised by the critics [...] want it made clear to the editors who accept my [novel] for serial publication that I must have my own way with regard to titles as well as to all the details of my tales" (qtd. in Buchanan-King, 11). The title, so insisted on by Wharton, refers to a Hudson River Bracketed architecture named the Willows in *Hudson River Bracketed* and *The Gods Arrive*. Wharton explains the term in the epigraph to *Hudson River Bracketed*: "A.J. Downing, the American landscape architect, in his book on Landscape Gardening (published in 1842) divides the architectural styles into the Grecian, Chinese, Gothic, the Tuscan, or Italian villa, style, and the *Hudson River Bracketed*" (original emphasis). Halo Spear, the heiress of the mansion, tells Vance the history of the Willows:

"It was our indigenous style of architecture in this part of the world" [...] "I perceive," she continued, "that you are not familiar with the epoch-making work of A. J. Downing Esqre on Landscape Gardening in America." She turned to the bookcases [...]: "Here— here's the place. It's too long to read aloud; but the point is that Mr. Downing, who was the great authority of the period, sums up the principal architectural styles as the Grecian, the Chinese, the Gothic, the Tuscan or Italian villa, and—Hudson River Bracketed. Unless I'm mistaken, he cites the Willows as one of the most perfect examples of Hudson River Bracketed (this was in, 1842), and—yes, here's the place: 'The seat of Ambrose Lorburn Esqre, the Willows, near Paul's Landing, Dutchess County, N.Y., is one of the most successful instances of etc., etc....'". (*HRB*, 69)

Though Wharton repeatedly attributes the term "Hudson River Bracketed" to Downing, in fact neither the phrase nor the Willows appear in his well-known *A Treatise on The Theory and Practice of Landscape Gardening*. He only mentions architectural styles such as the Grecian, Chinese, Gothic, Tuscan, and Italian. Instead, he uses "the Bracketed mode" to refer to many beautiful villas along the Hudson in Duchess County. Rinaldi and Yasinsac thus argue that "Edith Wharton crystallized (if not coined) the term 'Hudson River Bracketed' in her 1929 novel of the same name" (98). If we take Wharton's emphasis on the title and her life-long interest in architecture into consideration, then it is necessary to understand her intention in choosing to "crystallize" the architectural term for the novel. This book proposes that the Willows serves as the embodiment of the writer's expectation about the cross-fertilization of European heritage and American innovation.

The Bracketed mode dominated architecture in the eastern United

States, particularly the Hudson River Valley, in the middle nineteenth century. The ornate wooden bracket under the eaves was the chief feature of this architectural style. The Willows, as Vance describes it, certainly belongs to this mode. While walking on a green lane which leads up to the house, he sees that its front is veiled in the shadow of two ancient willows and balconies supported by "ornate wooden brackets". The sloping roof over the front door rests on "elaborately ornamented brackets" and "arcaded verandah" spans from "bracket to bracket" (*HRB*, 58). According to Downing, the Bracketed style was the most representative architectural mode that transformed European styles to adapt to the characteristics of American landscape.

If it is not the best and highest style of architecture which will be developed in this country, it has the merit of being the first that has taken a distinct shape and meaning in the hands of our countrymen [...] it has features similar in origin and use with the Swiss and Venetian styles [...] Its elements are simple and useful, but this simplicity and utility both spring from our circumstances and climate". (*The Architecture of Country Houses*, 393-394)

As Downing points out, the advantages of the Bracketed mode came primarily from the balance of European aesthetics with the Hudson Valley's geographical and climatic conditions. He further elucidates in *A Treatise on The Theory and Practice of Landscape Gardening* that this style "adapted to North America" the cultural images of Europe: "it awakens associations fraught with the most enticing history of the past" (405). By specifying the mansion's architectural style and its owners' Dutch and English ancestry, Wharton highlights the influence of European cultures upon the region and underscores the role of the Willows as a symbol of the combination of European conventions and American landscape.

In addition to its architectural style, the Willows is characterized by its harmony with nature. Downing states that one significant feature of the Hudson River Valley landscape is "the harmony of buildings and scenery": the scenery is as much a part of the architecture as the architecture is part of the scenery (*Treatise*, 78). The exterior of the Willows is dark brown, the color of the earth, which blends the house into its natural surroundings. When he sees the house for the first time, Vance is impressed by its organic relation to nature:

> its front so veiled in the showering gold-green foliage of two ancient weeping willows that Vance could only catch, here and there, a hint of a steep roof, a jutting balcony, an aspiring turret. The facade, thus seen in trembling glimpses, as if it were as fluid as the trees, suggested vastness, fantasy and secrecy. Green slopes of unmown grass, and heavy shrubberies of unpruned syringa and lilac, surrounded it; and beyond the view was closed in on all sides by trees and more trees. "An old house— this is the way an old house looks!" (*HRB*, 57)

Vance's portrayal of the Willows not only emphasizes its harmony with nature but also implies its long history. Such descriptions as "ancient weeping willows" and "heavy shrubberies of unpruned syringa" suggest the age of the house. His exclamation "this is the way an old house looks!" demonstrates that he has been captured by the temporality of landscape. In terms of "temporality", anthropologist Tim Ingold proposes that landscape is not a fixed or unchanging "backdrop to human activities"; rather, "landscape is constituted as an enduring record of—and testimony to—the lives and works of past generations who have dwelt within it, and in so doing, have left there something of themselves" (152). In other words, landscape displays the passage of time and records the lives of the people who once lived there. Looking at the exterior and interior of the Willows,

Vance senses the traces of the past left by generations of occupants: the ancient trees and flowers in the garden, the paths outside the house formed by people's daily activities, and the furniture with patina in the rooms all "laid a weight on his heart", reminding him of the bell of the Roman Catholic church in his hometown (*HRB*, 58). In "The Temporality of the Landscape", Ingold lists the church as a "monument to the passage of time" since "its bells ring out the seasons, the months, births, marriages and deaths" (169). Vance's analogy between the house and the church bell thus illustrates that the temporality of the Hudson Valley landscape makes him aware of the power of the past. For the first time in his life, the protagonist realizes the narrowness of his go-ahead hometown where people always associate stability with stagnation and look down on traditions: "Why wasn't I ever told about the Past before?" (*HRB*, 62). According to historian Anne Douglas, the attitude of Americans towards history in the 1920s was different from that of previous generations. Americans in the 1920s consciously shaped themselves as modern people and claimed that it was a time of "youth, freedom, and breaking with tradition", characterized by a rejection of the past (qtd. in Glennon, 56). Vance's transformed view of the past hence reflects the power of the Willows in resisting repudiation of history.

The Past that the Willows reveals to Vance refers not only to the history of the Lorburn family who have lived there since 1830, but also to the heritage of European literature. In the library of the previous owner—old Miss Lorburn, he reads Goethe and English poets such as Christopher Marlowe and Coleridge. A college graduate who only knows Americans poets such as Henry Wadsworth Longfellow and Walter Whitman, Vance learns that European classics are essential to his artistic creation and officially begins his professional career by writing a short novel about the Willows and Miss Lorburn during his stay in the Hudson River Valley. This experience completely alters "Vance's perspective, transform[s] his world from the staring flatness of a movie 'close-up' to a many-vistaed universe" (*HRB*, 95). Through linking the Willows to the protagonist's literary creation, Wharton reminds readers of such celebrities as Irving, Cole, and Downing who drew their artistic inspiration from the landscape of the Hudson Valley, thereby highlighting the region's significance as a birthplace of American literature and art. More significantly, like these predecessors who incorporated European cultures into American landscape, Vance on the one hand learns from European traditions, on the other hand gives the Willows new life with his novel which garners substantial popularity among young American intellectuals.

Although it is respected by the residents of Paul's Landing, the Willows is left vacant after Miss Lorburn's death. The new houseowner hires Vance's relatives, the Tracys, to ventilate the rooms and dust the books, but because he demands that everything be kept unchanged, nobody reads the books in the library. Having been abandoned for several years, the mansion is gradually forgotten by the locals. They talk about it indifferently: "Nothing particular. Just an old house" (*HRB*, 52). By comparison, Vance understands that "dusting a dead woman's books" is not "a more vital and necessary act than reading them" (*HRB*, 121). In his eyes, the landscape of the Willows links the past and the present. As Ingold puts it, the temporality of landscape tells humans that "the present is not marked off from a past that it has replaced or a future that will, in turn, replace it; it rather gathers the past and future into itself, like refractions in a crystal ball" (159). The temporality of the Willows teaches Vance that progress in the present does not always come at the expense of the abandonment of the past, as Midwesterners believe; rather, art cannot be produced in a cultural vacuum.

Vance's attitude towards the Willows reflects Wharton's view that modern literature is based on the tradition of the past rather than cut off from it. In *Tendencies in Modern Fiction* published in *Saturday Review of Literature* on January 27, 1934, she criticized the young generation of writers such as Virginia Woolf and James Joyce for their "rejection of the past": "so far as the new novelists may be said to have any theory of their art, it seems to be that every new creation can issue only from the annihilation of what preceded it. But [...] the accumulated leaf-mould of tradition is essential to the nurture of new growths of art" (*The Uncollected Critical Writings*, 170).

As Singley states, Wharton did not deny change or become out of touch with American culture in the 1920s and 1930s. What Wharton criticized was that modern writers ignored the past and sought newness blindly ("Change at Stake", 6). The writer shared her idea of the significance of the literary past with Marcel Proust and T. S. Eliot. In *The Writing of Fiction*, she summarizes that Proust's "strength is the strength of tradition. All his newest and most arresting effects have been arrived at through the old way of selection and design" (154-155). She also held a similar admiration for literary tradition as Eliot did. Eliot argues in "Tradition and Individual Talent" that the past tradition and modern innovation are complementary and a qualified writer must obtain "the historical sense":

> a perception, not only of the pastness of the past, but of its presence; the historical sense compels a man to write not merely with his own generation in his bones, but with a feeling that the whole of the literature of Europe from Homer and within it the whole of the literature of his own country has a simultaneous existence and composes a simultaneous order. (55)

The temporality of the landscape thus implies the dialectic relationship between the past and the present. On the one hand, Wharton argues for the relevance of tradition in contemporary life through the Hudson Valley mansion; on the other hand, she acknowledges that retreating to the past is not a good solution to problems. The Lorburns expect the Willows to stay the same because they are too caught up in their family's past glory to accept any change. It is Vance's critically acclaimed book about the Willows that breathes new life into the unoccupied mansion and sparks American readers' interests in the Hudson River Valley, the history of the Lorburns, and European classics in the library. Moreover, the Willows reflects Wharton's expectation for the cross-fertilization of European tradition and American innovation; while European literature provides Vance with the conventions essential for artistic inspiration and fills his lack of education, his literary creation in the library renders the neglected European classics popular among ordinary American readers. By emphasizing that Vance uses the books to create his own story instead of leaving them unread like the Lorburns do, Wharton demonstrates that the past should not be kept unaltered or passively accepted; instead, the past should be adapted to the present as much as the present is nurtured by the past.

Wharton's belief in the cross-fertilization of American and European cultures further illustrates her idea about the emerging globalization. Sociologist Roland Robertson located the origins of globalization in the period from the 1870s to mid-1920s; globalization, "the intensification of consciousness of the world as a whole" (8), was undergoing its crucial "take-off period" in the 1920s (59). Technological marvels such as the transoceanic steamship, the telephone, and the radio transformed travel and communication, led to the rise of international tourism in the United States, and rendered the world more closely-knit and accessible than ever before. America's economic and imperial forays into Latin America and the Pacific,

245

its active participation in the First World War, and increased prestige in international politics further reshaped the way Americans perceived their interconnectedness with other nations.

For Wharton, "the consciousness of the world as a whole" refers primarily to the relationship between Europe and the United States whose growing military, political, and economic power in the world led to a boom in its cultural exports during the interwar years. Jazz music and Hollywood movies, for example, gained worldwide recognition in the 1920s. Debates about the influence of American culture were common in Europe, as Europeans were both attracted by American popular culture and its economic innovations, and shocked by its excessive materialism and conformity. In France, where Wharton lived from 1907 until her death in 1937, intellectuals worried about "the Americanization of the world", the "development and spread of American or American-like products, techniques, and organizations throughout Europe", and "the superficiality of American popular culture and the materialism of the American business world" (Goedde, 250). Wharton also often complained that Paris had been more and more influenced by American lifestyle since the end of World War I: the city "is simply awful—a kind of continuous earthquake of motors, busses, trams, lorries, taxis and other howling and swooping and colliding engines, with hundreds of thousands of U.S. citizens rushing about in them and tumbling out at one's door" (qtd. in R. W. B. Lewis, *Edith Wharton: A Biography*, 420). As Glennon notes, the increasing impact of American culture led to "reinvigorated sense of exceptionalism" and "overt rejection of European tradition in the 1920s and 1930s" in the United States, which "was a source of great concern for Wharton" (172). In the essays published during this period, Wharton repeatedly warned that "it [was] a curious, and deeply suggestive, fact that America's acute [...] nationalism developed in inverse ratio to the growth of modern travelling facilities, and in exact proportion to the very recent Americanism of the majority of our modern literary leaders" (*The Uncollected Critical Writings*, 156). The writer's uneasiness about the ubiquity of American culture thus anticipates late-twentieth-century theorists' debate about "American cultural primacy" as a side effect of globalization (Lieber & Weisberg, 275).

In terms of literary creation, many critics in the 1920s and 1930s thought that American writers should focus on American topics. In "The Great American Novel", Wharton criticized the intellectual insularity in the United States with arguing that the standards of American novels constrain artists' imagination: "if his work is really to deserve the epithet 'American,' it must tell of persons so limited in education and opportunity that they live cut off from all the varied sources of culture which used to be considered the common heritage of English-speaking people" (*The Uncollected Critical Writings*, 152). When American business culture and technological innovation "internationalized the earth" (156), Wharton insisted that Americans should benefit from the "perpetual interchange of ideas and influences" on both sides of the Atlantic (157). Thus, the great American novel should be concerned with a wider geographical range: "Its scene may be laid in an American small town or in a European capital; it may deal with the present or the past, with great events or trivial happenings; but in the latter case it will certainly contrive to relate them to something greater than themselves. The ability to do this is indeed one of the surest signs of the great novelist" (157-158). In other words, Americans must cultivate a deeper appreciation of the history, culture, and social traditions beyond their national borders.

At the end of *The Gods Arrive*, when he returns to Paul's Landing after a long period of wanderings in Europe and his Midwestern hometown, Vance senses his emotional "attachment" to the Willows as soon as he sees the surrounding landscape: "The old house had been his fairy godmother, and it was only now, as he looked at it again, that he understood" (*GA*, 418). The "fairy godmother" alludes to the concept of The Mothers—the source of all life and poetic creation—in Goethe's *Faust*. Through linking the American landscape to the German canon, Wharton once again underscores the role of the Willows as an integration of European heritage and American innovation. The term " attachment " in environmental psychology refers to "a positive connection or bond between a person and a particular place " (Williams & Vaske, " The Measurement of Place Attachment", 831). According to Daniel R. Williams and Jerry J. Vaske, attachment as an emotion can be analyzed from two dimensions: place dependence and place identity. Firstly, place dependence is considered as a form of functional attachment which reflects "the importance of a place in providing features and conditions that support specific goals or desired activities" (831). Because of its beautiful scenery and rich collection of books, the Willows meets Vance's needs for creative inspiration and intellectual education as a writer. Secondly, place identity, an emotional attachment, refers to "the symbolic importance of a place as a repository for emotions and relationships that give meaning and purpose to life" (831). Vance's attachment to the Hudson River Valley deepens when he becomes acquainted with both the history of the Willows and European literature. After having travelled in Europe for three years, and then returning to the mansion, he realizes that the Willows has become a part of himself: "What he craved for, with a sort of tremulous convalescent hunger, was a sight of the Willows, the old house where his real life had begun" (*GA*, 416). His identification with the Willows and European literature reveals his understanding that American writers should learn from European traditions and pay attention to global issues.

Furthermore, Vance's attachment displays globalization's impact upon American identity: his transatlantic travels and associations with European intellectuals teach him that the concept of nation is more cultural than geographic. Every time when he reads in the library, Vance feels that he enters an international community of writers and thus develops a sense of belonging to not only the valley but also a transatlantic culture. His emotion echoes Jeffrey Jensen Arnett's explanation for psychological consequences of globalization. According to Arnett, globalization results in the development of people's "bicultural identities", meaning that "in addition to their local identity", people acquire a global identity that cultivates an understanding of foreign cultures and gives them a sense of belonging to a worldwide culture (777).

In her study of Wharton's view about American identity, Singley points out that during the post-WWI years the writer was influenced by French philosopher Ernest Renan who described nationhood as "common glories in the past, and a common will in the present" ("Race, Culture, Nation", 37). Renan regarded the "nation as a spiritual family" which embraced cosmopolitan ideals and transnational humanism, and his ideas about nation and nationhood helped Wharton come to terms with her own expatriation (36). In her opinion, residing in Europe afforded her with a more advantageous vantage point from which to observe American issues rather than separating her from her motherland. It was for this reason that, subsequent to her relocation to France in 1907, she continued to write extensively about the United States. Moreover, her expatriation also made her aware of the need for innovation in Europe. By comparing America and Europe, she drew attention to the deficiencies of American society and underscored the crucial role of European art and culture in counterbalancing the detrimental impact of business culture in America. In her 1936 tribute to Paul Bourget, Wharton elucidated that it was "only in seeing other countries, in studying their customs, reading their books, associating with their inhabitants, that one can situate one's own country in the history of civilization" (qtd. in Lee, 1004). Her sustained attention to American issues distinguished her novels on the relationship between America and Europe from those of Henry James who primarily depicted Americans' adventures abroad. In short, Wharton's distance from her native land deepened her understanding of it.

By describing Vance's attachment to the Willows—the embodiment of the cross-fertilization of American and European cultures, Wharton expresses her expectation in her last completed novel that the combination of Americans' vitality and the rich history of European cultures will create great American writers. Vance's return to the Hudson Valley at the end of the book and his maturity as a qualified writer demonstrate Wharton's belief that the exposure to European cultures will free Americans from their intellectual narrowness. From her perspective, an exemplary American is one who manifests a genuine curiosity towards diverse cultural traditions and demonstrates a willingness to incorporate them into his or her own culture, one who merges old traditions and modern innovations.

In summary, drawing on the valley's multicultural history and its significance in American literature and art, Wharton portrays the Willows as an idealized mansion which embodies the cross-fertilization of European and American cultures. Although he used to overlook the importance of the past, the temporality of the landscape in Paul's Landing enables Vance to understand the dialectic relationship between the past and the present: the present is nurtured by the past, while the past must adapt to change. Furthermore, his attachment to the Willows and identification with European cultures display the impact of emerging globalization upon American identity: he develops a sense of belonging to not only the valley but also a transatlantic intellectual community. Wharton's delineation of the Willows thus illustrates her expectation that the cross-fertilization of European heritage and American innovation can serve as a counterbalance to intellectual parochialism and repudiation of history in American society.

4.4 Summary

In her last two completed novels, *Hudson River Bracketed* and *The Gods Arrive*, Edith Wharton expresses her views on how Americans should cope with the impacts of social transformations by creating an idealized landscape of the Hudson River Valley. Building upon the significant role of the Hudson River Valley in American literature, art, and architecture, the author endows this region with distinctive features in her novels: the harmony between landscape and technology, integration of natural beauty and artistic beauty, and fusion of European heritage and American innovation. Through contrasting the idealized Hudson landscape with the protagonist Vance's bleak Midwestern hometown, Wharton underscores that Americans' domination over nature leads to their emotional numbness. She also points out that Americans suffer from the adverse effects of social transformations such as standardization, human-nature alienation, and repudiation of tradition. More importantly, her portrayal of the Hudson landscape reveals her expectation that Americans can find aesthetic redemption from the power of nature, art, and history.

Chapter Four analyzes the Hudson River Valley landscape in the two novels, including the suburb, the forest, and the old mansion, in order to investigate how the writer deals with the deleterious effects of social transformations on American society in the 1920s and 1930s with her fictional creation of idealized landscape. To begin with, Paul's Landing, a suburb in the Hudson River Valley which is close to New York City, liberates Vance from the standardizing influences of social transformations and revitalizes his sensibility suppressed by standardization and mechanization. While the monotonous suburb in his Midwestern hometown reflects

Americans' worship of technology and machinery, Paul's Landing is characterized by the coexistence of natural landscape and technology. Although Vance's initial disappointment with the landscape of Paul's Landing reveals his Taylorized mindset which prioritizes efficiency and conformity, the harmony between machinery and natural beauty in the valley gradually teaches him that technology is the means to improve human life rather than an end of human existence. His sensibility that has been repressed by the mechanical Midwestern life is thus activated by his experience of nature's aesthetic value. Secondly, the enchanted scenery, especially the forest in the Hudson Valley, is depicted as a combination of natural beauty and artistic beauty, a remedy for human-nature alienation. When the rise of the West challenged the cultural dominance of the Eastern United States at the turn of the twentieth century, Wharton argues that the pioneers' values have turned into unrestrained instrumental rationality through depicting the sterile Midwestern landscape in Vance's hometown. Under the influence of capitalism's expansionist logic, Midwesterners are alienated from nature. By comparison, she connects the Hudson River Valley landscape with the first national school of art in the United States and highlights the importance of the East in defining American identity. Initially, Vance's instrumental way of seeing the world results in his emotional distress. The aura of the forest in the valley, nevertheless, cultivates an intersubjective relationship between him and nature. Vance's exaltation manifests that the power of nature and art in aesthetic redemption allows him to break free from the grip of instrumental reason and restore his emotional energy. Moreover, the Willows, an old mansion in Paul's Landing, embodies the cross-fertilization of European heritage and American innovation, and counterbalances the intellectual parochialism and disregard for history that characterize twentieth-century American society. With its architectural style which displays the combination of European conventions and American landscape, its harmony with nature, and its association with European masterpieces, the building demonstrates the history of the Hudson Valley and the heritage of European literature. The temporality of the landscape teaches Vance the dialectic relationship between the past and the present. His attachment to the Willows and identification with European cultures further reflect the impact of emerging globalization upon American identity.

To sum up, Wharton's depiction of the Hudson River Valley illuminates her solution to the challenges posed by social transformations in the United States. She envisions an ideal model that combines landscape, art, and history, and blends European and American cultures, with the aim of redeeming the increasingly materialistic and standardized American society. As demonstrated in this chapter, Wharton's view of nature has its roots in European Romanticism and American Transcendentalism, and her concern about the spiritual numbness of modern people shares similarity with the next generation of American modernist writers such as Sinclair Lewis and T. S. Eliot. Therefore, her reflections on social transformations showcase the transitional position that she occupies in the history of American literature.

However, Wharton's idealized Hudson River Valley landscape is flawed in several significant respects. Firstly, her criticism about the Midwest comes from stereotypes and her idea about the superiority of the American East implies her bias as a Northeastern elite. Secondly, her emphasis of European influences on the valley ignores the cultures of the non-whites such as Native Americans and African Americans. In addition, the history of the Willows implies that the owners' wealth is based on their ancestors' colonial exploitation in other countries. For example, the money for building the mansion partly comes from their great-great-grandfather's business with the East India Company. Critics also points out Wharton's Orientalism via investigating the exotic Eastern decoration in the Willows (Toth, 232). Lastly, Wharton's expectation about the power of landscape

253

in aesthetic redemption seems too utopian to be realized in early-twentieth-century American society. Despite the above limitations, she provided an alternative perspective for thinking about social transformations in the United States when most Americans were intoxicated by technological progress and economic prosperity.

Chapter Five   Conclusion

The landscape in Edith Wharton's novels is not merely the setting for the stories, but a lens through which the experiences of Americans are refracted during the crucial transition period between the post-Civil War era and the 1930s. Primarily adopting a perspective of landscape studies in cultural geography, this book investigates Wharton's depiction of New England landscape in her six novels, with the aim of providing new interpretations for her works and advancing interdisciplinary research that applies theories from cultural geography to Wharton studies.

5.1   Major Findings

Based on the analysis of New York cityscape, rural New England landscape, and idealized Hudson River Valley landscape, this book presents the following findings:

Firstly, Wharton's depiction of New England landscape in the selected novels sheds light on the impacts of social transformations upon Americans' lifestyles and mentalities at the turn of the twentieth century. The transformation of New York cityscape is enabled by the displacement of Old New Yorkers with the new plutocrats due to the socio-economic restructuring during this era. The changes in the urban landscape—represented by the streets, the opera houses, and the hotels—reflect the rising importance of individuality, the increasing accessibility of leisure, and growing geographical and social mobility in New York's transition from a nineteenth-century Victorian City to a twentieth-century modern one. Wharton's portrayal of the urban landscape illustrates her skepticism toward social transformations. She believes that the above-mentioned transformations result in detrimental impacts on Americans, including selfishness and irresponsibility, decline in cultural taste, and disregard for traditions, morality, and history. As Americans navigate the tides of social transformations, there is a noticeable shift in the regional identity of rural New England, changing from a decaying backwater to rural idyll in urbanites' eyes. Old New England's transformed image is molded by the notions of class, race, and gender. The ways Americans view key elements of old New England landscape—the villages, the mountains, and the vernacular architecture—are shaped by the power relations between the urban leisure class and rural poor, US-born Anglo-Saxons and immigrants from Ireland and Italy, and men and women. Wharton's delineation of rural landscape reveals that old New England's transformed identity is an invention of urban residents as a remedy for the negative effects of social transformations. In the writer's view, resorting to a romanticized old New England which cloaks and perpetuates class, gender, and racial inequalities is an ineffective approach to addressing the challenges of social transformations. Wharton articulates her perspectives on how Americans should cope with the impacts of social transformations by envisioning an idealized landscape in Hudson River Valley which is characterized by the harmony between landscape and technology, integration of natural beauty and artistic beauty, and cross-fertilization of European legacy and American innovation. Under the influence of capitalism's expansionist logic, Americans' domination over nature alienates themselves from it and contributes to their emotional numbness. Wharton's depiction of the suburb, the forest, and the mansion indicates her expectation that the aesthetic values of landscape can counterbalance the widespread negative effects of standardization, mechanization, human alienation from nature, and neglect for history in American society.

Secondly, Wharton's delineation of New England landscape reflects the societal transformations in the United States between the postbellum years and the 1930s. This period encompassed the Gilded Age, the Progressive Era, and the Roaring Twenties, which represented a crucial transitional phase and a period of rapid growth in American history. This book finds that the characters' experience in the novels demonstrates significant socio-economic, political, and cultural transformations. The socio-economic transformations mainly include industrialization, urbanization, globalization, standardization, mechanization, agricultural commercialization, as well as the expanding geographical and social mobility. Within the political domain, notable transformations such as immigration and debates regarding national identity can be seen. In terms of cultural values, the characters undergo substantial influences from the growing importance of individuality, new notions of leisure, the rhetoric of social progress, disregard for history etc. Wharton's scrutiny of those social transformations displays her critique of unrestrained capitalism when the priority of economic determinants undermines taste, humanism, and tradition.

Thirdly, the analysis of the landscape in the novels demonstrates that Wharton's attitude towards social transformations in the United States undergoes changes. The writer's transition from skepticism towards social transformations to acknowledging its inevitability leads her to place greater emphasis on seeking solutions to mitigate its adverse effects, rather than solely criticizing it. Her perspectives on tradition evolves as well. In *The House of Mirth* and *The Custom of the Country*, she expresses her shock at Americans' indifference to history and appeals to the importance of the past. Then she discusses the peril of being trapped in the past and disconnected from modern world in *Ethan Frome* and *Summer*. Finally, in *Hudson River Bracketed and The Gods Arrive* she places greater emphasis on the continuity between the past and the present. Towards the end of her career, the writer also adopts a more positive attitude towards America, as evidenced by her placing hope for the future in a young American from the Midwest. Though she continues to critique modern American society, her affinity for it emerges more clearly in her writing of the 1920s and 1930s. The changes in Wharton's attitude can be attributed to a combination of objective and subjective factors. In terms of objective reasons, the international influence of the United States continued to ascend in the aftermath of World War I. Additionally, France, where Wharton resided as an expatriate, was increasingly influenced by American culture. These factors prompted her to reassess her perspective on social transformations in America. Regarding subjective reasons, the trauma of World War I and the successive loss of intimate friends in the 1920s made Wharton yearn for the bygone days in America, thereby alleviating her criticism of the country.

Fourthly, Wharton's writing on New England landscape illustrates her inheritance from European and American Romanticism, as well as her similarities with the next generation of American modernist writers. As has been explained in chapter four, the author learns from Goethe, Coleridge, and Ruskin about the detrimental impacts that industrialization imposes upon nature and human sensibility. She is also significantly influenced by American Transcendentalists' emphasis on nature's sacredness and its spiritual strength to resist the materialism of American society. Different from her Romantic predecessors who advocate human beings' spiritual connection with God in nature, Wharton pays special attention to nature's aesthetic value as a revitalizing antidote. Unlike contemporary naturalist writers such as Frank Norris, she acknowledges human agency rather than embrace environmental determinism and social Darwinism. Moreover,

258

Wharton's investigation of the spiritual crisis faced by modern individuals and her envision of aesthetic redemption in landscape bear resemblances to the subsequent generation of American modernist writers. For instance, while the protagonist in Sinclair Lewis's *Babbitt* regards his experiences in the wilderness of Maine as a means to resist the standardized urban life, in *The Old Man and the Sea*, Ernest Hemingway constructs coastal landscape as an aesthetic utopia which frees himself from an alienated American society. Compared with the younger writers, Wharton places greater emphasis on the significance of cultural heritage from both sides of the Atlantic. Therefore, Wharton's depiction of landscape exemplifies her significant contribution to American literature as a writer who builds upon the past traditions and paves the way for the next generation of artists.

5.2 Significance and Limitations

This book scrutinizes the dynamic interrelationship between the Americans at the turn of the twentieth century and the different types of New England landscape, and its significance lies in the following aspects:

First of all, this book adopts a new critical perspective to study how Wharton's delineation of landscape reveals the impacts of social transformations upon turn-of-the-twentieth-century Americans, which demonstrates that landscape in her writing is much more than a "metaphor" (Whaley, 235) or "view of aesthetics" (Dean, x). Primarily employing the perspective of landscape studies in cultural geography, this research sheds light on the complex socio-economic, political, and cultural forces that shape individuals' perceptions of their surroundings. This study also illuminates the effects of social transformations on people's emotions, ideologies, and aesthetics.

Secondly, this book's research on landscape in Wharton's novels indicates that it is narrow to label her as an Old New York novelist. Her works encompass the regions of both the Northeastern and Midwestern United States, and explore the lives of Americans from diverse social classes, genders, and ethnicities. The writer's description of landscape also suggests that she does not hold a conservative attitude towards social transformations. Additionally, the examination of her post-WWI novels, such as *Hudson River Bracketed* and *The Gods Arrive*, displays that Wharton does not detach from the reality of American society due to her exile in France, which elucidates the significance of drawing Wharton scholars' attention to the writer's later works.

Thirdly, this research provides a case for landscape studies in American literature. In current literary cases of landscape studies, critics tend to prioritize the examination of rural landscape while overlooking that of urban landscape. Those studies mainly interpret literary representations of landscape as timeless idylls or myths of national consciousness. This book's attention to urban and suburban landscape thus broadens the application of landscape theories in literary criticism. Furthermore, due to the common association of landscape with pastoralism in scholarly discussions of local color literature, landscape is often seen as the antithesis of social transformations. These studies not only oversimplify the relationship between rural and urban areas, but also overlook the rich historical and cultural context of American local color literature and its close connection to social transformations. Therefore, the analysis of landscape and social transformations in this book provides new perspectives for the study of American literature.

Fourthly, Wharton's scrutiny of the effects of social transformations encountered by Americans at the turn of the twentieth century provides insights into the related social issues in today's America. Since the publication of economist Thomas Piketty's influential book *Capital in the Twenty-First Century* (2014) , it has become widely acknowledged that Americans are living in a "second Gilded Age". Wharton's critique of class division and conspicuous consumption has foreseen the culture of affluence and economic inequality in contemporary American society. Her ambivalence towards a changing class structure also helps people better understand the civil divisions that culminated in the Capitol Rotunda in January 2021. Besides, the author's cosmopolitan critique of nationalist fervor remains enlightening when the anxieties about immigration, white hegemony, and changing demographics continue to vex American culture. Moreover, the fierce indictment of the limitations imposed upon women's lives in her novels is still pertinent to today's America, as evidenced by the Me Too movement and the popularity of trophy wives. As renowned Wharton scholar Emily J. Orlando recently put it, Wharton's writings "provide the tools to critically examine the vicissitudes of the complicated, fractured world as we advance into the third decade of the new century" (*The Bloomsbury Handbook to Edith Wharton*, 3). Wharton's contemplation on social transformations in the United States at the turn of the twentieth century holds relevance for the current social development in China as well. Industrialization, urbanization, and globalization have similarly brought about significant transformations to China, and Chinese people are dealing with the feelings of alienation and estrangement resulting from rapid development. Therefore, Wharton's reflections on social transformations and her proposed solutions in the novels offer valuable references for examining contemporary Chinese society.

Despite the above-mentioned contributions, this book has its limitations. The present study lacks scope and variety to produce a more comprehensive analysis of New England landscape and social transformations in turn-of-the-twentieth-century United States. Because of Wharton's class and racial identities, this research mainly focuses on the impacts of social transformations upon middle-and upper-class white Americans. Thus, future studies can encompass a broader geographical range by including the works of additional American writers from that time period.

References

Adamson, Joseph, and Hilary Clark. "Introduction: Shame, Affect, Writing." *Scenes of Shame: Psychoanalysis, Shame, and Writing*. Eds. Joseph Adamson and Hilary Clark. Albany: State University of New York Press, 1999: 1-34.

Adorno, Theodor W. *Aesthetic Theory*. 1970. Trans. Robert Hullot-Kentor. London: Continuum, 2002.

Allen, Garland E. "The Misuse of Biological Hierarchies: The American Eugenics Movement, 1900-1940." *History and Philosophy of the Life Sciences* 5.2 (1983): 105-128.

Althusser, Louis. "Ideology and Ideological State Apparatuses (Notes towards an Investigation)". *Lenin and Philosophy and Other Essays*. Trans. Ben Brewster. New York: Monthly Review Press, 1971: 142-147, 166-176.

Ammons, Elizabeth. The Myth of Imperiled Whiteness and *Ethan Frome*. *The New England Quarterly* 81.1 (2008): 5-33.

---. *Edith Wharton's Argument with America*. Athens: University of Georgia Press, 1980.

Anderson, Ben. "Affect and Emotion." *The Wiley-Blackwell Companion to Cultural Geography*. Eds. Nuala C. Johnson, Richard H. Schein, and Jamie Winders. West Sussex: John Wiley & Sons, 2013: 452-464.

Anderson, Donald, and Judith Saunders. Edith Wharton and the Hudson Valley. *The Hudson River Valley Review* 23.1 (2006): 1-5.

Anderson, J. L. "You're a Bigger Man": Technology and Agrarian Masculinity in Postwar America. *Agricultural History* 94.1 (2020): 1-23.

Andrews, Malcolm. *Landscape and Western Art.* New York: Oxford University Press, 1999.

Archer, John. Country and City in the American Romantic Suburb. *Journal of the Society of Architectural Historians* 42.2 (1983): 139-156.

Arnesen, Eric. Whiteness and the Historians' Imagination. *International Labor and Working-Class History* 60 (2001): 3-32.

Arnett, Jeffrey Jensen. The Psychology of Globalization. *American Psychologist* 57.10 (2002): 774-783.

Askins, Kye. Crossing Divides: Ethnicity and Rurality. *Journal of Rural Studies* 25 (2009): 365-375.

Aspden, Suzanne. "Introduction: Opera and the (Urban) Geography of Culture." *Operatic Geographies: The Place of Opera and the Opera House.* Ed. Suzanne Aspden. Chicago, IL: The University of Chicago Press, 2019: 1-11.

Atha, Mick, et al. "Introduction." *The Routledge Companion to Landscape Studies.* 2nd ed. Eds. Peter Howard, et al. New York: Routledge, 2019: xix-xxviii.

Augé, Marc. *Non-Places: Introduction to an Anthropology of Supermodernity.* Trans. John Howe. London: Verso, 1995.

Bailey, Brigitte. Aesthetics and Ideology in *Italian Backgrounds. Wretched Exotic: Essays on Edith Wharton in Europe.* Eds. Katherine Joslin and Alan Price. New York: Peter Lang, 1993: 181-200.

Ball, Andrew J. "'Christianity Incorporated': Sinclair Lewis and The Taylorization of American Protestantism." *Religion & Literature* 50.2 (2018): 1-25.

Banta, Martha. *Taylored Lives: Narrative Productions in the Age of Taylor,*

Veblen, and Ford. Chicago, IL: The University of Chicago Press, 1993.

Barillas, William David. "Aldo Leopold and Midwestern Pastoralism." *American Studies* 3.7 (1996): 61-81.

---. *The Midwestern Pastoral: Place and Landscape in Literature of the American Heartland*. Athens: Ohio University Press, 2006.

Barnett, Clive. "Cultural Turn." *The Dictionary of Human Geography*. 5th ed. Eds. Derek Gregory, et al. Chichester: Wiley-Blackwell, 2009: 134-135.

---. "Impure and Worldly Geography: the Africanist Discourse of the Royal Geographical Society, 1831-1873." *Transactions of the Institute of British Geographers* 23.2 (1998): 239-251.

Barringer, Tim, et al. *Picturesque and Sublime: Thomas Cole's Trans-Atlantic Inheritance*. New Haven: Yale University Press, 2018.

Bartky, Sandra Lee. *Femininity and Domination: Studies in the Phenomenology of Oppression*. New York: Routledge, 1990.

Batcho, Krystine Irene. NOSTALGIA: The Bittersweet History of a Psychological Concept. *History of Psychology* 16.3 (2013): 165-176.

Bauer, Dale. *Edith Wharton's Brave New Politics*. Madison: The University of Wisconsin Press, 1994.

Beard, Charles, and Mary Beard. *The Rise of American Civilization*. New York: The Macmillan Company, 1927.

Beckert, Sven. *The Monied Metropolis: New York City and The Consolidation of the American Bourgeoisie*, 1850-1896. New York: Cambridge University Press, 2001.

Bell, Michael M. Did New England Go Downhill? *Geographical Review* 79.4 (1989): 450-466.

Benert, Annette. *The Architectural Imagination of Edith Wharton: Gender, Class, and Power in the Progressive Era*. Madison, NJ: Fairleigh

Dickinson University Press, 2007.

Berberich, Christine, Neil Campbell, and Robert Hudson. "Introduction." *Affective Landscapes in Literature, Art and Everyday Life: Memory, Place and the Senses.* Eds. Christine Berberich, Neil Campbell, and Robert Hudson. New York: Ashgate Publishing, 2015: 1-20.

Berleant, Arnold. *The Aesthetics of Environment.* Philadelphia, PA: Temple University Press, 1992.

Beuka, Robert Andrew. *SuburbiaNation: Reading Suburban Landscape in Twentieth-Century American Fiction and Film.* Diss. Louisiana State University, 2000.

Birdsall, Richard D. Berkshire's Golden Age. *American Quarterly* 8. 4 (1956): 328-355.

Blair, Sara. *Henry James and the Writing of Race and Nation.* New York: Cambridge University Press, 1996.

Bondi, Liz, Joyce Davidson, and Mick Smith. "Introduction: Geography's 'Emotional Turn'." *Emotional Geographies.* Eds. Liz Bondi, Joyce Davidson, and Mick Smith. Hampshire: Ashgate Publishing Limited, 2007: 1-16.

Boyd, Ailsa. "From the 'Looey Suite' to the Faubourg: The Ascent of Undine Spragg." *Edith Wharton Review* 30.1 (2014): 9-28.

---. *Home of Their Own: Representations of Women in Interiors in the Art, Design and Literature of the Late Nineteenth Century.* Diss. University of Glasgow, 2002.

Boym, Svetlana. *The Future of Nostalgia.* New York: Basic Books, 2001.

Bramen, Carrie Tirado. The Urban Picturesque and the Spectacle of Americanization. *American Quarterly* 52.3 (2000): 444-477.

Bratton, Daniel. Edith Wharton and Louis Bromfield: A Jeffersonian and a Victorian. *Edith Wharton Review* 10.2 (1993): 8-11.

Brook, Isis. "Aesthetic Appreciation of Landscape." *The Routledge*

Companion to Landscape Studies. Eds. Peter Howard, et al. New York: Routledge, 2019: 39-50.

Brown, Dona. *Inventing New England: Regional Tourism in the Nineteenth Century*. Washington, D.C.: Smithsonian Institution Press, 1995.

Brown, Richard D. *Modernization: The Transformation of American Life*, 1600-1865. New York: Hill and Wang, 1976.

Buchanan-King, Mindy Leigh. *Edith Wharton and Romanticism: A Study of the [Bracketed] Artistic Self*. Diss. The University of Charleston, 2019.

Buell, Lawrence. *New England Literary Culture: From Revolution through Renaissance*. New York: Cambridge University Press, 1986.

Bunnell, Tim. "Urban Landscapes." *The Wiley-Blackwell Companion to Cultural Geography*. Eds. Nuala C. Johnson, Richard H. Schein, and Jamie Winders. West Sussex: John Wiley & Sons, 2013: 278-289.

Bush, Ronald. Pound, Emerson, and Thoreau: "The Pisan Cantos" and the Politics of American Pastoral. *Paideuma: Modern and Contemporary Poetry and Poetics* 34.2 (2005): 271-292.

Cadle, Nathaniel. *The Mediating Nation: American Literature and Globalization from Henry James to Woodrow Wilson*. Diss. The University of North Carolina at Chapel Hill, 2008.

Campbell, Brad. The Making of "American": Race and Nation in Neurasthenic Discourse. *History of Psychiatry* 18.2 (2007): 157-178.

Carlson, Marvin. *Places of Performance: The Semiotics of Theatre Architecture*. Ithaca, NY: Cornell University Press, 1989.

Carso, Kerry Dean. "To loiter about the Ruined Castle": Washington Irving's Gothic Inspiration. *The Hudson River Valley Review* 24.2 (2008): 23-42.

Chen, Wei-Han. Black Urban Modernity of the Harlem Renaissance: A Dialectical Negotiation between Urban Individuality and Community in

Toni Morrison's *Jazz*. *Wenshan Review of Literature and Culture* 7.1 (2013): 119-148.

Cheng, Xin. Fashionable Things: On Edith Wharton's *The Custom of the Country*. *Foreign Literature Review* 4 (2015): 187-201.

---. New Directions of Wharton Studies in the 21st Century. *Contemporary Foreign Literature* 2 (2011): 161-167.

Clarke, Deborah. *Driving Women: Fiction and Automobile Culture in Twentieth-Century America*. New York: Johns Hopkins University Press, 2007.

Clayton, Daniel. On the Colonial Genealogy of George Vancouver's Chart of The North-West Coast of North America. *Ecumene* 7.4 (2000): 371-401.

Cloke, Paul, et al. Deprivation, Poverty and Marginalization in Rural Lifestyles in England and Wales. *Journal of Rural Studies* 11.4 (1995): 351-365.

---. "Rural Landscapes." *The Wiley-Blackwell Companion to Cultural Geography*. Eds. Nuala C. Johnson, Richard H. Schein, and Jamie Winders. West Sussex: John Wiley & Sons, 2013: 225-237.

---. Rural Poverty and the Welfare State: A Discursive Transformation in Britain and the USA. *Environment and Planning A* 1995 (27): 1001-1016.

Clubbe, John. Interiors and the Interior Life in Edith Wharton's *The House of Mirth*. *Studies in the Novel* 28.4 (1996): 543-564.

Cogan, Francis B. Weak Fathers and Other Beasts: An Examination of the American Male in Domestic Novels, 1850-1870. *American Studies* 25.2 (1984): 5-20.

Cohn, Jan. The Houses of Fiction: Domestic Architecture in Howells and Edith Wharton. *Texas Studies in Literature and Language* 15.3 (1973): 537-549.

Cole, Thomas. Essay on American Scenery. *American Monthly Magazine* 1 (1836): 1-8.

Coleman, William L. From Villa to Studio Thomas Cole's Drawings for Cedar Grove. *Bulletin of the Detroit Institute of Arts* 90.1/4 (2016): 16-31.

Coleridge, Samuel Taylor. *The Complete Works of Samuel Taylor Coleridge.* New York: Harper & Brothers, 1856.

Colin, Clément, and Sandra Iturrieta Olivares. Nostalgias for a *Barrio*: Narratives of Generational Loss from Esperanza Neighborhood in Valparaiso, Chile. *Social & Cultural Geography* 23.2 (2022): 292-308.

Conforti, Joseph A. *Imagining New England*: *Explorations of Regional Identity from the Pilgrims to the Mid-Twentieth Century.* Chapel Hill: The University of North Carolina Press, 2001.

Conron, John. *American Picturesque.* University Park: The Pennsylvania State University Press, 2000.

Cooper, James Fenimore. *The Last of the Mohicans.* Buffalo, NY: Broadview Editions, 2009.

Cosgrove, Denis, and Daniels Stephen. "Introduction." *The Iconography of Landscape.* Eds. Denis Cosgrove and Stephen Daniels. Cambridge: Cambridge University Press, 1988: 1-10.

---. *Social Formation and Symbolic Landscape.* Madison: University of Wisconsin Press, 1998.

Cresswell, Tim. *In Place/Out of Place*: *Geography, Ideology, and Transgression.* Minneapolis: The University of Minnesota Press, 1996.

Cross, Gary. Crowds and Leisure: Thinking Comparatively across the 20th Century. *Journal of Social History* 39.3 (2006): 631-650.

Croucher, Sheila. Contesting America in a Global Era. *Globalized*

Identities: The Impact of Globalization on Self and Identity. Eds. Iva Katzarska-Miller and Stephen Reysen. New York: Palgrave Macmillan, 2022: 157-184.

Culhane, Paul J. *Public Lands Politics.* Baltimore, MD: Johns Hopkins University Press, 1981.

Cusack, Tricia. *Riverscapes and National Identities.* New York: Syracuse University Press, 2010.

D'Amore, Maura. "'Close Remotenesses' along the Hudson: Nathaniel Parker Willis's Suburban Aesthetic." *Early American Studies* 7. 2 (2009): 363-388.

Daniels, Stephen. *Fields of Vision: Landscape Imagery and National Identity in England and the United States.* Cambridge: Polity Press, 1993.

Darby, Wendy Joy. *Landscape and Identity: Geographies of Nation and Class in England.* Oxford: Berg, 2000.

Davis, Fred. *Yearning for Yesterday: A Sociology of Nostalgia.* New York: The Free Press, 1979.

Dean, Sharon L. *Constance Fenimore Woolson and Edith Wharton: Perspectives on Landscape and Art.* Knoxvill: University of Illinois Press, 2002.

Despotopoulou, Anna. Monuments of an Artless Age: Hotels and Women's Mobility in the Work of Henry James. *Studies in the Novel* 50. 4 (2018): 501-522.

Dimuro, Joseph A. Lay of The Land: Edith Wharton's Unmapping of New York. Unpublished Conference Paper Presented to Modern Language Association Convention. New York, January 4, 2018. Accessed 9 May 2021.

<https://mla.confex.com/mla/2018/meetingapp.cgi/Paper/3026>

Dinerstein, Joel. Modernism. *A Companion to American Cultural History.*

Ed. Karen Halttunen. Malden, MA: Blackwell Publishing Ltd, 2008: 198-213.

Dizikes, John. *Opera in America: A Cultural History*. New Haven: Yale University Press, 1993.

Domosh, Mona. A Method for Interpreting Landscape: A Case Study of the New York World Building. *Area* 21.4 (1989): 347-355.

---. "Those 'Gorgeous Incongruities': Polite Politics and Public Space on the Streets of Nineteenth-Century New York City." *Annals of the Association of American Geographers* 88.2 (1998): 209-226.

---. *Invented Cities: The Creation of Landscape in Nineteenth-Century New York and Boston*. New Haven: Yale University Press, 1998.

Downing, Andrew Jackson. *A Treatise on the Theory and Practice of Landscape Gardening, Adapted to North America*. New York: George P. Putnam, 1850.

---. *The Architecture of Country Houses*. New York: D. Appleton-Century Company, 1850.

Dreiser, Theodore. *Sister Carrie*. Auckland: The Floating Press, 2009.

Dulles, Foster Rhea. *America Learns to Play: A History of Popular Recreation 1607-1940*. New York: D. Appleton-Century Company, 1940.

Duncan, James, and Nancy Duncan. (Re) reading the Landscape. *Environment and Planning D: Society and Space* 6.2 (1996): 117-126.

---. Landscape Taste as a Symbol of Group Identity: A Westchester County Village. *Geographical Review* 63.3 (1973): 334-355.

---. *The City as Text: The Politics of Landscape Interpretation in the Kandyan Kingdom*. Cambridge: Cambridge University Press, 1990.

Dunwell, Frances F. *The Hudson: America's River*. New York: Columbia University Press, 2008.

Dyer, Thomas G. *Theodore Roosevelt and the Idea of Race*. Baton Rouge: Louisiana State University Press, 1992.

Dyreson, Mark. Nature by Design: Modern American Ideas About Sport, Energy, Evolution, and Republics, 1865-1920. *Journal of Sport History* 26.3 (1999): 447-469.

Edmonds, Mary K. "'A Theatre with All the Lustres Blazing'—Customs, Costumes, and Customers in 'The Custom of the Country'." *American Literary Realism*, 1870-1910 28.3 (1996): 1-18.

Eliot, T. S. "Tradition and Individual Talent." *The Egoist* September (1919): 54-73.

Emerson, Ralph Waldo. *The Complete Essays and Other Writings of Ralph Waldo Emerson*. NY: The Modern Library, 1950.

Endy, Christopher. Travel and World Power: Americans in Europe, 1890-1917. *Diplomatic History* 22.4 (1998): 565-594.

Evans, Anne-Marie. Public Space and Spectacle: Female Bodies and Consumerism in Edith Wharton's *The House of Mirth*. *Inside Out: Women Negotiating, Subverting, Appropriating Public/Private Space*. Eds. Teresa Go mez Reus and Ara nzazu Usandizaga. Amsterdam: Rodopi, 2008: 107-124.

Evelev, John. *Picturesque Literature and the Transformation of the American Landscape*, 1835-1874. New York: Oxford University Press, 2021.

Faherty, Duncan. *Remodeling the Nation: The Architecture of American Identity*, 1776-1858. Lebanon: University of New Hampshire Press, 2007.

Farland, Maria. "Ethan Frome and the 'Springs' of Masculinity." *Modern Fiction Studies* 42.4 (1996): 707-729.

---. Modernist Versions of Pastoral: Poetic Inspiration, Scientific Expertise, and the "Degenerate" Farmer. *American Literary History* 19. 4

(2007) : 905-936.

Fick, Annabella. The Waldorf-Astoria and New York Society : Grand Hotel as Site of Modernity. *Anglo-American Travelers and the Hotel Experience in Nineteenth-Century Literature : Nation, Hospitality, Travel Writing*. Eds. Monika M. Elbert and Susanne Schmid. New York : Routledge, 2018 : 129-138.

---. *New York Hotel Experience : Cultural and Societal Impacts of an American Invention*. Bielefeld : Transcript Publishing, 2017.

Finnigan, Jonny. *The New York Hieroglyphs : Urban Ekphrases in New York Novels of Edith Wharton*. Diss. University of Glasgow, 2008.

Fischer, Claude S. Changes in Leisure Activities. *Journal of Social History* 27.3 (1994) : 453-475.

Fishman, Robert. *Bourgeois Utopias*. New York : Basic Books, 1987.

Föllmer, Moritz. The Sociology of Individuality and the History of Urban Society. *Urban History* (2019) : 1-16.

Ford, Ben. The Presentation of Self in Rural Life : The Use of Space at a Connected Farmstead. *Historical Archaeology* 42.4 (2008) : 59-75.

Foster, John Bellamy. *Ecology Against Capitalism*. New York : Monthly Review Press, 2002.

Fredrickson, Barbara L., and Tomi-Ann Robert. Objectification Theory : Toward Understanding Women's Lived Experiences and Mental Health Risks. *Psychology of Women Quarterly* 21 (1997) : 173-206.

Freud, Sigmund. The Uncanny. *The Uncanny*. Trans. David McLintock. London : Penguin, 2003 : 121-162.

Fryer, Judith. *Felicitous Space : The Imaginative Structures of Edith Wharton and Willa Cather*. Chapel Hill : The University of North Carolina Press, 1986.

Galland, Olivier, and Yannick Lemel. Tradition vs. Modernity : The Continuing Dichotomy of Values in European Society. *Revue*

Française de Sociologie 49.5 (2008): 153-186.

Garb, Tamar. Gender and Representation. *Modernity and Modernism: French Painting in the Nineteenth Century*. Eds. Francis Frascina, et al. New Haven: Yale University Press, 1993: 219-289.

Ghee, Joyce C. *Building in Dutchess: Reading the Landscape*. Poughkeepsie, NY: The Dutchess County Department of History, 1986.

Gilbert, Sandra M. Life's Empty Pack: Notes toward a Literary Daughteronomy. *Critical Inquiry* 11.3 (1985): 355-384.

Gindro, Sandro. Ethnicity. *Dictionary of Race, Ethnicity and Culture*. Eds. Bolaffi Guido, et al. London: Sage, 2003. 94-98.

Glennon, Jenny Lynn. *American Ways and Their Meaning: Edith Wharton's Post-War Fiction and American History, Ideology, and National Identity*. Diss. University of Oxford, 2011.

Goedde, Petra. The Globalization of American Culture. *A Companion to American Cultural History*. Ed. Karen Halttunen. Malden, MA: Blackwell Publishing Ltd, 2008. 246-262.

Golden, Hilda H. *Immigrant and Native Families: The Impact of Immigration on the Demographic Transformation of Western Massachusetts, 1850-1900*. Lanham, MD: University Press of America, 1994.

Goldsmith, Meredith, and Emily J. Orlando. "Introduction. Edith Wharton: A Citizen of the World." *Edith Wharton and Cosmopolitanism*. Eds. Meredith L. Goldsmith and Emily J. Orlando. Gainesville: University of Florida Press, 2016: 1-18.

Goldthwait, James Walter. A Town That Has Gone Downhill. *Geographical Review* 17.4 (1927): 527-552.

Gordon, Sarah. *Passage to Union: How the Railroads Transformed American Life*. Chicago, IL: Ivan R. Dee, 1934.

Grant, Madison. *The Passing of the Great Race*. New York: Scribner's,

1916.

Grosz, Elizabeth. *Jacques Lacan: A Feminist Introduction*. New York: Routledge, 1990.

---. *Sexual Subversions: Three French Feminists*. North Sydney: Allen & Unwin, 1989.

Groth, Paul. *Living Downtown: The History of Residential Hotels in the United States*. Berkeley: University of California Press, 1989.

Gschwend, Kate. The Significance of the Sawmill: Technological Determinism in *Ethan Frome*. *Edith Wharton Review* 16.1 (2000): 9-13.

Guardiano, Nicholas L. *Aesthetic Transcendentalism in Emerson, Peirce, and Nineteenth-Century American Landscape Painting*. Lanham, MD: Lexington Books, 2016.

Halttunen, Karen. From Parlor to Living Room: Domestic Space, Interior Decoration, and the Culture of Personality. *Consuming Visions: Accumulation and Display of Goods in America*, 1880-1920. Ed. Simon J. Bronner. New York: W. W. Norton & Company, 1989: 157-190.

Hartley, Florence. *The Ladies' Book of Etiquette and Manual of Politeness*. Boston, MA: G. W. Cottrell, 1860.

Harvey, David. *The Urbanization of Capital*. Oxford: The Johns Hopkins University Press, 1985.

Hawkins, Harriet. Picturing Landscape. *The Routledge Companion to Landscape Studies*. (2nd ed.) Eds. Peter Howard, et al. New York: Routledge, 2019: 206-214.

Hays, Samuel P. *The Response to Industrialism*, 1885-1914. Chicago, IL: The University of Chicago Press, 1995.

He, Yan. A Naturalistic Interpretation of *Ethan Frome* in the Context of Modernism. *Fudan Forum on Foreign Languages and Literature* (Fall

2010)∶ 36-40.

Hobsbawm, Eric. Mass-Producing Traditions∶ Europe, 1870-1914. *The Invention of Tradition*. Eds. Eric Hobsbawm and Terence Ranger. New York∶ Cambridge University Press, 1983∶ 263-307.

Hood, Clifton. *In Pursuit of Privilege∶ A History of New York City's Upper Class and The Making of a Metropolis*. New York∶ Columbia University Press, 2016.

Hoskins, Gareth. Poetic Landscapes of Exclusion∶ Chinese Immigration at Angel Island, San Francisco. *Landscape and Race*. Ed. Richard H. Schein. New York∶ Routledge, 2006∶ 95-112.

Howe, Daniel Walker. American Victorianism as a Culture. *American Quarterly* 27.5 (1975)∶ 507-532.

Howells, William Dean. *A Hazard of New Fortunes*. New York∶ Harper & Bros., 1890.

---. *Suburban Sketches*. New York∶ Hurd and Houghton, 1871.

Hubka, Thomas C. The New England Farmhouse Ell∶ Fact and Symbol of Nineteenth-Century Farm Improvement. *Perspectives in Vernacular Architecture* 2 (1986)∶ 161-166.

---. *Big House, Little House, Back House, Barn*. Hanover, NH∶ University Press of New England, 1984.

Hudson, Edward Christopher. *From Nowhere to Everywhere∶ Suburban Discourse and the Suburb in North American Literature*. Diss. The University of Texas at Austin, 1998.

Hudson, Nicholas, et al. Foreword. *The Bloomsbury Handbook to Edith Wharton*. Ed. Emily J. Orlando. London∶ Bloomsbury Academic, 2023∶ xiii-xix.

Huntington, Samuel Phillips. The Change to Change∶ Modernization, Development, and Politics. *Comparative Modernization∶ A Reader*. Ed. Cyril E. Black. New York∶ The Free Press, 1976∶ 25-61.

Husband, Julie, and Jim O'Loughlin. *Daily Life in the Industrial United States*, 1870-1900. Westport, CT: Greenwood Press, 2004.

Ingold, Tim. The Temporality of the Landscape. *World Archaeology* 25.2 (1993): 152-174.

Irland, Lloyd C. New England Forests: Two Centuries of a Changing Landscape. *A Landscape History of New England*. Eds. Blake Harrison and Richard W. Judd. Cambridge, MA: The MIT Press, 2013: 53-69.

Irving, Washington. A Letter of 'Geoffrey Crayon' to the Editor of *The Knickerbocker Magazine*. *Miscellaneous Writings* 1803-1859. Ed. Wayne R. Kime. Boston, MA: Twayne Publishers, 1981: 104.

Jackson, J. B. *Discovering the Vernacular Landscape*. New Haven: Yale University Press, 1984.

Jackson, Kenneth T. *Crabgrass Frontier: The Suburbanization of the United States*. New York: Oxford University Press, 1985.

Jacobs, Jane. *The Death and Life of Great American Cities*. New York: Vintage Books, 1961.

Jacobsen, Ann. Edith Wharton's Houses Full of Rooms. *Women's Studies* 44.4 (2015): 516-536.

Jacobson, Joanne. The Idea of the Midwest. *Revue Française D'études Américaines* 48 (1991): 235-245.

Jacobson, Matthew Frye. *Whiteness of A Different Color: European Immigrants and the Alchemy of Race*. Cambridge, MA: Harvard University Press, 1998.

Jaher, Frederic Cople. Style and Status: High Society in Late Nineteenth-Century New York. *The Rich, the Well Born, and the Powerful: Elites and Upper Classes in History*. Ed. Frederic Cople Jaher. Urbana: University of Illinois Press, 1973: 121-133.

James, Henry. *The American Scene*. New York: Penguin, 1907.

Jamison, Phil. *Hoedowns, Reels, and Frolics: Roots and Branches of Southern Appalachian Dance*. Urbana: University of Illinois Press, 2015.

Jarvis, Kimberly A. Women and the White Mountain: Changing Visions of Nature in New England, 1830-1930. *A Landscape History of New England*. Eds. Blake Harrison and Richard W. Judd. Cambridge, MA: The MIT Press, 2013: 71-89.

Junod, Sarah Elizabeth. *Manly Martyrs and Pitiful Women: Negotiating Race, Gender, and Power in Salem Witchcraft Tourism Since* 1880. Diss. University of California, 2020.

Jurca, Catherine. *White Diaspora: The Suburb and the Twentieth-Century American Novel*. Princeton, NJ: Princeton University Press, 2001.

Kaplan, Amy. *The Social Construction of American Realism*. Chicago, IL: The University of Chicago Press, 1988.

Kassanoff, Jenni A. *Edith Wharton and the Politics of Race*. New York: Cambridge University Press, 2004.

Kearns, Gerry. The Imperial Subject: Geography and Travel in The Work of Mary Kingsley and Halford Mackinder. *Transactions of the Institute of British Geographers* 22.4 (1997): 450-472.

Kerber, Linda. The Republican Mother: Women and the Enlightenment—An American Perspective. *American Quarterly* 28.2 (1976): 187-205.

Kilborne, Benjamin. The Disappearing Who: Kierkegaard, Shame, and the Self. *Scenes of Shame: Psychoanalysis, Shame, and Writing*. Eds. Joseph Adamson and Hilary Clark. Albany: State University of New York Press, 1999: 35-52.

Kimmel, Michael S. The Contemporary 'Crisis' of Masculinity in Historical Perspective. *The Making of Masculinities*. Ed. Harry Brod. New York: Routledge, 1987: 121-151.

---. *Manhood in America*. New York: Oxford University Press, 2006.

King, Moses. *King's Handbook of New York City* 1892: *An Outline History and Description of the American Metropolis.* New York: Barnes and Noble Books, 1892.

Kinloch, Graham C. Irish-American Politics: Protestant and Catholic. *America's Ethnic Politics.* Eds. Joseph S. Roucek and Bernard Elsenberg. Westport, CT: Greenwood Press, 1982: 197-216.

Kirsch, Geoffrey R. Innocence and the Arena: Wharton, Roosevelt, and Good Citizenship. *American Literary Realism* 51.3 (2019): 200-219.

Klimasmith, Betsy. The "Hotel Spirit": Modernity and the Urban Home in Edith Wharton's *The Custom of the Country* and Charlotte Perkins Gilman's Short Fiction. *Edith Wharton Review* 18.2 (2002): 25-35.

---. *At Home in the City: Urban Domesticity in American Literature and Culture.* Lebanon: University of New Hampshire Press, 2005.

Koprince, Susan. Edith Wharton's Hotels. *Massachusetts Studies in English* 10 (1985): 12-23.

Kracauer, Siegfried. The Hotel Lobby. *Postcolonial Studies: Culture, Politics, Economy* 2.3 (1999): 289-297.

Kutchen, Larry. The "Vulgar Thread of the Canvas": Revolution and the Picturesque in Ann Eliza Bleecker, Crèvecoeur, and Charles Brockden Brown. *Early American Literature* 36.3 (2001): 395-425.

Laoire, Caitríona Ni. Winners and Losers? Rural Restructuring, Economic Status and Masculine Identities among Young Farmers in South-West Ireland. *Geographies of Rural Cultures and Societies.* Eds. Lewis Holloway and Moya Kneafsey. New York: Routledge, 2004: 283-301.

Leach, Nancy R. New England in the Stories of Edith Wharton. *The New England Quarterly* 30.1 (1957): 90-98.

Lears, T. J. Jackson. *No Place of Grace: Antimodernism and the Transformation of American Culture* 1880-1990. New York: Pantheon

Books, 1981.

Lee, Hermione. *Edith Wharton*. New York: Vintage Books, 2007.

Lewis, R. W. B. *Edith Wharton: A Biography*. New York: Harper & Row, 1975.

Lewis, Sinclair. *Main Street*. New York: Harcourt, Brace, and Company, 1920.

Lewis, Tom. *The Hudson: A History*. New Haven: Yale University Press, 2005.

Li, Jin. *Toward Self-Realization: A Critical Study of Edith Wharton's Eight Novels*. Beijing: Qunzhong Press, 2005.

Lichtenstein, Diane. "Domestic Novels of the 1920s: Regulation and Efficiency in *The Home-Maker*, *Twilight Sleep*, and *Too Much Efficiency*." *American Studies* 52.2 (2013): 65-88.

Lieber, Robert J., and Ruth E. Weisberg. Globalization, Culture, and Identities in Crisis. *International Journal of Politics, Culture, and Society* 16.2 (2002): 273-296.

Liming, Sheila. *What a Library Means to a Woman: Edith Wharton and the Will to Collect Books*. Minneapolis: University of Minnesota Press, 2020.

Lindner, Christoph. *Imagining New York City: Literature, Urbanism, and the Visual Arts*, 1890-1940. New York: Oxford University Press, 2015.

Locatelli, Angela. Emotions and/in Religion. *Writing Emotions: Theoretical Concepts and Selected Case Studies in Literature*. Eds. Ingeborg Jandl, et al. Bielefeld: Transcript Verlag, 2017: 77-98.

Lovett, Laura L. *Conceiving the Future: Pronatalism, Reproduction, and the Family in the United States*, 1890-1938. Chapel Hill: The University of North Carolina Press, 2007.

Lynch, Kevin. *The Image of the City*. Cambridge, MA: The MIT Press,

1960.

Marcuse, Herbert. Ecology and the Critique of Modern Society. *Capitalism Nature Socialism* 3.3 (1992): 29-38.

---. *Counter-Revolution and Revolt*. Boston, MA: Beacon Press, 1972.

---. *Negations: Essays in Critical Theory*. Trans. Jeremy J. Shapiro. Boston, MA: Beacon Press, 1968.

Marsh, Robert M. Modernization and Globalization. *Concise Encyclopedia of Comparative Sociology*. Eds. Masamichi Sasaki, et al. Leiden: Brill, 2014: 331-341.

Marx, Leo. *The Machine in the Garden: Technology and the Pastoral Ideal in America*. New York: Oxford University Press, 1967.

---. "Pastoralism in America." *Ideology and Classic American Literature*. Eds. Sacvan Bercovitch and Myra Jehlen. New York: Cambridge University Press, 1986: 36-69.

Matthias, Bettina. *The Hotel as Setting in Early Twentieth-Century German and Austrian Literature: Checking in to Tell a Story*. New York: Camden House, 2006.

Maynard, Barksdale W. Thoreau's House at Walden. *The Art Bulletin* 81.2 (1999): 303-325.

McCarthy, Jessica Schubert. Modern Critical Receptions. *Edith Wharton in Context*. Ed. Laura Rattray. New York: Cambridge University Press, 2012: 103-113.

McConachie, Bruce A. New York Operagoing, 1825-1850: Creating an Elite Social Ritual. *American Music* 6.2 (1988): 181-192.

McDermott, William P. The Dutch in Colonial Dutchess—Declining Numbers—Continuing Influence. *The Dutchess County Historical Society Yearbook*. Eds. John and Mary Lou Jeanneney. New York: Dutchess County Historical Society: 1985. 5-19.

McDonald, Bryan. Considering the Nature of Wilderness: Reflections on

Roderick Nash's "Wilderness and the American Mind". *Organization & Environment* 14.2 (2011): 188-201.

McDonald, Gail. The Mind a Department Store: Reconfiguring Space in the Gilded Age. *MLQ: Modern Language Quarterly* 63.2 (2002): 227-249.

McQuire, Scott. Urban Space and Electric Light. *Space and Culture* 8.2 (2005): 126-140.

Meagher, Timothy J. *The Columbia Guide to Irish American History*. New York: Columbia University Press, 2005.

Meinig, D. W. Symbolic Landscapes: Some Idealizations of American Communities. *The Interpretation of Ordinary Landscapes*. Ed. D. W. Meinig. New York: Oxford University Press, 1979: 164-192.

Miller, Angela L. *The Empire of the Eye: Landscape Representation and American Cultural Politics*, 1825-1875. Ithaca, NY: Cornell University Press, 1993.

Mindrup, Emilie F. "The Mnemonic Impulse: Reading Edith Wharton's 'Summer' As Propaganda." *Edith Wharton Review* 18.1 (2002): 14-22.

Mitchell, Don. "Landscape." *Cultural Geography: A Critical Dictionary of Key Concepts*. Eds. David Atkinson, et al. London: I. B. Tauris, 2005: 49-56.

Mitchell, Jean. "L.M. Montgomery's Neurasthenia: Embodied Nature and the Matter of Nerves." *L. M. Montgomery and the Matter of Nature (s)*. Eds. Rita Bode and Jean Mitchell. Montreal & Kingston: McGill-Queen's University Press, 2018: 112-127.

Mitchell, W. J. T. "Imperial Landscape." *Landscape and Power*. Ed. W. J. T. Mitchell. (2nd ed.) Chicago, IL: University of Chicago Press, 2002: 5-34.

---. "Introduction." *Landscape and Power*. Ed. W. J. T. Mitchell. (2nd ed.) Chicago, IL: University of Chicago Press, 2002: 1-4.

---. "Preface." *Landscape and Power*. Ed. W. J. T. Mitchell. (2nd ed.) Chicago, IL: University of Chicago Press, 2002: vii-xii.

Montgomery, Maureen E. *Displaying Women: Spectacles of Leisure in Edith Wharton's New York*. New York: Routledge, 1998.

---. "Henry James and 'The Testimony of the Hotel' to Transatlantic Encounters." *Anglo-American Travelers and the Hotel Experience in Nineteenth-Century Literature: Nation, Hospitality, Travel Writing*. Eds. Monika M. Elbert and Susanne Schmid. New York: Routledge, 2018. 149-165.

Moore, Robbie. *Hotel Modernity: Corporate Space in Literature and Film*. Edinburgh: Edinburgh University Press, 2021.

Morris, Lloyd. *Incredible New York: High Life and Low Life from 1850 to 1950*. New York: Syracuse University Press, 1951.

Mowl, Graham, and John Towner. "Women, Gender, Leisure and Place: Towards a More 'Humanistic' Geography of Women's Leisure." *Leisure Studies* 14.2 (1995): 102-116.

Mulvey, Laura. "Visual Pleasure and Narrative Cinema." *Film Theory and Criticism: Introductory Readings*. Eds. Leo Braudy and Marshall Cohen. New York: Oxford University Press, 1999: 803-816.

Mumford, Lewis. The Wilderness of Suburbia. *The New Republic* 7 (1921): 44-45.

---. *Pentagon of Power: The Myth of The Machine*. New York: Harcour, Brace Jovanovich, 1967.

Nash, Catherine. Reclaiming Vision: Looking at Landscape and the Body. *Gender, Place and Culture* 3.2 (1996): 149-170.

Nicholls, Angus. Goethe, Romanticism and the Anglo-American Critical Tradition. *Romanticism on the Net* 10 (2003): 31-40.

Nicolaides, Becky M., and Andrew Wiese. The Transnational Origins of

The Elite Suburb. *The Suburb Reader*. Eds. Becky M. Nicolaides and Andrew Wiese. New York: Routledge, 2006: 13-24.

O'Brien, Sharon. *Willa Cather: The Emerging Voice*. New York: Oxford University Press, 1987.

O'Connor, Alice. Modernization and the Rural Poor: Some Lessons from History. *Rural Poverty in America*. Ed. Cynthia M. Duncan. New York: Auburn House, 1992: 215-234.

Olin-Ammentorp, Julie. *Edith Wharton, Willa Cather, and the Place of Culture*. Lincoln: University of Nebraska Press, 2019.

Olwig, Kenneth R. Recovering the Substantive Nature of Landscape. *Annals of the Association of American Geographers* 86.4 (1996): 630-653.

Orlando, Emily J. "'One Long Vision of Beauty': Edith Wharton and Italian Visual Culture." *Edith Wharton Review* 36.1 (2020): 25-47.

---. "Introduction." *The Bloomsbury Handbook to Edith Wharton*. Ed. Emily J. Orlando. London: Bloomsbury Academic, 2023: 1-18.

---. "The 'Queer Shadow' of Ogden Codman in Edith Wharton's 'Summer'." *Studies in American Naturalism* 12.2 (2017): 220-243.

Panniter, Tara K. *Home Away from Home: The Summer Place in Turn-of-the-Twentieth Century American Women's Literature*. Diss. New York University, 2006.

Pells, Richard H. *Radical Visions and American Dreams*. New York: Harper & Row, 1973.

Penn, Theodore Z., and Roger Parks. Nichols-Colby Sawmill in Bow, New Hampshire. *The Journal of the Society for Industrial Archeology* 1.1 (1975): 1-12.

Pennell, M. Melissa. "'Justice' to Edith Wharton? The Early Critical Responses." *Edith Wharton in Context*. Ed. Laura Rattray. New York: Cambridge University Press, 2012: 93-102.

Peters, Scott J., and Paul A. Morgan. The Country Life Commission:

Reconsidering a Milestone in American Agricultural History. *Agricultural History* 78.3 (2004): 289-316.

Pile, Steve. Emotions and Affect in Recent Human Geography. *Transactions of the Institute of British Geographers* 35.1 (2010): 5-20.

Piott, Steven L. *Daily Life in the Progressive Era*. Santa Barbara, CA: Greenwood Press, 2011.

Pratt, Mary Louise. *Imperial Eyes: Travel Literature and Transculturation*. London: Routledge, 1992.

Qiao, Xiufeng. "'The Darkness of the Soul': Landscape and Melancholy in John Ruskin's *Modern Painters*." *Foreign Literature Review* 2 (2022): 181-195.

Raphael, Lev. *Edith Wharton's Prisoners of Shame: A New Perspective on Her Neglected Fiction*. New York: St. Martin's Press, 1991.

Richardson, Judith. *Possessions: The History and Uses of Haunting in the Hudson Valley*. Cambridge, MA: Harvard University Press, 2003.

Rickly-Boyd, Jillian M. Authenticity & Aura: A Benjaminian Approach to Tourism. *Annals of Tourism Research* 39.1 (2011): 269-289.

Rinaldi, Thomas E., and Robert J. Yasinsac. *Hudson Valley Ruins: Forgotten Landmarks of an American Landscape*. Lebanon, NH: University Press of New England, 2006.

Risinger, Jacob. "Boston and Concord." *Ralph Waldo Emerson in Context*. Ed. Wesley T. Mott. New York: Cambridge University Press, 1976: 3-11.

Roberts, David. Aura and Aesthetics of Nature. *Thesis Eleven* 36.1 (1993): 127-137.

Robertson, Roland. *Globalization: Social Theory and Global Culture*. London: Sage, 1992.

Robinson, John P. "'Massification' and Democratization of the Leisure Class." *The Annals of the American Academy of Political and Social*

Science 435.1 (1978) : 206-225.

Roediger, David R. "Becoming White: Irish Immigrants in the Nineteenth Century." *American Immigration and Ethnicity*. Eds. David A. Gerber and Alan M. Kraut. New York: Palgrave Macmillan, 2005.

Rogers, Brandon. The Politics of the Picturesque: The Marches Settle Van Rensselaer's New York City. *American Periodicals* 12 (2002) : 75-88.

Rose, Christine. *Summer*: The Double Sense of Wharton's Title. *ANQ: A Quarterly Journal of Short Articles, Notes and Reviews* 3.1 (1990) : 16-19.

Rose, Gillian. *Feminism and Geography: The Limits of Geographical Knowledge*. Cambridge: Polity Press, 1993.

Rose-Redwood, Reuben S. *Governmentality, the Grid, and the Beginnings of a Critical Spatial History of the Geo-Coded World*. Diss. The Pennsylvania State University, 2006.

Rosk, Nancy Von. "Spectacular Homes and Pastoral Theaters: Gender, Urbanity and Domesticity in *The House of Mirth*." *Studies in the Novel* 33.3 (2001) : 322-350.

Ross, Edward Alsworth. Italians in America. *The Century* October (1914) : 439-445.

---. The Value Rank of the American People. *The Independent* November (1904) : 1061-1064.

Rostow, W. W. *The Stages of Economic Growth: A Non-Communist Manifesto*. Cambridge: Cambridge University Press, 1960.

Rotundo, E. Anthony. *American Manhood: Transformations in Masculinity from the Revolution to the Modern Era*. New York: Basic Books, 1993.

Rowley, Thomas. The Value of Rural America. *Rural Development Perspectives* 12.1 (1996) : 2-4.

Ruskin, John. *Modern Painters*. Vol. 4. New York: John Wiley & Sons,

1883.

Ryan, James R. Visualizing Imperial Geography: Halford Mackinder and the Colonial Office Visual Instruction Committee, 1902-1911. *Ecumene* 1.2 (1994): 157-176.

Ryden, Kent C. The Handselled Globe: Natural Systems, Cultural Process, and the Formation of the New England Landscape. *A Landscape History of New England*. Eds. Blake Harrison and Richard W. Judd. Cambridge, MA: The MIT Press, 2013: 37-50.

Saisselin, Remy G. *The Bourgeois and The Bibelot*. New Brunswick, NJ: Rutgers University Press, 2010.

Sandoval-Strausz, A. K. *Hotel: An American History*. New Haven: Yale University Press, 2008.

Sartre, Jean-Paul. *Being and Nothingness*. Trans. Hazel E. Barnes. New York: Routledge, 1966.

Sauer, Carl Ortwin. The Morphology of Landscape. *Land and Life: A Selection from the Writings of Carl Ortwin Sauer*. Ed. John Leighly. Oakland: University of California Press, 1983: 315-350.

Saunders, Judith P. "Wharton's *Hudson River Bracketed* and Coleridge's 'Kubla Khan': Re-Creating Xanadu in an American Landscape." *Connotations* 24.2 (2014): 187-216.

Sauter, Billeter Irene. *New York City: "Gilt Cage" or "Promised Land"? Representations of Urban Space in Edith Wharton and Anzia Yezierska*. Bern: Peter Lang, 2011.

Schaffner, Anna Katharina. *Exhaustion: A History*. New York: Columbia University Press, 2015.

Schein, Richard H. A Methodological Framework for Interpreting Ordinary Landscapes: Lexington, Kentucky's Courthouse Square. *Geographical Review* 99.3 (2009): 377-402.

---. "Normative Dimensions of Landscape." *Everyday America: Cultural*

Landscape Studies after J. B. Jackson. Eds. Chris Wilson and Paul Groth. Berkeley: University of California Press, 2003. 199-218.

---. "Race and Landscape in the United States." *Landscape and Race in the United States*. Ed. Richard H. Schein. New York: Routledge, 2006: 1-22.

Schuyler, David. *Sanctified Landscape: Writers, Artists, and the Hudson River Valley*, 1820-1909. Ithaca, NY: Cornell University Press, 2012.

Schweitzer, Marlis. *When Broadway Was the Runway: Theater, Fashion, and American Culture*. Philadelphia: University of Pennsylvania Press, 2009.

Scobey, David M. Anatomy of the Promenade: The Politics of Bourgeois Sociability in Nineteenth-Century New York. *Social History* 17. 2 (1992): 203-227.

---. *Empire City: The Making and Meaning of the New York City Landscape*. Philadelphia, PA: Temple University Press, 2002.

Siddall, Stephen. *Landscape and Literature*. Cambridge: Cambridge University Press, 2017.

Sies, Mary Corbin. The City Transformed: Nature, Technology, and the Suburban Ideal, 1877-1917. *Journal Of Urban History* 14.1 (1987): 81-111.

Simmel, Georg. "The Metropolis and Mental Life." *On Individuality and Social Forms*. Ed. Donald N. Levine. Chicago, IL: University of Chicago, 1971: 11-19.

---. *The Philosophy of Money*. Trans. T. Bottomore and D. Frisby. New York: Routledge, 1990.

Singley, Carol J. Change at Stake: Teaching Edith Wharton's Late Fiction." *Edith Wharton Review* 29.1 (2013): 1-7.

---. Race, Culture, Nation: Edith Wharton and Ernest Renan. *Twentieth*

Century Literature 49.1 (2003): 32-45.

---. *Edith Wharton: Matters of Mind and Spirit*. New York: Cambridge University Press, 1995.

Skaggs, Carmen Trammell. *Overtones of Opera in American Literature from Whitman to Wharton*. Baton Rouge: Louisiana State University Press, 2010.

Skillern, Rhonda. "Becoming a 'Good Girl': Law, Language, and Ritual in Edith Wharton's *Summer*." *The Cambridge Companion to Edith Wharton*. Ed. Millicent Bell. New York: Cambridge University Press, 1995: 117-136.

Smith, Sidonie. *Moving Lives: Twentieth-Century Women's Travel Writing*. Minneapolis: The University of Minnesota Press, 2001.

Snowman, Daniel. *The Gilded Stage: A Social History of Opera*. London: Atlantic Books, 2010.

Snyder, Katherine V. *Bachelors, Manhood, and the Novel: 1850-1925*. Cambridge: Cambridge University Press, 1999.

Solie, Ruth. *Music in Other Words: Victorian Conversations*. Berkeley: University of California Press, 2004.

Spain, Daphne. Gender and Urban Space. *Annual Review of Sociology* 40 (2014): 581-598.

Stearns, Harold. "Preface." *Civilization in the United States: An Inquiry by Thirty Americans*. Ed. Harold Stearns. New York: Harcourt, Brace, and Company, 1922: iii-2.

Steen, Ivan D. Palaces for Travelers: New York City's Hotels in the 1850's As Viewed by British Visitors. *New York History* 51.3 (1970): 269-286.

Stephenson, Liisa. *Reading Matter: Modernism and the Book*. Diss. McGill University, 2007.

Stilgoe, John R. *Borderland: Origins of the American Suburb*. New Haven:

Yale University Press, 1988.

Stokols, Daniel. Instrumental and Spiritual Views of People-Environment Relations. *American Psychologist* 45.5 (1990): 641-646.

Stone, Alison. Adorno and the Disenchantment of Nature. *Philosophy & Social Criticism* 32.2 (2006): 231-253.

Street, George. *Mount Desert: A History*. Boston, MA: Houghton, Mifflin & Co., 1905.

Sun, Wei. *Elite Tradition and Culture of Consumption: On Edith Wharton's "Old New York" Novels*. Chengdu: Sichuan University Press, 2014.

Surdam, David. *Century of the Leisured Masses: Entertainment and the Transformation of Twentieth-Century America*. New York: Oxford University Press, 2015.

Susman, Warren. *Culture as History: The Transformation of American Society in the Twentieth Century*. Washington, D.C.: Smithsonian Institution Press, 2003.

Szymanski, Dawn M., Lauren B. Moffitt, and Erika R. Carr. Sexual Objectification of Women: Advances to Theory and Research. *The Counseling Psychologist* 39.1 (2011): 6-38.

Tallack, Douglas. *New York Sights*. Oxford: Berg, 2005.

Thoreau, Henry D. "Economy." *Walden*. Ed. Jeffrey S. Cramer. New Haven: Yale University Press, 2004: 1-77.

Tickamyer, Ann R. "Rural Poverty." *Handbook of Rural Studies*. Eds. Paul Cloke, Terry Marsden, and Patrick Mooney. Thousand Oaks, CA: Sage, 2006: 411-426.

Tischleder, Bärbel. The Deep Surface of Lily Bart: Visual Economies and Commodity Culture in Wharton and Dreiser. *Amerikastudien / American Studies* 5.4 (2009): 59-78.

Tolia-Kelly, Divya P. Fear in Paradise: The Affective Registers of the English Lake District Landscape Re-Visited. *Senses and Society* 2.3

(2007): 329-352.

Tönnies, Ferdinand. *Community and Civil Society*. 1887. Trans. Jose Harris and Margaret Hollis. Ed. Jose Harris. Cambridge: Cambridge University Press, 2001.

Toth, Margaret A. Orientalism, Modernism, and Gender in Edith Wharton's Late Novels. *Edith Wharton and Cosmopolitanism*. Eds. Meredith L. Goldsmith and Emily J. Orlando. Gainesville: University of Florida Press, 2016: 226-250.

Totten, Gary. "'Inhospitable Splendour': Spectacles of Consumer Culture and Race in Wharton's *Summer*." *Twentieth Century Literature* 58.1 (2012): 60-89.

---. Edith Wharton's Geographical Imagination: A Response to Judith P. Saunders. *Connotations* 26 (2016/2017): 91-101.

---. The Dialectic of History and Technology in Edith Wharton's *A Motor-Flight through France*. *Studies in Travel Writing* 17.2 (2013): 133-144.

Tuan, Yi-Fu. *Landscapes of Fear*. New York: Pantheon Books, 1979.

Turner, Frederick J. Middle Western Pioneer Democracy. *Minnesota History Bulletin* 3.7 (1920): 393-414.

Turner, Victor. *The Ritual Process: Structure and Anti-Structure*. Ithaca, NY: Cornell University Press, 1977.

Valentine, Gill. "The Geography of Women's Fear." *Area* 21.4 (1989): 385-390.

Van Der Werf, Els. "'A Woman's Nature is Like a Great House full of Rooms': Edith Wharton's Personal and Fictional Representation of Homes." *Home Cultures* 6.2 (2009): 179-197.

Van Engen, Abram C. *City on a Hill: A History of American Exceptionalism*. New Haven: Yale University Press, 2020.

Veblen, Thorstein. *The Theory of the Leisure Class*. New York: Macmillan,

1899.

Vidler, Anthony. *The Architectural Uncanny: Essays in the Modern Unhomely*. Cambridge, MA: The MIT Press, 1999.

Vogel, Steven. "On Nature and Alienation." *Critical Ecologies: The Frankfurt School and Contemporary Environmental Crises*. Ed. Andrew Biro. Toronto: University of Toronto Press, 2011: 187-205.

Waid, Candace. *Edith Wharton's Letters from the Underworld: Fictions of Women and Writing*. Chapel Hill: The University of North Carolina Press, 1991.

Wang, Lin. *The Literary Map of American Cities: Centered on New York, Chicago, and Los Angeles*. Beijing: China Social Sciences Press, 2018.

Ward, Joseph A. "'The Amazing Hotel World' of James, Dreiser, and Wharton." *Leon Edel and Literary Art*. Ed. Lyail H. Powers. Ann Arbor, MI: UMI Research Press, 1988. 151-160.

Waterman, Jayne E. The Midwest, the Artist, and the Critics: Edith Wharton's *Hudson River Bracketed* and *The Gods Arrive*. *Midwestern Miscellany XXXVIII*. Ed. Jayne E. Waterman. East Lansing, MI: The Society for the Study of Midwestern Literature, 2010. 69-84.

Waterton, Emma, and Steve Watson. *The Semiotics of Heritage Tourism*. Bristol: Channel View Publications, 2014.

Watson, Jay. *William Faulkner and the Faces of Modernity*. Oxford: Oxford University Press, 2019.

Weber, Max. *Economy and Society: An Outline of Interpretive Sociology*. 1921. Trans. Guenther Roth and Claus Wittich. Berkeley: University of California Press, 1968.

Weil, François. *A History of New York*. Trans. Jody Cladding. New York: Columbia University Press, 2004.

Welter, Barbara. The Cult of True Womanhood: 1820-1860. *American*

Quarterly 18.2 (1966): 151-174.

Wermuth, Thomas S., and James M. Johnson. "Four Hundred Years of Hudson Valley History." *America's First River: The History and Culture of the Hudson River Valley*. Eds. Thomas S. Wermuth, et al. New York: SUNY Press, 2009: 1-9.

Westbrook, Perry D. *The New England Town in Fact and Fiction*. East Brunswick, NJ: Associated University Presses, 1982.

Westphal, Bertrand. *Geocriticism: Real and Fictional Spaces*. 2007. Trans. Robert T. Tally Jr. New York: Palgrave Macmillan, 2011.

Whaley, Ruth Maria. *Landscape in the Writing of Edith Wharton*. Diss. Harvard University, 1982.

Wharton, Edith, and Ogden Codman, Jr. *The Decoration of Houses*. New York: W. W. Norton & Company, 1897.

---. *A Backward Glance*. New York: D. Appleton-Century Company, 1934.

---. *Ethan Frome*. New York: Charles Scribner's Sons, 1911.

---. *Hudson River Bracketed*. New York: D. Appleton and Company, 1929.

---. *Summer*. New York: Bantam Books, 1917.

---. *The Custom of the Country*. New York: Charles Scribner's Sons, 1913.

---. *The Gods Arrive*. New York: D. Appleton and Company, 1932.

---. *The House of Mirth*. New York: Charles Scribner's Sons, 1905.

---. *The Letters of Edith Wharton*. Eds. R. W. B. Lewis, Nancy Lewis, and William R. Tyler. New York: Charles Scribner's Sons, 1988.

---. *The Uncollected Critical Writings*. Ed. Frederick Wegener. Princeton, NJ: Princeton University Press, 1996.

---. *The Writing of Fiction*. New York: Octagon Books, 1925.

Whelpton, P. K. A History of Population Growth in the United States. *The Scientific Monthly* 67.4 (1948): 277-288.

Whitney, Gordon Graham. *From Coastal Wilderness to Fruited Plain: A History of Environmental Change in Temperate North America*, 1500 *to the Present*. Cambridge: Cambridge University Press, 1994.

Wiebe, Robert H. *The Search for Order*: 1877-1920. New York: Hill and Wang, 1967.

Williams, Daniel R., and Jerry J. Vaske. The Measurement of Place Attachment: Validity and Generalizability of a Psychometric Approach. *Forest Science* 49.6 (2003): 830-840.

Williams, Raymond. *The Country and the City*. New York: Oxford University Press, 1973.

Williamson, Jefferson. *The American Hotel*. New York: Arno Press, 1975.

Wilson, Harold Fisher. *The Hill Country of Northern New England*: Its Social and Economic History, 1790-1930. New York: Columbia University Press, 1936.

Wilson, Richard Guy. Introduction: What is the Colonial Revival. *Recreating the American Past*: Essays on the Colonial Revival. Eds. Richard Guy Wilson, Shaun Eyring, and Kenny Marotta. Charlottesville: University of Virginia Press, 2006: 1-10.

Wilson, Sarah. "New York and The Novel of Manners." *The Cambridge Companion to the Literature of New York*. Eds. Cyrus R. K. Patell and Bryan Waterman. New York: Cambridge University Press, 2010: 121-133.

Wolff, Cynthia Griffin. "Cold Ethan and 'Hot Ethan'." *College Literature* 14.3 (1987): 230-245.

---. *A Feast of Words*: The Triumph of Edith Wharton. New York: Oxford University Press, 1977.

Wood, Joseph Sutherland. "New England's Legacy Landscape." *A Landscape History of New England*. Eds. Blake Harrison and Richard W. Judd. Cambridge, MA: The MIT Press, 2013: 251-267.

---. *The New England Village*. Baltimore, MD: Johns Hopkins University Press, 2002.

Worster, Donald. *Dust Bowl*. New York: Oxford University Press, 1979.

Wortham-Galvin, B. D. The Fabrication of Place in America: The Fictions and Traditions of the New England Village. *Traditional Dwellings and Settlements Review* 21.2 (2010): 21-34.

Wylie, John. A Single Day's Walking: Narrating Self and Landscape on the Southwest Coast Path. *Transactions of the Institute of British Geographers* 30.2 (2005): 234-247.

---. "Landscape." *The Dictionary of Human Geography*. (5th ed.) Eds. Derek Gregory, et al. Chichester: Wiley-Blackwell, 2009: 409-411.

---. *Landscape*. Abingdon: Routledge, 2007.

Xiao, Sha. Picturesque: A Keyword in Critical Theory. *Foreign Literature* 25 (2019): 71-84.

Xie, Ronggui. The Female Tragedy in American "Pyramid": A Review of Edith Wharton's *The Age of Innocence*. *Foreign Languages and Literature (Quarterly)* 3 (2006): 203-207.

Xiong, Tianyu, and Min He. On the Development of Edith Wharton's Female Consciousness Through Lily and Ellen. *Foreign Languages and Literature Research* 2.3 (2016): 57-62.

Xu, Hui, and Qiqing Guo. Spatial Transformation and Life's Vicissitudes: New York in Wharton's Fiction. *Foreign Languages Research* 5 (2013): 97-101.

Yang, Jincai, and Liming Wang. Marriage in the Old New York Society—On Edith Wharton's New York Novels. *Collection of Women's Studies* 61.5 (2004): 48-52.

Zhang, Hui. On the Picturesque and Morality. *Foreign Literature Studies* 3 (2023): 18-31.

Zhou, Ming. "'The Land of Strangers': Archaeology, Native Americans, and Spatial Politics in Turn-of-the-Century American Literature." *Foreign Literature Review* 1 (2022): 32-68.

Zhu, Hejin, and Tiesheng Hu. The Dispute over Individual Ethics and Collective Ethics: The Ethical connotation of the House Image in Wharton's *The Age of Innocence*. *Journal of Northeast Normal University (Philosophy and Social Sciences)* 6 (2012): 155-158.